# THE STOLEN CHILD

Sanjida Kay is a writer and broadcaster. She lives in Bristol with her daughter and husband. *Bone by Bone* was her first thriller.

Also by Sanjida Kay

*Bone by Bone*

# THE STOLEN CHILD

## Sanjida Kay

CORVUS

Published in trade paperback in Great Britain in 2017 by Corvus, an imprint of Atlantic Books Ltd.

10 9 8 7 6 5 4 3 2 1

A CIP catalogue record for this book is available from the British Library.

Trade paperback ISBN: 978 1 78239 691 8
E-book ISBN: 978 1 78239 693 2

Printed and bound in Great Britain by Clays Ltd, St Ives Plc.

Corvus
An imprint of Atlantic Books Ltd
Ormond House
26–27 Boswell Street
London
WC1N 3JZ

www.corvus-books.co.uk

*To Jasmine*

*Come away, O human child!*
*To the waters and the wild*
*With a faery, hand in hand,*
*For the world's more full of weeping*
  *than you can understand.*

'The Stolen Child', W. B. Yeats

# LONDON

# MAY

She's coming! She's going to be early! I half knew it, felt it in my bones. Thank goodness Ollie believed me and helped me get the nursery ready. We have all the essentials: a cot, a buggy, a pile of nappies, Sudocrem, an adorable rabbit with Liberty-print ears. Babygros. A Moses basket. Blankets. Bottles. A mobile that sings and cascades coloured lights across the ceiling.

'Zoe! The taxi's here!' Ollie shouts.

He's standing looking out of the window of our first-floor flat. He has his coat on already and is holding mine for me.

As he carefully slides my jacket over my outstretched arms, I say, 'I haven't finished the mural!'

The mural is my way of trying to keep calm during the pregnancy and I wanted it to be finished and perfect before she arrived. It's on the nursery wall and it's of Ilkley Moor, where I grew up: the Cow and Calf rocks at sunrise, a friendly giant called Rombald striding through the purple heather. Ollie kisses my cheek.

'It looks wonderful. She'll love it just as it is. And you'll have time to finish it when she's here.'

We already know we're having a girl.

'I won't!' I say, my voice rising in pitch. 'Babies never sleep. They're up all night. I'll be too tired to paint!'

'Newborns sleep all the time. Especially bottle-fed ones,' says Ollie, steering me towards the door, his arm around my waist.

He's the youngest child in his family and I have no siblings, so what do we know? But Ollie has read the most enormous stack of books about babies so maybe he's right. I tried, but it made me even more stressed. What if she gets colic, roseola? Has a febrile seizure?

'The bag!'

'I've got it,' he says. He packed it weeks ago, just in case.

'What about—?'

'I've put your handbag in and I've got money and my phone. I'll grab the car seat. We don't need anything else.'

He smiles gently at me. The seat is already by the door. Ollie said we should bring it just in case we can take our baby home straight away. Ollie researched the best one to buy online. He joined forums on Mumsnet and BabyCentre and took out a subscription to *Which?*. I found one in a charity shop, but he was horrified and made me take it back. Apparently it's not safe to buy second-hand baby car seats.

'I can manage,' he says, carrying everything. 'Careful on the stairs.'

He's noticed the tears blurring my vision. In the car he holds my hand. He tells the driver we need to get to hospital as fast as possible. The man looks at me in the rear-view mirror and then at the baby seat. He looks puzzled for a moment, and then he smiles.

'Hold on to your hats, ladies and gentlemen,' he says. He's wearing a turban.

We drive past a kebab shop, a Polish grocer, a newsagent with red peppers and oranges stacked in Tupperware bowls outside, and then he veers abruptly down a side street, hurling us over the speed bumps. Red-brick blocks of flats merge into white and brown Victorian semis with palm trees and mock orange trees in the gardens and we shoot onto Chatsworth Road opposite a storefront full of succulents and Kilner jars and a Spanish deli with jamon in the window. Just before the traffic lights, past a pizza restaurant that looks like an upmarket pub, the driver takes a sharp right. The baby seat tilts forwards. I glance in the window of a toy shop with a pink wooden castle, all fairy-tale turrets and gold flags, on display.

I've lost my bearings.

'Almost there,' says Ollie, squeezing my arm.

The young woman at the hospital says, 'It's going to be an emergency Caesarean.' She leans forward. 'The baby is at risk if we don't operate.'

'She's premature,' I say. 'Four weeks. It's too early—'

'They'll take good care of her. She'll be put straight into an incubator.' She takes my hand in both of hers. I try and recall her name. Sarah. That's it. I should have remembered.

She says softly, 'We did warn you this was likely to happen, Zoe.'

I nod and gulp back hot tears. Ollie passes me a tissue. I blow my nose. I don't want my baby to be cut out. Surgically removed as if she were a tumour. Put into a box. I want to hold her in my arms, still slick with blood and mucus.

'We're prepared,' he says, and takes my hand, lacing his fingers through mine.

The wait is interminable. The smell of boiled eggs and slightly burnt mince drifts down the corridor from the cafeteria. It makes me feel even more nauseous. I grip Ollie's hand so hard my nails cut his palm. He winces and gently removes it from my grasp. He puts his arm round me instead.

'It's going to be okay,' he says, whispering into my hair.

I squeeze my eyes shut and push away the pain of those years of longing and miscarriages; forget the blood, 'Scissor Sisters' playing on the radio as the surgeon bends over me, tears running into my ears. That's all in the past. It's finally happening. This is what we've always wanted. We've been together for eight years, since I was nineteen and Ollie was twenty, and now we're going to have a baby at last. We're going to be a family.

I can't stop myself. 'What if. . .' I say.

We've been over this endlessly, with each other, with officials and doctors. We've been told all the risks. It's been brutally spelled out to us. She's so premature she might die. She could be brain damaged. They told us to wait before we gave her a name. They said if we named her, it would make it harder. But we ignored them. We're going to call her Evelyn Catherine Morley. Catherine after my mother; Evie for short.

I remove Ollie's arm so I can look at him properly. He has blue eyes and dirty-blonde hair that flops over his forehead. Mine would be the same colour but I've been dying it since I was at university. 'Natural blonde' it says on the packet. I've just done my roots because I know, once Evie is here, I won't have time. Ollie's expression is kind. He's listened to me and reassured me patiently for months.

'Don't worry,' he says again. 'It will be all right.'

How does he know? It was far from all right in the past.

The room we're in is painted white with grey linoleum and terrible pastel-coloured paintings on the wall. I imagine telling my daughter about those paintings one day, when she's old enough to understand how we waited for her to be born with such love and hope: *Stippled, like the French Impressionists*, I'll say, *but fake, modern, vacant. Do you know what I mean? When you're waiting for someone as important as your baby to be born, you want everything to mean something.* And she'll open her eyes wide and say, *Did you know, Mummy, some artists even use scribbling as a technique?*

'I love you,' Ollie says.

'I love you too.'

'It's going to be okay.' He kisses me on the forehead. 'We're going to take our daughter home very soon.'

I can't believe how tiny she is. Her entire body could fit in one of Ollie's hands. We press our faces against the incubator.

Ollie has tears in his eyes. 'Evie Cathy Morley,' he says. 'Our daughter.' He hugs me tightly. 'We did it,' he whispers.

We aren't allowed to touch her yet. She's encircled by tubes. There are flashing lights and beeping monitors next to her trolley. She's wearing a cream cap to keep her head warm. It would fit a doll. She's turned away from us, so I can't see her face. Her body is emaciated, arms and legs like sticks, ribs winging out with each strenuous breath. She's covered in downy hair. I walk round to the other side so I can look at her properly. I feel a hot flare in my chest: fear or love. I can't tell.

I bend down so I'm level with her and peer in. It's so hot in here, I can barely breathe. A shock of black hair juts out from beneath her hat. There's something odd about her features. Something is not quite right. I struggle to inhale. Something is wrong. Seriously wrong. Evie opens her eyes for the first time since we saw her. They're large and unfocused, enormous in her minute face. They're too far apart and a colour I can barely describe. But they're definitely not blue. Her skin is pale brown. She doesn't look like our child. She doesn't look like a baby at all. Not a human one. Sarah puts her hand on my shoulder. I'm hyperventilating.

'She may have Foetal Alcohol Syndrome,' she tells me. Sarah has been our case worker throughout the pregnancy. 'It's normal in a situation like this. We'll run tests later, when she's stable. Right now,' she says, 'Evie is being treated for drug addiction.'

Ollie is openly weeping. We knew it was likely, but we still hoped she'd be okay. He reaches for me, tries to pull me closer.

'Is she going to make it?' he asks.

Sarah hesitates. 'We don't know yet. But the team here will do everything they can to save her. To cure her. It's why we chose this hospital,' she reminds us. 'They specialize in treating the babies of drug addicts.'

I stand up abruptly. I need some air. I have to get out of here. I'm shaking with rage.

I could kill Evie's mother.

# SEVEN YEARS LATER


# ILKLEY

# AUGUST, SATURDAY

Ben's helping and I can feel my stress levels rise. He's managed to smear icing from his wrists to his elbows and his chocolate grin is as wide as the Joker's. I glance at the kitchen clock. In forty-two minutes the first guests will arrive. We're still icing Ben's birthday cake. I'm trying to get the buttercream to stick to the sponge and not my knife without ripping off the surface; Ben is sucking the beater. I haven't changed out of my jeans that sag at the knees and Dad's old shirt yet and there are still balloons to be blown up, party bags to be filled, cocktail sausages and cheese-and-pineapple sticks to be skewered. I sprinkle sugar stars randomly over the top of the cake and plonk two candles in the middle. Ben looks happy.

It's a far cry from Evie's second birthday. By then she was already talking in full sentences, demanding a princess cake. Ollie ordered one from Bettys. It cost a fortune and it was beautiful – pale pink icing fell like folds of fabric, a tiny sugar princess rising from the midst of her Victoria sponge ballgown. The cake was so sweet it set your teeth on edge. I look up, hoping to see Evie. The kitchen is at one end of the house. When we moved in, Ollie had the partition wall knocked down and now the whole downstairs space is open. Light floods through from Rombald's Moor behind us and the hills on the far side of the valley. I'd hoped she'd help – enjoying her role as a big sister; cutting the crusts off cheese sandwiches and wrapping up the yo-yo and the bubbles for pass-the-parcel – but she's nowhere to be seen.

'Evie! Evie?' I shout.

She loves making cakes. And it's not like her to miss out on the chance of licking the bowl. There's no sign of her and I feel uneasy. She's been behaving oddly round Ben for the past few months now.

Bella, who's finished lapping icing sugar off the chair Ben is standing on, clicks across the polished wooden floor towards the garden. We always had English springer spaniels when I was growing up; after my mum died, I bought a liver and white puppy to remind me of her.

I rinse out the dishcloth and wipe Ben with it. It's not hygienic, but I'm running out of time.

'Chocolate,' he says happily, pointing to his mouth.

I've invited too many toddlers. What is it that BabyCentre says? You should have the same number of guests as the age of the child? It seemed a bit unfair for Ben to have only two kids at his party and I couldn't just invite some of his friends and not others. In the end, I asked everyone at his nursery – and nearly all of them are coming. Is there any point in changing Ben? I roll his sleeves down and smooth his blond hair flat. The cowlick curl at the front bounces up. I give him a cuddle and kiss his fat cheek and he wriggles away from me, desperate to run after Bella. Unlike Evie, who was always so still as a small child. Almost unnaturally so.

I look at the clock again. Where the hell is Ollie? He said he had to go back to work. On a Saturday. On the day of Ben's party. I'd protested as I was wrestling with the Sellotape and flowery wrapping paper that was all I could find in the house at 10.30 last night. He'd made a face and said it was unavoidable.

'I'll go early, catch the first train. I'll be back, don't worry,' Ollie had said.

He didn't say whether he'd be back in time to help or if he was planning to arrive as the party was going to start. He'd left before I'd stirred, shutting the front door too hard, waking Ben and sending

Bella into a flurry of barks. I clear up the chocolate icing and streaks of butter from the work surface. The entire kitchen is stainless steel – the tops, dishwasher, fridge. Ollie insisted and it looked brilliant until the kids got their hands on it. Now it's covered in smeary fingerprints. I chuck the bowl and beater in the dishwasher and I'm just making a start on chopping the cheese into cubes, when the doorbell rings. I swear and wipe my hands on my trousers. In my head, I'd imagined myself welcoming the first parents and their children with Ben clinging to one leg, wearing his tractor top, Evie in that polka-dot dress I love, and I would look chic, with glossy hair, in kitten heels, skinny jeans and my new Breton top. Some chance.

Before I can reach the hall, Andy shouts, 'It's only us,' and half falls in with his two children, Sophie, who is Evie's best friend, and eight-month-old baby Ellen.

'So lovely to see you,' I say, embracing Gill, his wife.

'We thought you might need some help,' she says. 'Sophie. Go and find Evie.'

Gill unpacks her bag. She's brought brownies and flapjacks, all home-made and chopped up into bite-sized squares, a bumper pack of Hula Hoops and a huge, almond-studded fruit cake from Bettys.

'For the grown-ups,' she adds.

I feel as if I've known Gill and Andy forever. We met at Leeds University. Andy studied History of Art with me. I used to be Gill's best friend but I hardly ever see her these days. She's a lawyer.

'I don't know how you found the time,' I say, taking a flapjack. Gill works even longer hours than Ollie.

'Ollie's working?' she says, looking around for my husband.

I make a face. He hasn't replied to my texts asking him when he'll be here.

'I'll do this while you change,' she adds, eyeing my outfit, and getting mugs, a cafetière and coffee out of the cupboard. 'Andy, love, put the party playlist on.'

I can't find my stripey top so I end up wearing my favourite shirt that's worn a bit thin in patches, and ballet pumps. I had my hair cut short after Ben was born and now it's grown into a ragged bob. It's still blonde but my beige roots are showing through. It's definitely not glossy. I give my hair a quick brush and tuck it behind my ears. Gill's hair is immaculate: recently highlighted, smooth and as shiny as oiled teak.

By the time I come back downstairs, the first families have already arrived. Andy is surrounded by toddlers and is blowing up balloons. Songs from *The Jungle Book* are playing, Gill has laid the rest of the party food out on paper plates on one of the worktops in the kitchen. Ben is shrieking with delight and wiggling to 'I Wanna Be Like You'. Ollie hasn't arrived and there's still no sign of Evie but I assume she's in her bedroom with Sophie.

'Let's play musical statues!' I say, cranking up the volume so the toddlers will start dancing. I begin twirling and stamping my feet until they join in.

I pass the remote to Andy and take the laundry basket – now full to the brim with presents for Ben – upstairs so they'll be out of the way of little people who might be tempted to start opening them. I catch sight of Sophie, curled up in an armchair, watching something on the iPad.

'Sophie? Where's Evie?'

She shrugs and doesn't look at me. 'She didn't want to play with me.'

'Evie?' I call.

I can't hear anything. When was the last time I saw her? I leave the presents on the landing and climb the stairs to her room, but she's not there. I check my studio, the bathroom and our bedroom, but there's no sign of her.

'Evie!' I shout more loudly, in case she's hiding somewhere and can't hear me above the sound of 'Colonel Hathi's March'.

I push open the door to Ben's room. I give a little scream, floored by the sight that greets me. Evie is hard to spot at first. She's at the far end of the room, balancing on the end of Ben's bed. She looks guilty for a second and then defiant.

'Evie! What have you done?'

I can't quite make out what it is at first. The room is full of streamers criss-crossing the space from Ben's bed to the wall and back again – like those crazy webs made by spiders given drugs. There are things hanging from them. I duck under one. She's unwound balls of wool in all different colours and tied the ends to the furniture. She's attached postcards to the skeins with yards of Sellotape and, dangling from the bottom of the cards, are socks. She's stapled one of Ben's socks to every card! A jumble of thoughts goes through my mind all at the same time: it's so bright and dense I feel as if it'll bring on a migraine; it's going to take a hell of a long time to clear up; Ben's socks are ruined. A less logical part of me is applauding the unbridled creativity of the sock-stapling. I also feel like shaking her. Hard.

She jumps down from the bed.

'It's a surprise for Ben,' she says.

'Evie. It's Ben's party.' I try not to shout. 'Why are you doing this when you could be downstairs joining in?' Is it really something she thinks Ben will like (he probably will) or is she being deliberately naughty and attention-seeking because it's his birthday? I sigh. 'What is the matter with you?'

She shakes her long brown hair over her shoulder and frowns at me.

'You always ruin everything,' she mutters.

'Come with me, right this minute.'

I take her hand and pull her along, giving her a little push towards Sophie when we get back to the sitting room. I'll have to talk to her after the party. I call Ollie but it goes straight to voicemail. I leave him an angry message.

An hour or so later, all the children are sitting in a line at small wobbly tables and chairs that I've borrowed from several parents. They've exhausted themselves with pass-the-parcel and musical chairs, they've burnt off their sugar rush and they're reaching the end of lunch. It's suddenly quiet. Even the parents have stopped talking. I light the candles on the birthday cake and carry it over. Late summer sunlight, angling off the steep moors behind us, slants through the French windows. The children look up and start to sing.

Ben is shouting, 'Cake!' over and over.

He's my longed-for son, the one I felt I'd waited a lifetime to meet, the baby I thought I'd never have, the child I love so much I feel my heart might burst. I'm singing and smiling and my eyes are filling with tears, and then I look up and catch sight of Evie. She's standing, half in the shadows, where the old dining-room wall used to be, wearing a dress I've never seen before. She's watching me and she's scowling.

I set the cake down and Ben rounds his rosy cheeks and blows. He looks like a pudgy blond cherub from a Michelangelo fresco. One candle flickers and wavers and Ben tries again, showering spit over the cake. Everyone cheers. Evie folds her arms over her thin chest. She's scrawny, with bony knees. Her hair is dark, her skin is the colour of milky tea and her eyes are streaked green and brown. She doesn't look like anyone else in my family. Normally adoption agencies like to match children to parents who could be their real ones – but after the initial shock, it never bothered me – she's my daughter and I love her. Then Ben arrived, long after we'd given up trying to have kids of our own, with his eyes like his dad's and a dimple in his chin the same as mine. Maybe it's started to matter to her. I want to hug her tightly, but Ben shouts, 'Chocolate! Mine!' and suddenly I'm surrounded by toddlers sticking fat fingers into the icing and grabbing sugar stars.

Everyone leaves shortly afterwards, clutching cake in sticky napkins and a party bag, the parents hyped on caffeine.

'That lasted a lifetime,' I say to Gill and Andy, laughing. 'Will you stay for a glass of wine?'

Gill hesitates. Her free time must be so precious, but Andy is already looking for glasses. I pull a chilled bottle of Chardonnay out of the fridge and unscrew it. The first few sips go straight to my head. I didn't manage a proper breakfast, just Ben and Evie's leftover toast, and since then I've been snacking on a healthy combination of Gill's fruit cake and Hula Hoops.

'Leave it. I'll do it later,' I tell Gill, who's started to pick up hummus-smeared plates.

I throw open the French windows and we walk out into the garden. It's such a gorgeous day.

Our house is the last one on Rombald's Lane. It's tall and thin and made from the dark millstone grit that all the factories round here are built from. The garden is long and thin too, and at the end of it is a small bridleway that runs past the golf course, and beyond that is Rombald's Moor, the famous Cow and Calf rocks on the skyline, threatening to topple over and tumble down the hill.

Andy cradles Ellen on one hip, holding his glass with the other hand. Sophie, overcome with tiredness, folds herself onto Gill's knee as she sits at the trestle table. Bella's tail thumps against my leg. Ben races around on a bright yellow digger. I'm relieved it's over and glad it went well. I try not to let my annoyance with Ollie mar this perfect moment, this small oasis of calm. It's early afternoon, but it feels much later. It's as if autumn is already upon us and yet it's still August. The last day of August. My late summer baby, I think, looking at Ben, his halo of hair gleaming golden in the sunshine.

'She's been a bit out of sorts,' says Andy.

I think he's talking about Sophie, but he nods his head towards Evie, who's playing at the far end of the narrow garden.

'She's probably just jealous of all the attention Ben had today,' says Gill.

'You could be right. It was okay when he was a baby and he was small and cute but now he takes her toys, wants to play with her—'

'Tell me about it! She thinks she's too grown up to be with a little one,' says Gill, giving Sophie an affectionate squeeze.

I look at Andy. He knows Evie better than Gill does. He wrinkles his brow. He doesn't think that's the real reason for Evie's behaviour.

'She has been asking a lot of questions about her parents too. Her biological ones.' I lower my voice and hope Sophie doesn't understand what we're talking about.

'Yeah, she's at that age where she could be starting to think about the, you know, her place in your family, why she looks different.'

He looks awkward as if he might offend me.

'I hope I haven't been spending too much time with Ben,' I say, biting my lip.

Gill snorts. 'You could spend twenty-four hours a day with them and it wouldn't be enough.'

'Like you do, love?' Andy says lightly.

I take my glass of wine and walk over to Evie. There's a tree in the corner – I'm not sure what kind – but it has a fat, knobbly trunk and low branches. Evie loves it and is always making dens in its split innards; now she's swinging from one of the branches and talking to herself. I can't remember if she ate anything at the party.

'Evie, sweetheart,' I call.

She jumps and turns. Her eyes are wide apart and she looks like a startled animal, a cat maybe; there are grass stains on her knees. She's wearing a blue and silver dress – I think it's a copy of Elsa's, the princess in *Frozen*. I didn't buy it for her. I want to ask her where she got it from, but I don't want to upset her. She's frowning at me.

Maybe she borrowed it from a friend? I hold out my arms, trying not to spill my wine, but she backs away.

'What is it?'

'Nothing. I'm playing a secret game. I don't want you to come over here.'

'Can I play too?'

'It wouldn't be a secret then, would it?'

I change tack. 'Did you enjoy the party?'

'Not really.'

'I'm sorry you didn't have fun. You love icing cakes and parties! Weren't you feeling well?'

'No! Can't you even give me five minutes peace?'

I'm startled to hear Ollie's phrase being repeated by a seven-year-old and I want to laugh, but that would make her feel undignified.

I carefully set my wine glass down on the lawn and it promptly topples over, spilling my Chardonnay. I lunge at Evie and grab her and tickle her, trying to dispel her bad mood. She screams and kicks and not in a playful way. And then she bites me. I cry out and let go. I look down at the wet patch on my shirt and feel raised welts of teeth marks in my skin. I'm about to tell her off when Ollie steps into the garden.

'Hello, everyone,' he calls. 'Christ, it looks like we've been hit by a tornado. How can a few toddlers make that amount of mess?'

I follow his gaze and see that from one end to the other, the house is a chaos of wrapping paper and bits of rubber from burst balloons. The mini chairs are upended, there are heaps of messy plates on every surface and half-eaten bits of pineapple and sausages and crushed crisps strewn across the floor. He's frowning – presumably because we haven't cleared up and we're out here drinking wine. I scowl at him – he can hardly turn up after the party's over and complain about the state of the dining room. I want to ask him why the hell he didn't get back in time, but I need to deal with our daughter first.

'Evie. . .' I say.

She runs away from me, her shiny dress slippery against my palm as I reach for her. When she's upset she normally goes to Ollie, but she races past him and into the house. I hear her clatter up the stairs. Those high-heeled silver sandals aren't hers either.

'I'm sorry I'm late,' says Ollie. 'Work was manic. We've got a deal going through and I couldn't get away.' He raises his eyebrows at me. 'What's the matter with Evie?'

'She's—'

'Being Evie?'

Ollie retrieves my toppled glass and refills Andy's. He doesn't catch my eye. He doesn't want me to make a fuss or tell him off for missing the party in front of our friends.

'Cheers!' he says, chinking a bottle of beer against Andy's glass, and he kisses Gill on the cheek.

He's right. I should let it go. He said he couldn't help it. And Evie is just a little jealous. She'll be fine after she's had a slice of cake and Ollie's made a fuss of her. Ben has had a brilliant time. My husband hands me my glass, full to the brim with green-gold wine, and I stifle my resentment and attempt to smile at him. I mustn't lose sight of what we have – two beautiful children; an amazing house that I never, in a million years, thought we'd be able to afford; Gill and Andy, my best friends – and this perfect day. I take a deep breath and feel my shoulders relax. I can smell the faintest trace of heather, drifting down from the moor.

I don't get Ben to bed until almost 8.30 p.m. That's after clearing up the detritus from the party, unravelling the carnage Evie had created in his bedroom, two hours of putting him in his bed, finding him wandering down the landing, cuddling him, tucking him back in. In the end, I ignored him and he fell asleep curled round his tractor at the bottom of the flight of stairs to Evie's bedroom. I carry him gently back to his own room. For a moment I kneel by his bed and rest my head on the duvet. I tell myself it's just to check he's still sleeping. He snores loudly and snuffles and grunts like a hedgehog. I'm so tired I could stay here. Ben has dropped his afternoon nap and, because he's sleepy, he's cranky in the afternoons and I have no respite – no chance to catch up on emails or even have a cup of tea, go to the toilet or have a shower by myself – and he's not going to bed on time either. It makes no sense – he needs to rest. On the worst nights I find myself pleading with him to go to sleep. Ollie won't get up with Ben because he says he has to have a clear head for work. I'm an artist and somehow Ollie thinks it's okay for me to paint even when I feel slightly insane.

I force myself to rise and tiptoe out of his bedroom. I go downstairs and pour Ollie and me a large glass of Merlot. Ollie's lit the first fire of the year – it's already chilly now the sun has set.

He glances at his watch and does a double take that would be funny if he were smiling. 'Jesus. I'm meant to be at The Bar.'

'You're going out?'

'Work,' he says, patting his pockets for his phone and wallet. 'I'm sure I told you. Thank God I persuaded them to meet me in Ilkley and not Leeds. I won't be late. Sorry, darling. I know I left you to deal with the party on your own.'

His tone implies it was some dreadful chore, and not a joyful occasion he should have wanted to be there for.

'Do you have to go?'

'Yes. Sorry.'

'But you've already been out all day. You missed your son's second birthday!'

'I said I was sorry. I told you, I've got an important deal I need to finalize. Believe me, I'd much rather lie on the sofa with you.'

He kisses me on the cheek.

I bite my lip. I don't want to become one of those women who nags or moans. I pour his wine into my glass and put on my favourite movie, *Gone with the Wind*, to stop myself from feeling angry with him. I kick off my slippers and curl up alongside Bella in the corner of the sofa. I bury my hands in her soft fur and she sighs contentedly. I sip my wine and congratulate myself on surviving a two-year-old's birthday party without a jot of help from my husband.

# SEPTEMBER, MONDAY

A shaft of sunlight angles into the kitchen and lights up Evie's pale green eyes as she sits at the table eating her cereal. She looks beautiful and ethereal. How did she come to be *my* daughter? What did I do to deserve her as well as Ben? I lean over and kiss her.

'Mummy!' she says. 'You've just wiped yogurt on my face.'

The mornings are always stressful. Since Ollie leaves before anyone is awake, I get no help from him. Today I'm even more distracted than usual – I need to go and see my agent at the gallery in Ilkley. I have a solo exhibition in early spring. I've fallen so far behind in the amount of paintings I need to produce, I have heart palpitations thinking about it.

I was beginning to be recognized at least – by other artists and the owners of art galleries – when I unexpectedly fell pregnant with Ben. Now, although having a family of my own was all I ever wanted, I don't want to lose my status as an artist, such as it is. I'm finding it hard to balance painting and looking after the two of them. Ben goes to nursery every morning at the school Evie attends, but by the time I get home, clear up the wreckage in the kitchen and take Bella for a walk, I barely have an hour or two at most. Some days it feels as I've only just picked up my brush before I have to set it down again.

I'm feeding Ben Weetabix and it's going everywhere, running down the inside of his bib and onto his clean clothes. Bella is whining and scratching at the front door. Evie finally finishes her cereal and stirs the milk round and round, closely examining the concentric ripples she's creating.

'Evie,' I say, more sharply than I intend. 'Go and get ready for school. Make sure you've washed your face and brushed your teeth.'

She slides off her seat. I start wiping the beige mush off Ben's face and am dimly aware of Bella's tail thumping, which means Evie is with her and not getting ready. I look up and see Evie in the hall. She's put her coat on, wrapped a scarf round her neck, and is sitting on the floor, trying to jam her boots on. Her hat is lying next to her.

'Evie!' I shout.

'What?'

'You haven't even brushed your —' And then I stop.

'But you said, you said, get ready for school!'

She flings her hat at the front door, her face crumples and she starts that sobbing-howl I'm so familiar with.

I take a breath. It's my fault. I said it in the wrong order. She's obeying me exactly – getting ready for leaving the house first and then she would have gone upstairs and brushed her teeth. And now she's crying because she's done something wrong and she's not sure what or why I'm angry. I lift Ben down from his high chair and go and give her a hug. Ben puts his arms around her too but she pushes him away. I dry her tears and unwind her scarf and help her out of her coat.

'Go to the bathroom, give your face a wash with soap and brush your teeth for two minutes using the egg timer. And then come down here and we'll both get ready to go to school together,' I say gently.

She takes a juddering breath and nods. I start bundling Ben into his all-in-one suit. There isn't a name for what's wrong with Evie. It's as if she has fragments of disorders. I think this one – having to hear everything in the right order and having difficulty processing information – is a touch of dyspraxia. And maybe she has an element of dyslexia too. The doctors can't find anything wrong with her and, I hate to admit it, if she'd been my biological child, I would probably have laughed it off as Evie's quirkiness, which is what Ollie does. Instead, I blame her real mother. She's damaged Evie in some indefinable way.

It amazes me how children live entirely in the present. By the time I'm wheeling Ben in the buggy down Rombald's Lane, Bella on the lead attached to one handlebar, Evie is dancing alongside me, singing and chatting. The resentment towards Ben over his party has gone, there's no trace of her tears a few minutes before and she's back to being my lively, lovely, sunny daughter, bestowing magic kisses on her brother.

'Evie kiss,' he laughs, and blows a raspberry back at her.

She skips almost all the way to school. At the gates, she gives me a bear hug, almost crushes Ben with an affectionate squeeze, and races off, waving over her shoulder. Her teacher, Jack Mitchell, is waiting at the door to her classroom, welcoming the children.

'Hey, Evie!' he shouts. 'What did you make this weekend?'

He crouches down next to her and I can hear her telling him in great detail about the chaos she created in the Ben's bedroom. Evie loves Jack. He's one of those gentle, kind, funny men that children gravitate towards. He's a child-man, I think, his development arrested somewhere along the line so that he's perfectly in tune with under-nines. Jack has known her since she was about Ben's age as he used to work in the nursery and he often babysits in his spare time. It's not the done thing, I know, but in a small town like this, everyone is grateful to him for his help.

'It sounds like an installation piece,' he says, and she nods gravely.

Jack completely ignores me – he's so focused on Evie – but I'm used to that now and I'm grateful. Who else would listen to her endless tales of Meccano and magic? This year Jack's got a new teaching assistant, Hannah White. She's talking to the children inside the classroom. I don't know her that well yet but Evie seems to get on with her too. Hannah looks up and sees me.

'Mrs Morley? Have you got time for a quick word?' she asks.

I think of Jennifer Lockwood, my agent, waiting for me, and nod reluctantly. It's bound to be about Evie's spelling. Or her maths.

'Perhaps you could come inside for a moment? I can't leave the children and Mr Mitchell has agreed to keep Evie occupied,' she adds, smiling at me. Her teeth are small and perfectly straight.

She turns to go into the classroom. If she and Jack have already arranged this between them, perhaps it's more worrying than I thought. I take Ben out of the buggy and he rushes in excitedly, heading straight for the piles of boxes meant for junk modelling. Hannah hands me Evie's exercise book. She's curvy, her waist is tiny: a perfect hourglass figure. She's wearing a brocade dress, with short, square sleeves in a demure navy. Her legs are bare, even though there's a slight chill in the air and her sandals are tan. It's the perfect take on the practical yet professional look. I stifle my jealousy. If I cared enough, I'd do something about it, I tell myself.

The book is open at a story Evie's illustrated with a princess in a thin, spiky castle. On the next page the princess is holding the hands of a man and a woman who are on either side of her and she's beaming. I try not to be shocked at Evie's atrocious spelling.

It begins, 'wuns up on A tim thEr wuz a PrinSEs...'

Is Hannah going to remonstrate with me about the amount of time I spend practising spelling with Evie? I continue to read. The princess lives with her nasty, wicked stepmother and father. Instead of being rescued by a prince, she sets off across the moor in search of her real parents. She's accosted by a giant and a witch, but she defeats them with her magic wand that turns into a sword, and finds her true mother and father. Everyone lives happily ever after.

'It's so imaginative, don't you think?' says Hannah. She smoothes one lock of her long straight blonde hair behind her ear. She has green eyes. Her cheeks are round and plump with youth. She looks as if she's barely out of college but she must be in her mid-twenties. 'Even her spelling has improved.'

'Hmm,' I say.

'What do you feel about the content?' she says, her expression serious.

I flush. I feel as if it's an obscure test and I'm failing.

'I was thinking,' Hannah says slowly, 'that Evie must be working out some of the issues she has?'

'Issues?'

'Yes. With being adopted.'

'Oh.'

I look back at the story. The princess has dark hair and green eyes. Her parents have yellow hair and blue eyes. Even the wicked witch and the giant are blonde. When the girl finds her real parents, they all line up at the end, like peas in a pod, with identical sparkling emerald eyes and long black hair.

'We adopted Evie as a baby. She hasn't known anyone else in her life apart from us.'

My voice has taken on a defensive note. I glance over Hannah's shoulder. Ben has strewn cardboard boxes and polystyrene bits all over the carpeted area at the back of the classroom.

'Research shows that children who are adopted from birth still feel a sense of loss,' Hannah says. 'After all, they've known their real mother since conception. They form a bond with her in the womb and that's cemented during birth.'

'She's just feeling a little insecure and jealous about Ben, that's all,' I snap. 'It was his birthday at the weekend.'

How could Evie have 'formed a bond' with the woman who tried to kill her when she was a foetus?

A girl comes and wraps herself around Hannah's leg and the teaching assistant bends down and hugs the child and says softly, 'Sweetie, I'm talking to Evie's mummy. I'll be with you ever so soon.'

Hannah's smile is filled with empathy and concern and I immediately feel bad for speaking sharply.

'We could try play therapy with Evie if you like?' Hannah says.

'Play therapy?'

'I worked with kids in a developing country before, before I came here. Their lives are really tough, you know, in comparison... I mean, many of them had lost their parents or their brothers and sisters to disease or war. And the abuse, especially of the girls... It's a safe way of getting kids to act out what happened or how they feel using play to express their emotions.'

'Oh. That must have been quite hard for you though. To hear what happened to those children?'

I hadn't realized Hannah had worked overseas. It sounds a million miles away from the middle-class angst in Ilkley.

'Yes, it was. Heartbreaking.' She gives a little sigh and a half shrug as if shaking off terrible memories. 'We could have a go with Evie. I could do some role-playing with dolls or get her to write another story?'

I hesitate. I don't want Evie to feel it's a legitimate concern, for teachers to start making a fuss because she's been adopted.

'We love Evie just as much as if she were our biological daughter,' I say.

Hannah inclines her head. 'Of course, you do, Mrs Morley.'

'Zoe, please. And thank you for bringing this to my attention,' I add, feeling awkward when she's only trying to help. 'Just, you know, keep an eye on her. Let me know if anything else like this comes up.'

'I will,' she says, but her words are drowned out by Ben, who's fallen over and has started crying.

Hannah walks me to the door.

'By the way, Mr Mitchell says to tell you that next Saturday is fine. And I wanted to say that I'm also happy to do any babysitting if he's busy and you need someone.'

Jack has agreed to take the children on Saturday afternoons to give me more time to paint, since Ollie seems to be working longer hours at the weekends, but any extra help is always welcome.

'Thank you. I'm sure Evie would be delighted,' I say, and Hannah beams.

After I've dropped Ben off at nursery, I head to Brook Street. I want to reassure Jennifer Lockwood that the painting is going well. As I approach the gallery, I feel anxious. If someone other than me has noticed that Evie is behaving oddly, perhaps something really is wrong? I'm also nervous because, if I'm honest, I'm a bit intimidated by Jenny. She's warm, but also efficient and business-like. Ollie describes her as an iron fist in a velvet glove. I badly want this exhibition to be a success.

I tie Bella up outside and go in. The gallery is beautiful: a white, open space. It's flooded with light sliding off the moor: clear and chill. In my waxed Barbour jacket and paint-streaked jeans, I feel dowdy compared to Jenny. As usual, she's in navy, wearing her signature red lipstick. She's talking to someone so I look around. It's an exhibition by an artist who paints birds in meticulous detail; every feather seems to glow. The backgrounds are an impressionistic blur of colour, the paint running and seeping across the canvas.

The cobalt-blue of a sunbird; the lime-yellow of a spiderhunter, all impossibly exotic here in the heart of Yorkshire.

The man Jenny was talking to is staring at me. He's tall and broad, built like a soldier, not an artist or a dealer. He has dark hair in rough curls and he's unshaven. His green-brown eyes are piercing. There's something leonine about him. He's scowling and I wonder if I've inadvertently interrupted his chat with Jenny or maybe Bella has upset him, scratching at the gallery door.

Jenny appears from behind a huge vase of proteas and kangaroo paws. 'Let me introduce you two. This is Harris, one of my artists, and this is—'

'Zoe Butterworth.'

He has a Bradford accent. He strides forward and holds out his hand. He clasps mine firmly. His palm is warm, his fingers calloused.

'Oh,' I say, flustered. 'How did you know?'

'I like your work,' he says.

'How are you, Zoe?' asks Jenny, giving me a kiss on the cheek.

'Very well, thanks. I hope I'm not interrupting.'

Harris says, 'We're done.'

'I came to show you a couple of photos I took on my phone of my latest painting. I'm sorry I didn't answer your emails—'

'I know you're busy, Zoe.' Jenny smiles. 'I'm not concerned. Your paintings are wonderful and I'm sure you'll get them done on time.'

She still holds her hand out for my mobile though. I give it to her and, to my surprise, Harris stands next to Jenny and leans over to look at the screen.

'It's good.' His tone is terse but I find myself welcoming this one word of praise more than any effusive outburst.

Jenny nods in agreement. 'Get in touch when you're ready to bring them in,' she says. 'I can't wait to see them all together.'

———

Harris follows me out of the gallery. As the door swings shut behind him, he says, 'Do you want to go for a coffee?'

I look at him in astonishment and he regards me calmly. He still hasn't smiled. He doesn't explain himself or try to persuade me further. He strokes Bella's head and undoes her lead from the hook on the wall, before passing it to me. He's waiting for a response.

'Okay,' I say. 'That would be lovely.' I grin foolishly.

He turns and marches down the street and I almost have to skip to keep up with him. I dodge passers-by, trying not to get in a tangle with Bella's lead. He doesn't ask me where I want to go. He passes Costa and Bettys – I imagine they would be too twee for him – and The Bar, where I would have gone if I wanted a decent coffee, and veers sharply down a little side street. I'm curious now, I can't think where he has in mind. He ducks swiftly through the last doorway before the mini arcade along Back Grove Road. It's a tiny cafe I've never noticed before. There are only three small booths with wooden benches and on the short counter there's a lemon-yellow plate with chocolate brownies and a blue one of coconut macaroons; a spiral of cucumber slowly spins in a jug of water. That's it. But the smell is overwhelming: there are at least eight different kinds of coffee in burlap sacks with labels saying which *fazenda* they're from.

'How do you take your coffee?' he asks.

'I'll have a latte.'

He looks disgusted and then, not hiding his distaste, says, 'Do you want a cake?'

I shake my head, although I would quite like a macaroon, and slide onto one of the benches. Bella ducks underneath and sits on my feet. Harris squeezes himself in on the other side and stares frankly at me. I start feeling uncomfortable. What am I doing here with this strange man? I should be at home painting. I calculate how much time I have left before I need to pick up Ben. Harris's coffee is black with a thin skin of froth on the surface; it looks lethally strong.

'What kind of painting do you do?'

He shakes his head and his curls tremble.

'I'm a sculptor. I make things out of scrap metal. Things you might find on the moor. Or not find.' I look puzzled and he says, 'When you look at one of my sculptures, you could imagine discovering it on the moor. It wouldn't be out of place. Like it belonged. Or it grew. Or the earth ejected it.' He shrugs. 'Hard to describe, isn't it? One's art.' He reaches into his jacket pocket and pulls out a flyer. 'My exhibition opens soon. Will you come to the preview?'

He pushes it towards me. There's a picture of him in black and white, looking brooding, and a photo of one of his sculptures, raw and rusty and somehow tortured. His hand, stretched across the table, his fingertips still touching the corner of the flyer, are like something sculptural too – the digits long and sturdy, covered in a web of cuts and scars and callouses. I want to reach out and touch him. I'm still looking at the invitation, wondering how to respond. Is he being so forward because I'm an artist too, represented by the same gallery? I want people to come to my exhibitions but somehow I can't muster the chutzpah to invite random strangers let alone the parents I know from the school run. And when they do come, I'm so nervous I can't bring myself to promote my art properly.

He laughs suddenly and I look up. His teeth are very white against the olive of his skin. Is he from here? Perhaps he's spent years abroad and developed this sun-baked, wind-burnt look.

'Too soon?' he says, sliding his hand back and gripping his coffee mug. 'I've only just met you but I feel like I've known you forever. I've been following your work. Jenny took me on recently – poached me from another gallery – and I saw she represented you too. I thought I'd run into you sooner or later.'

'Following my work?' I echo.

'Aye. I can see the connection we have to the moor. It runs through everything you do. There's something stark about your work. Dark – even in the paintings with the prettiest colours. *Sunset over the Twelve Apostles. Dawn at Black Beck.'*

He's quoting the names of paintings I did four years ago. The Apostles are twelve stones set in a circle at the peak of Rombald's Moor, dating back to Neolithic times. They might have been part of a ritual to worship the sun. In my picture, the silhouettes of the granite blocks are set against a sky suffused with salmon-pink and primrose. Jenny had told me I needed to lighten my work up a bit, use a greater tonal range. I'd sell more, she'd said.

'It doesn't matter how bright the sky, you can feel the crushing emptiness of your life faced with that wide, open space,' he says, as if reading my mind. He leans forward. 'When I look at your paintings, I can sense it. The danger. The way you can lose yourself on the moor. Slip silently into a peat bog. We have so little wilderness left – but there's some that's wild and untamed right here.'

I nod. It's exactly what I believe, what I try to portray in my work. The unthinking cruelty of nature, running alongside our so-called civilization.

'People usually talk about the colours; they buy my paintings to remind them of Yorkshire or because the sky goes with their sofa,' I say. 'They don't see the brutality. They say things like, "You must really love the moors." I don't. I don't love them or hate them.'

'It's got nothing to do with *liking*. They're always there, as much a part of you as your bones or the blood in your veins.'

I look at him in surprise. It's as if he's finished my sentence for me. And then I can't help myself. I beam at him, and Bella, as if sensing my change in mood, wags her tail against our legs.

'I've been watching your progression as an artist,' Harris continues, stroking Bella's head. 'It was all there at the start – the ideas, the concepts. But you're bringing it all together. Making it come alive.'

'Yes!' I say. 'It's as if it's become, not easy, because it's never easy, but harmonious. I don't mean the colours—'

'No,' he agrees. 'The concept. It's fused. There's no discord between what you're trying to achieve and the composition of your pictures.'

I can't remember the last time I was able to speak to anyone about my work properly – maybe at university? Just afterwards when I was at that shared studio? Ollie is and always has been supportive, but he doesn't get it. He doesn't see any real difference between me and one of his clients – who freezes flowers and photographs them – except I make less money. Jenny sells my pictures at a high price, but I don't paint fast enough to be rich. It's not about the money, even if that's all that matters to Ollie.

'Aye, you're a rare talent, Zoe Butterworth,' he says, and I glow with pride.

For all his gruffness, Harris is surprisingly easy to talk to – and, I have to admit, I'm stupidly pleased that another artist has taken the time to look at my paintings. I finish my latte and start to think about getting back. He notices immediately.

'Can I get you another?'

I should go. But it's so wonderful to talk about art I can't bring myself to leave.

'I'll get it,' I say, starting to rise.

'No.'

He orders another latte, returning with two coconut macaroons.

'Must be hard trying to work with two little ones.'

I look at him in surprise. How does he know?

'Article in the *Telegraph* magazine.'

I remember it. There was a photo of me with Evie, holding Ben. He was about six months old at the time, and I was feeling this desperate need to get back to my painting – but I didn't have any childcare: Ben seemed far too little to put in a stranger's hands. It had been Jenny's idea – to increase people's desire to own one of my paintings precisely when I couldn't supply any. And it worked. People are clamouring for another Zoe Butterworth picture, she tells me. When I married Ollie, I took his name – Morley – but kept my own for my art work. I like the distinction. The photographer, who was local, had made us stand in Well's Walk, me leaning against one of the little bridges over the beck, Ben on my hip; Evie had looked like a jungle sprite, peering through the foliage of a giant agapanthus.

'It's tough if you can only work in the mornings when your daughter's at school and your son's at nursery.'

I nod, biting into a macaroon.

'What about your husband? Can he help out?'

I shake my head. 'Ollie's an accountant. His clients are artists – people in fashion, music, art – interesting careers but sporadic incomes. A nightmare for the tax man. I'm sure you know what it's like. He's away a lot,' I add.

The macaroon is delicious, crisp on the outside and meltingly gooey in the middle. Bella can smell it and whines. I give the last bit to her.

'We used to go out together – you know, fashion shows, book launches – but he's taken on a lot of celebrity clients. When I have gone with him, they act like I'm less than nobody. The wife of their accountant...' I tail off. I can't believe I've told all this to a complete stranger. There's something about Harris though – the quality of the way he listens, perhaps.

'So he's got money but he won't help you,' he says, and I catch my breath because the way he's put it sounds brutal. 'It's not just about the time, is it? It's the headspace. As an artist, you need the freedom to think and feel. Switching from being a mother to a painter for a couple of hours and back... Can't be easy.'

I nod. Harris leans forward and stares at me so intensely I want to look away but I'm unable to.

'You have to. You're a brilliant artist. Never forget it.' He sits back and takes some coins from one of his pockets and lays the money by his cup as a tip. 'I'll let you get on. I know you've work to do.'

Almost before I've taken breath, he's gone. I bundle myself into my coat, fumbling for Bella's lead. I feel bereft. He left so quickly. I didn't even take his number or email address. He did leave the flyer though. I slip it into my pocket and start to walk home. I can't see any sign of Harris. I follow the winding path through Well's Walk, past where the photographer took our picture, up to the edge of the moor and then alongside the tarn. Three mallard ducks plop into the water when they see Bella and she gives a low bark that's almost a growl. I'm hardly conscious of where I'm going. I'm thinking about Harris. His intensity. The way he seemed to understand me and my painting. It feels like a heavy cloak has slipped from my shoulders and, for a few minutes, I'm so light, it's as if I'm floating. I'm once more madly, passionately in love with painting; full of confidence and can-do. I imagine my exhibition open night: my pictures hanging on those pure, white walls, people sipping wine, the heady buzz of conversation.

Can I do it? Could I pull it off? The deadline is so close. The familiar anxiety starts again – how to find the time, how to create the mental clarity for inspiration; even fitting in the simple, practical details of ordering new linseed oil, taking more photographs as background material, seem insurmountable problems. I take a deep breath. I will make it happen. I can do this. I see Harris's strange hazel eyes gazing at me as I form this resolution; shafts of green woven through his iris. What an odd name he has – Jenny never gave me his surname and his first name sounds like a last name. It only says Harris on the flyer too. Harris. Like Madonna. It makes me giggle – he's the last person to remind anyone of the pop star.

Normally I come off the tarn path at Cowpasture Road and head to our house along the street, but today I cross the beck and double back onto the moor. There's a hum, low as ultrasound, of bees hovering over the bilberry bushes. I emerge on Hangingstone Road and follow the bridle path that runs alongside the surreal green of the golf course. There's almost no point in going home – when I get there I'll have to turn round and leave again. I'll drive to pick Ben up, I decide, and at least Bella will have had a good run.

As I walk along the bridle path, I feel the hairs on the back of my neck tingle, and a shiver, the way a horse twitches, crosses my shoulder blades. Bella gives her strange growling bark again. It feels as if someone is watching me. But there is no one here. There isn't even anyone standing on the Cow and Calf rocks like there normally is. The backs of our neighbours' gardens are all discreetly hidden behind thick hedges – no one could be spying on me, unless they were looking out of an upstairs window. I reach our garden and stop. One of the things we plan to do is put up a wooden fence and plant a hedge, as well as fitting a gate so we can access this lane directly from our lawn. Now, standing outside our house, I can look right through the wire and into our kitchen; I can see my studio and Ben's bedroom next to it; Evie's attic window above them. And so could anyone else standing out here.

'Your story,' I say to Evie that night as I sit on her bed, 'the one you wrote for Miss White? It was really good. I was wondering, do you feel as if you're like that princess, looking for her real parents?'

She wanted to have the attic bedroom even though it's the furthest one away from the rest of us and, although it's large, the eaves slope down sharply so that not even a child can stand beneath them. We store a lot of junk up here and I worry that Evie will go into the loft space. The floor isn't properly stable over the old beams.

Evie regards me as if I'm stupid. She blows her hair out of her eyes and falls backwards onto her bed.

'It's just a story, Mummy. There aren't any giants or witches. Are you going to read *Charlotte's Web* or not?'

I give up questioning her, and after both children are finally asleep, I sit on the sofa waiting for Ollie. I've poured myself a large glass of wine and I'm looking through Evie's fairy tale. I'm not sure that Hannah is right – Evie's spelling seems as bad as ever.

Ollie kisses me on the cheek. His face is cold. I watch him surreptitiously as he hangs up his trench coat and threads his suit jacket onto a hanger. As he walks to the kitchen, he picks up toys and drops them in the row of wooden wine boxes on wheels that he's lined up on one side of the dining-room wall.

'Good day? Anything for tea?'

'Not yet,' I say, yawning.

He searches for something to defrost in the freezer.

'Hannah White wanted to talk to me today. She's Evie's teaching assistant.'

'Oh yeah?'

He turns the oven on. It's a Smeg in brushed stainless steel and the settings are so complicated I can barely use it for anything more advanced than grilling cheese on toast.

'She thinks Evie's worried about being adopted.'

Ollie snorts in response.

'Have a look at her story.'

He pours himself a glass of red wine and joins me on the sofa, turfing Bella onto the floor.

'Her spelling is appalling.'

He hands me back her exercise book. The timer pings and he slides something frozen in a silver foil tray into the oven. I can't help thinking that Harris would not set a timer to make sure the oven is hot enough before putting a ready meal for two in to cook. And then I feel a bit mean. Ollie is home late again and he's probably starving. I've been nibbling the children's leftovers.

'Do you think we should be worried?'

'No, of course I don't. We're not wicked step-parents. She's being creative. Look at her princess wielding a sword. It's a modern twist on a fairy tale. And she's obsessed with that giant, what's his name, the one that lives on the moor. Rombald. God, why do these bloody people have to interfere?'

I look again at her drawing of the stepdad. She's coloured him in so hard, the paper has flaked away. He's wearing a grey suit and a navy tie and in his hand is a briefcase. I look at Ollie's shale-coloured suit jacket hanging by the door. It looks expensive. He never used to dress like that for work. The lining is a pale-oyster silk. All my clothes are smeared with yogurt or ketchup. Maybe Evie doesn't see Ollie as her real father because he's never here?

I try to think back to when Ollie first became like this – so busy all the time, home late, working on Saturday, checking emails on his phone when he's supposed to be playing with the kids. Has he become ambitious? Or is there another explanation? It doesn't seem that long since he used to come home early while Evie was still awake and swing her over his head and tear round the garden with her. Ollie's work was never something he took this seriously. It's crept up on me and I've got used to feeling a little like a single mum. It's been that way since Ben was born. So Evie could associate

Ben's birth with Ollie disappearing out of her life, and she also feels resentful of the attention I give her brother.

'Maybe she's becoming more aware of what it means to be adopted?'

'For Christ's sake, Zoe, she's seven,' he says.

He kisses me on the top of my head and picks up his jacket before going upstairs to get changed.

I've been searching for you since you were born. There hasn't been a single day when I haven't missed you or thought about you. Seven years. It's taken me seven years. I would never have given up – I hope you realize that when you're older and understand what I've been through. Sometimes I thought I would never find you, but I always knew that God was on my side, and He would help me put this wrong right.

As the Lord says, 'My success can only come from Him. In Him I trust, and unto Him I look.'

I never gave up looking for you but, at times, I was sad and felt hopeless.

On one of those occasions, I visited my parents in Yorkshire: where we come from, you and I. They don't make me happy, my parents, your grandparents, but we are getting on better now. My mother told me some details about your fake mother she'd never mentioned before. I was able to track her down. That was how I found you. It was two years ago. I was walking home along the edge of the river, past the park, feeling the weight of my life pressing down on my shoulders. I knew you lived here by that stage, you see, but I hadn't managed to find your address yet.

I saw a little girl standing at the top of a slide. I couldn't see your face – your hair was haloed by light. I felt my breath catch, my heartbeat quicken. You slid down, your dress rising. I remember you were wearing shoes with clear sequins and embroidered strawberries. I felt the old sadness rise in me; you seemed about the same age as my daughter and I was reminded, yet again, of what I had lost.

You turned to look at me. I don't think you realized our connection; maybe I caught your eye because I was standing so still, watching you. The shock of recognition hit me, like a blow to my chest; a left hook to my stomach. You smiled. Your green eyes glowed. You still had your baby teeth. You were – and are – so beautiful. I was absolutely certain, like I know the feel of the breath in my body, the beat of my heart. You, the little girl on the slide, were my daughter. You were five years old. I had finally found you.

I sat on a park bench and pretended to read a paper. I watched you and watched you, drinking you in, like a thirsty man craves water in a desert. You have the same colour eyes as me. You certainly don't look like your adopted mother, father or your baby brother. I was relieved to see that you were healthy and happy – although you are painfully small and thin for your age. I've been worrying all this time – what if your pretend parents didn't care for you or didn't love you? They do. They do love you – I can see that. But then, they're well off. They can afford to buy you nice things.

I followed you home. I couldn't bear to lose you again. Over the next year, it took hard work to get close to you, but I was energized, I had a purpose once more. And nothing was going to get between me and my daughter again.

Later, when I was able to speak to you, you told me that you left London when you were little. It's ironic that you've been here all along while I was on the other side of the world. Now that I know you better, I can see you're not as happy as you looked then, that carefree day in the park. You're troubled. It's sad to see it in a child – but how could you not be? For your entire life, you've been in mourning for your real parents. You lost something so profound, the day you were born, that you have never been able to recover.

I watch you: in the playground, walking home from school, in your bedroom at night. You are like a beautiful bowl that has been cracked. There's a fragment missing. I will heal you. I will mend you. I am your flesh and blood. I'm the lost piece in your life. No one can love you as much as I do. No one else knows how you feel like I do; no one else sees your loss.

Every day is a bitter-sweet joy. I watch you as often as I can, but I have to maintain my distance. Your fake parents touch you, hug you, kiss you. I can never get close enough. Even when I'm right next to you, I'm not near enough. The relief I felt on finding you was tarnished, because the old bitterness and rage rose up again.

They stole you from me. They took you away for seven years. Your entire lifetime. A life sentence. The waiting has been endless. The watching. The planning. Now, finally, I'm almost ready. I've got a few things to take care of and then we can be reunited.

Make no mistake, my darling. I am coming for you.

I will take you back.

# TUESDAY

I leave the buttery crusts of toast and puddles of spilt milk – the detritus from breakfast – and head to my studio. It doubles as the guest bedroom so I keep the sofa bed covered and roll up the carpet to prevent everything getting splattered with paint. It's at the back of the house, looking over our garden and up to the Cow and Calf rocks. I notice that the slope of bracken encroaching the moor is already starting to turn a crisp burnt umber.

My exhibition is going to feature a series of abstract paintings of the moor, paired with a line from Emily Brontë's *Wuthering Heights*. I *think* I've finished the painting that I was working on, the one I showed Jenny. It's hovering over that fine line of being done and looking overdone. I move it to one side. I wish, for what feels like the thousandth time, as I get out my brushes and my paint, that I had more time and, more importantly, someone to talk to about my work, someone who gets it and gets *me*, what I'm trying to achieve. A small voice whispers in my head that perhaps Harris is that person.

I take a deep breath and try to focus. I pull out photographs and sketches that I hope will inspire me. I grew up near Burley, the next village along, so the moor has always been part of my life. It's like a muse: the colours of the heather and the sky; how you can see the savagery of the wind in the way the dwarf pine trees are bent double; the bleak lines of the landscape in winter when everything save the moss and the grass are dead, stones like bones, poking through a thin skin of bilberry bushes, rushes reflected in black bog water.

I lay out all my materials. I use cheap brushes as I go through them so quickly. Most of them are worn down. I throw them in the bin. I'll need to get more from the art shop on Hawksmoor Street. I top up my jars of Zest-it, Liquin and linseed oil – I buy these in bulk – and check I don't need any more oil paints. I pace around my studio, glancing at the photographs and the sketches, the new large white canvas solidly in place on the easel. I can't concentrate at all.

My mobile rings and I jump. I don't recognize the number.

'Hello?' I say.

There's a pause. 'It's Harris.' His voice is deep.

'Harris?' I stutter. And then I can't help myself. I smile.

'I got your number from Jenny. I hope you don't mind me calling. I was thinking – you finished your painting, the one you showed me – so you must be starting another one. When I've got a new piece of work to do, I find it hard to get going. I thought maybe a walk would help. It's beautiful on the moor.'

How did he know? I haven't had this before, this intuitive understanding of how I work. Ollie gives me a look when I say I've been walking, as if I've been shirking, instead of realizing it's all part of the process, how I create new work. I look at my watch. I've got just enough time. I know from experience that standing here in front of a blank canvas is a waste of energy.

'Yes,' I say and I can hear the warmth in his voice when he replies.

We arrange where to meet. He hangs up without saying goodbye.

It *is* a beautiful day. It feels like early autumn – the sky is a brilliant blue and cloudless, the rowans fringing the moor are bowed with orange berries already, but the heather is still blooming: the flowers have faded to a vintage rose; clouds of pollen fall from the bells as we brush past. The smell is intoxicating. Bella sneezes and bounds ahead. Harris seems more alive here, not as solemn. He laughs, and his eyes glow green in the sunshine. We talk about our work; he knows so much about mine, I'm flattered.

In his presence, I feel able to stop as often as I want to take photos. I'm inhibited about doing this with Ollie as he sighs or strides ahead impatiently. Harris isn't patient – I can see he's a restless man – it's more that he's attuned to this landscape; he's thinking about his own work, absorbing, observing. I can't let Bella off the lead – there are sheep on the moor – but Harris takes her so I can concentrate on my pictures without her pulling me off-balance.

I tell him I'm worried about completing all the paintings in time for the exhibition. He shakes his thick mane of hair.

'Don't be. You'll do it. But make yourself and your work a priority. Get more childcare. Do whatever it takes, get whatever you need. This is going to be your best exhibition, your greatest work yet.'

I look at him in astonishment. How can he tell? How can he be so sure? As if I've spoken, he continues, 'When you've had a break, your work leaps forward. All that time, you think it's been wasted, but it hasn't. Your mind has been working. And once you start, you unleash all that creative energy. You'll see.'

He's talking about me, the gap I've had from midway through my pregnancy, when I was too sick to paint, until recently, when Ben started at nursery. But it sounds as if he's also talking about himself.

'Did you take a break from your art?' I ask.

'Aye. A long one. I went abroad for a few years.'

We're following the Millennium Way. Below us is Panorama Drive, which leads to a reservoir and Heber's Ghyll. The houses here are grand, with gardens that open directly out onto the moor. I imagine how that might be – to step out of your house and within minutes you'd be surrounded by bog myrtle and sundews; curlews and green plovers.

'Where did you go?'

'The Hunza Valley in Pakistan.'

I must look blank because he explains. It's a magical place, he says: a lush, fertile valley sliced through the middle of the Kharakorum Mountains, where the people grow apricots and, legend has it, lead long and healthy lives. It's the origin of the myth of Shangri-La, Harris adds, a Himalayan utopia hidden from the rest of the world. He worked on an organic farm. He makes it sound so idyllic, I'm jealous. My life here in Ilkley with two children is prosaic.

'How long were you there?'

'Seven years. I've not been back long.'

It explains his sunburnt, wind-darkened skin; why he seems foreign in spite of his Yorkshire accent.

'I made sculptures when I was out there, but they were small and I didn't have the right tools – or enough scrap metal – to create the kind of pieces I wanted to. But now I'm back, the work I've done has scale and power. You'll see,' he says, turning to me and smiling.

He's assuming I'm going to the preview of his show. He's right. I *am* going to go. I won't be able to keep away. I'm surprised that the work he's showing isn't about the Hunza Valley, but when I ask him, he says shortly, 'No. It's about here. This place. This is what I've missed,' and he gestures to the moor surrounding us and strides ahead of me. It's exactly how I would feel if I were him.

We stop at the Swastika Stone. It's a flat piece of pockmarked granite on the edge of a small cliff. It's ringed by metal railings so that you can't stand on it. Carved in the centre is a loose shape, vaguely like a swirly swastika. It's thousands of years old.

'It's a symbol of peace,' says Harris, as we perch on nearby stones. 'You see the same ancient sign in India too.'

I'm so at ease with him that I take out my sketch book. Harris has brought a flask of coffee. He pulls a jam jar of milk out of his rucksack, even though he doesn't drink it, and tops up my cup. He sits with his arm round Bella, as if she's his dog. It's so clear I can see all the way across the valley, to the moor on the other side, the slow climb up Simon's Seat above Bolton Abbey; a line of white wind turbines on the crest of a hill. I feel a peace that I haven't known for years with this virtual stranger.

After a while, he joins me, leaning over my drawing. For once, I don't mind another person seeing my incomplete work. He looks back at the view and nods approvingly.

'You've captured the shape of the hill perfectly. The feel of the place. I can almost hear the wind singing through them blades.'

He's so close to me, I can feel the heat rising from his skin, where he's rolled his sleeves to his elbows.

'I'm so pleased I found you,' he says softly. 'I've waited a right long time to meet you.'

I blush and duck my head. But I feel as if I'm blossoming, unfurling like a flower in the warmth of his attention. The picture I'm going to paint will be good: I can already sense the atmosphere of it, the dusky pinks and burnt oranges as summer bleeds into autumn.

That evening I heat up a goat's cheese and spinach tart and empty a bagged salad into a bowl. I stopped at Tesco's on the way home and picked up some olives and sun-dried tomatoes from their deli. It's not quite proper cooking – not like the shepherd's pies with their buttery mash and the unctuous chicken casseroles that Ollie's mum makes and he wishes I did – but the salad looks a little more interesting now. I also bought pizza – Evie's favourite food. She gave me a quick hug around one of my legs and said, 'Thank you for such a nice tea,' before she ran off to her room.

Now, as I lay the table and even light a candle, I notice there's a little smear of ketchup where she'd pressed her face against my hip.

Ollie comes in with a gust of cold air and a flurry of autumn leaves.

'Smells good,' he says. I expect him to be delighted he doesn't have to start cooking, but he peers in the oven and frowns. 'You've got it on too high.'

'It's got more dials than the cockpit of a plane. You need a PhD in engineering to figure out how to use this thing!' I try and keep my voice light.

He adjusts the temperature and the timer and loosens his tie. It's the colour of heather.

'New tie?' I ask, running my hand down his chest.

'Yes,' he says, turning away and reaching for the wine. 'I've had back-to-back meetings all day. I'm shattered.'

He takes a sip and makes a face.

'What's wrong? Has it been open too long?'

That hardly seems likely in our house.

He shakes his head. 'It's not that nice. Was it on special offer by any chance? There is a reason for that, you know.'

He pours us both large glasses and sticks the bottle in recycling.

'When did buying wine for four pounds ninety-nine become a crime?'

'Old habits die hard,' he says. 'We can afford to get decent plonk, Zoe.'

He goes upstairs to change and I sigh. My phone beeps. It's a text from Harris. I unlock my mobile quickly, my heart skipping a beat. It makes me smile, it's so in keeping with his character: terse but kind. It reads:

You'll save time if you buy prepared canvases. More expensive, but worth it. Call this guy. Tell him I told you to ring. He'll give you a discount. Harris.

I lean against our flashy new oven, letting the warmth seep into me. There's a phone number and a website. Preparing canvases takes so long it would free up a lot of my time if I bought them already stretched onto a wooden frame and primed with acrylic paint. I click through to the website. You can order online. It's so expensive, though. Should I really be spending that kind of money when I can do it myself?

I think about Harris sitting on the moor, his arms wrapped round Bella, saying fiercely, 'Make yourself and your work a priority… Do whatever it takes.' There was such conviction in his voice. He believes in me. I glance towards the dark end of the house. Ollie still hasn't reappeared. I re-read Harris's text. My husband hasn't asked me a single thing about my day. I wonder how much his new tie cost. Or his suit, for that matter.

I'll do it, I decide, I'll get them tonight, and I feel a rush of excitement.

# FRIDAY

I've been thinking about him every day. I check my mobile obsessively in case he calls or texts. I have his phone number now so I could ring him. But what would I say? I only met him four days ago. Four days. It feels as if I've known him forever. Yet not well enough to send him a text saying, 'Coffee?' without an excuse, because it *is* only four days since Jenny introduced us. I'm acting like a teenager. I drop Ben at nursery and Evie at school. Neither Jack nor Hannah says anything to me – hopefully that means Evie hasn't drawn any more pictures of wicked step-parents and vengeful, sword-wielding princesses.

As I leave the playground I have that prickling sensation again, running across the back of my neck, as if someone is watching me. I stop on the pavement and look around. Parents and toddlers flow past me. A child scoots over my foot. And there is someone watching me. He's standing perfectly still on the other side of the road. In the hazy autumnal sunshine, I can't see his features, only his outline. He's tall, broad-shouldered. He holds up one hand in greeting. It's Harris. For a second, I wonder if he's a figment of my imagination, as if, by wishing, I've conjured him. I raise my hand too and step into the road without looking, as if I'm being reeled towards him. Something inside me is liquefying.

He turns as I reach him and we fall into step. He hasn't even said hello.

'Thanks for your text about the canvases. I've ordered some.'

I'm speaking too fast, gabbling my words.

'I hope my friend gave you the discount,' he says, holding the door to the cafe open for me.

The smell of freshly ground coffee and newly baked cinnamon buns envelops me. I slide into the seat where we sat last time. Harris returns from the counter with a latte and an Americano for himself.

'I've been thinking about you,' he says, and I go still. 'How are you getting on with your new piece?' he asks, rubbing Bella behind her ears.

He means he was thinking about my painting. I'm not sure whether I'm disappointed. I make a face.

'I haven't started yet. The walk helped,' I add, in case he thinks I didn't enjoy it, or it wasn't useful.

I take a sip of the coffee and try to breathe more slowly; my heart is racing. There is no small talk with Harris. A moment later, the waiter passes over a plate of cinnamon rolls, steaming gently. I bend my head over the plate and inhale the scent of the spices and hot bread. Harris breaks one in half and hands it to me. His fingertips, gritty with sugar, graze mine. I take a bite and the warm dough and caramelized almonds coated in maple syrup melt in my mouth. My senses are so heightened, it's as if I haven't tasted anything before. Harris is staring at me. I lick the sugar from my lips. The intensity of his gaze is unnerving and I drop my head. I'm drawn back, hooked by a strange flaw in his right eye, a deep green fleck in his iris. His nose is long, fine; he's unshaven; I'm struck again by his strength, the set of his jaw.

'I've brought you some things. From the moor. I thought it might help.'

As he reaches to one side, I look at him more frankly. He's not dressed in black, as I'd first thought when I saw him silhouetted on the other side of the road. He's wearing brown moleskin trousers, so soft I want to stroke them, and a thick shirt and a jumper the colour of moss. There are dark hairs at his throat. I imagine what he might be like without his shirt, and I immediately think of Ollie, whose pale skin has grown puffy, his stomach dough-like, from too little exercise and too much alcohol. I feel bad for being disloyal. I try not to stare at Harris's chest.

Harris opens his leather messenger bag and lays a couple of objects on the table in front of me. They're wrapped in white tissue paper. He unfolds the first one carefully. I watch his hands, mesmerized. They're large and strong. Did the scars come from his metal-work? Inside is a twisted branch. It's so wind-blasted it looks like driftwood. It's grey, burnished, as if it's been cast of silver, with a ruff of lichen that's equally sculptural. I pull the other parcel towards me and peel back the stiff paper to reveal a small skull. It's thin, with a snub nose. Harris turns my hand over. His are warm; his grip is firm. He places the skull in the palm of my hand. There are four canines; the top two are so long and curved I can feel them pricking my skin. There's a green tinge round the eye socket and in a fine line across the cranium. I'm not sure what animal it's from.

'Stoat,' Harris says, as if I've spoken out loud. 'They hunt grouse and partridge. I found it behind my house. I buried the body in the furze until it was just bone.'

His hand is still beneath mine, supporting it. I think of him seeing the small dead creature and digging a tiny grave for it. Planning ahead for all those months just so he'd see the skeleton. Or maybe he severed the animal's head and that was the only part he buried.

'It's been waiting for you all this time. Like I have.'

I shiver and he releases me. I set the skull down, the white paper crinkling around it, incongruous against this ancient, primordial-looking creature's bones. What does he mean – he's been waiting for me? For a friend to talk to? Or does he mean something more? I try and pull myself together. All of a sudden, this feels dangerous. Harris feels dangerous. I'm married, I remind myself. I have two children. I lick my lips again and taste salt and sugar and a trace of cinnamon. Harris leans back in his seat and smiles at me and I stare at him, transfixed. Perhaps this is what the stoat's prey feels like.

Harris drains his coffee and slides some coins onto the table.

'I can see you want to get on,' he says. 'You've work to do.'

I nod. I can't trust myself to speak. I haven't thanked him or asked him about his own art, his approaching exhibition. By the time I've got my coat on, and Bella back on the lead, he's gone. I wonder where he lives. I touch the crenellations swirling from a knot in the wood, run my finger down one sharp tooth. I rewrap these found objects and put them in my bag. How did he know exactly what I would need? The scene I've been imagining in my mind turns darker, more sombre. I'll have to get more raw umber.

Ollie texts to say he's got a drinks engagement after work and not to wait up. I grit my teeth and swear under my breath. Why is he never home? We need to have a proper conversation about how seldom he's here with me and the kids; our relationship is practically non-existent. I put the children to bed. I'm so exhausted, I follow them shortly afterwards. I must have fallen asleep straight away, because when I jolt awake, it's after midnight. For a moment, I think Ollie is home, but his side of the bed is cool, the sheets smooth. Something must have woken me. I rise and pull my dressing gown around me. I check Ben. He feels hot when I lay my hand against his forehead. I pull the covers down a little and move his toy lion. He opens and closes one fist; fat fingers curling like a starfish. I stand at the bottom of the stairs up to the attic where Evie sleeps, but I can't hear anything.

Shadows play across the landing as the moon's light is fragmented by tree branches. It's streaming through the window in my studio, where the door is half open. I go in. I placed Harris's gifts on the sill; now the moon picks out the contours of one empty eye socket in the stoat's skull, gilds the gnarled driftwood. I look outside. It's so bright I can see our garden clearly: an abandoned truck lies on its side; shadows from the table and benches are elongated across the lawn. The dark edge of the moor and the Cow and Calf rocks are crisp against the blue-black sky. I can't see anyone outside, watching us. As I shut the door behind me, I hear a noise. It came from the hall. I feel the hairs rise on the back of my neck. If it was an intruder, surely Bella would have alerted us? The sound comes again: a low murmur as if someone is whispering.

I creep quietly down the stairs. When I'm halfway, I pause. The next stair creaks. Bella whines and thumps her tail as she senses my presence. There's a shape on the sofa, haloed by light from the TV. Ollie. I click on the lights and blink in the brightness. He turns round and squints at me.

'What are you doing?' I ask. I'm angry he frightened me.

He gestures at the TV. He's watching *Suits* with the volume turned right down. It's his favourite show: an American series about some hot-shot lawyer who hires a college drop-out with an eidetic memory who's never been to law school.

'Trying to unwind,' he says.

I used to think Ollie loved the series because of its morality: the brilliant young lawyer, Mike Ross, takes on cases and clients that no one else will fight for. Now, as I watch Ross and Harvey Specter squaring up to each other, I wonder if it's something else that attracts him: naked ambition, raw greed and the lifestyle that only the super-rich can afford.

'Why are you doing this?' My voice is high and tight.

'Doing what?'

He rubs his eyes and sits up. He's still in his suit and it's rumpled, the tie loosened. It's another one I haven't seen before: chrome-yellow with a soft sheen. He can't help glancing at the screen.

I shake my head, my anger growing.

'You're never here.' I sound like Evie, but it's too late. So much for waiting for the proper time for a chat. 'You're out all the time. You even work every bloody Saturday. I feel like a single mother. I'm juggling my painting, two children, the dog.'

'I'm doing it for us!' he says, his voice rising. He tries to speak more quietly. 'We're a family of four now. I've got to be responsible for all of you. If I'm made partner, we'll be financially secure. I'm working all these bloody hours for you. For us.'

So that's what this is all about. Partner of the firm. Behind Ollie's head, the *Suits'* CEO, Jessica Pearson, strides through her firm, graceful as a panther, in six-inch heels and a necklace that cost more than a month's salary.

'I never asked you to.'

'You didn't have to. It's obvious. Your art is— Well, it's brilliant, Zoe, but it doesn't bring in much money. And it's erratic. You have no idea when you'll sell a painting or how much for. You're not business-minded about it. I love that about you, I really do, but don't you see? You doing what you want to do and not worrying about how much you're earning puts more pressure on me.'

I can't believe what he's just said. I pull my dressing gown more tightly around me.

'Have you forgotten I'm raising two children, with no help from you, and my work has to fit in around them? Maybe I could earn more, be more "business-minded", but it's pretty bloody hard when I only have a couple of hours a day to knock out a masterpiece.'

He sighs and interlocks his fingers behind his head, stretching. A joint in his spine cracks.

'We're not poor,' I continue. 'I was poor when I was growing up. I know what it feels like. We're far from that. You don't have to do this, Ollie. You don't have to work this hard. I'd rather have less money and have you at home more.'

He pauses the DVD. A woman with a perfect cleavage and fuchsia-pink lips wavers on screen.

He says carefully, 'I know how tough it was for you. Don't you realize – I don't want that for our children? But you've no idea. What all this costs.' He gestures to the smeary stainless-steel units. Presumably he means everything, not just the new kitchen, and I have a pang of guilt when I think how much I spent ordering canvases and paying for delivery.

'If it's that bad, we should downsize.'

'No,' he says, 'it's not that bad. We're fine. You're right – we're comfortable. This is what I've always wanted. A big house with a garden, by the moor. You've got your studio. It's what I've worked for. But I need more, Zoe, don't you see? I want our kids to have the best. Not to have to scrimp and save and eat beans on bloody toast every day like you did. A private education. No student loans. For us to be secure in our old age. Maybe even have a holiday abroad when I've made partner. You don't bother about these things, you never have. You're like your dad. Happy to live in the moment. I'm the one who's forced to think about our long-term security. Our children's future.'

I don't know whether to be affronted or pleased that he thinks I'm like my dead, alcoholic dad, whom Ollie never met. Affronted, I decide.

'What's happened to you?' I say.

Where did the man I married go? It's as though now Ollie's doing the accounts for minor celebrities, he wants what they have. And then I can't help myself; I think of Harris. I cannot picture him picking silk ties in some expensive boutique in his lunch hour, let alone wearing one. Ollie presses play and we both watch as Harvey Specter stands in his soulless apartment with the best view in New York, and tells his brilliant, ex-junkie associate, that he doesn't care about caring, only about winning.

# SATURDAY

I love my work. In a funny way, I only realized how important it was to me when Evie was little and I no longer had all the time in the world to spend all day thinking about a painting instead of getting on with it. Talking about it with Harris reminds me of how passionate I used to be. Thanks to him, I'm trying not to feel guilty about asking Jack to look after Ben and Evie this afternoon so I can get on with painting. Ben is ready to go and I've already loaded his nappy bag and buggy into the car, but Evie hasn't responded to my increasingly annoyed shouts.

She's outside playing. I walk across the lawn. The day is cold. The sky is bright blue and there are long lines of clouds criss-crossed over the moor where planes have passed. Bald, damp patches proliferate; what should be flower beds round the edges are ragged with couch grass and small, ugly bushes grown woody. Ollie wants to hire a landscape gardener but I think we should do it ourselves. It seems such a waste of money to pay someone to put a few plants in. Maybe, after my exhibition, it can be my summer project. Evie is by her tree. It's a chestnut, I remember now, a little diseased. We ought to get rid of it – half the leaves have withered as if autumn has come early to one side. She's humming tunelessly and poking sticks into something dangling from the lowest branch.

It looks like a bird's nest, but spiky, without the cosy contours of a robin's, say. The twigs are bound with bits of ribbon, balloon strings, and some garish gold thread that was wrapped round one of Ben's presents. Inside the tangle is a tiny, naked doll resting on a cushion of lichen, her blonde hair matted. I know I should be thinking how creative Evie is, but some of her sculptures are a bit creepy. I go closer. I don't want to touch it. I'm being ridiculous, but there's something about the abandoned doll, a smudge of dirt on her cheek, that makes me shiver. Maybe it's put me on edge already, because I have the sensation that something is tiptoeing down my spine. I feel as if we're being watched again. Bella lifts her nose and sniffs. The wind stirs the curls at the nape of her neck. I look around but I can't see anyone else. I go to the fence and scan the bridle path, but there is no one here. I glance at the house next door; the upstairs windows are dark and stippled with the reflection of the dying bracken on the hillside.

I turn back to Evie and her monstrous nest. 'Come on, sweetheart. It's time to go. Didn't you hear me calling you?'

She narrows her green eyes at me, as if she's only just noticed me prowling around.

'Where are we going?' she asks.

'You're going to Jack's so I can do some painting. Remember, we talked about it this morning?'

'I don't want to go,' she says. She puts one hand behind her back.

'You'll have fun at Jack's house,' I say, going towards her.

Ben appears at the French doors.

'Plane,' he says. 'Sky,' pointing at a white vapour trail.

He crawls down the steps, smearing algae and rainwater across his trousers. Evie sidesteps. She's holding something, trying to hide it in the folds of her skirt. It's sharp-edged, white, not a piece of ribbon or string.

'Jack is waiting for you. Please go inside and get your coat.'

She half turns as if to obey and I'm about to run after Ben – he's going to jump in a puddle – when the thing she was clutching flutters to the ground between us. It lies, garish and glittering, on the grass. I catch the word *Daughter* in looping handwriting in sparkling-pink paint on the front before Evie snatches it up. Her birthday was three months ago. Ollie and I didn't give her a card like that.

'Can I see it, please, Evie?'

She shakes her head.

'Who gave it to you?' I ask again.

She doesn't say anything.

'Evie. Give me the card, right now.'

Her lip starts to quiver and her eyes fill with tears. She hands it to me. It's made of thin, cheap card, the kind you might find in a newsagent's or a corner shop. I open it. Inside in blue Biro someone has written:

*Hello my darling,*

*I'm your real father. I've been searching for you ever since you were stolen from me. I love you so much.*

*Daddy*

I go cold. I read it again and again. My chest tightens and I can't breathe. *Stolen. Your real father.* The words ring in my head like tinnitus.

'Evie. Who gave this to you?'

She shrugs. 'My daddy. My real one.'

'But who? Who was it?' I shout.

She starts to cry properly and runs inside and up the stairs. I see my reflection in the windows. My face is bleached of colour. Not only did Evie's mother choose not to stay in touch with us, she never told us who Evie's father was. I wheel around as if the man, as if her father, is here, standing in the bridleway. There is no one in the lane. The wind whistles through the hollow heart of the tree, making Evie's sculpture spiral. A laugh rings out and my head snaps up. It's only a couple of golfers, their jumpers garish in the grey light. Ben splashes in the puddle on the patio and screams as the cold water soaks him.

I haul everything back out of the car and ring Jack to cancel. I put the stairgates on and Ben in his room to play, then go to find Evie. I sit on her bed. She ignores me. Evie is building another sculpture, this time out of Meccano. It's one of the strange, spidery creatures she often creates; she does it when she's feeling perturbed and it seems to calm her. Because of her problems, she can often feel a little perturbed. I realize that's what she might have been doing in Ben's room at his party – calming herself. And maybe getting a letter from her 'daddy' could have made her feel anxious.

'Shall I tell you the story of you?' I say, hugging my knees to my chest and wishing my daughter would let me cuddle her.

She nods, barely perceptibly.

'A long time ago, before you were even a twinkle in anybody's eye, your daddy and I really, really wanted a baby girl. We tried and tried to have a baby but we just couldn't.'

The more I tell this tale, like a fairy story instead of an offering from the Brothers Grimm, the easier it gets.

'Then we met a kind young woman who was pregnant with a baby girl and she said we could have her baby because we didn't have one of our own. And so we waited and waited, and you grew bigger and bigger inside her and, one day, we got a phone call to say that you were ready to come out. So we rushed to the hospital—'

'In London?' asks Evie.

She doesn't look at me but she's stopped screwing bits of plastic together.

'Yes, love, this was when we were living in London. You'd decided to come early!'

I say this brightly and brush away the sick feeling I always get at this point. Today when people look at Evie they see an elfin beauty; an otherworldliness. I find it hard not to see the scars of those early weeks when she was floating in an opiate miasma: the wide-set eyes, the fairy-features, her thin frame – she still wears clothes designed for a five-year-old – are they all marks of foetal drug abuse? The doctors never could tell us.

'You were so tiny, you had to live in a box. You looked like a little elf! Daddy and I spent every minute at the hospital staring at your beautiful little face and watching you grow. And then, one day, the doctor opened the box and gave you to me.' Evie has now shuffled over and is half leaning against me. I slip off the bed next to her and put my arms around her. 'And from the moment I held you in my arms, I loved you,' I say.

I will never tell her about the doubts and uncertainties I had. There was something unnatural about her, as if she wasn't wholly human. I know that sounds like a terrible thing to say and I hated myself for feeling that way at the time. Thankfully Ollie loved her right from the start and, after the first few months, I did too. But perhaps she knew. They say the first six months are crucial, don't they? Maybe she sensed the lack of love in me.

Sometimes I say we chose Evie; sometimes I tell her she was a gift, but I always end by saying how precious she is to us and that she is *our* daughter. Normally this story makes her happy.

Before I can get to that bit, she interrupts.

'But what about my daddy? My real one?'

'I don't know who he is, Evie. The young woman who gave you to us didn't tell us who your original father was. But Ollie is your daddy. He's looked after you and loved you since you were born.'

I stroke her hair. Ben has lost patience with being in his bedroom and has come to find us. He pushes the door open and makes a beeline for the sculpture.

'Lego!' he shouts with delight.

Before I can reach him, he grabs one end and knocks it over. It breaks into several pieces and Evie starts her screaming-howl and throws herself full-length on the floor.


'Jesus.' Ollie rubs his hand over his face, holding the card as if it's contaminated. I waited until both children were in bed to tell him. 'Why would anyone do this to a child?' he asks.

He turns the card over in his hands, its glittery surface catching the light, re-reading the poisonous words inside.

*'I've been searching for you...'*

I know them by heart. Who would send such a thing to our daughter?

'Do you think it could be a joke? Maybe someone at school who's heard she's adopted?' he says.

A child then, seeing Evie, like a reversed Midwich cuckoo, an impostor fledgling in this blonde family nest.

'It seems a bit of a sick thing for a kid to do.'

I tell him Evie found the card in the garden.

'Could be a coincidence. Not even meant for her.'

'No,' I say flatly.

'If they've screwed up, given out our contact details to some idiot who wouldn't even admit to having a daughter before she was born...' he says.

A muscle clenches in his jaw. He leans forward and throws the card in the fire.

'Don't!' I grab it, flapping it to put the flames out. It's scorched but hasn't burnt. 'I'm going to speak to the adoption agency on Monday. We might need it as evidence.'

Does he think I'm being too dramatic? He's always been the one to reassure me – that everything with Evie would work out and I needn't worry so much. He's been right so far – her brain scans have all been normal. I still believe there could be something wrong with her that the doctors haven't properly diagnosed.

'How could her father have tracked her down?' I ask.

I don't feel as if we – Evie, Ben and I – are safe any more. Should I tell Ollie the feeling I've had, that we're being watched? Would he believe me?

Ollie shrugs. 'Let's see what the adoption agency has to say,' he says, as he puts another episode of *Suits* on.

I want to ask him more about the card. What it means. I'm frightened. I know Ollie thinks this kind of 'talking around an issue' is pointless because we don't know who sent it or how he found Evie. He used to have the patience for it but not any more. Talking about it would help me deal with it, though, make me feel less jittery. I open my mouth to speak, but Ollie grunts with laughter. I'm not sure what's worse – my husband chortling minutes after I've shown him the card that our daughter received from a man who believes his illegitimate child was stolen from him and has tracked her down seven years later – or Harvey fucking Specter's smug face.

# MONDAY

I have a churned-up feeling in my stomach. The words from the card we found on Saturday spin round and round in my head. '... *you were stolen from me...*' I'm shattered. I haven't been able to sleep for the last two nights. How does he know where we live? How did he find Evie? Is he definitely her father or is it a ruse to lure a small child to him – any small, pretty child? She's so precious – and so vulnerable. She's seven, for God's sake. What can she really understand about errant fathers who change their minds regarding their illegitimate children? The unfairness of it makes my cheeks burn. I tried again yesterday to talk to her properly about the card and explain that she's loved, but Ben was such a handful and it was impossible. Now is definitely not the right time, we're on our way to school.

Just before we get there, Evie sprints on ahead. I wish she'd stay with Ben, Bella and me. I glance around. The cars passing us are going slowly as they approach the junction. He could be in any one of them, tailing us. My palms become cold and slippery. I expect Evie to stop and wait for us at the bottom of the road, but she doesn't – she sprints round the corner, out of sight.

'Evie!' I shout.

I start to run. Bella thinks it's a game and races ahead, tugging on the lead. I can't control her and the buggy and it starts to tip over.

'Evie!' I yell again.

I yank Bella back and right the buggy. We reach the corner. My heart is pounding. Evie is standing a few metres away, waiting for us. She looks puzzled.

'Please don't run away like that—'

'Evie run,' says Ben.

'I wasn't running away!'

'I couldn't see you! Just stay where I can see you, okay?'

She pouts and drags her feet the rest of the way. She sullenly slopes into school without saying goodbye. I'm marching purposefully from the playground when I see Harris. He's waiting for me on the other side of the road. I stop. My heart clenches and a slow smile spreads across my face. Warmth courses through my body, like standing in front of a fire after a bracing walk on a chill day. I need to tell him I can't go for a coffee today. I have to get back, dig out Evie's case notes, call the adoption agency.

When I reach him he says, 'Do you want to walk back through Heber's Ghyll? It's a bit of detour but it'll not add too much time to your journey.'

I stare up at him. His dark curls are tousled by the wind; he has day-old stubble. He looks weathered, craggy; his green-brown eyes are kind.

'You look like you could do with clearing your head.'

I nod wordlessly. He takes Bella's lead from me and we follow the back roads through Ilkley, along wide, tree-lined roads, through narrow snickets carpeted with gold larch needles, past high stone walls and gardens where the last roses of the year bloom. We reach the wood, which connects the town to the moor. The winding path alongside the ghyll will eventually emerge at the end of Panorama Drive, alongside the reservoir and below the Swastika Stone. It's steep and in some places there are flights of stone steps, edged with moss. Harris strides ahead of me. I can see the muscles in his thighs as he climbs. The deep water is brown with peat, and edged with foam and ferns. I like the way Harris feels no need to speak.

We pause before we reach the moor. There's a semicircular granite wall at the top with a wooden bench set into it. By the time I reach him, he's already pouring coffee for us from his Thermos.

'You didn't paint much this weekend,' he says.

It's a statement, rather than a question and I relax back against the cold stone. I don't need to explain or justify myself with Harris. There's no judgement in his words: I don't have to feel guilty. I briefly consider telling him what happened but he doesn't know that Evie is adopted. It would be a long explanation. I don't want to be the kind of mother who talks about her children the entire time. I want Harris to be for me. I want him to be mine. There's nothing else in my life that I don't share with Evie and Ben and Ollie. I'm surprised how fiercely I feel; how possessive I am of him. He passes me a coffee and the mug is so small that our hands collide, our fingers merging. He steadies my wrist so I don't spill it and, when he lets go, I can still feel the impression of his fingertips against my skin.

'What about you?' I ask.

'Aye, I'm working like a dervish, trying to get it all done before the exhibition. I needed to clear my head too,' he says, and smiles at me.

Bella lies down at his feet, resting her head on his hiking boots. He strokes her gently.

'Fewer distractions than you. I can work all night if I feel like it.'

I sigh, remembering those days, alcohol and caffeine-fuelled, high on white spirit and the sheer thrill of painting. Out of nowhere I have an image of Evie's doll, lichen-stained, her bare limbs twisted, clawing her way out of her cage of twigs. I shut my eyes.

'Tell me about the Hunza Valley,' I say, and he does.

He describes cobalt skies, cherry blossom, the way the leaves turn gold and vermillion in autumn, women in marigold shalwar kameez carrying glacier-water, donkeys laden with panniers of chillies and apricots. His words wash over me like a tonic, clearing the thoughts crowding my mind.

'When you stand right in the centre of the valley, you're surrounded by five snow-capped mountains. It feels like you're in the heart of the earth and no one else but you exists.'

Like a fairy tale, his word pictures replace the dark greens of this dank, primordial wood.

'Thank you,' I say, and he doesn't ask why, as if he has seen my distress and knows how to help me forget, just for a moment.

He stands and stretches out his hand, pulls me to my feet and enfolds me in his arms. I inhale him. He smells of newly planed wood and oil.

'I'm glad I met you, Zoe Morley,' he murmurs into my hair. 'I knew you'd be a kindred spirit. My kindred spirit.'

He releases me and we emerge into a shale-grey sky. I need to get home but I'm torn, confused by his embrace. He sounded as fiercely possessive as I feel about him: *my kindred spirit*. Does he want to come back with me? I wish I could stay longer with him but I can't. I have to make that phone call.

As ever, he seems to intuitively discern what I'm thinking because he hands me Bella's lead and says, 'I'm heading this way,' inclining his head towards the moor.

He bends down and kisses me on the cheek. His stubble scratches me. He cups my face for a moment between both his hands and then he's gone. I watch as he strides away, towards the Swastika Stone and the bent pines on the horizon.

I touch my cheek with my fingertips, where his lips were. And I can't help but be pleased he thinks we're alike. I feel bereft without him. I try to put him out of my mind so I can think what to say to the adoption agency. When I reach our garden, I stop opposite the chestnut tree. The fence here is warped, as if Evie had been pushing it with her feet, her back against the tree trunk. I bend down and that's when I see it. There's a hole. Someone has cut the wire. It's quite neat and the strands have been bent so that a person reaching their arm in – or out – would not cut themselves. It's directly opposite the fissure in the tree. There's something poking out of the hollow at its base. Inside the cleft, the earth is smooth where Evie has worn it flat. There's a cup and saucer and a small plate with a glossy green leaf on it, as if she's been playing tea parties. And next to them is a parcel, covered in pink sparkly paper. Maybe it was one of Ben's presents that somehow got mislaid. I push my arm through the hole and pick it up. Bella nudges me with her cold nose but I ignore her. Could Evie have deliberately taken it and hidden it out here because Ben was getting all the attention last Saturday? But how many of the parents I know, even the most politically correct ones, would give Ben something wrapped in pink glittery paper? I turn it over in my hands. It's light and knobbly. There's no gift tag but instead a plain white sticker, the kind you'd use to readdress envelopes or paste on jam jars. It's the same blue Biro, slightly smudged, and the identical handwriting that was on the card. It says:

*To my daughter,*
*All my love,*
*your daddy*

My breath catches in my throat and I shiver. I stand up and tear it open. Inside is a My Little Pony, the colour of a rose, shiny plastic hair for its mane and tail. He doesn't know her, he doesn't know her at all, I think angrily. She likes Lego – but not in kits – sharp, new pencils, polished stones... I march to the end of the bridleway; before I reach our road, I turn and look back. Her father must have been here, in our garden. Watching us. Waiting for us to leave, or to go to bed and turn out the lights. Even though I've been walking fast, I'm suddenly freezing.

I hide it in the same kitchen cupboard that I've put the card. I fetch Evie's case notes and ring the adoption agency. If we can trace her biological mother, she might be able to help us find the father. But when I finally get through after a long wait, I'm transferred to three different people. I grow increasingly anxious because, at this rate, I'm going to be late to pick up Ben. The woman I end up talking to is sympathetic.

'You know Evie's biological mother didn't sign up to the letterbox scheme,' she says.

If both parties agree, the real and adoptive parents – or the child – can send a letter once or twice a year to an agency that will forward the letter on. Photos aren't allowed any more, since it's now too easy to track a child down through social media.

'But if we sent a letter in, you could forward it?'

'We don't have her details. She didn't leave an address when you adopted Evie. Even if she had got in contact, we wouldn't have been able to match her to Evie. No one can access your daughter's original birth certificate until she's eighteen.'

I know this already. I was hoping there was something I'd missed or forgotten.

The woman reminds me that Evie's father was never listed on the birth certificate. 'There's no way her biological father could trace your daughter through us since we can't even link your child to her biological mother. Not until she's eighteen,' she repeats. 'The man that's sending Evie the cards and presents – you need to find out how he's got hold of your address.'

'I have to call the police,' I say, more to myself than her, my breath quickening.

'You do, love,' she says.

I check my watch. I'll have to ring them on my way to pick up Ben.

———

Evie runs straight past me and Ben when she sees us in the playground after school, standing beside Andy.

I call after her. 'We're going to Sophie's house. Had you forgotten?'

She nods, but she doesn't look particularly pleased. Sophie is her best friend. Evie doesn't have many friends and usually she looks forward to Mondays and having Sophie to herself. Andy and Gill live nearby, on Queen's Road. It's a quiet, leafy street that seems a million miles away from the town centre even though it's only a few minutes' walk from the many shops and restaurants in The Grove.

On the way there, Evie resolutely ignores Sophie and walks with Andy, chatting to him. I'm relieved – I don't want her out of my sight even for a moment – but I worry the girls have had an argument. I look around. Now that we've left the roads near the school, it's quiet. There's hardly anyone here. I still have a shivery sensation that creeps along my collar bone. Are we being watched? Behind us is an elderly couple. He's leaning on a stick and she has her arm in his. She smiles at me. On the other side of the road is a man, maybe in his thirties. He looks across when he catches me staring. Evie's father could be anyone. He could be anywhere.

I walk faster so I can be closer to Evie. She's describing what she did at school, which she never tells me.

'Do you believe in magic?' she suddenly asks Andy.

He stops so he can concentrate better on what she's saying.

'What kind of magic?'

'All kinds. The kind where you wave a wand and make a spell and your dreams come true?'

'What do you think?' he asks her.

Sophie is waiting for us up ahead, swinging round a lamp post and looking impatient.

'I expect magic doesn't exist,' she says. 'No one is going to make my dream come true.'

'You don't know that!' Andy glances back at me and raises his eyebrows. 'How about you tell me what your dream is?'

Evie shrugs and runs off. When she reaches Sophie, she starts spinning round and round, her arms outstretched, her head thrown back, until she gets dizzy and collapses on the pavement, screaming with laughter. It's so shrill I want to put my hands over my ears. She seems so unstable. I wonder with a sick feeling if this is the first card and the first present she's been sent, or if there are more and we have missed them. Missed the impact they're having on our daughter.

We reach Andy and Gill's house – it's modern, surrounded by lush grounds and feels palatial – although Andy, Ellen and Sophie frequently create a small tsunami of mess that Gill complains about. Andy butters scones for all of us and makes a pot of tea. After the kids have eaten and been wiped down, Evie and Sophie run upstairs and we barricade Ben and Ellen in one corner of the sitting room by pushing the sofas together. I splodge jam on our scones and top up our mugs.

'I found a present today,' I say.

The girls are out of earshot, but I still keep my voice low.

'A present?' Andy says, smiling.

'Yes.' I swallow uncomfortably. 'From Evie's biological father. In the tree in the garden. And a card on Saturday. He's cut a hole in the fence so he can hide them for her.'

'Oh God. That's stalking! How the frig could he have tracked you down? Have you spoken to the adoption agency?'

I nod. 'They say there's no way he can trace her through them. Ben!' I retrieve him. He's pushed Ellen over and is lying on her head. Fortunately, she thinks it's funny.

'And there's nothing on the birth certificate?'

'No. Not that we're allowed it until Evie turns eighteen. The girl, Evie's biological mother, was a drug addict so I don't know, I'm guessing she slept around, maybe she didn't even know who the father was. She could have been a prostitute. I mean, by the time you're an addict, you'll do anything for drugs and cash, won't you?'

Andy says nothing. I'm probably starting to sound too right wing for him.

'I guess what I'm saying is I have no idea who her father could be, or what sort of man he is. No one we would know. I mean, what kind of man sleeps with a drug-addled prostitute? Not anyone that would wind up living in Ilkley, that's for sure.' I rub my hands over my eyes. 'I just don't know what we're facing. How dangerous he could be. How much it's going to upset Evie.'

Andy still hasn't said anything. I wonder if I've offended him. Back in our university days he was going to be a poetry-quoting rock star and Gill was training to be a human rights lawyer, and now here they are – Andy is a house husband and they live in a demi-mansion bought with the proceeds of his wife's career in corporate law. Usually it's only after a few drinks that Andy gets piously liberal. But then, I have no right to talk. Back then I dreamed of winning the Turner Prize; being a 'commercial' artist whose art matches people's cushion covers was a total sell-out.

'I slept with a prostitute once,' he says, gripping his mug with both hands and staring into it.

'What?' I spill tea on my jeans. I pull Ben off the back of one of the sofas, just before he nosedives onto the wooden floorboards.

'Tractor,' he says with delight and starts smashing the toy into the skirting board.

'I'm not proud of it,' Andy adds, as I return to my seat. 'It was when I wasn't with Gill—'

'But you two met at university—'

'Okay, well, we took a break, if you remember. When Gill was doing her final year of training, I went off the rails a bit. Tried drugs I'd never done before. And other things.'

I'm too stunned to know what to say.

'I'm telling you because it means Evie's father could be anyone. Sure he could be some pimp from Leeds, but he could equally well be someone like—'

'You?' I say.

'I was going to say, someone like our neighbours. The man across the street. Who happens to live in Ilkley. It's not as uncommon as you think, Zoe, middle-class men sleeping with prostitutes.'

I slump back on the sofa. I can't seriously believe that someone like Andy could be Evie's father. I try not to think of Andy, the Andy I know with his dark wavy hair and a pot belly, the Andy with fantastic legs from five-a-side football once a week, with a propensity to get drunk and quote Oscar Wilde, whilst looking as camp as a rugby forward – *that* Andy, sleeping with a call girl. I shut my eyes and an image of Ollie comes into my mind. My Ollie, who's become obsessed with celebrities and stardom, who has a tendency to have one too many glasses of red if anyone semi-famous is buying; my Ollie, from whom I also took a break towards the end of university. It was more than a year after we graduated before we got back together.

'I've called the police.'

Andy puts his hand on my shoulder and he's about to say something when there's a loud wail and Evie runs over and throws her arms around me, sobbing loudly and dramatically in my ear, smearing tears on my top.

'Evie cry,' Ben says and comes toddling over.

'I want to go home.'

Andy and I exchange glances. The girls are always so tired after school: Sophie deals with it by becoming almost catatonic and flopping in front of CBBC, whilst Evie goes for melodrama.

'What is it, love?'

'It's Sophie,' she wails. 'She's not my friend any more.'

This also happens, usually about once every six weeks and then it all blows over and they're inseparable again. I start gathering myself, ready to prise Ben away from the train set he's now bashing, steeling myself for a long conversation on the way home with Evie about who said what to whom.

'She said I'm not part of the family. Only Ben is your real child. Only Ben is a Morley.'

There's a single moment of silence. Evie breaks it with a hiccup and then Andy, as angry as I've ever seen him, stands up and yells, 'Sophie! Sophie, come here right now!'

I make cheese on toast for Ben and Evie when we get home. After I've cleared up the tea things and got them both bathed and put Ben in bed, and then back in bed several times, I go up to Evie's room. We're reading *Charlotte's Web* again, but tonight I keep the book on my lap instead of opening it.

'How are you feeling about what Sophie said?'

Evie shrugs. 'Okay, I guess.'

'It was a hurtful thing to say but I'm sure she didn't mean it.'

'She said sorry. She's still my friend. Are you going to read the book?'

'In a minute, love. I don't want you to be upset by what Sophie said. You *are* a Morley. You're just as much a part of this family as Ben is. In fact, you've been a Morley for a lot longer than him.'

'Six years!' she says triumphantly.

'Well – seven minus two is?'

She shrugs again. 'We're on chapter five.'

Once the children are in bed, I stand in the window with the sitting-room lights off, watching the empty street, too agitated to settle to anything. It's all perfectly normal, a quiet, suburban cul-de-sac, with neat front gardens, but I see it differently now. Is he out there, hiding behind the manicured shrubs? Crouching in the shadows of the parked cars? Watching us? Ollie walks up the path to our house, his head bowed. He doesn't see me in the dark. He looks weary. We could all do with a break, a proper holiday. Perhaps after the exhibition we could go somewhere warm. Try and rekindle our marriage. He gives me a kiss when he sees me standing waiting for him.

'I found a present outside in the tree,' I say.

'What?'

The two lines above the bridge of his nose deepen.

Ollie has always looked youthful – permanently stuck in his twenties or early thirties. But I realize that he has aged – he still has plenty of floppy hair with no signs of baldness – but now he has these deep furrows in his forehead, fine lines around his eyes, creases running from his nose to his mouth. When did that happen? How did I not notice?

'From Evie's father. It's the same writing as the card.'

He rubs his hand over his eyes. 'Did you give it to her?'

'Of course not!'

'What is it?'

'A pink pony.'

He snorts in disgust. 'Have you spoken to her about it?'

I shake my head. 'Not yet. I didn't want to get her worked up just before bedtime.'

'Good. Don't tell her. It'll only upset her. Where was it?'

I tell him about the hole in our garden fence and he swears.

'We ought to call the police. What if he tries to speak to her?'

'I have. And the adoption agency. There's some food in the oven.'

I'm trying not to think about the awful possibility that Evie's birth father has already talked to her. She *said* she hadn't seen him when I asked her about it on Saturday.

Ollie comes back after a couple of minutes and sits next to me, his plate of shepherd's pie balanced on a tea towel on his knee. He forks in a mouthful of food. It's too hot and he exhales sharply. I bought a ready-made one. I'm feeling guilty at the amount of time I've been spending with Harris; the amount of time I'm spending thinking about Harris.

'What did the police say?'

'They're going to come round and speak to us. I phoned this afternoon so I expect they'll come tomorrow.'

'And the agency?'

He hadn't expected they'd have anything useful to say and when I explain that they can't give us any information and haven't passed on our contact details to anyone, he nods.

'That's what I thought. Her birth mother said she didn't want to stay in touch with Evie. She made that abundantly clear. But how the hell has her father found us?'

I don't have an answer. He jabs at the remote and turns the ten o'clock news on. I want him to talk to me about it, what it means, what we should do, how we should reassure Evie, but Ollie is tired and hungry and has already tuned out. I remind myself that this is how he unwinds – by watching TV late at night.

I think about my conversation with Andy today, how he slept with a prostitute when he separated temporarily from Gill. Ollie and I have never really spoken about the time we split up. It was in our third year when the pressure of our finals and my end of year exhibition all seemed too much. I met someone else – I'm sure Ollie did too. I know he partied hard for those first few months in

London when he started working as a trainee accountant. He told me he'd dabbled in cocaine and Ecstasy for a bit. I look at him out of the corner of my eye. Could Ollie have slept with a prostitute? Is Andy right, is it something a lot of men do? I try to push the thought away. Even if Ollie had, he wouldn't have been unfaithful when we got back together. He's just not the type. Is he? I would never have thought Andy was either. It's a coincidence that Ollie has the same strange clumsiness as Evie. He's so precise in some ways – with numbers, figures, oven dials, Lego instructions – but physically he's the opposite. He can suddenly overbalance, knocking someone's glass out of their hand, plates slithering to the floor, as if he isn't quite aware of where he ends and the rest of the world begins. It's always endeared Evie to him – she looks like a sprite and is as uncoordinated as he is.

I take his plate and my wine glass through to the kitchen. It's dark and Ollie is in a bubble of blue light from the TV at the far end of the house. I don't think he can see me. I can't help myself. I stand on a chair to reach the highest cupboard in the corner where I've hidden the pony. I take the garish parcel down and peel back the scrunched paper. It's actually a unicorn, not a pony. It's intended for a fairy-tale princess; its mane falls to its hooves, there are flowers and stars on its rump. It's revolting and I thought Evie would hate it when I first saw it. But now I'm not so sure. I think of her story of the princess, all the illustrations surrounded by hearts and magic wands. If I gave this to her, she'd love it. Perhaps we don't know her as well as we thought we did.

# TUESDAY

'Could you hold the strap?'

I hold it out to Evie. It's a lead that's attached to the buggy. You're meant to loop it round your wrist in case you let go of the handle and your precious baby rolls away from you.

Evie looks at me as if I'm daft. 'Mummy! I'm not five years old!'

'Okay, but don't run too far ahead. And make sure I can see you!'

She skips, scuffing the first leaves that have fallen. She jumps in a puddle and black mud splatters over her tights. Ben chortles. She tries to make him laugh again by tossing handfuls of dead horse-chestnut leaves in the air and finding another puddle to leap into. She's all angles – thin arms and legs, bony joints. I don't say anything. I want her to stay close to me and if I tell her off about everything else she's doing, that one instruction will be drowned out.

It's quiet in the suburbs. It's too cold for people to be in their gardens; and it's not a thoroughfare so few cars drive by. I look past decaying roses and through the first flush of Michaelmas daisies, blazing a glorious purple, into the darkened windows of the houses we walk by. Who lives here? Are they watching us? Did one of our neighbours do something seven years ago that he now regrets? How little we know of the people who surround us.

I use the traffic when we reach Cowpasture Road as an excuse to get Evie to hold on to the buggy and she does it without complaint because she wants to wave a dirty leaf over Ben as she whispers a spell. Her feet get in the way of the wheels and she trips Bella up too but I bite my tongue. I wish she would hold my hand. When we reach school, she waves goodbye without letting me kiss her and runs off.

Ben calls, 'Bye bye bye,' after her, but she ignores him.

Hannah White is at the door to her classroom and she smiles warmly at Evie. 'Is that a magic wand?'

'Yes! I've turned my brother into a toad!' she says.

'Oh, I can see that! I love his golden eyes!'

She's on Evie's wavelength. I would have told her not to drag a muddy leaf into the classroom.

'Morning, Mrs Morley,' she says to me.

'Hi, Miss White. Is it possible to speak to Jack? Sorry, Mr Mitchell.'

'I'm afraid not, he's in a meeting until around eleven. Is there anything I can help you with?'

I hesitate and then say, 'Actually, yes. It's to do with Evie so it would be good if you knew too – and you can pass it on to Mr Mitchell.'

'Of course.' She steps to one side so that we can talk without anyone overhearing us. 'What is it?'

She looks concerned. She seems to have such natural empathy – even though it must be overwhelming sometimes, being surrounded by so many children and their concerns, not to mention their parents'. She brushes her hair over her shoulder and fixes me with her large green eyes. She's wearing the same brocade dress as the other day, but in a different colour and with sheer tights. I try not to dwell on how mumsy I feel compared to her.

'We've discovered a card from her father – her biological father, that is. And a present.'

'Oh, how upsetting for you. Is Evie okay?'

'I'm so worried. I spoke to the adoption agency.'

'Were they helpful? What did they say?'

I shake my head. 'They don't know who the father is or how he could have got in touch. I mean, we can't even find out who her mother is, so—'

Hannah puts a hand on my arm. 'I'm so sorry.' She hesitates. 'Have you—?'

'Yes, I've called the police. I haven't seen anyone yet. I'll let you know what they say.'

She says, 'Yes, do. I'll keep an eye on Evie.'

I nod my thanks. Hannah squeezes my arm and smiles, then bends down to talk to Ben.

That afternoon, when we get back from school, two police officers are waiting outside the house. They introduce themselves as PC Ian Carr and PC Harry Priestley. They look as if they're in their early twenties and my heart sinks.

'She doesn't know about the latest development,' I say, inclining my head towards Evie, hoping they'll get the hint.

PC Carr has thick dark hair; his black eyebrows, almost meeting in the middle of his forehead, crease.

Priestley nods. 'No problem, Mrs Morley. We'll wait until you're ready to answer questions.'

I sit Ben in his high chair and give him a bag of apple crisps and a box of raisins, which will occupy him for a short while. He starts counting them but he doesn't know his numbers yet, so he sounds like a small sergeant major, muttering, 'One, two, one, two,' under his breath. I send Evie up to her room with a glass of milk and a slice of bread and honey. She doesn't make a fuss as normally I don't let her take food out of the kitchen.

'Would you like a cup of tea?'

'Only if you're making one,' Priestley says, as Carr cuts in, 'Milk and two sugars.'

Priestley is not as striking as his fellow officer; he has a round, pudgy face and pale blue eyes, but he seems sharper. I talk as I brew the tea – telling them about Evie's adoption and the gift from my daughter's 'real' father.

'Can we see where you found them?' Priestley is on his feet immediately.

I slide open the French windows and lead them into the garden.

'She was playing with the first card out here, and then yesterday I found a present addressed to Evie that she doesn't know about.' I show them the broken tree. 'He pushed them through a hole in the fence,' I explain.

It's been mended. Someone has bent the metal strands back and fastened chicken wire over the top. I feel a surge of relief and love for Ollie – he must have done it after I'd gone to bed. I picture him at night, clutching a torch and secateurs, his breath in a freezing cloud around him.

'No other cards or gifts?'

I shake my head.

'Could anyone have seen the intruder,' asks Carr, 'other than yourselves?'

I shake my head. 'Not from here. The neighbours might have noticed someone on the bridle path, but that wouldn't be suspicious. It's a right of way and it leads to the golf course and then the Cow and Calf rocks.'

They both look up. There's a man standing on the top of the granite block, stark against the sinking sun. As we watch, he turns and walks back towards the moor.

'I don't suppose you have CCTV?' Carr asks, and I shake my head again.

After we've returned to the kitchen and they've exhausted their questions over the cups of tea, Priestley asks if they can speak to Evie. I hesitate.

'I don't want her to know there was a present,' I say, trying to keep the agitation out of my voice.

'We won't mention it, Mrs Morley,' Priestley assures me.

I go and fetch Evie. She sits on the sofa next to me and holds my hand. Priestley crouches beside her and Carr takes the armchair opposite. Ben is delighted to have two men in the room and brings Carr a stream of trucks, diggers and trains. Priestley is holding the card we found on Saturday.

'I was admiring your lovely card,' he says. 'Who's it from?'

She gives him one of her hard stares.

'My real daddy,' she says. 'It says so inside,' she adds, in case he's illiterate as well as dim.

'And who is your real daddy? Do you know?'

She shrugs. 'My daddy's called Ollie, but I don't know who my real one is. The one that gave me away.'

I think about the story I always tell her – of the kind lady who gave her to us. I suppose that must be how she imagines her father – as a kind man who gave her away too, as if she were a gift. Only now he wants her back.

'Can you tell us how the card got there?' asks Priestley.

She shakes her head.

'And have you found any other cards, or anything else, in your special hiding place?'

'Mum, can I watch CBBC now? You said I could.'

'If someone you don't know tries to give you a card or a present, please don't take it. Can you be very grown up and tell an adult straight away? Like your mum. You won't get into trouble.'

She nods and squeezes my hand, looks up at me beseechingly. I put the TV on. It's the Waybuloos, cartoon characters with enormous eyes who do yoga and float about and I'm reminded again of how unnaturally far apart Evie's eyes are and what could potentially have caused her to look the way she does.

At the door, Priestley says, 'We'll alert the community police team and get them to do a routine patrol round here. We'll speak to all your neighbours, see if they've seen anyone acting oddly round your house. Keep an eye out for anything unusual and get in touch if you do notice something out of the ordinary. Or if another package turns up.' He glances towards Evie, but she's too engrossed in the television to pay him any attention. 'You might want to think about security – getting some kind of alarm and CCTV installed. And,' he hesitates, and then says, 'I'm sure you do it anyhow, and I don't need to tell you this, but I'd make sure you know where your daughter is, and who she's with at all times.'

I nod. 'Is there any way to track him down? Her biological father?'

'From what you've said, it doesn't look likely,' says Carr. 'We need to see if we can catch him – if he does come back. With an increased police presence in the area, he'll most likely be deterred from approaching you again.'

Priestley gives me a card with the Ilkley police station number and address. It's just round the corner from the school. I lock the door behind them. I'm shaken by our conversation. The officers have confirmed that this is serious and I'm not worrying unnecessarily, but they haven't made me feel safer or given me any confidence that they'll find the man who's stalking us.

# WEDNESDAY

I've just dropped the children off at school when the text comes through:

Coffee? I'm in the cafe on Back Grove Rd. H.

I hurry there as fast as I can. I want to see Harris, feel his reassuring presence. There's a strength about him that makes me feel secure, if only temporarily. When he sees me, he grins and kisses me on the cheek. It's as if something has unlocked inside him since our walk through Heber's Ghyll: he's warmer, more at ease.

'Zoe,' he says, and just the way he says my name makes me feel special.

For the first time since I met him, he seems tired.

'I've a commission to make a sculpture that'll go on the moor,' he says, when I ask him if he's still working on his exhibition. 'It'll replace the cairn above the Valley of Death.'

He starts to talk to me about the link between art and walking. He quotes Richard Long and someone called Rudi Fuchs. He says he wants to create something that isn't separate from the landscape, but is part of it and over time it'll alter and change as the world around it changes. At least, that's what I think he's saying, but I feel giddy on caffeine and his passion. He's leaning towards me, his hands sketching patterns through the sugar grains on the table, and he's so close I could touch him if I moved slightly.

He stops talking abruptly and gazes at me. A blush starts to flare across my cheeks. He picks up my hands in his.

'There's something wrong, isn't there?' he says slowly. 'Something's still stopping you painting.'

I nod. And then it all pours out. About Evie. Her adoption. How her real father has found her and is sending her these creepy messages and has left her a present. That he's been watching us, he's broken into our garden and formed some kind of bond with Evie. He could be involved with drugs. Prostitutes. Or he could be anyone. A nice middle-class man with a seedy habit. The police arriving yesterday.

'Like two boy scouts. What do they know?' I say.

He listens carefully and doesn't interrupt. He's still holding my hands and he squeezes me so hard it almost hurts. He says, 'You know the man that's leaving these things for your daughter might not be her father?'

It's my worst fear. I've been trying not to think about it. He grips me tighter, forcing me to face it.

'You said it would be hard to track Evie down. Her own mother doesn't know where she is. This man may not be related to her at all.'

The implication – that a paedophile could be stalking our daughter – becomes more concrete when Harris spells it out. He's right. We have no way of knowing if he's her father or not. Have the police considered this possibility? I try to calm down. Boy scouts or not, I'm sure they will have, it's probably part of their training.

'Keep her close,' Harris says. 'I'm sorry to hear some bastard is targeting your daughter like that. But you have to channel what you're feeling into your work.'

He interlaces his fingers between mine.

'You are beautiful, Zoe,' he whispers.

The desire and rage in his eyes is so fierce I think that he's going to yank me across the table towards him and kiss me. Tears fill my eyes. I can't remember the last time Ollie told me I was beautiful. But although I want Harris, I have to think of Evie. I sit back and slide my fingers from his.


I need to move the canvases Harris recommended I buy out of my studio so they don't get paint on them. After I've picked Ben up from nursery and given him his lunch, I make sure he has plenty of toys in front of him. I carry the canvases up to Evie's room. I'm going to store them in the attic, out of the way of sticky fingers, until I need them. I have to do three trips, piling them next to her bed. Ben starts crying when he notices that I'm not with him so I heft him upstairs too. Evie's Meccano sculpture is still lying on the floor from when he broke it and he starts to play with the pieces. I must remember to help her rebuild it. I open the cupboard door under the eaves that leads to our storage space and switch on the light.

I crouch to get inside. Ollie has put some plywood boards over the joists near the door. It's a temporary solution and they wobble slightly. I don't want to overbalance and land on the insulation. My materials for creating canvases are already stored here – the wood for the frames, a roll of ten-ounce cotton duck, a tin of acrylic primer. I ferry the canvases in, one at a time, and stack them up like giant playing cards. There's not enough room on the plywood board – I'm going to have to shift the roll of fabric over to one side. I peer through the open cupboard door to check Ben is still okay and then I restack the canvases so I can reach the cotton. As I pull it away from the wall, something tumbles out. It's a Princess Elsa doll in a frost-blue dress. There's something else there too. I run my hand down the gap between the roll and the wall and pull out toys. Toys that I've never seen before. A flat tin box filled with colouring pencils. A teddy with a handkerchief neck-tie. A pink purse with a felt flower sewn on the front. My breath quickens. I back out, leaving everything else where it is, banging my head. How long has this been going on for? Not only has Evie been receiving these presents but she's deliberately been hiding them from us.

I grab Ben and run downstairs with him, slipping on the last step, twisting my wrist as I grab the bannisters to stop myself falling. I have an overwhelming need to have Evie close to me, to hug her hard. Instead, I cuddle Ben and kiss him. He wriggles and giggles, trying to escape.

'Evie, love,' I say, taking both her hands in mine. 'I found some toys in the attic. I won't be cross. Please tell me where you got them from.'

She snatches her hands away and wraps her arms round her scrawny chest. We've just got home from school and we're sitting in her bedroom, fixing her Meccano sculpture. Ben is doing laps of her bedroom and the landing outside, chugging like a steam train.

'They're mine. You shouldn't have been looking at them.'

'I was putting my canvases away in the attic and I saw them. Where did you find them? Did someone give them to you?' She doesn't say anything. 'Were they in the tree?'

She nods. 'They're from my daddy. The real one.'

'Oh, sweetheart. Why didn't you tell me? Or the policeman when he asked you?'

'I didn't lie,' she says with spirit.

I'm about to tell her off when I realize that's she's right. She didn't answer PC Priestley, and none of us noticed. She bursts into tears and throws her arms around my neck. I think of the pile of presents, next to Evie when she's lying sleeping in bed. I want to throw them out. They feel poisonous.

'It's okay.' I try to soothe her. 'Your daddy, your real, true daddy is Ollie. He loves you more than anything in the whole world. Did you see the man who left those things for you?'

Her hot tears trickle down my neck when she shakes her head. 'I hid them because I didn't want Ben to get them,' she sobs. 'I want them to be special, just for me. You make me share my toys with him and he spoils everything.'

I look up in time to see he's stopped running round the room and is concentrating on pulling the arm off one her dolls. I let go of Evie and snatch the doll from Ben before he can do any damage and he starts to scream. He's so loud, I barely hear Evie.

'And he's not, you know.'

'Who's not what?' I ask, trying to contain Ben and keep the toy out of his reach.

In a small, tight voice, she says, 'Ollie's not my *real* daddy. And you're not my real mummy.'

Evie's words hit me like a blow to the solar plexus. I want to take her in my arms, but I'm wrestling with Ben.

I'm still thinking what to say to her, when she tilts her chin defiantly and says, 'I want my other mummy.'


I've worked myself into a fury. It doesn't help that I had a glass of wine while I was trying to get Evie and Ben into bed, as I thought it would help me calm down. What it actually meant was that I couldn't be bothered to cook tea and I'm now at the end of a second large glass on an empty stomach. I want to shout and scream at Ollie; that he's never here, that he's not protecting Evie, that he's not being a proper father. I'm taking my rage and my hurt out on him, I realize that, but why is he not here to soothe my feelings after my daughter can so casually dismiss me and all the love I've given her? I think of all those nights at the hospital, watching over her as she slept in the incubator. It hits me, as I'm tidying away Ben's toys, and wiping gunk off the table, that maybe Ollie is having an affair after all. It would explain why he's always home so late. The weekends. His distraction. Maybe even the new suits.

I pause, clutching a toy telephone on wheels to my chest. I have an image of me and Ollie dancing. We're at a friend's house, in their sitting room. A Eurythmics song is playing. We're in our early twenties. It's a year or two since we graduated. Ollie loves to dance but he normally doesn't because he's clumsy. Now he's so drunk or happy – we've just got back together again – he doesn't care. He pulls me into his embrace, flings me out again, twirls me round, sending other people flying, stepping on his best friend's foot. Ollie sings along to the lyrics, belting out the words in an unexpectedly loud baritone. I'm laughing so hard my stomach hurts. The music changes and there's a slow number. I expect him to stop, collapse on the sofa, but he doesn't. He holds me tightly and looks deep into my eyes. They're so blue. I see he's not drunk, only a little tipsy, and the way he's staring at me makes my stomach contract. Once, Ollie used to look at me like that all the time. Once, I would have done anything for him. Of course, Ollie being Ollie, as he leans in for a kiss, trips on the rug and falls, dragging me with him and knocking over a girl carrying two large glasses of red wine. I chuck the phone in one of the toy boxes and it rings, plaintively.

I'm pouring another glass of Chardonnay when I hear his key in the lock. I walk into the sitting room.

'Have you considered that he might not be her father? He could be a paedophile.'

Ollie doesn't say anything. He shrugs off his coat and hangs it up. Unties his brogues and slides them off. Sets his briefcase down. He runs his hand through his hair and says, 'Yes.'

'Yes? Why didn't you say?'

'We don't know. Whether it's her real father or not. I didn't want to worry you even more.'

He comes and puts his arms around me. I can't smell anything strange on him. He smells like he always does as the end of the day, of trains and newsprint. When I kiss him, I taste beer on his breath. Has he been drinking on the way home? Not that I have any grounds to complain.

'Has something else happened?' he asks.

I tell him about the presents I found in the attic.

'You should get on to the police again,' he says.

'*I* should get on to the police? She's your daughter too!'

'Sorry, I didn't mean it like that. I've had a long day. What I meant is, it's hard for me to make private calls when I'm at work, and it's easier if you do it because you're here and you know when it's the best time for the police to come and see you. But I can take time off if you want me to go to the station?'

The anger drains from me and I start to cry.

He hugs me and says, 'It's going to be okay. Let's get a takeaway. We should eat something. Shall we order a curry?'

# TWO WEEKS LATER

# THURSDAY

It's the evening of Harris's preview and I'm getting ready to go out, full of nervous excitement. There haven't been any more cards or presents over the past couple of weeks. Maybe whoever it was has been scared off because the police know he's out there. Evie hasn't mentioned her real parents either. I have a knot in my stomach every time I think about it. I barely let her out of my sight when she's not at school and I check the damaged tree in the garden twice a day. And every man I see on my way to and from school, as I'm buying groceries, as I walk Bella, I stare at, wondering – could it be him?

My work is progressing well though – I've almost finished the painting I started after telling Harris what's been happening. It's as if he really did unleash something in me, gave me permission to be an artist, to be myself, to let go of my worries, even if only for a little bit. It sounds hokey, but it's true. I've stopped feeling bad about asking Jack to look after Evie and Ben on Saturday afternoons – and they had a brilliant time last weekend. I took Hannah up on her offer too and she's here now, putting both of them to bed.

I asked Ollie if he wanted to come tonight. I thought it might be like the old days, when we'd dress up, talk bollocks about Art, pretend to be toff reviewers from the *Sunday Telegraph*, drink too much cheap wine, stagger home up Cowpasture Road. But nothing has changed. I've barely seen him. So it's no surprise he said he had to work late.

'You go,' he'd said. 'It'll be good for you to meet potential clients. It's not long until your show. Network.'

I'd made a face. He knows I hate the idea.

'Really, you should do a social media course, or a business module. You haven't even got a Twitter account. This is all the stuff you need to be doing *now*, before your exhibition opens.'

'That's why I have Jenny,' I'd said, 'so I don't have to.'

This afternoon he'd sent me a text saying:

**Have a good time. Don't forget to schmooze. XO**

At least he'd remembered. As for Harris – I've seen a lot of him over the past few days. We've got into the habit of meeting for a coffee after I've dropped the children at school and nursery, at the tiny cafe behind The Grove. Even though I know I have to work, even though I'm desperate to return to my painting, I'm always the one who lingers. Harris drains his Americano and smiles and reminds me I need to go. I wonder if he realizes: if he's smiling because he knows I'm torn between wanting to stay and wanting to paint. And he quite likes the power he has over me.

The taxi beeps. I've treated myself, instead of walking there with my heels in my handbag. It's early and I'm not ready. I hop round our bedroom, trying to put my strappy sandals on and push my new dangly earrings in. I've gone for a low-key luxe look – that's what I hope it is, anyhow: smart skinny jeans and a silk sleeveless top with beads round the collar.

'Is everything okay?' I ask Hannah, poking my head round the bathroom door.

The bath is really deep and Ben and Evie are in together, screaming with laughter. There's a lot of water on the floor and the bath mat is sopping wet. She smiles, her face flushed from the heat, small tendrils of honey-coloured hair curling in the steam.

'All good,' she mouths over the noise. 'Don't worry. I've got your mobile number.'

I nod and hesitate. At this rate she's not going to be able to get either of them to bed, they're so excited.

'Have fun!' she shouts and turns back to the children.

My mouth is dry when the taxi pulls up by the kerb in Brook Street. For a moment, I hesitate, looking in. The gallery is a white box of light blazing into the street; the sunset, clouds the colour of a split watermelon, are reflected across the windows. It's packed. I panic – I won't know anyone apart from Harris and Jenny and they'll be too busy to speak to me. I always feel shy, tongue-tied in this kind of social situation. I wish Ollie were with me. But then I see Harris. He's talking to someone, a glass of red in his hand and, as if he becomes aware of my gaze, he looks directly at me and smiles. As soon as I walk in, I'm glad I came on my own.

Jenny air-kisses my cheek and passes me a flute of Prosecco and a catalogue before she strides away to greet the next arrival. Harris is at my elbow immediately.

'Who are all these people?' Coldplay is blaring out of the speakers and he has to lean in to hear me. He shrugs, as if they're nothing to do with him.

'I'm glad you came,' he says, and his breath is warm against my ear. 'I've missed you. Shall I show you round?'

He cups my elbow, his knuckles grazing my waist. I'd like him to, but I shake my head.

'You need to mingle.' There's a couple hovering; I can imagine them living in a mansion in Middleton, the wealthiest part of Ilkley. She's wearing gold stilettos and a cream fitted dress; he's in grey, a watch that cost more than my car, peeking out from beneath his well-pressed shirt. 'I'll look around and catch up with you.'

He nods reluctantly. I wander over to the first piece, standing sentinel at the entrance. It's large, around seven feet high, and made out of scrap metal, rusted, sanded smooth and glazed in places. Close to, I vaguely recognize some of the individual parts – cogs and wheels, valves and bolts, springs and blades. When I step back, the crowds shifting around me, it looks like a tree, bent in the wind; one of the lone pines perhaps, crippled by the wind, out past the Swastika Stone. The varnish has the effect of making it seem damp – a squall of rain has passed, or a heavy mist drifted through its twisted boughs. I'm aware that Harris is watching me. Even as he talks to the power couple and then moves smoothly on to a man I know is an art dealer from Harrogate, his gaze follows me. I walk on to a creature – possibly constructed from a tractor's innards with broken teeth and staring eyes; a gollum that's arisen from the peat bogs. I glance at the catalogue. There's a photo of Harris – the one where he looks dark and brooding – and I smile as I read the sanitized blurb about him. I look up the listing for the sculpture I'm staring at and its price tag is so steep I'm astonished. My back is to Harris but I can feel his eyes piercing my shoulder blades. A blush spreads across my cheeks. I walk on to a second room in the art gallery, connected to the first by an archway. For a few moments, I'm sheltered from his gaze.

At a visceral level I understand his work. It's as if he's trodden in my footsteps, seen what I've seen, felt what I've felt, as I've criss-crossed the moors countless times. There's a small room off to one side. That's where I am, looking at the last sculpture, when Harris says, 'What do you think?'

He stands next to me, contemplating it, almost from my perspective. He hands me another Prosecco and takes a sip of his wine. He's completely still, waiting for my answer. If I say his work is good, I know his lip will curl. Anything else is going to sound measured, too arts-student-like. I think back to my first reaction, when I saw the photos for this exhibition.

'They look tortured,' I say.

He throws his head back and laughs. A few people stop talking and look at him. He turns to me abruptly and I realize how important my response was to him.

'Aye, they do. They are.'

I'm about to make a joke about the time he spent in Shangri-La and how it was wasted if, on his return from this Himalayan paradise, he could only dream up such anguish, but he's looking at me so intently, I can hardly breathe.

'Let's go outside. I need some fresh air.'

'Don't you need to speak to more people?' I say — prospective buyers have been practically lining up to talk to him — but he shakes his head and strides ahead.

The crowd parts for him; they've had too much to drink and are too deep in conversation to notice his departure. He walks to the back of the large middle room and towards a white door, flush with the wall. I've never noticed it before. He holds it open for me and I step through. I've been represented by Jenny for seven years — since we adopted Evie, and Ollie and I were still living in London and thinking about moving to Ilkley — but I've never seen this part of the gallery. We're in a short corridor leading to a galley kitchen and a small office. A waiter assembling canapés moves to allow us past. Jenny's leather jacket, like a shed snake skin, hangs from a hook on the wall and there's a rail of outfits with beautiful heels in Perspex boxes beneath each one. So this is how she looks immaculate all the time, I think, staring at them curiously. Harris takes my hand impatiently and pulls me through a back door.

The cold is a shock. The night is clear and every star is sharp and bright as steel. We must be facing towards Back Grove Road but I can't see anything — there's a fence around some bins and a couple of hard plastic chairs. We're completely hidden. I take a sip of Prosecco. I've drunk too much and eaten nothing and my head is expanding, my feet have left the ground. Harris has ditched his glass somewhere. He leans in and kisses me. I'm caught off-balance. He takes my glass and then he cups my face between his hands and kisses me again. This time it's long and slow. His lips are soft, his palms rough. I can taste the wine on his tongue. I feel as if I'm dissolving into him. It's unbearably tender and yet urgent, impatient. He sits on one of the chairs and pulls me onto his lap. He cradles my head in one large hand, the other slides round my waist.

I think briefly of Ollie and then I don't care. It feels so right. I haven't been kissed like this for years.

'I've wanted to do that since the day I first set eyes on you,' he says, and breathes in my ear, nuzzles my neck.

I know, I think, I've always known. I had never imagined I would cheat on Ollie – but now I can admit to myself this is what I've wanted to do since I met him. I lose track of how long we are here, how long we kiss. There's a noise and a beam of light spreads across the Tarmac – one of the waiters has opened the back door and is leaning out to smoke a cigarette. I pull away from Harris, take a deep breath. After the heat of his mouth, the air is so cold it burns my throat.

'I have to go –' I say, '– the children – I have a babysitter.'

I can't see his eyes but I can tell he's looking at me and his grip is tight and hard. For a moment I think he's not going to let me go and I don't want him to. He releases me and stands. He takes my hand and leads me round the fence and into the glare of the car park and street lights.

'I'll walk you to the taxi rank,' he says.

He stops beneath the awning of a shop on Brook Street and pulls me into the shadows. He kisses me one last time and crushes me against his chest. I can hear his heart beating; it echoes in my ribs.

I cross over the road. I climb in a cab and, as I drive off, he's still standing there, his hands in his pockets, his head lowered, watching me. He doesn't wave.

# FRIDAY

Evie is outside, wearing her princess dress even though it's growing chilly. I can't make my mind up whether she's playing in the old tree because it's her favourite spot or because she's expecting another present. I wish I could talk to my mum about Evie. It's been three years since she died, but I still miss her. I put Ben in front of CBeebies. I know I've only got about ten minutes. I prop my laptop on the kitchen work surface, so I can keep an eye on Evie, and open Google. There must be a way of finding Evie's real mother. Her first name was Jane. She was living in London when she gave birth. My fingers hover over the keyboard. Is that it? Is that all I have to go on? They didn't tell us her surname. Jane. Not a name you'd associate with a junkie. But then, she was somebody's lovely little girl once too. She might even have made that name up. 'Jane' signed away all rights to Evie when she was born; I'm pretty sure she was pressured by social services. The adoption agency doesn't have an address for her. So how can I find Jane from London seven years later? Maybe the hospital would have records? They'd be confidential though.

I rest the tips of my fingers on the keys. I touch the J. And then I can't help it. I think of Harris. The feel of his skin. His thumb pressing against my lips. How he smelled: of wood smoke and leather; red wine and cinnamon. His tongue pushing against mine. In spite of what I'm meant to be doing – searching for the birth mother of my adopted daughter to try to find out who her real father might be – my mind yet again drifts to last night. I feel a surge of desire.

I want to phone Andy, tell him all about it like I always do when anything exciting happens to me. But I can't. He'd see it for what it is: a betrayal of Ollie. I pull myself up short. I'm married. I have two children. I know next to nothing about Harris other than that he understands me and I understand him on some deep, intuitive level. It's all become so complicated, and I yearn for the way Harris makes me feel: that life is simple and art is everything. Could it work? Could I have an affair? Would I leave Ollie for him? Would Harris care for my children? I shudder when I think of the heartache and the complications – how could I take Evie and Ben away from Ollie?

When I got home late and slightly drunk last night, my vision a little blurry, rattling the key in the lock, Hannah had already left and Ollie was in bed. He stirred when I slid beneath the sheets but he didn't wake. He was up before me, out of the house before 6 a.m. And since then, I've been thinking of Harris constantly, turning his name over in my mind, reliving the gallery visit as if it's a hyper-real dream. Ollie is my husband, I tell myself sternly. He does not deserve this. But my heart isn't in my self-admonishment.

Ben comes barrelling towards me, clutching one of Evie's dolls in his hand. My time is up. I look outside and, at first, I can't see Evie. She was right by the tree just a few minutes ago. Ben trips on a chair leg and falls, banging his head on the sharp edge of a kitchen cabinet. He howls. I pick him up and hug him. He hasn't cut himself but the bump starts to swell almost immediately: the size of a wren's egg, blue-green against his pale skin. I run cold water on a dishcloth and hold it against his head. He tries to push it away and fights and kicks against me. I struggle to hold him. I still can't see Evie.

The doorbell rings. I tuck Ben on my hip and hand him the doll he was playing with as I go to see who's there. I'm nervous about leaving Evie when I don't know exactly where she is. Andy's on the path outside. There's a sheen of sweat on his forehead and he looks uncomfortable.

'Andy! Do you want to come in for a cup of tea?'

'I can't stay. I've left both the girls in the car.' He nods towards his Volvo, parked diagonally across the pavement. Sophie waves at me and Ben. 'I drove over straight away, as soon as I found it.'

'Found what? Is something wrong?'

I glance behind me, wondering if Evie has appeared, and when I look back Andy is holding out a parcel. It's small and thin and rectangular, wrapped in cheap paper with pink butterflies on it. It's been torn open but I can see the sticker and the writing in blue Biro, a looping capital 'D' beneath his thumb. A shiver courses through me like a glass of icy water on a cold day.

'Present,' says Ben, trying to reach it.

'It was in Sophie's room,' Andy says, sounding apologetic. 'She said Evie had it in her school bag and she must have left it behind when you were at our house on Monday.'

'Oh God,' I say, taking it from him and trying to keep it away from Ben. 'Have you looked inside?'

He nods guiltily. 'It was open already. I'm sorry, Zoe. I've got to go – I'm in the middle of getting the girls their tea. But call me later if you want to talk.'

I take it from him.

'I'm sorry,' he says again, and he dashes back down the path.

Is he sorry because it's another present from Evie's father, or that he looked to see what it was? Or is it what's inside that makes him pity me? I hope it's something innocuous like a colouring pad. To my relief, I spot Evie. She's sitting on the step by the sandpit, so close to the French windows I'd missed her. I step into the garden. The light is a rich orange, the colour of marmalade, and pulls out copper highlights in Evie's dark hair. She frowns at Ben.

'That's *my* doll!'

'He's just playing with it.'

Uncharacteristically, Ben holds out the doll for her. She grins and takes it, kissing him on his fat tear-streaked cheek. I put Ben down and sit next to her, holding the package in my hands.

'Where did you get that?' she asks.

'I was going to ask you the same question. Andy brought it round. He said you'd left it at their house.'

She snatches it from me.

'Where did you get it, Evie?'

She shrugs. 'I found it.'

'Where?'

'It was there.'

She points to the wooden bench in front of us. It's even closer to the house than the last hiding place.

'Who's it from?' I ask, although I already know the answer.

'My real daddy. Look.'

She turns it over and shows me the sticker and the smudged handwriting.

'Evie, love, I asked you to tell me if you found another present.'

'I knew you'd take it away from me,' she mutters.

'May I see?'

She clutches it to her chest and then relents. She slides a small red book out and passes it to me. The cover is soft leather and has been embossed with a gorgeous pattern; the title, in gold, glints in the sun. The pages are the colour of cream. It has beautiful illustrations and clear, easy-to-read prose. Evie leans over and her breath is hot on my wrists, the ends of her hair drape across my arm.

'He's even written to me inside,' she says, and turns over the frontispiece. In a flowing script, quite different from the Biro on the card and presents, it says:

*To my darling daughter,*
 *Let this be the guiding light for our journey together,*
 *with all my love,*
 *Daddy*

I snap the book shut; my heart stutters in my chest. The red book is small and light, just right for a child's hands, but in my own, it feels unbearably heavy.

It's a Muslim prayer book.

☪

I watch you. I've seen you grow and develop over this past year. You're flourishing, my darling, now that I'm in your life. I know you will bloom when we're together all the time. Not long now, sweetheart, we're almost there.

Nothing can make up for all the years I've lost. You're a little girl: a person. I've missed the chance to shape you; to cradle you as a baby, to watch as you took your first steps, to hear you speak your first words. I've missed all your birthdays. I didn't light the candles on your cakes, I never taught you to count them, or witnessed your delight as you unwrapped your presents.

This is the closest that I can get to making up for those lost years: buying you gifts and leaving them in our special place. Sometimes I hide and watch as you discover the parcels I've left for you. You're so happy to find something for yourself that you don't have to share with the other child, Ben. No matter how they disguise it, or what they call you, you're not their daughter and he's not your brother. You don't belong with them, my child.

I love the way your face lights up when you tear open your presents. I know you have to hide these gifts so that they don't confiscate them, and, for now, it can be our secret. And one day, very soon, you'll be with me always and you'll be able to play with them openly and without shame. I've bought you a special present this time. I hope you will treasure it. I know you'll be entranced by the pictures. You won't understand it yet, because they haven't taught you what is right and good and essential in this life, but you will. I will teach you.

'This Book is not to be doubted...'

This book will be the blueprint, the map, the guiding light for our journey together, my love, my treasure.

# SATURDAY

I've finished my painting, the one I started after I met Harris, and I need to begin a new one. It'll help if I can draw inspiration from the moor. I want to ring him. I want to hear his voice. I want him with me. But I don't call. I've dropped Evie off at Jack's house for the afternoon. I could have left Ben too, but Evie needs some quality time with an adult who cares about her and who isn't me or Ollie. If she's going to talk to anyone about what's going on, it would be Andy or Jack. And I want time alone with Ben too, just the two of us. As usual, Ollie is at the office. Ben and I are going on an expedition so that I can take new photos and maybe do a few sketches. I can't manage Bella as well so I leave her behind, eyeing me sadly.

I wear a cross-body bag with my pencils and drawing pad, my camera, snacks, wipes, nappies and water for Ben, keys and my phone – I won't need any money – and I put him in a baby carrier on my back. He's so heavy, I struggle to catch my breath as I head straight out, past the golf course and up the hill towards the Cow and Calf rocks. I look around but there's no one else out – apart from the golfers – and, for once, I don't feel as if I'm being watched. Ben hums tunelessly and happily in my ear and waves a long stalk of grass. I join in and we sing 'The wheels on the bus'.

As soon as I held that little red book in my hand yesterday afternoon, I knew I had to end things with Harris. I cannot have an affair with him. My daughter could be in danger. I don't know what the book means. That her father's Muslim? I don't know enough about Islam to know what it signifies; all I know is that a man has invaded our privacy and is threatening to destroy our family.

Last night Ollie was at a northern movie premiere and came home after I'd gone to bed, and then this morning he left before I got up. I haven't had a chance to talk to him about it. But what I do know is that I cannot do anything that would take my focus away from my family right now. Evie has to be my priority. I have a terrible sick feeling when I think what I might have done – what I still want to do – which is to meet Harris. To be with him. To have sex with him. And while I'm in bed with him who knows what could happen to my daughter? Who might be spying on her? Thank God we've known Jack for five years, or else I would have no one I could trust to look after her.

I think about Ollie too. I know I love him. It just doesn't feel like love right now. It's not the burning desire that rages through me for Harris, or even the cosy intimacy Ollie and I used to have. We first got together when I was nineteen and he was twenty. After we split up, I told myself I wanted to have fun and to be free; really, the entire time we were apart I was anxious and stressed. When I had that brief relationship with a guy in his late twenties after I graduated, I spent most of my time wishing I knew where I stood with him. I know Ollie inside out. Or, at least, I used to. Even when I was in my early twenties I was certain Ollie was the man I wanted to be the father of my children; I thought he would always care for me and our family. Look after my mum. Walk the dog. Take the kids to the park. Ollie is dependable and reliable. I never saw him as my soulmate.

'Ben's on the bus jumping up and down, up and down, up and down,' I sing.

And now it feels like I've found my soulmate. I understand how Harris's mind works at an artistic level: I've got no idea whether he'd change the sheets if Evie wet herself in the middle of the night, if he'd teach Ben how to read, or bring me a cup of sweet tea when I come down with a migraine. And living with another artist would be erratic, chaotic, unstable. Children need security. I cannot continue to see Harris, I tell myself repeatedly, my footsteps keeping time with the chant in my head. Even if the thought of never seeing him again, never touching him, feels like losing my left hand.

It's a beautiful September day. It's definitely autumn. The sky is pale blue and although it's sunny, there's a chill in the air. The bracken is bronze across the lower slopes of the moor. We stop at the Cow and Calf rocks and I take a few snaps, although I have photographed this iconic landscape in every conceivable weather and time of day. I pass Ben some fruit Yo Yos, which he calls worms, and he unwinds them and sucks them and wipes his sticky hands on my shoulders. We set off diagonally across the moor, towards the archaeological dig and the Twelve Apostles, leaving Ilkley behind.

I don't know what to do with myself, with my feelings for Harris. Despite my efforts to convince myself, I can't deny that I'm drawn to him. A small voice whispers, 'What if he's the one?'

I'm passing up the chance of a lifetime; forgoing tempestuous happiness – because somehow I know stability is not one of Harris's strengths – in favour of domestic drudgery as the wife of an accountant. I'm exaggerating. I do know how lucky I am, what I could lose. I think of all that Ollie and I have been through – the years of trying for children; two miscarriages, one stillbirth, three years of being vetted for adoption, a year searching for the perfect child – a baby who would be ours virtually from birth – and then finding Evie; the trauma of wondering if she'd been brain damaged, the uncertainty of knowing whether her biological mother might change her mind in those early weeks; the gift of such a beautiful little girl and then being able to have a child of our own, too. It makes me pause for breath – our sheer bloody good fortune. I cannot jeopardize what we have, what we've fought so hard for. I must tell Harris that it's over and that I can't see him again.

We cross a deep peat bog; I take care to keep on the raised wooden walkway. I stamp my feet pretending to be a troll and make Ben laugh. With any luck he'll fall asleep – he's been so tired since he's stopped having his afternoon nap. On the ridge of the hill, by the Twelve Apostles, I take Ben out of the backpack and stretch. He runs in between the stones and I take photos, some with him, some without. The air has changed: there's an electric charge in the atmosphere and the sky has darkened to sheet steel. Normally I don't walk beyond the stone circle – but this was the whole point of my expedition – to venture deeper into the heart of the moor. Past this ancient Neolithic site, the land is flat and bleak and barren. The heather is bitten to the quick and shards of mica glitter on the paths. I want to reach the plateau. My pictures will be all sky and bare desolation. I'm half delighted at the strange colour of the clouds and half worried. I haven't brought any waterproofs and the weather can change so quickly.

Ben reaches for my hand and we walk further. I take a few more photos but he starts to cry. He's cold and I haven't brought any more warm clothes. It starts to rain. I hastily pack my camera away, wipe his nose and start to bundle him into the backpack. It's one of those cloth ones – the other has a heavy frame and I can't carry him in it. I crouch on the ground and push up with my thighs. I'm almost upright when there's a tearing sound and Ben falls. I half catch him but he still tumbles and twists – one foot trapped by the rucksack – and hits his head on the ground. He's screaming. I unfasten the carrier and shrug it off and hug him tightly.

'You're okay, my love, you're okay. There's my big, brave boy.'

I check for bumps and cuts and bruises but it's more the shock. I've grazed my hand against the stony ground where I cushioned his fall. One shoulder strap has sheared away from the buckle. I curse myself for buying a second-hand carrier from eBay. Ollie told me to get a new one but I couldn't bring myself to spend that kind of money on something we'd only use for a few months. I try and tie the strap, but it's not long enough and it wouldn't hold Ben's weight anyway. I pass him a flapjack, the last of my snacks. It starts to rain heavily, big drops that sting our faces. Ben begins crying again and drops the biscuit in the sand.

I feel the first twinge of fear. We're in the middle of the moor. No one knows where we are. It's pouring. It's cold. I don't have any food or any money. I have no more warm or waterproof layers. Ben can't walk far and I can't carry him for long. We can't go back the way we've come – it would take too long. Ben might get hypothermia. I push my wet hair out of my eyes and try to think. If we head straight across the moor, in a north-east direction, we might hit a path. I vaguely remember the Dales Way runs between Black Beck and Coldstone – it would take us down to Moor Road. From there we could hitch a lift, catch a bus, get some help.

'Come on, little man,' I say, and take his hand.

He follows me, snivelling. I bundle the broken carrier into my bag and check my phone. I don't expect there'll be a signal and there isn't. There might be one nearer the road though.

After a few paces, Ben stops and sits down. I cajole him and get him to his feet and we walk a little way. He stops again and starts to cry in earnest. The heather, even though it's short, is too deep for him to walk through. It's old, with hard, gnarled branches. I lift him up and balance him on my hip. He's too small for me to give him a piggyback – he can't hold on by himself. I can't see; my mascara has run and my eyes sting. I stumble, the heather scrapes my legs. I'm worried there might be a proper storm with lightening. We're on top of the moor and I'm the tallest object for miles around. My biceps feel as if they're being ripped apart. I put Ben down and shake my arms. He screams and stretches his hands towards me, his eyes shut against the rain.

He shouts, 'No, no, no, no,' and then, 'Mummy!'

Our hair is plastered to our skulls and we're soaked to the skin. Ben has one long dry patch down his front where he's been pressed against me, but that darkens as I take his hand and tug him a little way further on.

I step in a bog and leap back. Cold, muddy water seeps into my trainers. I pick Ben up again and hug him tightly against me, trying to keep him warm. I go faster but it only makes me slip.

'Home,' he says. 'Want home.'

I can't risk falling into one of the bogs or tripping on a stone. Sometimes there are small cliffs and steep gullies hidden in the heather. I should have stayed on the path. I might have met someone who could have helped me carry Ben. It feels as if I'm wading through treacle and I want to cry. I curse my stupidity: I've grown up next to this moor and have become too confident, too arrogant about my ability to navigate it. It's a wilderness, not a place for a child. We come to a stream. I don't know whether I've veered too far and hit Black Beck or if this is Carr or Coldstone – or maybe even another beck altogether, one of the many nameless waterways the moor is riven with. It's not deep but the banks for several metres on either side are boggy. I can't jump it. I follow the water's course a little way and then wade straight through it. I reach the other side, mud up to my knees, my feet squelching with water, panting with the exertion. I switch Ben to my other hip, and push on, gritting my teeth against the pain in my arms.

And then I see the path. It's ahead of us, over a small ridge in the heath. It's stony and not easy to walk along, but it'll be easier than stumbling through the heather. When we reach it, I put Ben down to relieve the pressure on my shoulders.

'You need to walk for a little way, love,' I say, pleading with him, and I hold out my hand. But he cries and keeps his raised, jumping as he tries to get me to pick him up. I take his fist and pull him along, wailing. At least we're on the Dales Way, but we're still far from the road. I check my phone. No reception. I'm shivering and cold water is running down my back. Ben falls backwards into a puddle. His shrieks reach a crescendo. I want to block my ears. I lift him up and kiss him. I'm starting to feel desperate. I have to reach the road. There has to be someone who can help us. I remember I didn't bring any money for the bus – even if one were to come.

The visibility has dropped. It's growing darker and sheets of rain obscure the path. I start to jog. My bag bumps uncomfortably against my hip, the camera hits my leg. I keep my eyes firmly fixed on the ground so that I won't trip. When I glance up, hoping that I'll see the road, there's a man on the path, walking towards us. He seems to flicker in the curtains of rain, like an illusion. My first thought is that it's Harris, but that's only because I've been thinking of him constantly. Of course, it can't be him. Why would it be? Still, it's another human being. I switch Ben to my other hip and speed up. His shape is familiar: spare, tall, broad-shouldered; the face, square-jawed, dark-haired. It *is* Harris. He's running up the hill towards me. I want to cry with relief.

When he reaches us, he takes Ben as if he weighs nothing and slings my bag over his shoulder. He grasps my arm and guides me down the path.

'What are you doing here?' I shout above the noise of the rain.

'I was out walking and I saw a woman and a child. Thought they must be in trouble. When I got closer I saw it was you.'

'In this weather?'

'It's only rain. Nothing could keep me from the moors. You should know that.'

He smiles at me and water drips from his eyebrows, runs down his cheeks. He stops and hands Ben back. He shrugs off his waterproof and wraps it round my son, puts his own woollen hat on Ben's blond head. He peels off his jumper and passes it to me. I shake my head but I'm so cold and wet I accept it. He takes Ben again. I think my son will protest at being held by this strange man, but he snuggles into Harris's chest. I wish Harris would hold me too. Ben finally stops crying.

'Good job I've got the Fiat. It's on the road. I usually take my pickup. Better for collecting scrap. Not so good for transporting waifs and strays.'

'Car!' Ben yells.

It's on the road below us, cherry-red, small and boxy. I'm astonished at the coincidence – that it's Harris who's rescued us – and relieved, but almost immediately I start to feel guilty. Will he be thinking of our drunken kiss? Does he expect more? Will he talk about it? I have to tell him it is over, whatever it is we are doing. My family mean everything to me. How could I ever consider breaking up our home and ruining the security Evie and Ben have? It doesn't matter how I feel about Harris; nothing is worth risking my children's happiness. I can't say anything now though, not right this minute, not when he's saved us from pneumonia, when he has Ben in his arms. Once we're in the car, he wraps a blanket around us and turns the heater on full blast.

'I can take you home. Or you can come back to my house. I live nearby. On the moor. Get yourself warmed up. Have a cup of tea. I can make hot chocolate for the lad.'

He has his hands on the steering wheel as he says this. He flexes his fingers and stares straight ahead. I hold my breath. It's like it was in the gallery. He's waiting for my answer as if everything rests upon it. I want to go home and have a hot bath. I want to get Ben into warm, clean, dry clothes. I want to see more of Harris. I want to know where he lives, to have some insight into his life. And I need to tell him it's over.

'Yes,' I say, and he knows what I mean.

He drives a short way, I can't tell how far, I can barely see through the fogged windscreen. There's a black disc hanging from the rear-view mirror with gold Arabic writing.

'What does it say?' I ask, pointing to it.

'"Peace". A souvenir from the Hunza Valley.'

I hug Ben to me and kiss him and hope we don't crash when he's not in a child seat. What would Ollie say about what I've done today? I check my phone – still no signal. At some point Harris turns off the road and we drive directly into the moor down a rocky track; the car bucks and tilts, the disc swings and twists, the gold calligraphy flashing dully. I look at him in surprise. I didn't know you were allowed to do this.

'It's the old Keighley Road,' he says. 'People used to drove their cattle and sheep along it.'

He's hunched, a big man in a small car, peering through a smudged gap in the clouded windscreen. It feels as if we drive for a long way through the moor.

When we finally stop, he comes round to my side and opens the door. He takes Ben and my bag again, and puts the blanket round my shoulders and runs with us to his house. I can't take it in, where we are, what it looks like; it's raining so hard. I have a sense of space around us, of emptiness and isolation, and then he's pushing me inside. The three of us stand in his hall, dripping.

'Take your wet clothes off. You'll catch your death. I'll run a bath. And get you something dry to wear.'

I don't question him. My fingers are so numb with cold I can barely peel Ben's clothes from him. My son is blue around his lips and shaking. Harris ushers us into the bathroom, where there's an old bath on lion's feet, with an inch or two of warm, bubbly water and clean towels. A couple of minutes later he comes back with a pile of clothes and then he leaves us. I soak Ben in the water and dry and dress him. The nappies in my bag are damp, but they'll have to do. There are even bath toys, which I give him to play with on the mat, and then I add more hot water and submerge myself. Why does Harris have children's toys and a set of clothes a woman and a small boy could wear? Is he married? Was he in a relationship? I've become involved with someone I don't know the slightest detail about. I have to extricate myself. As soon as I'm dry, I'll do it.

As I'm towelling my hair, I catch sight of my reflection in the mirror. It's unlikely Harris would still find me attractive. He's seen me, mascara streaked down my face, my hair plastered to my skull, and now I'm as rosy as a boiled lobster. I bundle our wet clothes into a heap. I'm wearing the clothes Harris left out for me: faded jeans and a striped, long-sleeved T-shirt with a grey cardigan. They fit well and are similar to the ones I've discarded. I shiver. Could they be his wife's?

Ben and I emerge. We're in what was once a peasant cottage, maybe a farming croft. It's small, the walls are thick and the stone floor is uneven. Indian rugs are scattered across the flags. Or – more likely – they're from Pakistan. Someone must have knocked down the internal walls for it's open plan: the kitchen is on one side; there are large armchairs and a sofa with orange and red cotton throws slung over them; garlands of dried marigolds hang from the beams. There's a fire in the hearth and a tiny, spiral stone staircase, which presumably leads to a bedroom in the eaves. Harris has cleared a low coffee table, sweeping piles of papers and art magazines onto the floor, and has laid out a pot of tea, scones, jam, butter and hot chocolate in a plastic cup for Ben. He looks up at me and smiles, and my stomach flips over.

'My sister has a boy about your son's age. She keeps clothes here for the two of them, so she's less to carry when she visits,' he says.

I relax my shoulders slightly, less concerned about the feel of the fabric against my skin. He pours me some tea and spreads butter and jam on scones for us. Ben runs over to him and within a couple of minutes he's sitting on Harris's knee with a chocolate moustache and butter on his chin. I don't quite know how to start, what to say. I'm nervous – I've no real idea where we are. I walk slowly round the room, letting the heat from the fire warm me. I glimpse the moor through mullioned windows: it's a blur of brown and green and grey. On the whitewashed walls are photographs. I look more closely. They're originals, signed by the artist – someone with an impossibly exotic name: Hajar Abyadh. Here, in this house on the heath, the colours are incongruous: azure-blue skies, snow-topped mountains, chillies ripening in the sun, trees laden with golden apricots, a girl with dark hair and almond-shaped green eyes; a tiny emerald pierces her nose. She looks uncannily like Evie.

'They're of the Hunza Valley.'

'Harris,' I say, turning to him.

It's as if he knows what I'm going to say. He still has Ben on his lap. He stretches out his hand to me. I'm torn. I long to take it, feel his palm, rough against mine. My legs are like milk. I feel a rush of desire. Perhaps it could work? He'd make a good father. But then Ben wipes his sticky face on his sleeve and slides to the floor. Full of sugar, he starts to shout and charge from one side of the room to the other and it's as if the spell is broken. I remember who I am, what I stand to lose.

'I'm sorry,' I say, 'about the other night. I mean, it was – wonderful. I wish— But I can't— I've got a husband, Harris. Two children.'

Harris is shaking his head. His curly hair is almost dry and he comes towards me. I back away. If he touches me I know my resolve will weaken.

'Thank you. For coming to our rescue today. And for making me feel more confident about my work. But we can't keep seeing each other. Even for coffee.'

I think I'm going to cry. I'll miss talking about art. I'll miss him. I miss him already and the life I might have had. I hope he'll try to persuade me. And I hope he doesn't. I bundle our sopping clothes into my bag. I call Ben and hold out my hand for him. He ignores me. Harris is right in front of me. He's too close, towering over me. His face is twisted with rage.

'You can't do this to me,' he says.

I step back but now I'm pressed up against the kitchen cupboards. This wasn't what I'd imagined. I'd thought he might be upset, that he might try to talk me out of it – or that he'd say it had all been a mistake – he should never have kissed me. His raw aggression is frightening. My desire turns to fear.

'I want you,' he says quietly.

His pupils have shrunk to pinpricks. My heart starts to beat harder, faster. The muscles in his jaw are clenched tight. I can't breathe. I can't swallow. His expression is glazed, as if he can no longer see me or what I meant to him. The hardness in his eyes is terrifying.

'Harris?' It comes out in a weak croak. I stretch out my hand tentatively towards him. I'm shaking. The strength that I admired now seems dangerous.

'Mummy,' says Ben, and comes toddling over, jealously wrapping himself around my leg, pushing in between Harris and me.

I have to get Ben out of here.

'I thought better of you. I thought you were special.'

He looks down at Ben. Please God, don't let him hurt my child. I put my hand around Ben's head, press him tightly against my thigh.

'I thought you were different.'

Harris is breathing hard. The handle from the drawer behind me digs into my back.

'You bitch.'

His voice is quiet but his anger is unmistakable. He moves slightly and I scoop Ben up and retrieve my bag and camera from where they've fallen on the floor.

'I'll drive you home.'

'No,' I say, too loudly, too sharply.

'Don't be daft. You're miles away.'

There's a sneer in his voice.

'I'll call a taxi.'

He laughs and makes a gesture to the outdoors. We're somewhere in the middle of Ilkley Moor. I wonder if he'll offer to let me use his phone, but maybe there's no landline.

When I say nothing, he says, 'Have it your way. Get out of my house. I never want to see you again.'

He opens the door and I stumble out. Despair comes flooding back – I'm right where I was before – in the rain, in the middle of the moor, with a small child. Harris slams the door behind us. I take a deep breath. We're unharmed. I start to run down the road, bumping Ben on my hip and he giggles, thinking I'm doing it on purpose.

I sing 'It's raining, it's pouring' to keep him chuckling, and he joins in.

I keep checking my phone. On a rise in the path I stop. I can see Ilkley spread below me. The Keighley Road winds through shorn grass and bilberry bushes and I know where I am. I've got mobile reception! Relief surges through me. I phone Jack Mitchell.

'Jack?' I shout, deliriously happy when he answers. 'Can you bring Evie and come and pick us up, please? We're on the moor. And then drop us all back at my house?'

And Jack, because he's kind and wouldn't remind me that the arrangement was for me to collect Evie myself, says, 'Aye, sure. You've finished taking your photos then. Whereabouts are you?'

As if it's all completely normal.

I tell him where to meet me. Below White Wells, I say. Drive up the moor road.

We can walk that far together, Ben and I.

# OCTOBER, FRIDAY

I've been miserable all week. Snapping at Ollie and the children. This morning is no different. I'm tired and I've got a searing pain in my temples. I can't stop thinking about Harris and my lucky escape. Maybe it was my fault. Did I lead him to believe we had a future together? And what if I hadn't said anything to him? If I'd waited to see what would happen between us instead of trying to head it off before it came to pass? I would have fallen in love with him. The rational part of me thinks how terrible that would have been: he's unstable, aggressive and I would have destroyed my family. I realize that now.

Ben is full of beans, running manically around, pulling a caterpillar on wheels behind him singing, 'Raining, raining,' while I try to chivvy Evie into getting ready. She eventually appears in the kitchen.

'I want toast,' she says, as she sits at the table.

'Please.'

'Uhhh, please. Not brown! You know I hate brown bread!' she shrieks when I put a couple of slices in the toaster.

'You ate it last week. We don't have any white bread.'

'But I didn't like it. I hated it. I've always hated it.'

'So you don't want toast?'

'Yes, with chocolate spread so I can't taste the brown.'

'We don't eat chocolate spread for breakfast,' I say, wondering if I've just made that up; perhaps I've been eating Nutella in front of the kids and setting them a bad example? And is jam really any different? It's full of sugar; at least chocolate spread has nuts in it.

'Cheerios, then.'

'We've got Shreddies or Weetabix.'

'That's so boring. Why can't we have nice cereal like at Sophie's house? Or when we went on holiday and we had Frosties.'

'Evie! Shreddies, Weetabix or toast!'

She sighs elaborately and asks for Weetabix but with warm milk. While I heat it, and spread butter on her toast for me, she starts needling Ben, pinching his knees and his elbows. I don't think she's deliberately trying to hurt him, but he starts crying.

'Evie! Stop it! You'll have to sit at the other end of the table if you do that again.'

She takes her cereal bowl and flounces into the garden. I wince at the blast of cold air that funnels into the house. My mobile beeps. It's a text from Harris. He sent me several messages at the start of the week, apologizing and asking me to ring him. He said he missed me. I didn't reply. I click on this text. It says, 'You fucking bitch.'

I delete all of them and switch my phone to silent. It's yet more proof of his temper. I start to feel nervous. What if he decides to confront me? I check the time – we're going to be late. I go outside and find Evie by the sandpit, humming tunelessly and staring into space.

'Evie! You need to go upstairs and wash your face and brush your teeth. Why are you sitting out here? You're such a daydreamer!'

'I am NOT! You need to say, "Brush my teeth and *then* wash my face" or I'll get it all wrong! And then you'll shout at me. As usual!'

'You're seven years old!' I yell. 'You're old enough to get washed every morning without having to be reminded by your mummy!'

I go back indoors, wipe Ben's face and the table, clear up all the breakfast stuff and get both of us into our outdoor things – I even manage to find my purse and mobile without a last-minute panic – but Evie still has not reappeared. I strap Ben into the buggy and put Bella on the lead. When Evie doesn't come, I run upstairs. She's not in the bathroom and she clearly hasn't washed because her facecloth and toothbrush are dry. I fling open the door to her bedroom but the room is empty. I start to feel anxious.

Downstairs, Ben, trapped in the pushchair, starts to scream, 'Out!' and drum his feet against the wall. I've reached the point where I want to scream and bang my head against the wall myself. I'm too hot in my winter coat and I feel faint. I look in my bedroom and the studio. I find her in Ben's room, half hidden by his bed. She's crouching on the floor and she turns and gives me a beautiful smile.

'Look, Mum, it's a space ship called Noah. It's going to take all the animals off the earth before the aliens destroy the planet. We're going to start a new world called Paradise Bottom.'

She gives a little giggle at the silliness of her stellar name. She's made a tall, thin, skyscraper of a sculpture out of Ben's Duplo, complete with Playmobil animals hanging onto ledges and peering out of windows.

'Evie! Ben is crying downstairs, in his buggy. We are all waiting for you! Again! Why can't you just do as you are told? For once in your life!'

Her face clouds and the light goes out of her eyes. She stands up and kicks her sculpture in the middle. Pieces of Duplo ricochet round the room.

'Evie! For God's sake!' I shout again.

There's a wail and a crash, and I turn and run down the stairs. Ben has managed to push the wall so hard, he's upended the buggy and is now upside down, still strapped in and yelling. He's hit his head on the hall floor, and when I right the buggy, there's a red mark. It's in exactly the same spot he banged his forehead on a kitchen cabinet last Friday, and right next to the bump when he fell out of the backpack.

'Look what you've done to your brother!'

Evie is slowly putting her coat on. Her voice is quiet and precise. She says, 'He's not my brother.'

'Of course Ben is your brother!' I kiss him but Ben continues to cry. 'Why would you say something like that?' I ask, as I manoeuvre him out of the front door.

'Because he's not. None of you are my real family.'

'Evie, we are! We *are* your family.'

'I hate you all,' she says. 'I'm going to run away and live on the moor.'

'Now you're being ridiculous,' I say, losing patience.

We walk to school in silence, apart from Ben, who sobs intermittently and says, 'Ow,' pointing to his head with one fat finger.

I need to try to talk to her, when I'm calmer and can work out what to say. By the time we reach the playground, I start to feel like a human being instead of a bomb. My heart rate has returned to normal and I've stopped thinking I'll shake her or slap her if I'm not careful.

'Evie,' I say, bending down next to her.

I want to tell her that she needs to be grown up and to take responsibility for getting ready by herself and that I'm sorry I shouted at her, because I love her – I love her to the moon and back – but before I can say anything, she says, 'You're not very nice,' and runs off to her classroom.

I feel horrible. I look around me, cringing in case anyone else has heard her. None of the other mums are paying me any attention, but then I see Hannah, standing in the door, watching me, and my cheeks burn.

As soon as I get home I go straight to my studio. I've been painting all week as if I've been possessed. I mix raw umber and burnt sienna together. This is my most abstract painting yet. It's set on the plateau beyond the Twelve Apostles and I've poured all my feelings of despair and anxiety into it – whether Ben and I would make it off the moor last Saturday. The sky dominates the picture; the stones look skyscraper tall although, in reality, they're small. They erupt at odd angles, like broken teeth, from dark earth. The sky, the soil, the stones, all meld into one. It's called, '*My love for Heathcliff resembles the eternal rocks...*'

The painting is full of Harris too. In spite of everything, my whole body aches when I think of him. I know he's dangerous and aggressive and I should be grateful that nothing too much happened between us. But part of me yearns to talk to him about art and to be held in his arms again. He made me feel passionate about my work, as if I'm a proper artist, worthy of recognition. I'm bereft without him even though I know I made the right decision – to sever any connection between us. I can't even remember the last time Ollie and I talked properly, or went out and had fun. It's taken Harris to show me how weak my marriage is, but that's no consolation.

Just a few more touches and I can put my painting aside – it's almost finished. I glance at my watch and go cold. It's five to twelve. I hadn't realized how late it is. Ben finishes nursery at midday. There's no way I'm going to get there on time. I quickly wipe my paints off with a rag and run downstairs. I slip on my ballet pumps – I should get out my boots now it's cold – and faff around for a couple of minutes trying to find my phone, purse and car keys. One day I'll leave them all out together in a handbag I can just grab.

Bella tries to come with me but I push her back inside and run for the car. I've forgotten my phone and I go back, unlock the house, retrieve it from the stairs; Bella escapes into the front garden and I have to catch her and lock up again, swearing under my breath at myself. I'm not too worried about Ben – he loves his teachers and he'll be happy with them until I get there – unlike Evie who always cried when I dropped her off at nursery at his age and was in a rush to leave as soon as she saw me coming. But the staff will be annoyed and I'll probably be fined.

As I'm driving down Cowpasture Road, my mobile rings. I glance at the number. It's the school. I snatch it up.

'I'm on my way. I'm almost there. So sorry! I'll just be a few more minutes.'

'Mrs Morley, it's Kate Stevenson.'

Kate is the head teacher. I'm really in trouble now. I glance at the clock on the dashboard. It's a quarter past twelve. Surely that's not so bad? I still have to park and get to the school though.

'Five minutes more? Honestly—'

'Zoe,' she cuts across me. 'It's Ben. There's something wrong with him. We've called an ambulance and it's just arrived. They're going to take him to Airedale. If you get here in the next couple of minutes, you'll be able to travel to the hospital with him.'

'Oh my God. What's happened?'

'We don't know. He's unconscious. Can you make it?'

'Yes.'

I throw down the phone and put my foot on the accelerator. I turn sharp left, cutting in front of a car driving along Bolling Road, which swerves and blares its horn. The Grove is full of cars and pedestrians. I drive aggressively down a street that's so narrow, with cars parked along one side, it's become reduced to single-file traffic. My palms are sweating and my heart is racing.

Thank God, the ambulance is still there, in front of the school. I pull in behind it, parking on the zigzag lines, and run over. I'm vaguely aware of Mrs Stevenson and Ben's nursery teacher standing on the pavement. I bang on the back.

'Are you Ben's mum?' the paramedic asks, as she swings the door open. 'We were just about to go. Get in, love.'

Ben is strapped to a stretcher with an oxygen mask over his face. He's blueish-white with a clammy sheen. He's unnaturally still. I reach out to him.

'Oh my God, oh my God,' someone is saying over and over, and I realize it's me.

'Mrs Morley, sit here, next to Ben. Strap yourself in. Good to go,' she shouts through to her colleague in the front.

I hold Ben's hand. It's cold and lifeless. The paramedic turns back to me. 'My name's Julie. Ben had diarrhoea and vomited at nursery. He blacked out and that's when the school called us. He hasn't come round since then. We're giving him extra oxygen. That's all we know at this stage. We need to get him to A & E.'

'What's wrong with him?'

'We don't know, love.'

I can't take my eyes off Ben. I'm vaguely aware of the siren; we're going terrifyingly fast. Sometimes Ben's fingers twitch and his eyelids flicker, but he doesn't open them. I hold his hand and feel his pulse flutter in his wrist, light and fast as a sparrow's. I can't take it in – the change between this morning and now is so enormous I can't grasp it. I smooth his hair back from where it's sticking to his forehead. It's damp with sweat but he isn't warm.

'Is he, is he going to be okay?'

I stutter over the words and start crying.

Julie isn't looking at Ben, she's studying a green screen. I hadn't noticed it before – or the wires snaking from Ben's chest.

'It's a heart-rate monitor,' she says soothingly. 'His pulse is erratic. As soon as we get him to hospital the doctors will be able to work out what's wrong with your little boy.'

I'm mesmerized by the flashing light. It follows a regular rhythm for a minute and then speeds up, faster, and faster, until my own breath increases too, and then suddenly it seems to stop, the light slowing to a hypnotic beat. I hold my breath. This is my son's heart.

I imagine that small muscle struggling in his chest. I feel sick. I call Ollie, my fingers fumbling, the phone slippery in my palm. There's no answer. I hang up and try again but still get voicemail.

'Jesus Christ, Ollie, answer your phone!' I leave a message this time: 'Ring me back immediately. It's Ben.'

I should text but I can't bear to let go of Ben's hand. I'll try him in a minute.

Ben is mercifully free of vomit, but he's wearing someone else's clothes, pumps slopping off his feet, stained camouflage combats that hang past his heels, a navy T-shirt with holes, mismatched socks. They make him look even more baby-like than he is, and uncared for. We swing round a corner so quickly the seat belt cuts into my stomach. Julie tightens the straps holding Ben down.

When we reach the hospital, a team of medics are waiting for him. Ben's rushed straight into A & E. I run alongside the stretcher. I can hear our paramedic shouting over the noise, telling one of the doctors what's happened. I catch Ben's name and something about an erratic heart rate, now falling, and low blood pressure. Ben is lifted into a bed and it feels as if a swarm of nurses descend on him, some jabbing needles in his arm; one leans over and pulls his eyelids open, calling his name. I stretch out my arm as if I'm going to stop them, stop all of this. A woman peels away from the throng around him and introduces herself as Dr Agnes Vang. She has bright-blonde hair scraped back from her face.

'Mrs Morley?' She has a sing-song voice and pronounces my surname 'Moor-lee'. 'Can you tell me if your son has a history of heart problems?'

'What?'

She repeats the question in exactly the same way. There is no cushioning here, no easing me gently in to the situation.

'No. Never. He's always been fit and well.'

'That was going to be my next question. Any history of illness?

Anything you can think of that could have triggered this response?'

'Blood pressure is dropping,' someone shouts. 'Heart rate is ...'

'Er, no.'

And then I remember that Ben bumped his head twice, no three times in practically the same spot – but surely that wouldn't cause—

'Any problems with heart disease in the—'

'I can't find a pulse. There's no pulse!'

'Start CPR.' It's a tall Asian man in a white coat. 'Give him ten millilitres of ten per cent calcium gluconate.'

'Do you wish to wait outside?' Dr Vang grips my elbow. 'It can be upsetting to see this.'

I have my hand over my mouth. I'm crying. A doctor is pressing my son's chest, trying to restart his heart. Someone runs across with a defibrillator and one of the nurses is shouting, 'Clear!' My son's small body leaps. I can't believe this is happening. I press forward but Dr Vang seizes my arm. The Asian doctor pushes his way forward, crushes Ben's chest, up and down, without a pause. It's so brutal I think his ribs will crack.

'Pulse check in two.'

I stare at the heart monitor. The line is random, like green static. Two minutes. The seconds pass like hours. I'm biting my lip, shaking with the effort of not screaming. Suddenly the monitor starts beeping. The doctor glances up and puts a finger to my son's neck.

'We've got a pulse!'

Ben's heart has restarted. He's alive. My son is alive.

'Get him to ICU now. Stabilize his blood pressure. Put him on the ventilator.' The doctor turns to me. 'I'm Dr Imran Kapur, consultant paediatrician. Come with me, Mrs Morley. Your son's being taken to the Intensive Care Unit. We've restarted his heart but his blood pressure is abnormally low. He'll be attached to a ventilator with a tube running into his windpipe to keep him breathing and his airway clear. We ran a preliminary blood test and Ben has massive amounts of potassium in his system, which is what we think stopped his heart. We've given him insulin to nullify its effects, but he's still in danger. Right now we need to stabilize the arrhythmia in his heart rate and bring his blood pressure up to normal. I'll hand you back to Dr Vang. She has more questions for you.'

Within minutes Ben is in a ward with needles inserted in his arms, wires attached to his chest; a tube is pushed into his stomach. A bag of fluid on a stand slowly drips into a vein. There are a couple of screens by his bed, monitoring his heart rate, blood pressure, breathing. I'm reeling from what Dr Kapur just said – I didn't take any of it in. I check my phone and want to hurl it across the room; Ollie still hasn't called back. I send him a message, my thumbs slipping across the letters; predictive text can't cope with my erratic spelling. There are other people in this ward, all equally as ill as Ben, but I try not to look at them and see how distressed the relatives are. Someone pulls a curtain part of the way round the bed to give us the illusion of privacy. There are three nurses, the consultant – Dr Kapur, Dr Vang, and another doctor from ICU – all leaning over Ben and talking. I can barely see him. I reach my hand between two of the nurses and stroke a tiny patch of skin on his arm. He's so small, there's barely any of him that isn't hidden by tubes and wires, punctured by needles.

'I need to make sure one more time,' says Dr Vang. 'You can't think of any reason why Ben could have collapsed?'

I shake my head. I tell her about the bumps to his head and she speaks to Dr Kapur.

'Is he allergic to anything?' she asks.

'No.'

I glance at the clock on the wall and my heart leaps. Evie will need to be picked up from school soon. Bella is still locked in the house. My car is illegally parked outside the school entrance and I'm sitting in Intensive Care, without my husband and with my baby boy, whose heart is possibly failing and who cannot breathe on his own. If ever there was a time when I needed my mum, it's now. I wish she were still alive. I imagine calling her. She'd be kind and soothing, like she used to be. She'd pick Evie up from school. She'd take my daughter home and let the dog out. Somehow she'd sort out the car. I start crying with self-pity.

'Check his kidney function in an hour,' Dr Kapur says.

I call and text Andy but I only get his voicemail. I need someone to fetch Evie now. Where the fuck is Ollie? I'm finding it hard to concentrate because I'm trying to listen to what the doctors are saying to each other and watch Ben and the heart-rate monitor.

'Could it be something he ate?' asks the ICU doctor.

'Mum says he's not allergic to anything.'

'Could be a toxin.'

'Anything he might have ingested at nursery?'

'What could he have got hold of? This age they put everything in their mouths.'

'Something in the playground?'

'Chemicals? In the toilets?'

I try calling some of the mums I know but I can't get through to anyone. It's that time of day when everybody is getting ready for the school pick-up, plus the reception here is terrible.

'We're running some more comprehensive blood tests now,' Dr Vang tells me. 'We will get the results shortly. In the meantime, we're giving him activated charcoal.'

'What? Why?'

'In case he's eaten something. He might be having an allergic reaction. The charcoal will help neutralize it.'

I call the school and speak to Audrey, the secretary.

'How is Ben?' she asks immediately.

'The doctors don't know what's wrong with him. They think he could have eaten something funny. He has Weetabix every single bloody morning! I can't...' Tears stream down my face.

'I'm so sorry.'

'I'm ringing about Evie. My husband hasn't arrived and I can't leave Ben. I can't find anyone to take her home.'

My voice rises with anxiety.

'Don't worry, Zoe,' Audrey says. 'I'll ask Mr Mitchell to stay behind with her. Have you got his number? You can ring him directly when you know when you'll be able to get here, or if you find someone to pick her up.'

'Thank you. Thank you so much. I've got his mobile.'

As soon as I ring off, my phone buzzes in my pocket. It's Ollie.

'Thank God. I've been trying to get hold of you all afternoon.'

'Sorry, I was in a meeting. I had my phone switched off. What's the matter with Ben?' His voice is tight.

'I don't know. He blacked out at nursery. He's still unconscious. They think it could be a reaction to something he ate.'

'Jesus. I'm on my way. You're still in Intensive Care?'

'Yes,' I croak.

I'm pathetically grateful that I won't have to deal with this on my own.

Dr Kapur comes over. 'Ben's stable and his vital organs seem to be functioning normally. His heart rate is low, but within a normal range. I'll be back in half an hour when we receive the results of the other blood tests.'

I nod. The space around Ben's bed empties as the three doctors leave. One of the nurses stays and pulls the curtain all the way round.

'There's nothing you can do for the minute, love,' she says, smiling at me. 'Do you want to get a cup of tea? I'll stay here with him.'

I shake my head. She finds a chair for me and I sit down next to Ben and hold his fingers. His hands are small and pudgy. Bruises bloom beneath his semi-translucent skin where the needles have pierced his arms or where the nurses couldn't find a vein. His eyelids, covered by a filigree of minute burgundy capillaries, flicker;

his lashes are thick and dark blonde. I touch the dimple in his chin that's identical to mine. I've never seen my child so still; even when he's asleep he normally moves, murmurs, clenches his fists. I can't believe his heart stopped. He was dead and now he's alive. Will he be the same person when he wakes? Will he still be my Ben?

Dr Kapur, Dr Vang and two nurses return. Dr Kapur is about to tell me something when Ollie bursts through the gap in the curtain around Ben's bed. He's pale and perspiring, his tie is loosened, his coat slung over his arm.

'I'm sorry. I caught a cab from Leeds – the traffic was horrendous – it's taken me ages. How is he? Oh God,' he says when he sees Ben. He freezes. He's finally realized how serious this is, I think, and I feel a jumbled mix of relief and anger.

'Mr Morley?' asks Dr Kapur, and shakes Ollie's hand. 'Ben is stable now that we've lowered the potassium in his blood – but it could climb again. However, I believe we've found out what's wrong with him and we have an antidote. We're administering it now.' He nods at the two new nurses, who are disconnecting one drip and attaching a new one. 'If it works, it should clear the toxin from his system.'

'Toxin?' says Ollie, reaching out to stroke Ben's head.

'The blood tests indicate that your son ingested a cardiac glycoside. Specifically an evonoside, most probably *Euonymus europeaus*.'

'What?'

I can't process what Dr Kapur is saying.

'The spindle tree. It's a common wild plant. It's often grown ornamentally too. Ben must have eaten some of the berries.'

'But you've got the antidote?' Ollie interrupts.

'Yes, this is it. If it works, your son should start to recover. I'll be back to check on him shortly.'

'Will he be okay?'

'It's too early to say, Mrs Morley. But we are optimistic.'

He puts his hand on my shoulder as he leaves. A nurse finds another chair for Ollie.

'Where the hell were you?' I hiss at him.

'I *told* you where I was. What happened?'

I describe the afternoon; I tell him Ben's heart stopped. I think he's going to hold my hand, apologize again for not being here, but he touches Ben's face and his gesture makes me feel lonelier and angrier than ever. We sit side by side and watch our son. Even with his eyes closed, you can still see that they're the same shape as Ollie's.

I google 'Spindle tree'. The website for the Woodland Trust comes up first. It says the spindle, *Euonymus europaea*, is common in hedgerows and woodlands. It's deciduous and flowers in May and June. If the flowers come early, it's thought a plague will break out. The wood is hard and creamy-white; in the past it was used to make spindles for spinning wool, but more recently it's used as charcoal for artists. There's a picture of the flowers, pink ballgowns with orange stamens poking, like petticoats, through the gaps in the fleshy petals. In autumn they close to form fat hot-air balloon-shaped berries. The name comes from the Greek, *Euonyme*, meaning 'Mother of the Furies' and is a reference to its poisonous nature. I read on, my heart fluttering. The berries contain glycosides, which cause vomiting, diarrhoea, cardiac arrhythmia, hallucinations and loss of consciousness. Can kill.

'How did Ben get hold of the berries?' I wonder out loud.

Ollie doesn't say anything. Ben does put just about anything in his mouth and the berries look enticingly like sweets. But on the website, it says they taste bitter. Wouldn't he have spat them out? I don't remember seeing a tree like that growing near us or at the school, and surely no one would plant a poisonous shrub in a children's playground?

Slowly a pink flush spreads across Ben's cheeks. His fists uncurl. He still does not wake up. My eyes fill with tears. I hold Ollie's hand.

'Is he going to be all right?' I ask, as if he would know. I'm hoping he'll reassure me as he always used to.

'How long has he been unconscious?'

I look at my watch. It feels as if a lifetime has passed but it's only just after five o'clock.

'About five hours,' I say.

Ollie frowns. I know what he's thinking. Will Ben recover? And if he does, will he have suffered any brain damage? Will his internal organs have been affected?

'Evie!' says Ollie, leaping to his feet.

'Jack stayed behind with her,' I say.

'What about Andy? Couldn't he pick her up?'

'I couldn't get hold of anyone,' I say. 'One of us needs to get her. She'll be worried. And Jack can't stay at school indefinitely with her.'

I don't want to leave my son. I want to be here when he wakes up. I want to look into those blue eyes and see that it's Ben and not some vacant shell of a child.

'You go,' says Ollie. 'You've been here for ages. You must be exhausted. I'll stay with him. I'll call you the minute there's any change.'

I want to protest. It's not as if I've done anything – just sat here talking nonsense to Ben and holding his hand. But Evie might feel she's being neglected in favour of Ben and that's the last thing we need when she's already so insecure about her place in our family. I nod reluctantly. Ollie empties his wallet of cash so I can pay for a cab. I've left everything apart from my phone and keys in the car. I kiss him and then Ben. His cheek is warm beneath my lips.

The taxi driver drops me off at the school, right by my car. It hasn't been towed or clamped but there's a piece of paper jammed in the windscreen wipers. My heart sinks. It's bound to be from an irate parent saying that I've had the audacity to park on the zigzag lines, or else a ticket from a traffic warden. I pick it up. It's a note, signed from Kate Stevenson, saying the car belongs to a mother of one of the children and, due to an emergency, she had to leave it parked illegally. There's a mobile number to contact her in case of any problems. How kind of her. I glance in the window. My wallet is where I left it, on the front seat. Thank God Ilkley is such a law-abiding town. I turn to the school gates, expecting – what? Evie to come running towards me? Evie could hardly see me from here, her classroom doesn't face this way. And that's when I realize. The gates are locked. Not just locked, but padlocked with a chain around them too. I shake them futilely. Perhaps I can get in the back entrance, where the nursery is. I walk round the side, quickly now, stuffing the piece of paper in my pocket.

The nursery gates are locked and chained shut too. The school looks closed, not just shut but with that closed-for-the-weekend look, as if no one will venture near until Monday morning. I briefly think about climbing the fence. I phone the school but there's no one there. Jack's mobile goes straight to voicemail too. My mouth is dry and I'm beginning to feel anxious again. My brain doesn't seem as if it's fully in gear. It's no surprise – I haven't eaten since breakfast. Jack would be unlikely to stay at school this late – it's past five o'clock. So he must have taken Evie somewhere – probably to his house. I call Jack again and leave another message, saying that I'm going to drive over.

I put my phone on the passenger seat in case he calls me back. It's not far to Jack's. He lives on Mornington Road, two streets away from where my mum's house was, in one of the red-brick two-up two-down terraces. Evie loves going there because it reminds her of her nan's. In fact, she probably begged him to leave school early. I start to feel better. I begin calculating how long it will take – I need to pick Evie up, drive home, feed her, feed the dog, pack a bag for Ben and Ollie, head back to Airedale. If I hurry, I can be there by eight.

I ring Jack's doorbell. There's no reply. I ring the bell again and listen. I can't hear footsteps or Evie's voice. I bang on the door. I try the handle but it's locked. I press the bell hard. It's definitely working, I can hear it ringing. I'm just about to phone Jack again, when a voicemail pops up. It's from him. Perhaps he's taken her to the park, although it's a bit late and cold to be there now. Or maybe they've gone to a cafe. I press play.

He says, 'Hi, Zoe, sorry I missed your call. The reception on the M6 is terrible, I'm in and out of signal.'

The M6? What the fuck is he doing on the motorway?

'Sorry to hear about Ben being poorly. I hope he's okay. I'm glad her dad managed to get here and pick up Evie though – I was getting a bit concerned. I'm heading up to the Lakes and I want to get there before it's dark.' The message breaks up and crackles. There's a final word, '– care.' And that's it.

I'm shivering. Jack is driving to the Lake District. He thinks Ollie picked up Evie? How would Ollie have managed that? *Could* he have picked her up? I feel as if I'm going mad. No, we definitely had a conversation about it and he gave me the money for the taxi. I call Ollie. I can feel the hysteria building inside me. There's no reply. He's probably talking to the doctors, but can't he see I'm trying to reach him? I ring Andy instead.

'Jesus, Zoe, I just got your message and your text. I'm really sorry – I was in a meeting about a new adult ed course the college wants me to teach. How's Ben?'

'Is Evie with you?' I blurt out.

'No. I was about to ring but it's so late I assumed you'd got someone else to pick her up.'

'Jack stayed behind with her at school but he's left me a message saying that he's on his way to the Lakes and Ollie collected her. But Ollie can't have done – he's in hospital with Ben!'

'Wait. Slow down. You're sure Ollie hasn't got her?'

'Yes! He was with me. He drove straight from Leeds to the hospital. He gave me the money to get a taxi so I could come here!'

'Could she be with anyone else?' Ellen is crying and I can hardly hear him. I start crying too. 'Another friend from school?' When I don't answer he says, 'Look, call the police. Right now. Just in case. Zoe? Zoe?'

I hang up and dial 999. The man I speak to tells me to go back to the school and wait there and he'll send over two officers. When I reach the playground, I pull the crumpled piece of paper out of my pocket with Kate Stevenson's number and dial.

'Zoe! How is Ben? Is he okay? I didn't want to ring you in case you were still in hospital—'

'Kate.' I interrupt her. 'Evie is missing. Jack says Ollie collected her, but he didn't. Ollie's in hospital with Ben. I've called the police.'

There's a long pause and then Kate says, 'Where are you?'

'Outside the school.'

'I'll be there as fast as I can.'

'I need you to phone every parent in Evie's class to make sure they haven't taken her home with them. I've rung Andy Glover already.'

'The contact details are in the office. I'll be with you in five minutes. Where's Jack?'

A patrol car pulls up behind me. 'The police are here. I have to go,' I say. I blow my nose and get out of the car to meet them.

'Mrs Morley?'

I nod.

'I'm DCI Jeremiah Collier.' Collier holds out his hand. Mine trembles in his. He's in his late fifties, a heavily built man with a barrel chest. There are broken red lines on his nose and his watery eyes are grey. 'This here's DS Justin Clegg.'

The younger officer looks as if he's in his late twenties, but I suppose he could be early thirties. He's tall and gangly, pale with ginger hair and a beaky nose. I hold out my hand to him too and he stoops awkwardly to shake mine. I grit my teeth. We're wasting time with formalities.

'I understand your daughter is missing,' says Collier. 'Evie Morley, is it? Can you start from the beginning, love? How long has she been gone?'

'I, I don't know,' I say.

I explain about Ben being taken to hospital and how that meant no one from our family was there to collect Evie.

'So her teacher, Jack Mitchell, remained behind with Evie at the school and then at some point, between three-thirty p.m. when school finished and five forty-five p.m., when you got the message from Mr Mitchell that he was heading to the Lake District without your daughter, Evie went missing. And Mr Mitchell said in his message that Ollie, your husband, picked her up. Are you absolutely sure your husband didn't fetch her?'

'Yes.'

Behind us, I can see Kate climbing out of her car and rushing over to the school gates, her coat flapping open. I think I'm going to be sick. I'm shivering.

'What time did Mr Morley reach the hospital?'

'I'm not sure. It must have been almost five, or maybe a bit after? We both talked to the doctor – Ben seemed to be in a stable state and he – Ollie – suggested I leave and collect Evie from Jack. He gave me the money for the cab. The taxi took, I don't know, half an hour? The traffic was bad.'

This is agony. I want them to start searching for her. Where the hell could she be? Why did Jack say Ollie had her?

'Mr Morley suggested you collect Evie?'

'He'd forgotten about picking her up. He never does the school run. When he remembered, I said I'd arranged for Jack to stay behind with her and that's when Ollie said I should get her and he'd stay with Ben.'

I've said all this already. Why aren't they doing anything?

'Have you checked with any friends or family members?'

I tell them I've asked Evie's best friend's dad already, and the head teacher is in the school, phoning all the parents of the other children in her class. Ollie's mum and dad and his brother and sister live in London and my parents are dead. There's no one else.

'Could she be at home?'

She could have walked there! Jack shouldn't have let her but it's still a possibility. I have an image of her standing on the doorstep of our house, cold and alone and frightened.

'I haven't been back. Not since taking Ben to the hospital.'

'Mrs Morley—'

'Zoe.'

'Zoe. You go home and check,' says Collier. 'We'll have a quick word with the head teacher and we'll meet you at your house. What's your address?'

I tell him and give him Ollie's mobile and mine. He hands me his card. 'We'll be with you shortly. Let's hope your daughter is there. Call me when you get home.'

The road is a blur; my eyes are filled with tears. Still, I drive like a lunatic up Cowpasture Road. My car is old with no fancy in-car phone system, so I balance my mobile on my knee and try Jack and Ollie again, without any luck. I pull into Rombald's Lane and desperately try to see round the corner of our cul-de-sac. There's no little girl standing outside the front door. I run round the back in case Evie's gone along the bridleway. It's deserted and the garden is empty. The wire fence is too high for her to climb over in any case. When I open the front door, Bella doesn't come bounding over to me like she normally does. She sidles, cringing and whining. I can smell it.

'Poor dog,' I say, fondling her soft, floppy ears, 'I know it was an accident. You've been locked in all afternoon.'

She wiggles her backside and wags her tail. I let her out into the garden, then fill up her water bowl and shove a handful of dog biscuits by her bed as I ring Ollie and Jack. Both calls go straight to voicemail. I try Airedale Hospital and, after an interminable wait, I'm put through to ICU.

'Ben Morley?' asks the nurse. She sounds harassed. 'I'll check.' She comes back on the line a couple of minutes later and her voice is warmer. 'Yes, love. He's come round and he's asleep. He's breathing on his own without the ventilator.'

'Oh, thank you, thank you so much. Is he... is he going to be okay?'

She hesitates and then says, 'You'll have to speak to the consultant, Dr Kapur. Your son had a heart attack, didn't he?' I start crying. It sounds so terrible, so final. 'Can you come in, love?' she says. 'Dr Kapur will be back in half an hour.'

'I'm afraid I can't,' I whisper. 'Can you get my husband to ring me? Oliver Morley. He's with Ben. I can't get through to him.'

'I'm very busy but I'll get a message to him at some point this evening.' She's written me off as an uncaring mother because I'm not in hospital with my son who's on life support.

'It's urgent,' I say. 'Please. Our seven-year-old daughter is missing. I was at the hospital when she got out of school and I don't know where she is.'

She inhales sharply. 'I'll go and speak to him now. She's probably with one of her friends. I hope you find her soon, love.'

I want to start searching for Evie. I want to be in hospital with Ben. I need to hear what Dr Kapur is going to tell us. I have to do something. Why would Jack say that Ollie had picked Evie up? And, as her teacher, he couldn't let her leave without handing her over to a family member. Could he have meant someone else? Perhaps one of the other dads? If Jack was desperate to go, he might have rung another parent and asked them to look after Evie. It seems like the most rational explanation. I have to cling to it because anything else is unthinkable. The doubts crowd in though – why wouldn't Jack have called and told me or texted? Why wouldn't the parent who has Evie have called me or Ollie or the school to say she's with them?

I'm hovering by the front door, trying to think what to do, and just when I can't bear it any longer and decide I'm going to start driving round Ilkley looking for her, I see a dark shape through the frosted glass in the front door, walking up the path towards me. My heart leaps. It could be one of the parents, bringing Evie back. I yank open the door.

The woman standing in front of me is petite and curvaceous with short, dark, curly hair. She has a tiny snub nose and large downturned eyes, which make her look melancholic. 'I'm the family liaison officer, Ruby Patel,' she says, holding out her hand to me. 'The JC's are on their way.'

I frown.

'Jeremiah Collier and Justin Clegg. They're a formidable team. Don't worry, we'll find your daughter. We'll find Evie. May I come in? I just want to run through everything once more.'

'That's all anyone has done! Ask questions. I need to look for my daughter.'

She inclines her pretty, heart-shaped face to one side. 'Believe me, when a child your daughter's age goes missing, we work fast, even if there's a possibility – as there is in this case – that another parent could have her. We've got two teams of officers driving round Ilkley searching for her right now. We've instigated a region-wide alert. All UK airports and ports have been notified and we've started going through CCTV footage at the station. I do understand, I really do, that you feel the need to do something but we are searching for her. The most helpful thing you could do would be to have a chat with me – make sure there's nothing important you haven't told us. Let's get that out of the way. And hopefully, in the meantime, we'll find out she's with another parent from the school,' she finishes, attempting to reassure me.

'But,' I say, 'you don't even know what she looks like. What she was wearing.'

'The head teacher told us. She spoke to Evie this afternoon about Ben being in hospital, and then again later on, to let her know that Mr Mitchell would be waiting after school with her, so she has a clear memory of Evie's outfit. Mrs Stevenson also gave us a printed and an electronic copy of Evie's school photo and that's what we've circulated.'

I can't remember what Evie was wearing today and that makes me feel terrible. I do remember the school photo. I hated it. The picture had been taken at the end of the day and no one had brushed Evie's hair or even smoothed it down and she had a spot of tomato ketchup on her cheek. She looked unkempt, unloved, and her smile was an unnatural rictus, showing her crooked incisors that are just starting to poke through the gaps left by her baby teeth. I stand back to let Ruby in. She wrinkles her nose as she steps past me.

'Sorry,' I mutter, 'the dog was in the house and I've only just—'

'It's okay. Let's get it sorted.'

She marches through the sitting room and starts pulling out kitchen roll and disinfectant from under the sink.

After she's cleared up the mess, she asks, 'Have you searched the house?'

'She couldn't have got in,' I say. 'The place was locked when I came home and she doesn't have a key.'

Ruby doesn't say anything. Does she think Ollie and I have done something to our child? After a moment, she starts peering inside cupboards and I join her. We look in every wardrobe and under the beds. I show her the attic space. Even though I know it's pointless, I still feel a frisson of hope every time I open a door. We're covered in dust and cobwebs and biscuit crumbs by the time we're through.

'Do you have a garage or a garden shed?'

It takes me a few minutes to find a torch and then we go out into the freezing night. I should have thought of looking here. Just in case. The shed is locked: no one has broken in. It's unnaturally neat: shelves with plastic stackable drawers full of screws and drill bits, a lawnmower and half a bag of sand. It's Ollie's domain.

When we come back inside, Ruby rubs her hands together and makes an exaggerated 'Brrrr' sound. She makes me a strong, sugary cup of tea, a plate of toast, and opens a can of dog food for Bella, and then says, 'Sit down, Zoe, let's have a chat.'

I cup my tea in both hands and stare at her.

'Talk me through your day.'

I recount the basics, but she takes me back to the beginning and asks me to describe every detail. I start crying as I tell her about Evie's beautiful sculpture – 'Paradise Bottom' – now shattered, the Duplo scattered round Ben's room.

'What's the last thing you and Evie said to each other?' she asks gently.

My tears come faster.

'She said she hated us and she wanted to go and run away and live on the moor.'

Snot is dribbling over my lip. Ruby hands me some kitchen roll.

'Did you talk any more on the way to school?'

I shake my head. 'Not really. I tried to speak to her when we got there but she ran off. I mean, ran into the classroom.'

Ruby gets up to make me another cup of tea. She asks about Jack: how long Evie has known him, if she likes him, how often he's babysat for us. I keep looking at the clock. Why hasn't Ollie phoned back? The nurse said she would tell him to ring me straight away and it's been ages. I rub a piece of spider silk off my elbow.

Ruby leans towards me.

'Do you trust Mr Mitchell?'

'Yes,' I say. 'Evie loves him. He lets her ramble on for hours, or helps her build elaborate sculptures. He never minds the mess she makes.'

Five years of caring for my daughter. It must count for something, surely? I do trust him but why hasn't he phoned me?

'He's not so good with adults.'

'What do you mean?' asks Ruby, and her voice sharpens.

'He's so focused on the child – on children – he doesn't have time for all the things that parents like, you know, discussing their child's homework or SATs. But I always thought that was a good thing.'

Ruby isn't wearing a wedding ring; she probably doesn't have kids and so she hasn't yet got lost in the minutiae of life in the school playground to the extent where, suddenly, every conversation is about them and you no longer know how to relate to anyone who doesn't have a child.

'He's a suspect?'

'Yes. He was the last person to see your daughter. He hasn't returned our calls and we have no idea where he is.' She takes a deep breath and fixes me with her large dark eyes. 'But the reality is that primary suspects in cases like this are usually the parents. Especially as Mr Mitchell said that your husband collected Evie from him.' I'm about to protest, but she forestalls me. 'I know that must be difficult to hear, but we have to eliminate that possibility, get it out of the way now, so we can concentrate on finding out who really has your daughter.' She looks at her watch. 'He'll be here any moment.'

'Who?' I ask.

'Your husband. A patrol car went to the hospital to pick him up.'

I look outside but it's dark and all I can see is my own pale reflection. I shudder. Is Evie out there, alone? And if she's with someone, who could it be? Ruby is right: Collier, Clegg and Ollie arrive a few minutes later. Ollie comes over and folds me in his arms.

'I'm sorry I didn't get your message earlier. And then the police arrived. There was hardly any signal on the way here and I thought I'd be here soon so there was no point—'

I pull him tighter to me so that he can't read in my eyes how hurt and angry I am with him.

'You should have called,' I say.

Just a simple phone call — the sound of his voice would have been reassuring — to know that we're going through this together.

'We'll find her,' he says, his voice hoarse.

There's a lump in my throat. 'How's Ben?'

'He's okay. He's sleeping. One of us should go back as soon as we can, in case he wakes up.'

I think about Ben in that ward, surrounded by beeping machines and crying children, his body ensnared by tubes and wires, waking up on his own.

'What does Dr Kapur say?'

'He says it's too early to tell for certain whether there will be any lasting effects. They diagnosed the toxin and treated it in time and it's reversible. But they won't know if he's suffered damage to his kidneys or his brain yet.' He reaches for my hand. 'He said kids bounce back.' His tone is hollow.

Collier clears his throat. 'Sooner we get on with this, the sooner you can get back to your son,' he says.

We all sit down, apart from Ruby who is making more tea.

'Kate Stevenson has called all the parents of children in Evie's class and I'm afraid no one said they took her home. I'm sure FLO Patel has briefed you on what we're doing already,' Collier says, 'but I want to assure you we are taking this extremely seriously, even though there's every chance we'll find Evie with someone she knows and there's simply been some sort of miscommunication. We have two teams of officers driving round looking for her; we've got officers visiting every one of the families who has a child in your daughter's class, as well as all the teaching staff. There's a team in the station who are locating the CCTV cameras in the area and going through that footage as we pull it in.

'We've scaled up the investigation since Ruby got here, and instigated a country-wide alert using the photograph of Evie that Mrs Stevenson gave us. All our airports and ports have been notified. No one will be able to leave the country with her. Our number one priority, though, is to track down Jack Mitchell, since he was the last person we know of to have seen Evie. But we do need to ask you a few routine questions, Mr Morley, so that we can eliminate you from our investigation.'

'And take a formal statement from you both,' chips in Clegg.

Ollie nods reluctantly.

'Take us through your day, Mr Morley – from 12.15 when your wife first heard that Ben was poorly.'

I should be with Ben, I think. Ollie can answer these questions on his own. I look across at him, wondering whether to interrupt. Ollie runs his hand through his hair. It's his trademark gesture but today his hair is greasy and it stays in a rumpled quiff.

'I was in a meeting. I didn't see Zoe's call or texts. I had my phone turned off. I got her messages at about four and I called her and then went straight to the hospital. We talked to the doctor about Ben, and then Zoe took a cab to the school to collect Evie. I stayed on. With Ben. That's it.'

'Airedale Hospital?'

'Yes.'

'What time did you arrive?'

'About five p.m. It took ages. The traffic was terrible.'

'A long meeting.'

It's a statement rather than a question.

'What?'

'From before twelve to four.'

'I had two. Back to back. It's not unusual.'

'And you didn't switch your phone on in between?'

'No. I forgot. Look what is this? My daughter is missing, my son is in ICU, and you're asking me about my phone?'

'The meetings were in your office? Where you work?'

Ollie nods, swallowing his anger. Collier leans back, his hands resting on his knees. Ruby brings a tray across. She's managed to find the half-empty bag of sugar at the back of the cupboard and some digestives, the boring biscuits we never get round to eating. I wonder if Ruby waited for this moment to intervene. Her skin is the colour of black tea; when she passes me a cup, I notice her hands are so dry, her knuckles are starting to crack.

Clegg says, 'Thank you, Mr Morley. We appreciate it's distressing for the parents of a missing child to be interviewed, but we can start to move on now.'

I see what they doing – a good cop, bad cop routine – Collier, older, grumpier, with his brusque, broad Yorkshire accent; Clegg, the junior partner, kinder, easier to talk to. There's an innocence, a naivety about him. A lot of women have probably opened up to him. He's safe. Not a man who'd hit on you or act aggressively; a beta to Collier's alpha male. Or maybe I've just watched too many detective box sets while Ollie was at fancy parties.

'So what are you doing about finding Jack Mitchell?' Ollie asks.

'Mr Mitchell's got his phone switched off, but I'm confident he'll turn it on or we'll find someone who knows exactly where he is in the Lake District,' says Collier. 'I've notified the Cumbria Constabulary and they have officers searching for Mr Mitchell's car.' He looks at us both carefully and says slowly, heavily, 'He's a prime suspect, and I know I've asked you this already, Mrs Morley – Zoe – is there anyone else you could think of who might have your daughter?'

He means, anyone who could have picked her up from Jack, someone kind and benevolent, but Ollie answers: 'Her father.'

The two officers stare at him. Ruby is watching me, gauging my reaction. I've been trying to avoid thinking or saying it, as if by willpower alone, by not paying it any attention, I could make it untrue. But I can't. The words are seared on my mind: *I've been searching for you ever since you were stolen from me.*

My heart squeezes painfully tight.

'Evie is adopted,' says Ollie, not looking at me. 'Her father recently contacted her. Look,' he says.

He goes into the kitchen and comes back with the card, the pink unicorn in its garish wrapping, the presents I found in the attic, the red prayer book he'd been too angry to look at when I eventually told him about it. He piles them all on the coffee table in front of Collier and Clegg. Something changes imperceptibly in the room. The focus of attention has shifted from Ollie and it's as if we are all on the same side now.

'We reported this to the police already. It looks as if you didn't do your job thoroughly the first time round.'

'I thought the name Morley rang a bell. Aye, I do remember this case,' says Collier.

Ollie ignores him. 'Do you mind if I go? Someone needs to be with our son.'

It should be me. I want to be with Ben. I don't want to be left here on my own, without our daughter. I open my mouth to speak.

Clegg jumps in. 'Mind if we take your phone, Mr Morley? And laptop. Just a routine check. Yours too, Mrs Morley.'

Ollie looks furious and mutters under his breath. He's about to protest and then thinks better of it. He slides his phone onto the table. He hugs and kisses me.

'Don't worry, we'll find her,' he tells me as he leaves. 'She'll be at someone's house, having a whale of a time.'

His words lack conviction.

I'm going through everything, all over again, with Collier and Clegg, for my formal statement, when the doorbell rings. I leap to my feet, spilling my tea across the table.

'It's the sniffer dog,' says Ruby. She looks at me apologetically. 'We need to do another sweep of the house. To be sure.'

I sit back down. Clegg lets them in: two officers and an Alsatian. Bella barks and crawls under my seat and whines, her tail thumping the chair leg. I can hear them walking around over our heads.

'What happens now?' I ask.

'Our teams are doing all they can and more than likely we'll find her soon,' says Collier. 'We'll keep searching through the night. Tomorrow morning, officers will start going door to door. We'll speak to everyone in Ilkley. We'll trace the route she could have taken home from school, in case she tried to come here by herself, and look through all the sheds, outbuildings, garages. But,' he sighs heavily, 'the moor is another story. You said you had an argument in the morning and the last thing your daughter said to you was that she was going to live on the moor.'

'It's just one of those things that children say! She's seven! Of course she didn't mean she was going to run away.'

'We can't rule it out at this stage, Mrs Morley,' says Clegg. 'The head teacher showed us a story Evie wrote today in her schoolbook, about a little girl living on the moor. She seems to write lots of stories where witches and giants roam around out there.'

I put my head in my hands. So they think it's my fault? Surely there's no way Evie would have tried to hide on the moor?

'We also have to consider the possibility that she's been abducted,' Collier continues, 'and if it's not Jack Mitchell, or his accomplice, the moor could be where the perpetrator has taken her. A wilderness like that, right next to a small town — it's the perfect place to conceal a child. So if we don't find her tonight, there'll be a large-scale search, with dogs, police officers, volunteers, tomorrow morning. Across Rombald's Moor.'

'We still hope we'll find her soon, though,' says Clegg, and he pushes my statement towards me to sign.

After they've left, along with the two officers and the sniffer dog, Ruby says, 'I know it's the last thing you want to think about right now, but we won't be able to keep this out of the news. In fact, it could be to our advantage. Collier will ask you and your husband to speak to the media. Does that sound like something you'd be willing to do?'

I close my eyes. This is too serious. I can't believe this is happening, to us, to me, to Evie. It's after nine o'clock. Evie has been missing since mid-afternoon. Someone has taken our beloved child. I nod.

'Anything. Whatever it takes.'

It's odd having a stranger in my house, using my kitchen. She's clearing up the tea cups, carefully stacking them in the dishwasher, replacing the sugar in the cupboard, wiping down the surfaces. She knows her way around already.

'Do you live locally?'

She shakes her head. 'Bradford.'

I wonder if she's Muslim or Hindu; if she lives with her parents. Would she know anything about the prayer book – what it means?

'It's best if you're not on your own tonight,' she says. 'Do you mind if I sleep on the sofa?'

'There's a spare bed upstairs, in my studio.'

'Well, if you're sure. Don't get up. I can make the bed myself.'

I start to explain where the sheets are and then I realize that she already knows. Around ten, Ollie calls from a payphone.

'Any news?' he asks in a low voice.

'No,' I say, and I choke and start crying, great gulping sobs, with snot and tears running down my face. 'Where is she?'

'I'll come home tomorrow morning,' Ollie says. 'If they don't find her tonight, I want to be there to search for her.'

'What about Ben?'

'They believe he's recovering, but like Dr Kapur said, they can't be completely sure. It's going to take time. His kidneys are working though.'

But they don't know about his brain, I think. How can you tell with a two-year-old? How certain could you ever be? Like Evie, you can't predict what your child might have been – could have been – if their brain had not been damaged when they were a baby.

'I'll call you tomorrow. I'm going to try to check Ben out of the hospital if I can.'

'I don't think we should risk it.'

He'll need to be monitored. I can't imagine Dr Kapur will want a child who's been poisoned to leave hospital so early. And what if anything goes wrong? But I want to look for Evie and I want Ben here, with me. I can't bear the thought of him in that ward, surrounded by beeping machines and distressed children.

'I'll only take him out if the doctor says it's okay,' Ollie reassures me. 'Is there anyone we can ask to look after him? Andy and Gill?'

'No, Ben might still be too ill for them to care for when they've got Sophie and Ellen to think about as well.'

We're both quiet for a few moments. A child is crying in the background.

'You really think it could be her biological father? Who's taken her?'

'I don't know,' he says reluctantly. 'But he knows what Evie looks like, where we live. It wouldn't be hard to find out what school she's at – he'd only have to follow you in the morning —'

'Don't,' I say. 'Stop.'

I know he's been watching us. How else was he able to leave the gifts and card without us seeing him? What other explanation is there for the strange sensation I've had walking along the bridleway or on the school run? I've led him right to Evie's school. He took her. And we let it happen – if I'd managed to get hold of Ollie earlier, he could have picked her up, or if he'd stayed in hospital with Ben, I would have fetched her. Either way, one of us should have been with her every moment of the day she was not at school. I should have tried harder to reach Ollie. He ought to have left his phone switched on. Or checked it. That's the whole point of having a mobile, isn't? It's not to play Candy Crush on the train or look at the stock market – it's in case there's an emergency. He should have protected her and he didn't.

After I've hung up, I force myself to think practically. If Dr Kapur does let us take Ben home, who could care for him while we search? Hannah White. She got on well with Ben when she babysat for us before, and she would know what to do if he showed any signs of needing a doctor. If she came to our house, Ollie and I could both look for Evie together. I'm too upset to call but I send her a text.

She replies almost immediately:

Of course. I'm so sorry. I can't imagine what you're going through. You WILL find her. See you in the morning. Hannah x

I go upstairs to Evie's room and stand looking out of her window onto the moor. It's hard to see anything beyond the black shape of the chestnut tree, the darker outline of the hillside, but then something moves, just beyond the garden. There's no moon and the sky is cloudy. I press against the glass and strain to see. Whatever it is, out there, is now still. It's about the height and shape of a man, standing waist-deep in bracken. The hairs on the back of my neck rise. Could it be Harris? Watching us. Watching me. Or the person who took Evie? I'm cold. My breath mists the glass. My heart starts to thump. I should wake Ruby. Go out there to check. I sway slightly and squint. I can't make it out. I must be mistaken. There is nothing there. Slowly my heart rate returns to normal. It's just a bush, stirring gently in the wind.

You're with me. We're together at last. I have tears of joy in my eyes because I have you in my arms, my darling daughter. I can touch you without censure, cuddle you, kiss you, stroke your soft, dark hair. You were so pleased to see me when I picked you up. You thought it was a game, a special treat, just for you. And it is, of course it is. I keep hugging and kissing you. I can't stop. I'm making your favourite meal: garlic bread and pizza, with ice cream, strawberry sauce and marshmallows. Fortunately, my limited cooking skills are just about up to it. You scream with delight when I tell you. You'll have a bath, really deep with tons of bubbles and a pirate ship, and then we're going to watch your favourite movie, *Frozen*, and eat popcorn. We'll stay up late. We'll watch the stars rise in the heavens and thank Allah for our new life together.

Once you've explored my flat, you start asking questions. About your mummy. I tell you that the woman is a fake. The man is also a fake. It's much better to be with your real parents, who love you more than life itself, who love you to the moon and back.

You giggle and say, 'To the end of the universe and back?'

'I love you to the end of the universe and back,' I tell you.

I'll put you to bed tonight and I'll watch you fall asleep. I'll be with you in the morning. I will be the last thing you see at night and the first person you see when you open those beautiful eyes of yours.

For now, we have to hide. I don't want them to take you away from me again. I cannot lose you. But it won't be long. We'll be able to escape and start a new life. Our own little family.

# SATURDAY: THE DAY AFTER

I'm numb with fear. I'm walking across the moor, searching for my daughter. We started below White Wells, at the bottom of the path I took with Ben to meet Jack and Evie, a week ago today. Police officers, sniffer dogs and volunteers all spread out in a line and we began slowly trudging up the hill, through rank grass and rush, until we reached the ragged line of heather. The scale of the operation, the number of officers and dogs, is impressive.

My heart sank when I saw the weather: it's cold and foggy. Ruby is next to me but I can only see a couple of the other officers, everyone else is lost in the mist.

Last night I lay on my bed in all my clothes and I must have slept but if I did, I don't remember. I only recall weeping until my eyes were raw, and throwing up. I rose at 5 a.m., layered on warm clothes, made a flask of coffee and packed more warm clothes and waterproofs in a rucksack for me and for Evie to wear when we find her. Ruby tried to persuade me eat a bowl of Weetabix and to stay in the house.

'She might come back here,' she said.

'I have to look for my daughter,' I said.

Ollie called to say he was on his way home with Ben and he'd join me as soon as he could. His money ran out before he could give me any more details so I'm hoping that meant Dr Kapur was happy for Ollie to take Ben out of hospital. I feel a tug drawing my child to me; I wish he were here with me, in my arms.

Occasionally, there's a break in the fog, and I catch sight of people I know – parents from school, Kate Stevenson, Andy. I'm grateful they're here, looking for Evie, but I don't want to speak to anyone. I have to hope and pray that we find her, but my mind, as cloudy as the day, can't take it in – that my child could be out here, on the moor. I'm shaking. If we find her, what state will she be in? If, somehow, she got lost, and ended up on the moor, could she have survived a night in October? Yes, I tell myself fiercely, yes. It was cold but it wasn't freezing. She *will* be alive. And if someone took her and discarded her afterwards, what kind of state would she be in then? I try and make my mind blank. I don't want to think about the possibilities. What someone might have wanted with a seven-year-old girl. What he might have done to her. I have to focus on here and now, one foot in front of the other, on finding my daughter.

'I keep imagining I'll see her,' I say to Ruby, 'like she's suddenly going to appear through the mist.'

I think of her gorgeous, snaggle-toothed grin, long dark hair sparkling with beads of moisture, her green eyes wide and excited. I can't hold onto the image. It shivers like a mirage and disintegrates.

'We'll keep looking until we find her,' says Ruby.

I can't remember what Evie was wearing the last time I saw her. Hysteria threatens to overpower me. I keep my eyes on the ground, searching for any trace of her. Searching for her. My boots are coated with dead heather blossom. Tears leak out of the sides of my eyes.

'Zoe. Zoe!'

It's Ollie's voice. I turn, elated, expecting to see him holding our daughter in his arms. He's on his own, tripping over heather roots and bilberry tussocks. He's out of breath. Once Ollie was fit – he used to row and play five-a-side football with Andy. He hugs me awkwardly, conscious of Ruby and the other officers stealing sidelong glances at him.

'No sign?' He doesn't expect an answer. 'Ben is okay,' he adds quickly. 'I couldn't leave him there on his own – and he's fine, he really is. You'll see.'

'But he almost died! What did Dr Kapur say? Exactly.'

'Same thing as before. It's too early to tell, but he's optimistic he'll make a full recovery.' Ollie hesitates and then says, 'He didn't want me to take him home, but he said he could see that under the circumstances we couldn't stay in hospital with him and we would want our son with us. He said if anything changes, no matter how slight, to call him and bring Ben in. And he also wants to see him for a check-up tomorrow. Hannah is with him now.'

'How does he seem to you?'

'Okay, honestly. Don't worry. Hannah is giving him breakfast. You wouldn't know he was unconscious for several hours yesterday. I mean, he's tired but—'

He doesn't want to say what we're both thinking – there are no signs of brain damage. He falls into step a metre or so away from me, taking the place of an officer who moves further down the line. I comfort myself with the thought that Dr Kapur would never have let Ollie remove Ben from hospital if there was a concern. I wish I was with Ben. I haven't been apart from him for a whole night before.

'I keep remembering the last time I saw Evie,' I say miserably. 'I told her off. I shouted at her. I said—'

'It's not the last time you'll see Evie,' Ollie interrupts. 'There'll be many more occasions where you'll scold her and where you tell her how much you love her. She knows you love her, that we love her.'

His mouth is turned down as he speaks. It's an effort to be this kind and reassuring towards me. We've done nothing but snap at each other lately. I stretch out my arm and he stretches his and we touch fingertips.

'If she's with her father—' I start to say.

'*I* am her father!'

'Sorry, love, I'm sorry. I mean —'

The fight leaves him quickly and he looks beaten: sallow and unshaven in this unkind light.

'If she's been abducted by her biological father, then we'll find her,' he says. 'She can't leave the country. They've alerted all the ports and the airports. No one can hide for long. They'll trace his credit cards, they'll catch him on CCTV.'

If they knew who he was, I think, but I don't say it. We have to hope that she *is* with her father because he'll love her and he'll care for her, won't he? Until we can track her down and take her back. Take her home. I don't say this either because I don't want to hurt Ollie's feelings even more. I dig my nails into my palms. I never used to censor myself in front of him. I always said the first thing I was thinking and waited for him to be my sounding board, my voice of reason, my rock in the middle of the night. But, recently, he's stopped being so patient with me. And, most of the time, I've felt so angry with him, I've been suppressing my feelings in case I lash out.

I look ahead but the fog isn't clearing. This is not the kind of day where it'll lift to reveal bright blue sky. It's dark, grey, the air is heavy with moisture so that there seems no difference between the damp fog and the fine drizzle that has started. I want to stamp my foot, shake my fist at God. Or someone. We're covering so little ground and so slowly, I start to despair.

We reach White Wells, the spa where Darwin is said to have taken the waters. There's a small cafe here and the owner must have been informed about the search because he comes out with free tea and coffee for the police and volunteers.

'I'm sorry about your little girl,' he says, as he hands me a cup. 'I hope you find her, love.'

I can't meet his gaze. I don't want to see his pity or my own wretchedness reflected back. I turn away so he won't see my tears.

Ollie puts a hand on his shoulder and says, 'Thanks, mate', and the poshness of his London accent here, in the middle of the Yorkshire Moors, as we accept kindness from strangers, grates on me.

I sit on a low stone wall facing towards Ilkley, though I can see nothing more than a few yards of shorn grass. I feel a stab of envy when I think of the families below me; even though I can't see a single house, I know they're watching television, cooking breakfast, their children are doing homework, playing in their gardens – they're unaware of the bliss in the everyday, oblivious that I'm outside, raging and crying because someone has stolen my child.

Ruby sits a little distance away on the same wall. It's as if she's my minder. Does she suspect me as well as Ollie? I suppose increasingly people have become aware of the violence within women too: in mothers. I remember my disproportionate fury with Evie simply because she didn't get ready for school on time. How I made her destroy her beautiful sculpture...

'How are you doing?' Ruby asks.

I give a juddering intake of breath and I try to answer but words fail me. If a child was lost here, or had been left on the moor, what would the chances be of finding her? Finding her in time. Finding her alive. I take a sip of my tea and throw up over my boots.

'Oh, Zoe, love,' says Ruby, and hands me a paper napkin.

I wipe my mouth and say, 'Why isn't there a helicopter searching for her?'

'The weather's too bad. Even if the pilot used the thermal-imaging camera, we wouldn't detect her.'

'Why not?' I rinse with my lukewarm tea and spit but I can't get the taste of vomit out of the back of my throat.

Ruby looks away from me as if she's embarrassed.

'A small child is about the same size as a sheep.'

I pour the rest of my tea away. I could kill every single one of those sheep with my bare hands.

––––

By midday we've checked the Valley of Death, with its treacherous cliffs and rocks, sharp as shark's teeth, above which, one day, Harris's sculpture will stand, and we're slogging through the bog leading up to the Twelve Apostles. Someone emerges from the mist and comes towards me, her hands outstretched. She grasps mine. Her eyes fill with tears. It's Mandy Kilvington's mum. Mandy is in Evie's class, but I can't think what her mum's name is. There's a terrifying blank where the answer should be.

'We are all so sorry. Evie was a precious child. We all loved her. Such a talented little artist.'

I can't stand her tone of voice and I snatch my hands away.

'Thank you for coming to look for her,' I say through gritted teeth.

'We couldn't possibly stay away. Julie, Heather and I, we're all here. Our daughters played with Evie all the time at school. We couldn't imagine – if my Mandy – if one of our children —'

I can feel Ruby's presence. She's hovering just behind my shoulder. Now she leans forward and offers her hand.

'I'm Ruby Patel, the family liaison officer. Thank you for coming to help, Mrs…?'

'Mrs Kilvington,' Mandy's mum says. She wipes her tears away with a tissue. 'The first twenty-four hours is crucial, isn't it? That's why everyone from Evie's class has come to help. Because we simply have to find her—'

I'm going to be sick again.

'Thank you,' says Ruby. 'It's actually forty-eight hours. But, as you say, time is of the essence. Shall we get back to looking for Evie?'

Mrs Kilvington narrows her eyes at Ruby and sniffs. 'If there's anything you need, anything at all, please call,' she says, seizing my wrist.

'Thank you,' I manage before turning away.

Ruby puts her arm around me and squeezes. 'There's always one, wants to turn everything into a drama all about them.'

'She said "played". Past tense.'

'Evie is missing, that's all we know,' says Ruby gently.

I look into her large, almond shaped eyes with their thick lashes. I can't read her, I can't tell what she really thinks. Evie has been missing for almost twenty hours.

'You could do with a break. We've got plenty of officers out here who are trained to do this job.' I'm about to protest, when she says, 'You can always rejoin the search party later. But you need to keep your strength up. I'll go and get your husband, he can walk you back.'

I haven't seen Ben since yesterday afternoon and I nod wordlessly. Ollie and I head towards the Cow and Calf rocks and then we drop straight down Hangingstone Road and along the bridleway to the back of our house. There's a litany running through my mind, 'Where is she? Where is she?' over and over. I bite my lip to stop myself from saying it out loud. Ollie doesn't hold my hand, or help me, as he normally would when I stumble on the uneven path, he's so wrapped up in his own grief.

He doesn't speak until we can see our house and then he says, 'I'm going to kill Jack Mitchell.'

I touch his arm. 'We just need to talk to him. There's something we're missing. It doesn't make sense – Jack saying you collected Evie.'

He nods and a muscle fires in his jaw.

Hannah is standing outside. Her face is white and pinched. She looks anxious. Ben is bundled up in his all-in-one suit, playing in the sandpit. Hannah must be cold. Then I realize – she's worried too, she's fond of Evie. As her teacher, she spends hours with her, she knows a different side of my child, a part of her personality we don't see.

'Is Ben okay?' I ask when we reach the wire fence.

'He's been on good form,' she says. 'I've tried to keep him quiet and not overtire him. But I thought he could do with some fresh air, you know, after being in the hospital for so long.'

Ben sees me and comes running over, his arms outstretched, and starts to wail, 'Mummy, Mummy, Mummy.'

I can't reach him – the fence is too high to climb or to lift him over. He has a bluish tinge to his skin and there are dark purple thumbprints beneath his eyes. The backs of his hands are criss-crossed with plasters. I crouch down and put my fingers through the mesh. I'm so relieved to see him – I can't believe we nearly lost him yesterday – that I cry too.

'Any sign of her?'

Hannah looks at Ollie instead of me and he shakes his head.

I run along the path next to our garden – I'll have to go through the house to get Ben. Ollie follows more slowly. My son staggers after me, on the other side of the fence, howling as if I've abandoned him again. When I reach the front garden, I pull up short. There are two satellite TV vans parked outside. Someone gives a shout and a mob of people with cameras swing towards us. Men start shouting, 'Mrs Morley, Mrs Morley, Zoe – how are you feeling? Any sign of your daughter? Mr Morley? Ollie?'

How does it feel to know that your seven-year-old daughter has been missing for an entire day? A child you love so much you cannot breathe, a child who has only ever been out of your sight for a few hours whilst she was at school? Ollie pushes past and takes the key out of my trembling hands. He slams the door behind us and I run through the house to reach Ben. I can still hear the journalists clamouring outside. I pick Ben up and cuddle him and gradually his sobs quieten.

'Thanks, Hannah,' Ollie says, and takes out his wallet.

She shakes her head and her long straight hair falls in front of her face.

'No, I couldn't possibly.' She looks at me and her expression is almost desperate. Her green eyes fill with tears. 'If you need me again – tomorrow – just call. But I hope...'

She doesn't finish the sentence. I can't look at her as she turns to pick up her bag. I can feel my face tightening, aching.

I carry Ben to the window to wave goodbye to her, but he won't; he snuggles into my neck instead. Hope. Yes, we have to be hopeful. We will find our daughter. I stare into his blue irises. Is it Ben in there? Or have we brought a shadow-version of our child back from the hospital?

I watch Hannah pull her scarf over her face and burrow through the mass of press camped outside our house. As she drives away, a patrol car pulls up and Collier, Clegg and Ruby get out.

'Ollie! It's the police. Maybe there's news.' But then my heart sinks. If they'd found Evie, she'd be with them.

Ollie has already figured that out and curses under his breath as he opens the door.

'Mr Morley,' says Collier, heavily, as he enters. He's being formal. This can't be a good sign. 'We have a few questions for you.'

Ollie swears out loud. 'Have you found Jack Mitchell yet?'

'We will. Shall we?'

He indicates the dining-room table. The four of them sit down and I extricate Ben from his outdoor clothes, wincing at the bruises on his arms. Collier turns a tape recorder on.

'You said yesterday that you had two meetings at work. You had your phone switched off from around twelve until four when you picked up your wife's messages and then you went straight to Airedale Hospital.'

'That's right. We've gone over this already. We're wasting time. You haven't even found Mitchell, the last person to see Evie!'

Collier ignores him. I join them, holding Ben on my knee. I don't want to let him go. I don't understand why Collier hasn't moved the investigation on. 'We checked your phone records. You made two calls from your mobile at two seventeen and two twenty-two p.m.'

'Haven't you got more important things to do than look at my fucking mobile?'

'You said your phone was turned off,' Collier repeats. 'At two thirty-six p.m. CCTV footage from your office shows you leaving the building. And there's no footage of you returning or exiting your office just after four when you said you left to go to the hospital.'

There's silence. Ollie looks startled. He glances at me and then away.

'So. You actually left the building at two thirty-six p.m. Which would have given you time,' Clegg says quietly, 'to drive back to Ilkley, collect your daughter from Mr Mitchell, hide her somewhere, and then go to the hospital to meet your wife.'

'No! That's not what happened. You can't seriously believe I kidnapped my own daughter?'

Collier leans forward. His hands are large and red, the skin flaking. 'Why don't you tell us what did happen?'

My heart is in my throat. That can't be right. How could Ollie have left his office just after two thirty but only reached Airedale two and a half hours later? Ollie is white. He licks his lips. He puts one hand on mine. I grip Ben tighter and he wriggles and starts to cry.

'You have to believe me,' he says, looking at me. 'I was in meetings, I left around four, like I told you.'

I jiggle Ben up and down to try to calm him. Ruby is immediately at my side.

'Do you want me to take him?'

I shake my head.

'I would never, never hurt my daughter. You don't really think I'd do anything to Evie, do you?' He's looking from me to Collier and Clegg and back at the officers.

'She's not actually your daughter, though, is she?' says Collier.

'She's my daughter! She is my fucking daughter!' he shouts and Ben howls more loudly.

I get a bar of chocolate from the cupboard and give it to Ben. I'm trembling and I think I'm going to be sick again. Could there be any truth in what they're saying? Why would he lie though? Why? I can't believe it. Ollie wouldn't—

'Where were you? Where the hell were you? Why did it take you so long to get to the hospital?' I shout.

'I did have a meeting,' he says, swallowing. 'I did switch on my phone and I got your message.' He looks ashamed. A pleading tone comes into his voice. 'But it sounded like you had things under control. There wasn't anything I could do right away. And my meeting was with a prospective client who runs an art gallery. It was important. If he wanted us to take on the gallery's accounts, it would be huge. It's The Ormond Gallery – a franchise. It would have meant the accounts for the entire business, nationwide, and most of the artists they represent. So I went to the gallery and then I took a taxi to the hospital. I didn't realize how serious it was with Ben or I would have cancelled. And I didn't tell you, because—'

'– you didn't want me to know that you put a work meeting ahead of our son's life,' I say.

'I really thought it was just—'

'Just what?' I snap. 'I ring you from an ambulance, to tell you that Ben is unconscious, the paramedics have no idea what's the matter with him and we're heading for A & E and you didn't think that was serious?'

He runs his hand through his hair. 'Then you left me another message and a text saying Ben was stable, you were in hospital... I didn't think another hour would make any difference – and if this meeting went well —'

'– you'd be made partner of the firm,' I finish for him.

'Chocolate,' Ben grins and gives me a sloppy, sticky kiss.

He's never eaten this amount in his life. He wipes his hands down my jumper.

'I'm sorry,' says Ollie. 'I'm sorry.'

'Can you verify this meeting?' asks Collier.

Ollie nods. He pulls a business card out of his pocket. It says The Ormond Gallery, in gold lettering. He turns it over to show the detective the number he's scribbled on the back.

'That's the owner's private line. His assistant called a taxi for me.'

He hands it to Collier who passes it to Clegg. Clegg immediately walks to the far end of the living room and dials the number.

'I had my phone on silent. I was checking all the way through the meeting. If Ben had got worse, I would have left, I swear. But he was in the best place he could be. And you were with him. Times like that, a baby needs his mum.'

'You...'

I can't bring myself to look at him. I get up and take Ben over to the sink to clean him up.

'Checks out, boss,' says Clegg after a few moments.

'Check him out too,' says Collier brusquely.

I assume he means the proprietor, in case he's lying. I have to believe Ollie even though I'm shocked at his callousness.

'On it,' says Clegg.

He returns to the window bay and I hear him arranging to meet the gallery owner.

'So now what?' I say. 'Now that you know my husband has not abducted our daughter.' I put Ben down and he toddles over to his toys in the corner of the room.

Collier says, 'Has *probably* not abducted your daughter. We haven't verified it yet. We're still trying to trace Mr Mitchell. We've got a team of officers covering the route from your house to the school – calling door to door, going through every shed, garage, outbuilding – like I said. We've broadened our search to the nearby villages and towns – Burley, Addingham, Guisley. We'll keep looking across the moor – it's such a large expanse of wilderness and we've only covered a fraction of it. No one can smuggle Evie out of the country – the alert on the ports and airports is still in place. More officers are going through CCTV footage back in the station.'

'Is that all?' I whisper.

It's no different to what Collier told us they were planning to do yesterday. There must be something they can do to find Evie's father.

'How can you still not know where Mitchell is?' asks Ollie.

'Believe me, Mr Morley, we're looking for him. The Cumbrian Constabulary have set up several stop-and-search points. They're checking cars, asking if anyone has seen him or Evie.'

The Lake District is such a vast area, I think.

'He could be bloody anywhere,' says Ollie, recovering some of his spirit.

Collier and Ruby exchange glances. She knits her hands together and takes a deep breath before gazing steadily at me.

'When a child goes missing,' she says carefully, as if this was a speech she'd rehearsed, 'the first thing that we do—'

'– is suspect the family. I know. You've wasted a lot of time on that already,' I interrupt.

Ollie looks at me gratefully. He thinks I've forgiven him.

'– is check the location of all the paedophiles in the area,' says Ruby.

I put my hand to my mouth.

'We go through the sex offenders' register and then we ascertain where they all were at the time of the child's disappearance. We've got a team who are working through our list of known offenders.'

I retch over the sink.

'In the meantime,' says Collier, 'we'll need a statement from the two of you. For the media.'

Ruby starts to rise from her seat. There are deep lines between her thick eyebrows.

'No!' I say to her, wiping my mouth. 'I don't want help.'

And I don't want to stand hand in hand with Ollie in front of the town's journalists, pleading for our daughter, while some pervert watches us and gets a kick out of our pain.

'Whether you like it or not, this will be all over the news before the day is out,' says Collier. 'Experience tells us it's best to speak to the press. If you can give a statement to the media it'll help take the pressure off. Unless you give them something, they'll keep badgering you until they get their soundbite – and it might help us find your daughter. I'll leave you to talk it through with Ruby,' he adds, rising stiffly to his feet. 'She'll set it up if you want to go ahead. Don't use your landline. Let the answerphone pick up. If we have news, we'll ring Ruby or call you on your mobile.'

I stand at the window and watch Clegg and Collier leave. Ollie lifts Ben up and sniffs his bottom, wrinkles his nose.

'Stinky,' says Ben.

I can't bring myself to turn around and face my husband. He takes Ben upstairs to change him. I blame him. If only he'd answered his phone. If only he'd been honest. If only he weren't so obsessed with work. If only he'd put his daughter first. Maybe the truth is, he stopped putting Evie first once Ben was born.

'Men can struggle to accept a child who isn't their biological offspring. It would be natural for him to feel less strongly about Evie,' says Ruby. It's as if she can read my mind.

Still, I'm shocked at how brutal it sounds when she says it out loud. It *is* what some of the adoption books say – that men don't bond as well as women do with children who aren't theirs.

I tell myself to stop Ruby speaking; her words are like a toxin seeping into my mind, and it's going to poison my feelings for Ollie.

'It's not true,' I say. 'Ollie has always loved Evie. Right from the start.'

More than I did, I think, but I don't say that. In those early, difficult weeks when she was in the incubator, and I could summon no feeling for her, I never doubted Ollie's love for that little baby.

Ruby changes tack. 'We need to talk about the media statement. I know it sounds bloody awful and it's going to be traumatic – but it might help. Even if you decide you don't want to do it, I still need to brief you.'

I clench my jaw so I don't say anything rude in response. She's just trying to do her job.

'I'll do it. I'll make sure Ollie does too. Go ahead and set it up.'

We have to do everything in our power to get Evie back, even if I have to pretend not to think about the paedophiles watching us, one of them perhaps knowing where Evie is.

Ruby is on the phone when my mobile rings. I jump. I'd almost got used to not having it but Clegg handed it back to me this morning. It's Gill. She was out with the search party this morning. Perhaps she's seen Evie. I snatch it up.

Gill sounds frantic. I've never heard her lose her cool like this before, even when she was at her most stressed, during finals at university. I can't make out what she's saying.

'Zoe? Are you there?'

'Yes, sorry. It's not a good time, Gill.'

The disappointment is making me bitter. Why the fuck is she ringing me with her problems right now?

'Zoe, please listen. I know this is really, really awful for you, but Andy is not involved.'

'I know,' I say. Why does she feel the need to tell me that?

She takes a gulp of air.

'We're at the police station. He's being questioned. The police think he could have something to do with Evie... with Evie's disappearance. But you know Andy would never—'

'What?' I say, 'Why would they think —'

'Because of the present. You remember, the prayer book? Andy found it in Sophie's room. It's got his fingerprints on it.'

'He took it out of the wrapping paper to see what it was.'

'That's right! That's why his prints are on it. But the police don't believe him. You have to tell them!'

'Okay,' I say. 'I'll speak to Ruby. She's our liaison officer. I'll call you back.'

'Thank you, Zoe, thank you.'

'What is it?' asks Ruby, putting down her phone.

Ollie brings Ben back downstairs.

'It's our friend, Andy. He's being questioned. He found one of the presents Evie received – the Muslim prayer book.'

Ollie looks shocked. 'I told Collier that.'

'So it's probably just routine, then,' says Ruby. 'They're talking to all the parents of the children in Evie's class.'

'But not formally. Not in the police station.'

She's silent.

'Andy's been our friend for years,' says Ollie. 'His daughter, Sophie, is Evie's best friend.'

I remember the conversation I had with Andy when I was trying to work out who Evie's biological father could be. He said he'd slept with prostitutes. He said it meant Evie's father could be anyone. And my first thought had been: *even you.*

'He's so fond of Evie,' I say out loud.

'That's right,' says Ollie. 'He's always loved her—'

'– like his own daughter.'

And we both look at each other and I hate myself for the way

I'm starting to be suspicious of anyone, even my best friend. But it is possible. It could just be possible.

'It was the only present that didn't appear in the garden,' says Ollie. 'It turned up in Andy's house. And the writing inside was different to the writing on the outside of the presents.'

I nod. I feel sick and then a huge and terrible rage overwhelms me. 'What do we do?'

'There's nothing you can do,' says Ruby. 'He's being questioned. Collier and Clegg will get to the bottom of it.'

'Gill wants me to tell them to release Andy.'

'You can't,' says Ollie, echoing Ruby. 'You mustn't.'

'If he didn't have anything to do with Evie's disappearance, they'll let him go,' Ruby says.

Andy wasn't there last night when I tried to call him. I rang and rang and he didn't answer. He didn't even pick up his own kids from school that day. What did he say he was doing? Teaching some adult education course? So he could... I put my hands over my ears as if I can somehow drown out my own thoughts. There is no one left I can trust.

'I need to keep looking for Evie,' I say.

Ruby hesitates and then nods. 'Have you got any folding steps?'

I'm so surprised I answer: 'In the garden shed.'

I put my walking boots on and grab my rucksack from where I'd left it yesterday, still filled with snacks and warm clothes for Evie, and kiss Ollie and Ben goodbye. Ruby marches into the garden and fetches the steps.

'Come on,' she shouts to me, as she positions them by the chestnut tree. We climb up, hold onto the trunk, step on a fence post and jump into the bridleway. It's such an ingenious way of escaping the journalists, I forget to tell her I don't want her with me.

'It won't take them long to figure out this path is here and then they'll be peering in your house from both sides,' she says matter-of-factly.

She unfolds an OS map and radios one of her colleagues.

'The search party is here,' she says, showing me on the map. 'Or is there somewhere else you want to go? Some place that's special to Evie perhaps?'

I've got a splitting headache. I'm nervous it's going to turn into a migraine. The last time I had one was just after Ben was born and it wiped me out for two days. I can't risk that happening now. My mind feels fuzzy and I'm not clear what Ruby is asking me: does she think Evie has run away and hidden in a place she loves? Or is this somewhere to go to remember Evie, almost like a memorial? Surely that can't be what Ruby means. I shake my head and stop abruptly: the pain has sliced right through from the front to the back of my skull. Why would Evie run away? She didn't mean what she said when we argued. I remember her story about the princess who escapes from her evil step-parents. I think of all the other stories she's written about the moor, mainly featuring Rombald's giant, who supposedly stamped on a rock that split into the Cow and the Calf. Kate Stevenson was right when she told the police that Evie is fascinated by this wilderness.

'Do you have any paracetamol?'

'No, sorry. And I wouldn't be allowed to give you any even if I did,' she says.

Her tone is sympathetic though. She hands me a bottle of water.

'Let's go up Hangingstone Road. That'll be the quickest way to reach them,' I say, ignoring her question about Evie.

'I can radio for a car if you like, to drive us to the edge of the moor. The journalists know what yours looks like and we don't want to go back down there.'

I shake my head again and grit my teeth at the pain singing through my molars. 'No, I want to look for her as we walk.'

It feels utterly futile, but I can't think of anything else I can do and I can't stay in the house while Evie is out here somewhere. I have to hold on to the hope that I might find some fragment of her clothing or something that would indicate she's been here. Ruby and I walk on opposite sides of the road. I take the edge by the moor; there's no pavement, but I scan the rush-filled ditch. The urge to hold Evie in my arms, to smell her hair again, is overwhelming. I have a pain in my ribs so sharp my breaths are shallow. We're walking in a capsule of mist that's growing darker by the minute. There's only going to be another hour or so of daylight. I stifle a sob.

We pass the car park below the Cow and Calf and even now, in the fog and drizzle, there are a few diehard tourists buying ice cream and cups of Yorkshire tea. I find it hard to believe that anyone is capable of doing anything even remotely normal when my daughter has been taken.

A little further on we go by the Cow and Calf Hotel and I turn away so I don't have to see the punters enjoying an early-evening beer as they watch Sky Sport. Maybe it's seeing those men with their pints, but I think of Jack and all at once I'm filled with rage again. Ollie's right. It was Jack, not Andy, who was responsible for Evie. How dare he hand her over to anyone else without talking to me first?

'Why the hell hasn't Jack got back to me?' I say to Ruby. 'I should never have trusted him with her.'

'Don't blame yourself, love. We don't know if he's taken her. And there was no reason not to trust him. He looks after loads of kids in that school. Not just Evie.'

'It's the perfect cover, though, isn't it? I mean if you're a paedophile. Perhaps he's been waiting for Evie to reach some kind of magic age and he can't contain himself any more. Ben getting sick gave him the opportunity he'd been waiting for. He told me

Ollie picked her up but, really, he's taken her. And we'll never see our daughter again.'

'Don't,' says Ruby. 'You mustn't think like that. We'll find him.'

I press my hands against my temples.

A little further on we reach the track that Harris drove down to take Ben and me to his house, and I hesitate. I can't see far because of the mist. It's stony and muddy and barely wider than a bridlepath. Ruby consults the map.

'We need to go a bit higher before we can cut across and join the search party,' she says.

She glances at her watch. I know she's thinking it's getting late and dark. I wonder if her own family are missing her. If she has a mum who'll keep her tea hot in the oven.

'Have you looked down here?' I ask.

'No. Not yet. The moor's so big and we haven't the man-power. The helicopter would have covered it if it hadn't been for this fog.'

I try to think rationally about why I want to search here. If someone took Evie, they'd probably have a car. This old drover's road is one of the few places you can take a vehicle part of the way across the moor. It leads to Harris's house – nowhere else – but still… if someone took her hoping to find a quiet spot… maybe she escaped… maybe they left her… terrifying scenarios are jumbled in my mind with images: Evie's smooth, unblemished skin, her naked body. I have to stop this.

'I want to look down here. I came this way last week. You can get a car down the track.'

Ruby crosses over the road to join me.

'Was Evie with you?'

She sounds hopeful.

I shake my head. Jack picked Ben and me up from the other side of the moor – just below White Wells, where the search began this morning. Ruby and I head down the track together. The stones are slippery. A curlew calls. The sound is so mournful it makes my whole body ache.

'Were you out walking?'

I wonder if she's checking up on me or making conversation.

'Yes – with Ben.'

Evie's fascination with the moor didn't extend to actually wanting to hike across it, I think.

'My backpack broke and then we got caught in the rain. This guy I know happened to be passing and he rescued us. He lives down here.'

I don't tell her how frightening the 'rescue' actually was.

'I didn't know anyone lived on the moor.'

'Neither did I. It was probably an old farming croft originally. It's quite far away – maybe a mile or so.'

She shivers. 'I can't understand why anyone would want to live out there. You'd be totally isolated.'

I do. I could imagine waking up each day and instead of looking out of the window and seeing the moor in the distance, you'd be in the heart of it, feeling the wind turn, the storm rage, the rain lash, hearing the plovers piping. But then, that is partly why I fell for Harris – this shared understanding of what matters to us. Even now, in spite of what happened, I miss him. I have to fight not to pick up my phone and dial his number right now; to tell him my beloved daughter is missing. He'd run to find me, I know he would; he'd hold me tightly, take me back to his house in the midst of the heath and shelter me where no journalists would ever find me. That fierce side of his personality would work in my favour: he'd be utterly ruthless to anyone who tried to hurt me. But, of course, I won't. And I can't forget the way he turned his anger on me; leaving me and my small son to struggle home through the rain on our own out of spite.

It's getting dark but I can't turn back, not yet. A sheep bleats close by and another answers. Something looms like a rock out of the mist and I startle, not sure if it's my imagination. It's half blocking the path. Ruby shines her torch on it but the fog scatters the beams and we're temporarily blinded. We go closer. There's a strange, acrid smell. It's a car, turned on its side. Ruby walks gingerly round it, flicking the torch over it. It's been completely burnt – the rubber flayed from the tyres, the paint scalded from its surface; there are pools of glistening oil and charred matter pock-marking the grass. The windows have been smashed and tiny chips of glass glisten in the beam of the torch. Ruby peers inside but it's empty. I walk a little way further on. There are tyre tracks here, the path has been churned into mud. The shape of the car nags at me. It's familiar. I feel a cold sensation in my ribs. Could it be Harris's? I spot something glittering in the dim light, caught in a stand of rushes.

'Stop!' shouts Ruby. 'Come back. Don't step on anything – not even the tyre tracks.'

I ignore her and walk a little further, off the path, into the rough grass. I pick it up and turn it over in my hands. It's a flat black disc, a little scorched, with gold letters. I swing round to face her. 'I know whose car it is.'

And now I'm ice cold all the way through to my core, because – what does this mean? That Harris was in a crash? That he could be hurt?

Ruby is already on the phone when I reach her.

'Forensics are on their way. Just in case,' she says, holding out an evidence bag for me to put the disc in.

'Why?'

'It could be nothing – but, well, don't you see? A burnt car on the moor the day after your daughter goes missing. If she was in this car, the driver would need to destroy it to get rid of the evidence.

I'll wait here for them. You go on back. I'll call another officer and tell him to meet you. Someone should be with you.'

I'm shaking my head.

'But I know whose car it is,' I repeat, 'and he wouldn't have taken Evie.' As simultaneously I'm trying to clear the images from my mind, of blood on the seat, of strands of Evie's hair, of Harris – and how angry he is with me.

Ollie is so pale he's almost green. His voice is hoarse and his eyes are red and raw-looking. He's eating a plate of toast when I get home. I can't face food. Even thinking about eating makes me feel sick.

'We found a car on the moor,' I say. 'Someone had burnt it – there's just a shell left.'

I look at Ollie and from the way his face sags I can see he's understood what finding the car might mean.

'Do they know whose it is?'

'Not yet.'

I don't want to tell him my hunch that it's Harris's – not until I know for sure. It could have been a coincidence, finding his 'Peace' disc by the path. I don't believe Harris would have taken Evie – I can't believe it. It's more likely he was in a crash, driving home late; maybe he was drunk. But if I say to Ollie that I recognize the car, he'll ask me how, and when I got into it. I won't know how much to say, where to draw the line. I never told him about my escapade on the moor with Ben. He doesn't know about all my meetings with Harris.

'It's probably nothing to do with Evie,' I add. 'They should be trying to find out who her real, her biological father is. And they still don't know where Jack is.'

He hugs me and speaks into my hair: 'I'm sorry. I'm so sorry.' He starts to cry, great jagged, gulping sobs that shake his whole body. I cling on to his chest tighter, harder. I can't look at him. He's brought this upon us – Ollie should have been there for us, for Evie. But right now, what I need from him is not an apology. I need him to be strong, for all of us.

You're not here. I can't believe it. I've looked everywhere. I want to howl with rage.

I had to leave you. It was part of the plan; I need an alibi so that I won't become a suspect. I begrudge every moment I'm away from you. I think of you every second that we're apart. You have everything you need here: toys and books and food. It broke my heart to see your distress this morning. You cried for your so-called mother and father and brother. I explained that I'm everything to you: I'm your mother, your father, your brother. I am your all. It won't take you long to realize the depth of my love for you. I can give you more than they ever could.

You wanted to go outside to play but I told you that you couldn't leave the house. You cried even more when I said I had to go.

'It's only for a little while,' I said.

Later, you'll be able to go outside as much as you please. I tried to tell you what our new life together would be like.

'It will be magical,' I said. 'There are mountains. They reach right up to the sky. There are beautiful flowers and there's snow on the highest peaks.'

I helped you dress up in the *Frozen* costume you'd been carrying around in your school bag.

'You can be a princess of ice and frost where we are going,' I said.

I kissed you and told you I would be back soon.

So I don't understand. How could you leave me? How did you even manage to get out? I'm terrified you'll be hurt or discovered. I'm going to search for you. I will look all night if I have to, but I will find you. I will not lose you again.

It's dusk and the light is fading fast. The wind has a bitter edge and slices right through my fleece. At least the fog is starting to clear. You weren't even wearing a coat. I clamber up the steep path, past the reservoir. I shudder when I think of its slippery sides and how deep it is. You're too sensible to go near it, aren't you? I hope you haven't gone into the wood either and got lost in the thick undergrowth or fallen into Heber's Ghyll. I pull myself up jagged boulders until I reach the top and I stand, panting, next to the Swastika Stone. My breath is rasping in my lungs, my throat feels raw. I climb on a large rock by this ancient pagan site and scan the moor.

It's October and the heather has died. The bracken is the colour of rust and the dried grass is ash-blond. I'm looking for a little girl in a shiny silver-blue dress, the colour of ice. Would I see you even if you were here? You're small for your age. The heather is dense, the bilberry bushes grown tall and leggy. It's foggy. You might have fallen, twisted your ankle; the tracks are strewn with stones.

It's grown too dark to see far. My heart is thumping in my chest, hard enough to hurt. What if I can't find you? I don't know if you can survive the night out here. I've brought a torch, but it won't illuminate much in this wilderness.

If we were walking here together, I'd point out the carnivorous plants that grow on this spot: sundews with sticky red leaves, eating insects to sustain them because the soil is so poor. If you were with me, I'd take you to the Doubler Stones, where, thousands of years ago, Neolithic peoples carved channels in the rock to drain away the blood from their sacrifices. I would show you where the plover nests, and the green hairstreak butterfly lays its eggs. I love this place. I love this land. It's part of me, it's part of who I am. But it's no place for you: a seven-year-old girl in a princess costume.

There are other dangers too. Old quarries. Jagged-edged cliffs. Sharp rocks and bogs that could suck you in. I know them all. I pass a stand of rowan trees; the fine, gold leaves brush against my face. The clouds obscure the moon and the first stars. I switch my torch on and its beam seems feeble; the darkness appears darker. I suppress my feelings. I can't show any weakness, not now. I have to find you, before it's too late. I have to find you before anyone else does.

And when I do, we will be together, for ever, my darling.

## SUNDAY: TWO DAYS AFTER

I can't sleep. I walk round the house. I stand next to Ben and listen to his breathing. He's sprawled across the bed, hands curled into loose fists, the covers pushed back. I replace them gently and crouch next to him, watching him, touching his forehead to check he's not too hot or too cold. Evie never sleeps like that. She always curls into a tight ball, the sheets wrapped around her. Ben snores: unbelievably loudly for such a small child. Evie is quiet; she was so silent as a baby I used to worry she'd stopped breathing in the night. I go into her room and lie down, my face in her pillow, and inhale her smell.

I'm still there when Ollie comes in to wake me in the morning. I jump when he speaks. My eyes are raw and my neck aches where I've been twisted into an uncomfortable position in the night. I hadn't realized I'd finally fallen asleep. My limbs feel like lead.

'It's time to take Ben to hospital,' he says.

His voice is raw. I rub my eyes and sit up. We're both still. He continues to stand in the doorway and I sit on Evie's bed, my head in my hands.

'I'll take him,' I say. 'You need some rest. We've got to meet Ruby at eleven at the police station for the briefing. The media statement is at twelve.'

He doesn't protest. He looks dead on his feet. I splash cold water over my face and go to wake Ben. I soak up the small pleasure of holding him, warm and sleepy in my arms. I carry him to the car and slide him into the seat. I've brought his breakfast with me, but I'm hoping he'll doze off again as we drive towards Silsden.

'Zoe! Zoe!'

Someone is shouting at me. I stand up too quickly and hit my head on the car door. My heart starts to beat faster. I hope it's good news. Two men are running towards me. The one nearest is clutching his phone, the one behind him is laden with cameras. I can't believe it. It's 7 a.m. I panic. I climb back in the car, crawling over Ben and slam the door shut and lock it.

'Zoe! Mrs Morley? Just a few questions? Have you found your daughter yet?'

I buckle Ben in. He wakes up properly and seeing the men leaning in the window shouting, the flash of the camera, he starts to shriek. I'm so angry I want to get out and punch them. I climb into the front seat and drive off as fast as I can. I grip the steering wheel hard to still the tremors in my hands.

Dr Kapur removes the stethoscope from Ben's chest.

'He's had a significant heart trauma and low blood pressure caused by the high dose of the toxin in his system, all of which can lead to neural damage. But we caught it fast and children can recover fully. Ben's brain scan was clear and his ECG readings were normal for more than twelve hours before we discharged him.'

I take Ben from Dr Kapur and kiss his cheek, tuck his top back in.

'So has he recovered? Is he going to be okay?'

'It's too early to say. Keep an eye on him and if you're worried about anything, no matter how slight, come back. Do you have any idea how he got hold of the spindle berries?'

'Blueberry?' asks Ben hopefully.

'I haven't got any, love. No. Unless he grabbed them from a garden as we were walking to school?'

'This will have to be followed up – the school playground and surrounding houses need to be checked, as does your garden. They're a common ornamental plant round here. Less common in the wild now.'

I remind myself that we're lucky: Ben could have died. He looks well. His kidneys and heart are functioning normally, Dr Kapur said. I glance at my son in the rear-view mirror as we drive back. He's staring vacantly out of the window. Children do that, don't they? Go into a zoned-out state in the car. And he's tired – he's had a traumatic time in hospital. But could it be more than that or am I being paranoid?

Just before 11, Ollie and I cross the road to the police station and that's when I see them. Posters of Evie. They're everywhere, on every lamp post and telegraph pole, pasted into the window of M&S and Smiths; plastered across the bus stop. It's her school photo and 'MISSING' in large black letters above it. There's a number to ring. Who has printed them? Will it work? Will someone see her with a man and remember her face?

We sit down in front of Ruby in the police station. She glances from one to the other of us. Ollie looks terrible. His hair is greasy; there are dark rings under his eyes and his skin is puffy. I know I'm no better. I've managed to have a shower, but I haven't had time to dry my hair and it drips onto the collar of my shirt. Ruby tells us that we should read the prepared statement and Collier will deal with any questions.

'I did a draft for you but it'll come out better if it's in your own words. No one knows Evie like you do.' She pushes the piece of paper over towards us. 'I'll give you a few minutes' privacy to go through it. By the way, your friend Andy? His alibi checked out, so he's been released.'

'Is he still a suspect?' I ask.

I have a thick, cold feeling in my stomach when I think about Andy. I didn't do anything to help him. And I can't help wonder whether he could be Evie's father; whether he really does know where she is. After all, if Jack was helping him, it wouldn't matter where Andy was at 5 p.m.

'Until we find Evie, everyone is a suspect.'

After Ruby closes the door, I turn to Ollie. He hasn't moved.

'"A lovely girl. Our darling daughter." Jesus.'

He wipes his eyes with his hand and I can hear the scratch where he hasn't shaved.

'We have to make it personal. We have to make it about Evie so that people will care about her. What shall we say?'

What *can* you say when your seven-year-old goes missing? When the child you love more than your own life has been abducted? Ollie continues to sit catatonically still. I can't do this. I can't do it by myself. I glance at Ollie again. I have to. I snatch up the pen and scribble furiously.

A few minutes later, Ruby returns. She reads what I've written and nods. 'It's good. I'll type it up for you.' She glances as me. 'I know it must be the last thing on your mind, but appearances are going to be important,' she says as gently as she can in her strong, Bradford accent. She hands me a brush and a small bag of make-up. 'The toilets are the second door on your right. There's a hand dryer. You might be able to dry your hair off a bit.'

I stand in front of the mirror. The powerful blast from the dryer has made my hair windswept and fluffy. The bags under my eyes are the colour of a bruise and the whites are bloodshot. My cheeks are gaunt and my skin no longer glows. In the harsh fluorescent lights I can see every line and broken vein and pore. I've aged ten years. I should care but I don't. I brush my hair and look inside Ruby's make-up bag. It's all wrong for me – black kohl, foundation in Caramel Toffee, Violet Plum lipstick, Sunblush bronzer. I use her mascara, a clear powder and lipstick, smudging it off so there's only the barest hint of pink.

The journalists are already in place when we enter. The small room is packed and everywhere I look lenses are being pointed and focused at us. A small sea of phones rises up to record our words.

'Ollie? Do you want to read it?'

He shakes his head. Ruby must have persuaded him to shave while I was in the toilets. He's cut his neck in three places and there's a spot of shaving cream on his ear. I try to hold his hand, but it's lifeless in mine. I glance at the faces in front of me. They look hostile. I feel my throat closing, my heart squeezing tightly. My hands shake as I hold the statement. Ruby passes me a glass of water and I take a sip. Most of the journalists are men. The women amongst them seem impossibly young and glamorous, wearing suit jackets and fitted dresses, bright red lipstick. I assume they're going to be presenting televised reports on Evie in a few minutes. I notice one woman who looks different, though. She's a few rows back. Her curly hair is in wiry corkscrews, threaded with grey. She could be in her fifties. She looks tough and she has an expression on her face that I can't quite read. It might be disgust. She catches me looking at her and her expression shifts instantly, to something warmer, more sympathetic. While everyone here is only thinking of what a good news story Evie will make, she's sorry for her, for me.

I clear my throat as Collier makes his announcement. He focuses on Jack Mitchell, the last person to see our daughter, and how it's imperative to call the police if anyone has seen him. He also gives out the number of the dedicated line for the newly created 'Finding Evie' campaign. When Collier's finished, I read out my statement. It's short and to the point: our beloved daughter has been missing since Friday afternoon.

'Evie is our beautiful, dark-haired, green-eyed child,' I say. I can hear the tremor in my voice. 'Like many seven-year-old girls, she's obsessed with princesses. We think she looks more like a fairy. She loves Lego and painting. She laughs easily. She has pretend tea parties in a tree in our garden and invites all her dolls. She wants to be an artist when she grows up. Please find her. Please bring her back to us. We miss her beyond measure. She is the love of our life.'

I choke over the last words and start to cry. Ruby grips my elbow and steers me out.

The room erupts with shouts of 'Mrs Morley! Zoe! Evie's mum!' and when I don't answer, 'Ollie! Mr Morley!'

Ollie stumbles behind me, like a man in a stupor. Ruby ushers us back into the room we were in earlier.

'That went well,' she says brightly. She pushes a box of tissues towards me and glances at Ollie. 'I'll get you both a cup of tea. DCI Collier will be in shortly. He wants to speak to you.'

'Is there news?' Ollie rouses himself.

'We don't know where Evie is, but he wants to keep you informed of our latest findings.'

'Jack Mitchell?'

'I'll get your tea; he'll be here in a minute.'

Collier and Clegg come in. Clegg smiles at me.

'Have you found Jack Mitchell?' Ollie asks before either of them can speak.

'We've found out who the car belongs to,' said Collier, sitting down and dropping a case file on the Formica table in front of him.

He looks tired too; the red veins in his nose more pronounced, the skin around his eyes is puffy. I don't suppose he's had much sleep either. He stretches a leg out stiffly to one side of the table; his knee creaks.

'A man named Harris.'

I knew it was Harris's car. I told Ruby. But is it relevant? Is it relevant to finding Evie? I can't help wondering if he was badly hurt in the crash. And then wishing I could talk to him.

'Haris Agni,' Collier adds, opening the file and taking out a photo.

He spins it round so we can see. It's a photo of Harris and underneath it says his full name: Haris, with one 'r'. So he does have a surname after all. Why does he spell his name differently? And then it hits me. This is a photo of Harris – *Haris* – in black and white, from the front and the side. A police mugshot. I can't take it in. There has to be some mistake. My lungs have been squeezed tight and I feel as if I will not be able to take another breath. I will drown on dry land in front of these men.

'Haris Agni was sentenced to seven years in prison for aggravated GBH. He was released getting on for two years ago after serving five years. It's suspicious – finding a burnt-out car on the moor the day after your little girl goes missing. That in itself would not make him a potential suspect, but there's more.'

I take a ragged gulp of air as he places a colour photo of Haris on top of the mugshot and alongside Evie's school photo. Ollie scrutinizes it and glances at me and then Collier. Ruby returns with mugs of tea. She must have made them herself, instead of going to the vending machine in the corridor. I don't want any more tea but I find myself taking the cup from her out of habit.

'There's a likeness, isn't there?' Collier says. He jabs his forefinger at Haris's face. 'Dark hair. Green eyes. Olive skin. The dates would match too. He was sent to Leeds Prison a month after your daughter was born.'

Clegg hands him something and he places it on the table too. It's Evie's red prayer book, the one Andy found, now in a sealed plastic bag.

'He's Hunza. Muslim. Originally from Pakistan.'

'So you think this man, Haris, could be Evie's father? And he abducted her? Took her in his car and then burnt it to get rid of the evidence?' asks Ollie.

'Aye. The car didn't crash. It was deliberately set on fire. Poured something highly flammable on it first, probably petrol.'

'And how are you going to find him?'

'We'll find him,' Collier says.

'I know this man,' I blurt out.

Collier looks pleased, as if he's forced some kind of confession from me before he asked.

'I told DCI Collier,' Ruby says.

I glance from her to Ollie.

'He's an artist. My agent represents him – Jennifer Lockwood from the gallery on Brook Street. Jenny introduced me to him when I had a meeting with her in September and then I went to his exhibition, the opening night.'

'That was him?' says Ollie, sounding incredulous. 'A thug – and he's passed himself off as an artist? How the hell did he manage that?'

I lick my dry lips. I want to tell them they've got it wrong because, if they're right, the truth is too horrible to contemplate.

'Jenny can't have known,' I say.

Collier shuffles through his notes. 'Ms Lockwood is aware of Haris Agni's history. She didn't want to make it public so they put together that story about his trip to the Hunza Valley.'

'What?' Haris and Jenny have both deceived me.

Collier looks over the rim of his glasses and then takes them off. 'She did some charity event and met him there. He was on day release. She saw his potential,' he adds drily.

It's too much to take in.

'What about Jack Mitchell?' Ollie asks again.

For a moment, Collier looks less sure of himself.

Clegg says smoothly, 'We've got police surveillance on his house twenty-four/seven. He's due back at work on Monday, so if he returns to Ilkley, we'll pull him in for questioning. And if he doesn't, we'll find him. They always screw up. Use their phones, their credit card, get caught on CCTV.'

'Jesus.' Ollie paces up and down our sitting room. 'Jesus. A convicted criminal could have taken Evie.'

He doesn't say, 'A convicted criminal could be Evie's father.'

It's as if my brain has stopped functioning, I can't think about Haris and what it all means. I have a vivid image of him placing a skull in the palm of my hand and telling me how he'd buried the animal until the flesh had fallen from its bones. As if it were waiting for me. In the darkness. Like he'd been waiting in the darkness of his prison cell for all those years. I shudder.

The house is gloomy. The curtains are drawn to stop the journalists, still camped outside, from peering in. Bella is whining and scratching at the back door. Hannah is giving Ben his lunch. She looks tired too. She pushes a curtain of hair behind her ear and frowns. 'What do you mean? Have the police got a lead?'

Ollie starts telling Hannah about Haris and the car Ruby and I found on the moor. I don't want him to tell her. I don't want everyone to know, not until I've worked out how to tell Ollie about my involvement.

'Ollie. Why don't you lie down for a bit?' I say.

He looks at me as if I'm a stranger, his eyes hard and glazed. Then his shoulders slump and his body sags. 'Just for an hour. Wake me up, won't you?'

'Thank you for this morning, Hannah. I don't know what we'd have done without you.'

'It's the least I can do.' Hannah gives me a hug. 'Let me know if you need me again. I'll text you tomorrow. Maybe I can come round after school.'

She's much shorter and slighter than me and feels fragile in my arms. She smells of lilies. I can't imagine wearing perfume again. I cannot imagine taking pleasure in anything as long as Evie is missing.

'How are you doing?' I ask Gill, when she answers the door.

Her eyes are red and her hair is limp. It's the first time I've seen her looking less than immaculate in years. I couldn't bear to stay in the house any longer and I want to keep searching for Evie. But I know I have to see Andy and Gill first.

'How long have we known each other?' she asks me. 'How many years have we been friends?'

Her voice wobbles and tears slide down her face. I dig my nails into my palms to stop myself from saying anything I'll regret later.

'You could have called, Zoe.' Tears drip off her chin. 'Andy loves Evie. We both love her. You could have rung the police. Told them that Andy would never harm her. We were there for hours—'

'Don't be daft, Gill.' Andy elbows his way past his wife, Ellen balanced precariously on his waist. 'It's not up to Zoe to clear my name. She's got more important things to worry about. How are you holding up, love?' He leans forward and kisses me on the cheek and Ellen reaches out one podgy hand to grab my hair.

I don't kiss him back.

'See! She doesn't believe us,' says Gill. 'Why don't you come in? Search the house. The police have already gone through everything, turned the whole fucking place upside down. But you never know, you might find something, something to show your best friend's—'

'Gill.' Andy puts his arm round his wife's shoulder. He looks at me. 'Do you want a cup of tea?'

I shake my head. 'I'm going to look for Evie.'

'I'll come,' he says, passing Ellen to Gill.

'No,' I say, 'I didn't come here for that. I just came—'

'I know,' he says. 'You don't have to explain.'

He picks up his boots from behind the porch door and walks to the car in his socks.

'See you later, love,' he calls to Gill.

She retreats inside without saying goodbye to either of us. I hesitate and then get in the car. The police no longer think he's under suspicion, do they? Three days ago I thought I could trust Andy completely, but now I don't trust my own judgement. Andy turfs Bella onto the back seat. She's whines and dribbles with excitement – she loves Andy. I drive to the far side of Ilkley. I have no real plan other than to walk on the opposite end of the moor to the search party. They're still out there, above our house, north of the Twelve Apostles. I can't face bumping into Mrs Kilvington or any of the other mums she's friends with. And it can't hurt to look somewhere else. Neither of us speaks.

It's not as foggy as it was yesterday and as we get close to the moor, I can hear the buzz of a helicopter circling overhead. I turn off at the Addingham junction and take a sharp left onto a farm track. I drive as far up it as I can and then abandon the car. Bella leaps out, delighted to be outside after being cooped up all weekend.

'They found a burnt-out car on the moor yesterday. It was on the news,' Andy says.

'I found it with Ruby, our family liaison officer. It belongs to a friend of mine – an artist. Turns out he wasn't who I thought he was,' I say. I wonder if I'm talking about Andy as well, even though we've slipped back into conversation as if nothing has happened between us.

'What do you mean?'

'The police have just told us his real name and that he spent five years in prison for GBH.'

'Jesus. He must have almost killed someone – very few prisoners actually serve a full sentence. His original sentence would have been even longer. Gill tells me this stuff,' he adds, as if apologizing.

I think about Haris: the suddenness of his rage when I didn't want to have an affair with him; how he could barely contain himself. He had wanted to hurt me. Bella tugs against her lead and I haven't the energy to tell her off. I let her pull me up the hill. It's grey and cold; there's a bitter wind. A grouse explodes from beneath my feet and it takes me all my strength to keep hold of the dog. Andy takes her lead from me.

'I went to his preview.'

Haris lied to me. To everyone. Everyone but Jenny, that is, I think bitterly. They reinvented him as Harris the sculptor, recently back from the Hunza Valley. It would explain how lean and hard he looks: seven years inside, working out. And why I haven't seen him around Ilkley or on the art scene before. I remember the signed, framed photographs of apricots and chillies, snow-clad peaks. He'd even bought the artwork to make his lie complete. Or maybe he had them anyway – if he really is Hunza.

'I guess it'll be on the news. Gill said you'd just done a statement for the media? That must have been fucking awful.'

We've reached a plateau and we stop and look around; I'm trying to catch my breath. Andy puts his hand on my shoulder. He's struggling to contain his emotions.

'I love Evie. I love her. I can't imagine what you thought when—'

'Don't, Andy. Please don't.'

'Okay, okay.' He blows his nose loudly. 'But for the record, I want to say it: I would never harm a hair on that child's head. And I know the prostitute thing must have crossed your mind but I'm not her father. I might have fooled around but—'

'I know,' I say, although I can't look him in the eye.

There's no way he could tell if he has an illegitimate child or not.

'We'll find her. We're going to find her,' he says.

I screw my eyes shut. I have to believe him. Or else I'll go mad. I turn back to scanning the ground for any minute hint that Evie has passed this way. Everything is a blur of green and brown. In front of us are the Doubler Stones. They're silhouetted against scuds of shale-grey clouds. There are two of them, taller than a man: flat stone heads balanced on precarious stems of rock, like windswept mushrooms. They look as if they've been weathered by wind and ice for aeons – the sections that have been shaved away by the elements have stripes of sandstone within them.

I climb up some rocks onto the taller of the two. On its surface is a complex pattern of rings and whorls and there are deep, round basins, full to the brim with rain water. Channels gouged in the rock lead from these strange indentations. Some say this was where Neolithic sacrifices were carried out and the grooves were to let the blood drain away. I scan the moor. It stretches before me, bleak, scoured by the wind. Nothing is moving. I cannot see a small girl, running through the heather. I jump down.

'The police think Haris is Evie's father,' I tell Andy. 'He was sent to prison seven years ago. She's seven. He's just been released. Now we start getting these cards from her dad, and there's a likeness – same skin colour, dark hair – he's got her eyes.'

I can't see her soft, child features in his chiselled face though, but maybe I'm clinging to an empty hope.

'Plus he's an artist,' says Andy softly.

My chest tightens. I think of Evie's Lego sculptures; the crazy birds' nests she builds from scraps, the naked doll within one. And I think of Haris's work, twisted and dark, as deformed and cruel as the Doubler Stones themselves. A kestrel hovers overhead, suspended, as if from a thread, and then razors its wings shut and plummets to the earth.

'Do you reckon he could have taken her? I mean, is he that sort of guy?'

The kestrel rises slowly, arduously, something tiny dangling in its talons. I never told Andy about my meetings with Haris. Perhaps I should have done. He'd have talked me out of it. *Would* Haris have taken her? He's fiercely possessive – if he thought she was his daughter, I could imagine him wanting to take back what he believed rightfully his. Or maybe it's his way of getting revenge. But he'd know it would destroy me. Surely he wouldn't do anything so calculated? That passion he'd shown, had it been love? Or only lust and madness.

'That's where he lives,' I say. 'You can't see it – it's where those trees are. He's got a croft behind them.'

Andy whistles. 'I always wondered who lived out there. In the middle of frigging nowhere.'

If Haris is Evie's father – or if he has taken her to punish me – then it's my fault. I welcomed his friendship, opened up to him, led him to believe I'd have an affair with him... I want to drag my wrists across broken glass. I pinch the backs of my hands. The pain is insignificant compared to the suffering that Evie is going through. The suffering that I've caused her.

I've been concentrating so hard on looking at the ground, searching for clues – a child's footprint in the mud, a long dark hair caught on a bilberry bush – that I miss it. It's Andy who calls me. I run over to where he's standing with Bella.

It's a low stone building, partly built into the hillside. It might once have been a shepherd's shelter, but it's been extended so it's about the size of a large garage. There's a corrugated-iron roof. The rust and the patina of algae have turned it the same shade as the drying heather that's encroaching on it. It blends so perfectly into the moor, you'd be hard-pressed to spot it even from a few metres away. There's a bare patch of ground in front of it, and a wide, well-trodden path leading for about half a mile downhill to the back of Haris's house. My heart starts to hammer in my chest and my throat constricts. The wooden door has a padlock holding it closed. Andy starts casting around for a rock to break it with. He scrabbles frantically in the ground to lift the stones but they're all sunk deeply in the soil.

I take my penknife out of my rucksack and snap open the screwdriver. The nails are rusty and deeply embedded in the door frame; when I finally get them out, the door sags open. Andy catches it. Bella starts barking. I step inside. I'm dazed for a moment and then my eyes adjust. It's surprisingly light. There are panels of clear plastic in the roof and long, thin windows cunningly set in the walls so that the space is filled with dim, muted light. I'm not sure what I'm looking at and my fear heightens.

'Evie?' I whisper and then I shout more loudly, 'Evie!'

There's a power cable snaking across the floor and Andy stamps on the round black switch attached to it. Suddenly the place is ablaze. There are four or five studio lights, the kind that you might find on a film set.

'What the fuck is this?' says Andy.

The room is filled with scrap metal: there are boxes of mattress springs, bolts, iron coils, chains and cogs and things that I have no name for nor knowledge of their origin. There are objects that look like instruments of torture: cutting blades and blowtorches. There's a low trolley with a flat wooden bed that Harris must use to transport his finished sculptures back to the house and pickup truck. I can't see Evie, but she could be hidden behind all this junk. I look at Bella to see how she's reacting. She's sitting next to me, half leaning against my leg. She's hot and panting. She's thirsty.

'It's Haris's studio.'

Andy starts tearing it apart, pulling away the sheets of metal, pushing over the boxes of scrap. There's an opening in the wall and I walk swiftly over to it, tripping on an old trowel and a wrench, once yellow, the paint chipped from it. Haris has sectioned off part of his studio so that it's almost like an office, running the length of the building. There's a small table and a chair with a gallon of water next to it, and a camping stove with an espresso maker. There's no sign of Evie. I slop some of the water into a mug and put it on the floor for Bella. As I rise to my feet, I notice the wall to my left. It's covered in photos, like a montage. My first thought is that it's a mood board to give Harris ideas for his sculptures, but the cold, sick feeling in my gut is telling me something different. I walk slowly towards it.

The pictures are all of me. There are photos of me looking glossy and groomed, professional ones that are in the public domain: there's the one taken for Jenny's website, and those the photographer took in Ilkley for the *Telegraph*. I've never seen the other pictures before. There are snaps of me drinking a coffee in a cafe, reading a newspaper, studying a shop window, walking on the moor. I'm not wearing any make-up and yet I look prettier than in real life. They must have been shot with a long lens and then blown up when they were printed: my edges have been smoothed; the sun highlights my hair; my face is over-exposed.

The noise stops.

'She's not here. I can't find her.' Andy's breathing hard. He comes to a halt next to me. 'Jesus Christ.' A drop of blood hits the floor. He's cut his hands searching for my daughter.

There's one photo, in the centre, where I'm pushing the buggy with Ben in it; his bright-blond hair gleams. I'm walking towards the photographer, my head turned away. But Evie is beside me and she's looking straight ahead, directly at him. Her lips are parted as if she is going to speak or smile. As if she knows him.

'The fucking monster!' he roars.

I hurtle back outside and take deep breaths as I wait for Collier to answer his mobile.

'Zoe?' Collier's tone is brusque but he sounds concerned. 'Where are you?'

'At Haris Agni's house.'

Below me are those twisted trees. I tell him where we are, what we've found.

'Are you sure she's not here?' I ask Andy, although I'm pretty certain she isn't. Bella isn't responding as if my daughter is in the studio. As if she's alive.

'What the fuck is that all about? Those pictures?'

I'm trembling. I don't want Andy to lose it. Not now. Not here. I start walking down the path towards Haris's house, hoping to meet Collier and Clegg on the way up. I don't want to stay in that studio a moment longer, with the evidence of Haris's obsession. He told me were kindred spirits, I remember now, and a taste of bile hits the back of my throat. He *knew* because he'd been watching me. Zoe Morley, he'd called me. He'd read that article in the paper, but it never mentioned my married name. Nor where my daughter was at school, and Ben had not even started at nursery then, yet he'd known where my children were: *'It's tough if you can only work in the mornings when your daughter's at school and your son's at nursery.'* He stalked me. He deceived me. He seduced me – in order to get to Evie.

Andy runs after me. 'Did you have any idea?'

I shake my head. A small, hard part of me is thinking – did Andy know? He was the one who found the studio. Is he acting a rehearsed role? Perhaps he and Haris were working together. I can't trust myself to speak. I'm not sure if I'll scream or cry if I open my mouth.

Halfway to Haris's house, I spot something. I grab Andy's arm. I can't help myself. I can't change the habits of friendship that have lasted my whole adult life. I point wordlessly at it. It's a fragment of material that's been snagged on a gorse bush. I pull it off and rub it between my fingers. It's shiny, synthetic, ice-blue. It's not from anything Evie wore to school on Friday. Andy's holding me tightly, gripping my arms so hard, he's bruising me.

'It's the dress,' he says. 'It's the fucking dress she was wearing on the day of Ben's party.'

The princess dress from *Frozen*. The one I'd never seen before. I start to breathe faster, wheezing gulps that lacerate my windpipe. She's out here. She's out here somewhere. Andy holds me until the police arrive.

It's late afternoon. I'm crouching on the sitting-room floor, surrounded by tipper trucks and tractors, trying to play with Ben as if nothing is wrong. I'm failing and he's being whiney and clingy. Ollie is clattering round the kitchen making coffee and sandwiches. The house smells odd. The breakfast bar is full of flowers. Carnations, chrysanthemums, lilies. Pity posies in hideously garish colours.

'They arrived when you were out,' says Ollie. 'They're from the parents in Evie's class. One of the mums – Mrs Kilvington – brought them. And a casserole.'

'A casserole?'

'Yeah. Chicken in white wine with a mushroom glaze. I put it in the fridge. She wanted to stay and wait for you.'

'Oh.'

The thought of chicken in white wine with a mushroom glaze made by Mandy Kilvington's mum makes me feel nauseous. Or is it the flowers? The smell is cloying. I sneeze.

'I told her she couldn't. You didn't want to see her, did you?'

I shake my head.

'Do you want a sandwich?' he asks.

He has that peevish expression you get when you've slept in the middle of the day but the amount of sleep you've had is insufficient. I remember it from the time Ben was a baby, snatching scraps when I could and it was never enough. Collier said they haven't found Haris: he's not at home and his pickup has gone. Yet. They keep saying 'yet'. Jenny says she doesn't know where he is either. I feel as if something has curdled inside me and it lies thick and cold, like broken jelly. I can't stop thinking about Haris and his creepy studio with the photo montage. How long has he been following me? Stalking me? Did he take Evie?

Ollie opens a can of tuna and the smell makes me bilious. He spills some of the liquid on the work surface and I know he won't wipe it up properly and will smear fish oil and crumbs across it and it'll stink.

I need to tell Ollie what I've found; it's going to look odd if Collier or Ruby speak to him when I haven't. I want him to comfort me. But I don't want to say what my part in all this has been. That I met up with Haris as often as I possibly could. That I kissed him. That I almost loved him. So I'm smashing trucks with Ben and trying to find the exact words, the correct phrase, the right amount of courage. I hope to God that scrap of Evie's dress is going to lead the police to her. Ollie is annoying me. He bangs every cupboard door, chinks each cup, rattles the spoons;

the bread knife grates against my teeth. I can feel my migraine, blooming just behind my eyes.

'You need to eat,' he says. 'When was the last time you ate anything? I'm going to make you one anyway.'

The thought of a tuna sandwich makes me want to retch.

'I said no thanks.'

'Cheese then.'

'No!'

And now I definitely can't say anything because it will come out as a shout or a scream. I know it's not wholly rational but right now I believe that none of this would have happened if Ollie hadn't been working so hard, if he'd been kind to me, if he'd been a proper father to Evie. If he'd been *present* I wouldn't have looked twice at Haris fucking Agni and Evie would never have started obsessing about her real parents.

I can hear myself speaking and for a moment I think I must have started talking to Ollie. I sound odd – like myself and unlike myself. And then I understand. I look up and see a picture of Evie on the TV and I put my hand over my mouth because how could I forget my gorgeous girl for even a second? Here we are, squabbling over tuna fucking sandwiches and there she is – almond-shaped green eyes, snub nose, lopsided grin, the hint of a dimple in her cheek. 'MISSING' is stamped over her face in large black letters.

The image cuts back to me and Ollie. I'm talking. I look terrible: the perfect image of a distraught mother: haggard and white as paste, hair like straw, eyes wild. This is the bit where I'm going to start to cry, any minute now, the end of this sentence... I get up to switch off the TV and then I notice Ollie sitting beside me in that room full of journalists. He's looking off camera. He's shaved and neat. You can't see the blood on his neck, where he nicked himself, or the grease in his hair. He looks presentable and completely detached. I never doubted my husband when

Collier and Clegg made their accusations. But now, seeing his remote expression, I start to wonder. Could he have hidden Evie somewhere? Is the guy who owns The Ormond Gallery in on this too and is he covering for him? It would explain why Ollie didn't come rushing when Ben was in hospital. What kind of man puts his career before his son's life?

The screen goes blank. Ollie is standing beside me with the remote in his hand.

'I was watching that!' I yell. 'Did you see yourself? You looked like you couldn't care less about our daughter.'

'What the hell? What do you think I'm doing right now? I'm going back out on that bloody moor to keep searching for her.'

'We wouldn't have to look for her if—'

'If what? If you'd arranged for someone trustworthy to pick our daughter up from school?'

I'm so shocked I'm speechless. Is that what he thinks? And why is it my responsibility – to be in hospital with our son as his heart is failing and organize childcare for our daughter too?

'I did. Her teacher. Who's been looking after her since she was tiny. Who could I have found that would have been more responsible?'

'Clearly you didn't because he's fucked off God knows where after letting our daughter be abducted by a fucking psychopath. Or else he's the psycho.'

Ollie starts cramming sandwiches into the plastic bread bag and stuffing them in his rucksack. His face is flushed. I've never seen him this angry before. I want to shout at him, for abandoning us during all the months leading up to Evie's disappearance, letting me struggle at home on my own – but I turn away; tears are running down my face.

'And as for that bloody press conference, I told you it was going to be a waste of time and you fucking insisted – you put us through it! What good has it done? It hasn't brought Evie back. The police are inundated with time wasters, reporting sightings of girls who look nothing like her. The paedophiles of Yorkshire are getting off on it as we speak. My Twitter account is jammed full of trolls telling me all the things they want to do to our daughter.'

He shoves his feet into hiking boots and grabs a jacket. As the door slams behind him, I hear the journalists, who are still camped outside, start to bay like a pack of hounds. My hands are shaking. Ollie has never spoken to me like that before. He's barely ever raised his voice. The unfairness of his outburst makes me want to punch him. I take Ben upstairs for a bath and try to calm down.

I've left the car on the farm track near the Doubler Stones, but, with Ollie gone, I won't be able to retrieve it. As Ben splashes, I think about Haris again. I have no idea where he could be. I really didn't know him well at all. I've called and texted him, asking him to get in touch, but he hasn't replied. How can I find him? And then I remember that he'd said he has a sister with a child the same age as Ben. Haris comes from somewhere around here originally. I grab the iPad and start googling Agni and Leeds and then Bradford. If she visits him, perhaps she lives close. Of course, if his sister has a son, she'd be married: she might have a different surname. I almost give up before I've started, but then three names come up and only one of them is a woman's – a Yasira Agni at Bradford University. Maybe she kept her maiden name, or she's a single mother? I click on the link. She's a post-grad in the English department, studying, 'W. B. Yeats: A Psychoanalytic Approach'. I try to enlarge her photo but it won't increase in size and it's hard to tell if she could be Haris's sister. I search for her on Facebook. She hasn't made her account private and I'm able to look through her photos.

Ben is flushed pink from the water and is taking full advantage of my lack of attention. He's making Captain Jack and his crew jump from their pirate ship and dive-bomb into the bathwater.

'Ben!' I shout, but he ignores me and continues to splash and shout.

I retreat to the far end of the bathroom to avoid the iPad getting wet. Yasira Agni is pretty. She has long, black, curly hair and pale green eyes; her skin is much darker than Haris's and the shape of her face is different – rounder, less defined, with a sharper nose. Could she be his sister? I can't tell and I'm starting to feel jittery. I should stop this and get Ben ready for bed. He's making booming and whooshing noises as his pirate ship blows something up. He's so loud, I can't think straight.

And then I find something. It's a photo of a child's birthday party – Yasira has her arms round a little boy. His face is lit up by two candles on his cake. His cheeks are full of air, ready to blow them out. I scroll to the next picture. The candles have been extinguished and Yasira is cutting the cake. It's a wider angle and you can see some of the guests sitting round the table – it's one of those mainly adults-only parties you can only get away with when your child is small. I'm about to give up and shut down the iPad, when I see him. He's on the far right-hand side of the picture, smiling at his sister and holding a glass of red wine. I enlarge the photo. It's definitely Haris.

I quickly put Yasira Agni's name into the search engine and, this time, 192.com comes up with her postcode. She's on the electoral register and if I sign up to the website, I'll be able to access her full address. I do it quickly. I can't believe I'm able to find out this much information about a complete stranger. Well, not quite a complete stranger any more. I know where she works, who her brother is, the age of her son, the poetry she likes to read, and that she's the same size as me with a similar taste in clothes. And now I know where she lives – 3, Stonechat Place, Little Horton, which is just behind the university. Yasira could walk to work.

I lift Ben out and dry him. There's no time to waste. Ollie may stay out with the search party all night. I put Ben into his pyjamas, plus thick socks and a fleece. I call a taxi.

Ben is excited to be going out at night, and points at the street lights, shouting, 'Moon. Stars.'

Once the taxi has dropped us off at the farm track where I left my car and Ben's buckled into his own car seat, he quickly falls asleep. I follow signs for the Alhambra and the university. We pass Bombay Stores. I remember going as a teenager and falling in love with the saris, reams and reams of tropical colours, shimmering with gilt and sequins. They seemed impossibly bright for someone like me to wear. I get lost in the maze of side streets. I wonder if Ruby lives round here too. I've barely asked her a thing about herself. It's not like me – but the truth is, I don't care. I want to find my daughter. I don't want to make small talk. But I ought to find out more about her, for Evie's sake. Haris is Muslim, Collier says. Ruby might be too and, who knows, there could be a conflict of interest; it might cloud her judgement.

It's early evening and it's cold: there's hardly anyone around, no kids playing out, no one I'd want to stop and ask for directions. I follow the birds: left onto Wheatear, along Plover, right on Curlew, a false turn down a dead end, before I find Stonechat. I park outside number three. The light is on, so I imagine Yasira must be home. Perhaps she's putting her little boy to bed or maybe he's already asleep. I unbuckle Ben and lift him out. He's hot and heavy. He nestles his head into the crook of my neck and snores softly.

I stand on the pavement. Sweat prickles across my chest, under my arms. I'm on my own with a sleeping two-year-old, about to knock on a stranger's door. I'm in a predominantly Muslim area and that alone makes me feel as if I've entered a foreign country. It's ridiculous, I know, but I can't help my unease. I look at the rows of houses either side of me. They're short, thin, crammed close together, built of millstone grit; they're no different to the house I grew up in, the kind of house my working-class mum lived in all her life and thought grand. These people might have originally come from somewhere else, but they're as Yorkshire as I am now.

My shoulders relax and I take a deep breath and knock on the door. There are footsteps and I wonder if Haris is here; if he might answer. My breath is light and shallow, mere sips of air. I hug Ben tightly. The door opens and Yasira Agni looks out. She stares at me and then glances up and down the street and then back at me. She looks tired. Her hair is caught in a messy bun. She's wearing shapeless jeans and a Breton top with worn Converse. I could have plucked the same outfit from my wardrobe and it reminds me that I still have her clothes at home.

'Can I help?' Her accent is like mine – West Yorkshire but smooth – in her case, polished after years of academia; mine is due to living with Ollie.

'I'm a friend of Haris's. Is he here?'

'No, sorry.' She shakes her head and starts to close the door.

'Please,' I say, walking towards her, 'Can I come in? Just for a minute. I need to talk to you.'

'I don't know who you are,' she says flatly.

'My name is Zoe Morley.'

'Zoe Morley.' Her eyes widen. 'I thought you looked familiar. I saw you on the telly. Your daughter...'

'Yes,' I say. 'It won't take a minute. Please.'

She glances at Ben and then steps back to let me in. We go into the sitting room, where a small boy with a shock of dark hair is lying on a leather sofa watching *In the Night Garden*.

'Thomas, go and sit on the armchair. You can lie him down there,' she says to me, pointing to the sofa. 'I'll get you a blanket. Do you want a cup of tea?'

I nod. I suddenly realize how hungry I am. I can't remember the last time I ate. Yasira comes back with a baby's blanket and I cover Ben with it. She turns the sound down a little and then goes to the kitchen. The boy has large eyes with thick eyelashes and stares at me with an unblinking gaze before Makka Pakka clinks his stones together and he's drawn back to the programme.

'Hello. I'm Zoe. This is Ben. He's the same age as you,' I say, but he ignores me.

There are toys scattered across the carpet, which is threadbare in patches and is covered with a Pakistani rug, just like the ones at Haris's house. Yasira returns with a mug of tea and a plate of buttered hot cross buns.

'I want one,' says Thomas, and she sighs and passes him a bun.

She's irritated, as if it's my fault he's tempted by them. I wish Ben would wake up and eat her bloody hot cross buns – surely it's not normal for him to sleep like this in a stranger's house with the TV on? *In the Night Garden* is his favourite programme. Is he floppy because there's something terribly wrong or because he's tired?

'It's hard to get them to bed when you're on your own. By the time you've finished clearing up the tea things, it's so late and you've no energy left.' She stops abruptly as if she might have offended me, talking about children when I've lost one. 'I'm sorry about your little girl. I hope you find her.'

I take a sip of tea so I won't have to make eye contact with her. I can't start crying now, in this woman's house.

'Are you Harris's girlfriend? No, you can't be. You're married. Were you having an affair? Is that why you're here?' Her tone is cold.

I shake my head. 'We were just friends. He's represented by the same art gallery as me. I'm trying to find him. He might know where Evie – my daughter – is.'

'And how would he know that?'

I hadn't expected her to be so tough. Having the same clothes and liking the same man – even if it's in different ways – don't give

214

you a shared connection, I remind myself. Now that I'm inside, I can see her house is very different to the one I grew up in. The living room opens into the dining room, which is dominated by a large oval table. The furniture is old fashioned, as if it came from a charity shop, but it's not chic. I search her for a trace of Haris: he, too would be abrupt to a stranger. It's only because I know him better than her, that I've seen he's also passionate and warm. And violent.

'Do you know where he is?'

'No.'

'The police are looking for him.'

For a second I see a flash of something in her face. Is it fear?

She drinks her tea and then says, 'I need to get Thomas to bed. I can't help you.'

She stands up as if I'm a recalcitrant student in her office and my time is up.

'They found his car. It was completely burnt. I didn't know if he'd been in an accident.'

She sits back down. For a moment she's stunned, but, when she speaks, her voice is controlled and icy again. 'If he'd been in a car crash he'd be in hospital. Our parents or I would have been informed. So the police must be looking for him in connection with your daughter's disappearance. Why?'

I don't know how much to say or how to phrase it so that I don't antagonize her further.

'Before Evie disappeared, we found cards and presents from a man claiming to be her biological father. One of the gifts was a Muslim prayer book.'

'So you've got a Muslim prayer book and a burnt-out car and you jump to the conclusion that the only dark-skinned person in Ilkley must have abducted your daughter? You people make me sick.' Her face is twisted in disgust. 'If he's really your friend, like you claim, you'd know that Haris would never do anything to harm a child.

He's not even that interested in children – apart from Thomas – and even then his attention is limited, shall we say.'

'He was my friend,' I say, 'but he told me he'd been in the Hunza Valley for seven years. He didn't say that he'd been in prison.'

I'm starting to feel desperate. I need her to help me. She jumps to her feet.

'Do you know how hard it's been for him? To get a job? To be recognized as an artist? What do you expect? Would you have bought a sculpture from him or rented a house to him if you'd known he was a convicted criminal?'

Ben wakes up. His eyes are wide and terrified. He starts to cry. I scoop him up and shush him.

'Please just tell me where he is.'

'I'm going to tell you something about Haris and then I want you to leave.'

She's speaking loudly, almost shouting at me, so that I can hear her over Ben's howls. It makes me feel even more frightened and angry than I am already.

'It's true that we're originally from Pakistan. Our grandparents are Hunza. They came to Bradford in the fifties. Our parents were born here. We – my brother and I – were born here. We are not Muslim. We weren't brought up as Muslims because our parents wanted us to fit in, to be integrated into society here. Haris is the least religious person I know. He drinks, for goodness sake. I doubt he'd know where Mecca was if you gave him a compass and a map! Our grandparents are dead. Neither of us has ever been to Pakistan. If you're looking for a Muslim, you're looking for the wrong person.'

She's trembling with anger. I get up too. She's standing too close to me, breathing heavily. There are dark circles beneath her eyes. I no longer feel any sympathy for her. Ben stops crying and starts to suck his thumb.

'I found pictures in Haris's studio.' I try to make my voice calm, measured. 'A whole wall covered with them. Nearly all of them were of me but right in the middle was a photograph of my daughter. She was looking at him. She knows him. If he hasn't got her then he knows where she is.' I jiggle Ben up and down and he grows heavier in my arms as he falls asleep again. 'Haris is a dangerous man, and you know it. I need to talk to him. I've got to find my child. If he turns up, you have to call me.'

I look for something to write with and, at first, she won't help me. When I pick up a crayon from the floor, trying not to drop Ben, she relents. She snatches it out of my hand and writes my mobile number down on one of Thomas's colouring books. She won't meet my eye as she opens the door for me. She doesn't say goodbye.

I found you. I have you in my arms again. The relief was overwhelming. My eyes filled with tears when I saw you. You were on the moor, by yourself. You were lost, you said. Your dress was in shreds and your poor arms and legs were scratched. You were shaking with cold, your skin rough with goosebumps. At first, you didn't want to come back with me. You cried and screamed and struggled. I hugged you and rocked you.

You don't love me as much as you said you did. Do you remember all those pictures you drew me, every one signed, 'Love Evie xxx'? It's no surprise. You haven't known me for long and you've been with them since you were born. They deceived you, telling you they were your true parents. It will take time. I knew this is what it would be like, but it's still hard to bear. I have to be strong. You are *my* daughter.

You said you wanted your mummy. I wanted to shake you, to make you see reason. I told you that woman was not your mother and never would be. You clung to me then because you were frightened of being on the moor in the dark. You thought I might leave you there. I know you're afraid of loss. It's a part of who you are. But I will change that. I will never leave you. I started to drag you home, tripping on heather roots and becoming ensnared in bilberry bushes. You were tired and cold and hungry. I had to carry you. You cried the whole way and your hot tears ran down the back of my neck.

When we got to my house, I had to give you something to calm you down. I didn't like doing it, but I can't risk anyone finding you, not now we are so close to getting away. Where I'm taking you, no one will ever find us. We'll have all the time in the world for you to grow to love me as much as I love you. You will forget them. My true spiritual home will heal you, as it once healed me.

# MONDAY: THREE DAYS AFTER

'Please tell me you're not going to work.'

It's 6.30 a.m. Ollie is dressed in his suit, pouring coffee into a thermal cup. He looks terrible. His skin is grey and papery. I wrap my dressing gown tightly around myself. I'm cold and the heating hasn't come on yet. I heard him get back about an hour ago and I expected him to come to bed, but I must have fallen asleep because when I woke, his side was still cold and I could hear him in the kitchen.

'I'm going to the office.'

'Ollie, please—'

'If that man – Haris Agni – took her, we're not going to find Evie on the moor. They've had a search party out there for two days and nights. A helicopter combed the entire area yesterday. There's no sign of anything alive out there save for the sodding sheep. They still haven't fucking found Jack Mitchell. They say he's due back at work today, but what are the chances he'll be there, waiting for them to pick him up?

'And I can't sit here and wonder which of those bastards has her and what they're doing to her. At least at work I won't have to think about it, even if it's only for a few minutes.'

His voice is hoarse. I hold him and he wraps his arms around me and rests his chin on my head. I squeeze my eyes shut and bite my lip, trying not to let the images flood into my mind that Ollie's words have conjured. If I let them in, my heart will break. Why can't he stay here with me and Ben? Ollie still doesn't know about the pictures in Haris's studio. I hadn't told him before he stormed off yesterday afternoon and Ruby – if she did see him – will have assumed he knew. Perhaps, if he was aware, he wouldn't be in such a rush to leave.

'I'm sorry about yesterday,' I mumble into his shirt.

'Me too.'

'There's something I need to tell you.'

I've got to say it to him before he finds out from one of the police officers – or sees it on the news.

'Shit. I'm going to be late for my train. Ring me if you hear anything.'

For a few minutes after he's left, I remain standing in the middle of the sitting room, unable to move. The house is completely quiet.

Then I hear footsteps and Ben calls, 'Mummy.'

He rattles the child gate upstairs. I'm not going to take him to nursery today. I can't let him out of my sight.

I open the gate and he looks up at me and says, 'Evie. Where Evie?'

'Oh, Ben, love.'

I bury my head in his soft, sleep-soaked body.

'Evie?' he says again, and starts to cry.

I hold him and rock him and ache for my daughter.


At 7.30, Ruby arrives.

'Don't get your hopes up,' she says immediately, taking in my tear-stained appearance. I must look as desperate as I feel.

'You've got Jack?'

She shakes her head. 'We found Haris late last night.'

She sounds almost triumphant. I turn away to hide my

disappointment and pull my dressing gown more tightly around myself. Ben is covered in Weetabix and I haven't washed let alone dressed. I must look terrible.

'He was staying with some friends in Leeds. He says he didn't even know Evie was missing – he hadn't seen the news. He said you tried to call him?'

I nod.

'He didn't listen to your messages – he says he deleted them straight away. We searched his friends' house but there's no sign of Evie. The forensic team are going over it now though; we'll let you know if we find anything.'

'He could have taken her somewhere else.'

'Yeah, he might have done. He's in custody. Collier is still questioning him – I wanted to let you know straight away. But so far there's no evidence that Evie has been in Haris's house or his studio.'

'What about the material – the bit of her dress that I found on the moor?'

'We haven't had the analysis back yet. We don't know if it is from her party dress.'

'And his car?'

'Too badly burnt to be able to tell if she'd been in it. He said he hadn't used it for several days – he'd left it in Ilkley. He had the pickup with him, parked outside his friends' house – there was nothing to suggest she'd been in that vehicle either.'

'How can you be so bloody sure? What about the pictures in his studio? How the hell did he explain them?'

'Shall I make us both a cup of tea? I know I could do with one.'

I shake my head, aware that this is not me. I've always been the sort of person to offer guests food and drink the minute they walk through the door. Ruby, though, is not my guest nor my friend and the last thing I care about right now is being hospitable.

'Can I put some toast on for us, too? I haven't had a chance to eat breakfast. By the way, here's your laptop back.' She slides it across the table.

I don't say anything. I'm shaking with the effort of keeping it together, of not yelling at Ruby. How can they believe Haris's lies? Why the fuck haven't they found Evie – or at least a trace of her? If I didn't have to look after Ben I'd be lying on the floor screaming. I suppose I can see why Ollie went to work.

Ruby makes the tea and by the time she's set it in front of me, I've managed to get my emotions under some sort of control.

'More, more, more,' says Ben.

I spoon the last of the Weetabix into his open mouth and start wiping up the gunk.

'The photos?'

She puts her mug down carefully and says, 'He had an explanation for them. You're not going to like it. It started when he was in prison.'

The toast pops up and she puts it on a plate, slides a couple more slices in.

'What started?'

'He wanted to relaunch his career as an artist. He met Jennifer Lockwood at a charity gala – she was giving a speech. She offered to represent him when he got out. He saw a photo of you on her website. What do you want on your toast?'

'I don't care,' I say, trying not to snap at her.

She spreads margarine on it and looks at me for a moment. 'Jam or Marmite?'

'Jam. Jesus. My photo?' I prompt her.

'Yeah. He said he couldn't get you out of his head. As you can imagine, he had a lot of time to think.'

She passes me a plate of toast and starts a round for herself. I take a bite and push it away. If I eat I'll be sick.

'He said he found out everything he could about you while he was inside.' Ruby sits opposite me. She hesitates and then says, 'He said he became obsessed with you. He'd planned it all quite carefully, Zoe. He followed you. Took photos. "Created an opportunity" to get to know you. I'm guessing that's shorthand for engineering an excuse to meet you.'

She stops speaking. She's waiting for my response. I turn away to lift Ben out of his high chair. I should be shocked but I'm strangely calm.

'It's all part of who Haris is,' I say with a shrug. 'He's obsessive, calculating, manipulative.'

And I'd bloody misread him as passionate, alluring, dangerously attractive. Ruby eats the toast fast with surprisingly large bites.

'If all he saw of me was a photo on a website, how would he know what I was really like? It's like reading a horoscope and believing it's all about you.' No wonder he was so angry when I didn't want to have an affair with him: in his mind I'd already left Ollie and moved into his house on the moor. Ruby finishes one slice and starts on the next. She's still waiting for me, hoping I'll carry on talking, tell her about my relationship with Haris.

'What about Evie? Was he using me to get close to her?' I ask.

She wipes the crumbs from her mouth.

'He says not. He says she's not his child. He didn't have a relationship with anyone prior to being sent to jail. The picture of her is coincidental – he was focused on trying to get photos of you. And obviously he denies sending the card or presents to your daughter.'

'Do you believe him? What does Collier think?'

'Let's wait and see,' she says. 'I'll let you know when Collier has finished questioning him. He's got an alibi – Clegg's checking it out now. The only thing we've got on him is that Harris can't prove he *didn't* send those cards and presents to Evie. His handwriting *is* similar and we've given the cards and a sample of his writing to a forensic handwriting expert. We're also running an analysis of his DNA – if he's Evie's biological father, we'll know tomorrow.' She carefully washes up her cup and her plate, instead of putting them in the dishwasher, and dries her hands.

'What about Jack?' I ask. 'Everyone is expecting him back at school this morning.'

She nods. 'There's a surveillance team waiting for him there and at his house. If he comes home or goes to work, we'll get him. I'm going to the station. I'll call as soon as I hear anything about Mitchell, and I'll drop by in the afternoon. Is there anything I can do for you now?'

I shake my head. I can't bring myself to speak.

'I'm sorry it's not better news,' she says, touching my arm.

'How are you?' I ask after a moment.

She stops as if seriously considering my question. I doubt she gets asked very often by the families she helps, but it can't be an easy job.

'I'm tired, but I'm doing all right.' She gives me a weak smile.

'You don't want to complain in front of me and Ollie. You think anything you might be going through will seem trivial in comparison—' I can't finish the sentence so I start again. 'But it's okay. I need to hear something normal, something every-day too.'

She ruffles Ben's hair and passes him his caterpillar toy, pulling it on its string in front of him.

''Pillar,' he says.

'Well, okay. Cases like this are hard. Emotionally and physically – long hours, and it's quite a commute from Bradford. I don't mind though. What's important is Evie, I can catch up on sleep later – finding her safe and well is what keeps me going.'

'And you live with your parents?'

'Yeah. I like being busy. Less time for them to tell me I'm too old and bossy to find a husband. My sister has a little boy. A year younger than your Ben. They live two doors up the road so my mum is distracted. Not on my case quite so much.' She hoists her bag onto her shoulder. 'I should go. Call me if you need me.'

'Are you Muslim?'

She stops in front of the door, with her back to me. For a moment she doesn't say anything. She puts her hand on the handle and I think she's going to leave without answering, but then she says quietly, 'Evil has no religion, Zoe.'

I pick Ben up and we watch her walking down the garden path, bantering with the journalists, who are drinking cheap coffee from Styrofoam cups, which they bought from the garage at the bottom of the hill, and eating Pukka Pies. The kind of journalists that don't hang around outside our front door, but have been inundating Ollie and me by email with requests for interviews, no doubt get their takeaway coffee from The Bar.

Ruby probably hates me now. She'll think I'm another prejudiced middle-class housewife. I don't care. I had to ask. I still don't know if it means she's biased against us or not. For now, I have to trust her. I wonder what Ruby knows, or think she knows, about Haris and me. She's certainly known that I knew Haris since the day we walked across the moor together and found his car. When was that? I can't remember. The days have blurred into a grey-green misery.

I answer a text from Hannah – no, there's no news. She's going to work, she says, but she can come over later if I need her to.

I write: 'Thanks. We're OK.'

I can't summon the strength to engage in small talk, even in a text, but she replies: 'It will be hard being at school without Evie. Thinking of you. Hx'

I want to turn my phone off so I won't notice any more texts, but I can't risk it. Collier might call. I carry Ben upstairs. Instead of dressing him in his bedroom, I go into Evie's room. I feel as if someone has punched a hole in my chest. I miss her so much. I lie down on Evie's bed and bury my head in the pillow. I inhale her smell. Ben thinks it's a game and comes barrelling over. He climbs on top of me and sits on my stomach and bounces up and down, giggling and dribbling. I start laughing and crying at the same time. At least he seems a bit more like himself.

My mobile rings. I sit up quickly, tumbling Ben to one side. It's Ruby.

'Zoe, we've found Jack,' she says. She's out of breath. 'Evie is not with him. He says her dad picked her up. He's sticking to what he told you on the phone. I don't know any more than that. He's being questioned right now. I can call you when I know more. Zoe?'

'Where was he? Why didn't he ring?'

'I'm not sure yet. I'll get back to you as soon as Collier finishes the interview.'

I text Ollie to let him know and lie back on the bed. I didn't think Evie would be with Jack, but as long as we didn't know where he was, there was hope he'd be able to explain what had happened to her. I don't understand why Jack is trying to put the blame on Ollie, though. I know Haris is Evie's father and I know he's taken her. I can feel it in my gut, just as I know that scrap of ice-blue fabric is the *Frozen* dress Haris must have given her. How could I not have seen it? He manipulated me, manipulated Evie and now he's manipulating the police. I have to find evidence. Where has he hidden her? Could Yasira be in on it too? Could she be sheltering Evie? I should have searched her house while I was there.

Ben grows bored by my lack of response and slides to the floor. He loves Evie's room. He pulls out a box of Lego and tips it out. He glances up at me, delighted by the noise and chaos, wondering if I'll tell him off like I normally do. I get up and I start looking at Evie's things. It's the only way I have right now of feeling close to her. I run my hands through the clothes hanging in her little wardrobe. On every surface there are objects she's collected: pebbles and shells, a tiny princess in a blue dress that you can take apart, a heart-shaped ring, pine cones, Moshi monsters and minute drawing pads, bead bracelets and a cupcake-shaped eraser. I find a shoebox full of torn sheets of paper – it's her box of spells. She'd written one for me too. She'd drawn snowflakes and ice crystals and a penguin wearing a crown.

'It'll make you Queen of Antarctica,' she'd said, pressing it into my hand. 'You must keep it somewhere very safe.'

'I'll be a bit cold there,' I'd laughed.

She'd looked at me with a serious expression and said, 'But, Mummy, your heart is so warm you'll never freeze.'

It occurs to me that the answer could be here somewhere. Evie's a hoarder. She hid the presents from me. I take her room apart. When every bit of modelling clay, every fragment of scrap paper and fabric, every piece of plastic, felt-tip pen and naked doll, is on the floor, I stop. I have a chaotic, artist's impression of my daughter's life: a magpie-like collection of anything that can be turned into a sculpture or a collage is here; her quirky seven-year-old heart laid bare.

I start to pull out some of her books. I can't believe I ever thought reading to her was a chore. I'd sit here some nights, fidgeting, thinking of all the things I needed to do, my voice hoarse, reluctant to read 'just one more chapter', wishing I could escape to my glass of wine. What did I have to do that was so important? What could be more important than reading my daughter a bedtime story?

I take down *Charlotte's Web*. I can't remember where we'd got to: as usual, my mind was on other things. I open the book at random and wish I hadn't as a line springs out at me: 'After all, what's a life, anyway? We're born, we live a little while, we die.' I snap it shut. I feel something trapped between the pages. It might be a bookmark;

now I'll know what the last words I ever read to Evie were. It's a card. I turn it over. On the front is a picture of an orange flower, like a flat-petalled marigold. It has a home-made feel to it, as if the sender has printed a photo and cut it out himself. Inside it says:

*My darling daughter,*

*Not long now until we can be together! Wait for my signal and then you'll know it's me.*

*All my love,*

*Daddy*

I drop it on the floor to stop myself from crumpling it into a ball and hurling it at the wall. Ben lets the doll he was playing with fall and comes running over, hand outstretched to grab it. I snatch it back up again and he starts to howl. I have to take it to Collier. It's proof – further proof – that Haris was communicating with her. I'm outraged. Collier and Clegg searched Evie's room and they missed it. I missed it too. There must be another letter, telling Evie what the signal was – and then we'll know how he persuaded her to leave with him. I go through everything all over again.

But there is nothing here that can tell me what the signal was or where she is now.

I hoist Ben on my hip and slap the card down on the table in front of Collier. 'I found it in Evie's room.' I can't keep the accusation out of my voice.

Collier pulls on a pair of latex gloves and balances his glasses on the end of his nose. They're gold-rimmed and their studiousness is at odds with his appearance: he looks like a gruff miner. After he's read the card, he puts it in an evidence bag. 'But you found nothing else?'

'No – nothing to say what the signal was.'

'Have a seat, Mrs Morley. I'm glad you've come in. Ruby, would you get Mrs Morley a cup of tea and some juice for the lad? And we could do with a top-up and some biscuits.'

'I know he took her,' I say, refusing to sit. 'Can't you see – the card's from him?'

Ben slides out of my grasp and I put him down. I've left Evie's room exactly as it was, as if it has been ransacked by a cat burglar, and driven to the police station. I tip a bag of toys out for Ben but he heads straight for Clegg and tries to tickle him with his pudgy fingers.

Collier sighs heavily. 'It pains me to say it, because the man's clearly a devious bastard – sorry,' he inclines his head towards Ben, 'but his alibi checks out. He says he went to Leeds City Art Gallery about a commission. He stayed with friends, who vouch for him, as does the curator of the gallery. And we've got him on CCTV entering and leaving. His meeting finished at ten to four on Friday, so it's conceivable that he could have driven to Ilkley in time to pick Evie up from Jack Mitchell.'

'He didn't use the pickup though – as that was parked outside his friend's house the entire weekend,' says Clegg, tickling Ben back, 'and the Fiat was stolen, driven across the moor and torched by joyriders. We found the boys who were responsible – two fifteen-year-old lads from Ilkley Grammar.'

'His mates are artists – they work with metal like himself – and he was making one of his sculptures in their studio,' Collier continues. 'He was there after the meeting with Leeds City Art Gallery, and most of the weekend, emerging only in the evenings to have something to eat and a few drinks. Several people dropped in to the house and called round at the studio; they all confirm his alibi. So, like I say, there's a possibility, but it's looking highly unlikely.

'The handwriting expert says there's only a twenty per cent chance the cards are from him. There's no fingerprints on them other than yours, your husband's and your daughter's.'

'What about the writing in the prayer book? That was different.'

'Our guy says it's written by the same person. The perpetrator used his left hand to address the parcels and make them look messier, more childlike. Maybe to deflect suspicion or make it harder to identify him by his writing.'

Collier slides his glasses into his jacket pocket.

'Haris says Evie isn't his child – and we'll find that out tomorrow one way or the other. He denies taking her, or being involved in her abduction in any way – he would say that, wouldn't he? But he has been remarkably forthcoming about other aspects of his life – like his obsession with you – volunteering information that doesn't put him in a good light.'

'Such as?'

I slide into the chair opposite Collier. Clegg is now distracting Ben by bouncing him and down on his lap and letting him almost fall to the floor and Ben's shrieking with laughter.

'I don't think you've been honest about your relationship with Haris Agni,' Collier says, folding his arms across his belly and leaning back.

Ruby returns with a tray filled with mugs of tea and a packet of biscuits.

Ben holds out his hand and shouts, 'Biscuit, biscuit.'

I move the squash she's brought out of his way and put his sippy cup on the table, but it's too late and he starts asking for 'Juice'.

'You still haven't found my daughter!' I say. 'I'm not the person you should be investigating!'

'Is it all right if the lad has one?'

Ruby mouths 'Sorry' at me.

My heart is pounding. Collier hands Ben a Garibaldi and takes one for himself.

'I hate these bloody biscuits.' He dips it in his tea anyway and says, 'Haris says you went to his house.'

'Yes, with Ben. I told Ruby that when we found his car.'

I can't actually recall what I said at the time. I remember thinking how much I *wanted* to be in his house, locked away from the media maelstrom, hidden in the heart of the moor.

'Haris says you and Ben got into difficulties on the moor and he came and rescued you. Took you back to his house to dry off. Gave you clean clothes.'

'That's right.' My breath is speeding up. If Haris has told them we had an affair they'll be distracted – they'll view him as my lover and stop seeing him as our daughter's kidnapper.

'Quite the knight in shining armour.'

'It was stupid of me to have gone out on the moor that day with Ben. I hadn't even brought waterproofs. I don't know what would have happened if he hadn't turned up.'

I'm cradling my tea in my hands. I haven't taken a sip yet. I should tell them what happened once I got inside. They'd understand what manner of man they're dealing with. But then I'd have to admit to almost having an affair with him and Ollie will find out. I don't want Ollie to be distracted by this too.

'Do you know how he knew where you were?'

'What?'

It's not what I expected Collier to say.

'He followed you. Watched you and the lad, saw you getting into trouble. But he didn't help you. Oh no. He left you on the moor. He went home. Got his car, drove along Hangingstone Road. Waited a little while longer so you'd be soaked good and proper. And then

he took himself across the Dales Way to meet you. To rescue you.'
There's a long pause. 'He thought you'd fall in love with him,' says
Collier finally.

'Don't you see?' I'm no longer surprised by anything I hear about
Haris. I lean across the table towards Collier. 'He used me. He used
me to get at Evie.'

'He was obsessed with *you*. He stalked *you*. He risked you and
Ben getting hypothermia so he could "save" you. But I doubt he
took your daughter. It was all about you, Zoe.'

'What does Jack say?' I ask.

'He's sticking to his story,' says Clegg. 'Says Evie left him just
before five to go to her daddy.'

Collier shoots him a look.

'Mr Mitchell says he was climbing in the Lake District. He'd
been camping with a friend, somewhere with no mobile signal.
He'd turned his phone off. He drove back on Sunday night – during
the night – intending to go straight to work. We picked him up
at his house. We're waiting for his lawyer so we can continue our
interview. We'll let you know as soon as we've questioned him
further.'

Ben slides from Clegg's knee and comes running over towards
me, his arms outstretched, his face crumpling. My time is up: his
attention span has run out. I could tell them the whole story, but
I see now that would still not be enough. I need proof.

There's a poster of Evie on the door of the newsagent's between
the police station and the school. I choose a plain cheese sandwich
for Ben. It's the only thing I can find that's vaguely healthy and
that he will eat. I need to keep him occupied for a little longer.
I pass the news-stand on my way to the till and I'm shocked to

see a picture of Ollie on the front page of the *Mirror*. I pick it up. The headline is one word: 'LIAR!!' The article quotes an expert who says that it's usually the father who is responsible for abusing and killing missing kids, particularly in cases where the child is not biologically his own. The journalist has plotted Ollie's route from work to the hospital and 'proved that Mr Oliver Morley had a window of opportunity to seize his adopted daughter'. I shove the paper back quickly before I can read any more. There's no way Ollie could have missed seeing this when he arrived at Leeds station this morning.

The girl behind the counter is watching me surreptitiously; her greasy fringe covers pallid skin and she has a line of red spots on the edge of her jaw. She twists her mouth as if attempting to smile and ducks her head so her fringe hides her face. I feel sorry for her: the awkward self-consciousness, the painful pimples – and then my eyes fill with tears. I hope one day Evie will be like this; that Evie will live to be a teenager, no matter how shy or acne-ridden.

Once back on the road, I follow the line of the moor, past the Cow and Calf rocks, until I find the turning that will take me across the heath to Haris's house. The spot where his Fiat was burnt is black and greasy, the rush-filled verge flattened and scored with tyre tracks. I drive slowly, my car bumping and grating over the stones. The sky is dark grey – it looks as if it's about to rain. Am I clutching at straws? Did Evie really walk along the path between Haris's house and his studio, or was it some other little girl in a shiny blue dress? Could Haris have taken her? It makes sense. If Haris was so obsessed with me and I chose to end our relationship, it's no wonder he tried to destroy my family. I think he poisoned Ben. He wanted to kill my son. But when that didn't work, he used Ben being on life-support as a distraction to take Evie.

The police must have finished the forensic work on his house, because when I reach it, there's no tape, no officers standing guard.

I park as close to it as I can and leave Ben in the car. The first drops of rain hit my cheek. The wind is bitterly cold. I try the door. It's locked, of course. I stand in the lea of the doorway and watch the rain start to fall in sheets, slicing through the heather.

Ilkley, so far below me, looks tiny. How did Haris feel, when he stood here? He must have enjoyed an untrammelled sense of freedom, after his years inside, with this wilderness around him, suburban domestication at his feet. Entitlement, too, a feeling that he was master of all he surveyed. Collier said that if Haris isn't Evie's father, they wouldn't be able to hold him any longer. He'll be released tomorrow, pending the DNA results. I want him locked up. Forever.

I wave at Ben and make a funny face through the window. He's scattered grated cheese over himself and wiped margarine down the sides of the car seat. I don't want to leave him, even for a minute, but it's raining hard now. I'll be quick. I glance at him over my shoulder as I run round the side of the house. Screening it from the rest of the moor is the stand of pines – the reason why you can't see the studio from here. There is a garden though. I can't imagine Haris is much of a gardener. He'd rather let it run wild. I peer over the mossy tumbledown wall. As I suspected, it's almost as much a part of the moor as the land outside. The grass is cropped short by the sheep and there's the odd shrub, grown leggy, since they haven't been pruned. It's an odd combination: moorland trees, like rowan, next to a dying lilac. I could imagine him hacking it down out of sheer spite, since its beautiful scented blossom doesn't belong here.

I need to get back to Ben. I lean against the wall and the lichen and algae stain my top. I'm wet through. Why have I come here? What can I hope to prove? The police have searched his house and studio extensively. There is, they've told me repeatedly, no sign of Evie, save that one scrap of princess dress I found skewered on a gorse bush. I remember the stoat and how Haris said he buried the body until the flesh had disintegrated from the bones.

I look around again and that's when I see it. It's another native bush, one that Haris might approve of. Unlike the lilac, shedding seeds like scales, this one is in full bloom, covered in glorious pink, fleshy flowers. It's a spindle tree: *Euonymus europeaus*. Each berry is a potent capsule of evonoside, the poison that stopped Ben's heart. I feel as if my own heart will implode. This is the proof I was looking for. How could Haris do this? To Ben, to me. To Evie. I want to drop to my knees in the heather and howl with rage.

When I get back to the car, Ben's face is red, his top lip curled. He's sobbing, aware that I've left him alone. I wonder if he remembers the hospital – the hours drifting in and out of consciousness – waking up in the night when neither of us were with him. I snatch open the door and unbuckle him from his seat; I hug him and rock him until he's quiet and I'm covered in cheese and tears.

I throw the branch in front of Ruby.

'This is what Ben was poisoned with,' I say.

She looks uncertainly from the stick dripping water onto the table, now dusted with pollen from the golden-orange stamens, back to me. After I'd got home, I phoned to ask her to come here.

'I found it growing outside Haris's house. He tried to kill Ben and then he took Evie.'

'Because you didn't fall in love with him after he rescued you and Ben?' She echoes Collier's words, her voice flat. She's trying hard not to look sceptical. Ruby isn't one to hide her feelings or sugar-coat her expressions. I have to tell her. It's the only thing that will convince her and Collier.

'We almost had an affair. We met nearly every day. We kissed. That was it. That day on the moor I told him it couldn't go any further and he was about to attack me. Then he let me walk back from his house with Ben in the rain. The person I called to come and "rescue" us was Jack Mitchell. Jack picked us up and took us home.'

'But he didn't hurt you?'

'No. I was frightened. I thought he might. You can see how intense he is. I didn't tell you because I wanted you to focus on finding Evie. Don't you see, Haris must have taken her. He wanted revenge.'

'And you didn't want Ollie to find out?' She sighs. 'Just because he's got a poisonous bush in his backyard, it doesn't mean he tried to harm Ben.'

'He had the motive.'

'I'll tell Collier.'

She hooks her bag over her shoulder and picks up the spindle. The description I read on the Internet is right: the wood is creamy where I've split it from the tree, hard and fine-grained. It would make perfect charcoal.

'Tell Collier what?'

The door bangs and Ollie comes in. He's drenched. His jaw is clenched tight. He throws his briefcase on the sofa and Bella, who's napping there, yelps. It's the middle of the afternoon – he must have left work early. He kicks off his shoes and yanks off his tie as he rants at Ruby.

'You're not keeping us in the loop, Ruby. Why the fuck do I have to find out from the local news that Haris had a bloody shrine to my wife? With a picture of Evie and my son. You've got the culprit. Why the hell haven't you found my daughter?'

Ruby can't help herself. She glances at me and then quickly looks back at Ollie, but it's too late. He pivots towards me.

'You knew? You knew and you didn't tell me?'

'I did try – last night, before you—'

'Jesus. You didn't try very fucking hard.'

'Finding that scrap of Evie's dress was more important.'

'More important than that psycho's scrapbook of pictures of our daughter?'

'There was only one photo of her. They were all of me. He was obsessed with me.'

Ruby is standing between us, clutching the branch of spindle flowers. In her long, dark trench coat and with her curly hair, she looks like a faun that's lost its way.

'You knew,' he says.

His blue eyes are hard and accusing. He is looking at me as if he has never loved me. My breath catches in my throat.

'I need to get back to the station,' Ruby says.

Still staring at me, he says, 'You're the fucking family liaison officer. Fucking liaise.'

Ruby stares squarely at me and raises her pointed chin.

'Are you going to tell him or shall I? He needs to know, Zoe.'

How dare she? She knows nothing about relationships. She lives with her bloody parents who have probably given up on the idea of arranging a marriage for her because she's too sodding old. Has she ever even dated?

'Tell me what?'

Ollie's speaking quietly but his voice is so cold I'm terrified. Ben starts to cry. For a moment we all stand there then I start to move.

'He probably need his nappy changed.'

Ollie looks tired again. He wipes the rain from his face with his sleeve.

'I'll do it,' Ruby says, and I remember her nephew is a toddler. She'll have had practice.

I turn back to Ollie.

'I kissed him,' I say.

That's all it takes, just those three little words. Ollie sinks into the sofa and puts his arms around Bella.

He says, 'You did this. You brought him into our lives.'

'Do you think I don't know that?'

We're silent until Ruby comes down and hands Ben to me. He's hot and smells of Sudocrem. For one moment he's still, his arms heavy around my neck; we're all still. Then Ben slides to the floor, as Ruby picks up her piece of spindle tree and Ollie leaps to his feet and kicks the TV screen. He collapses on the sofa, swearing. There's a shard of glass embedded in his foot. Ben starts crying, and I grab him, to get him away from the fragments, and it's only when the second drop hits my hand that I look down and see it's blood. A piece of the screen has cut open his cheek, just below his eye. I start screaming. Suddenly there's a lot of blood.

'This is all your fucking fault,' Ollie yells at me, attempting to pull the glass out of his toe and slicing open his hand.

Ruby calls an ambulance. By the time it arrives, she's locked Bella in the garden, cleared up the broken pieces of TV, wrapped a bandage round Ollie's hand and put a butterfly plaster across the cut on Ben's face. My hands are wet with his blood. I wash them in the sink as Ben shrieks and Ruby tells Ollie not to be a complete pillock and try and take the glass out of his foot himself again.

In the ambulance on the way to the hospital, she looks from Ollie to me and says, 'Listen to me. Collier and Clegg don't think that Haris took your daughter. If he's not her father, he will be released tomorrow morning. They don't have enough evidence to hold him. I suggest you two put this behind you, whatever happened between Zoe and Haris. You can deal with it in the future. Right now, you have to focus on finding your daughter. I'm going to suggest to the boss that he does a press release and you do another televised statement to the public. And this time, Ollie, you need to look like you bloody care.'

She shouts through to the driver and he stops, dropping her off near the police station.

———

Ben cried almost the entire time we were in A & E. The doctor put surgical tape across the cut; thank God he didn't need stitches. He's in a lot of pain. I'm furious with Ollie. Ben could have lost his eye. His distress makes it even worse; we're both on edge, but we're barely speaking to each other. Without Ruby, we have no buffer. I know Ollie feels guilty, not because he says anything or even apologizes for acting like a total idiot, but because he insists on holding Ben and trying to comfort him. Ben wants me to carry him. He's become much more clingy since his trip to hospital last Friday. I take him from Ollie as often as I can, partly because I want to keep Ben close, but also to prove that he loves me best and to make Ollie feel worse. Which makes me a complete bitch. And the entire time I feel as if I've been eviscerated. Evie has been missing for three days. The man we both think took her is in police custody, but in a few hours, he'll be a free man.

In the taxi on the way home, Ollie falls asleep, holding onto Ben's foot with his uninjured hand. Ben is in my lap and so Ollie's hand rests on my thigh. In other circumstances I'd think this was sweet. Now it makes me nauseous.

When we get home, Andy is standing waiting on the doorstep. He looks cold, as if he's been there for a while. He pats Ollie on the shoulder and gives me a kiss on the cheek, tickles Ben under the chin.

'What happened to you?' he asks Ben, and then looks at me with concern.

Neither of us says anything.

Ollie unlocks the door and says, 'I'll take him.' Ben has finally quietened and lets me hand him over. 'I'll put him down,' Ollie adds, not making eye contact with Andy. He limps upstairs.

'Everything all right?' asks Andy, and then looks stricken. 'I mean, apart from, you know, oh God, I mean, is Ben okay?'

'It's all right, Andy. Ben cut himself.'

Andy glances at the shell of the TV with its jagged edges where the screen was, and then back at me.

'Can I get you a drink?'

'Yes.'

I sit on one of the stools at the breakfast bar. I haven't bothered to take off my coat or switch on any lights. Andy doesn't put them on either. He pours us both a glass of wine. He must have brought it because Ollie and I have drunk everything in the house, even the sticky, eight-year-old Limoncello bought on our last trip to Italy. I can't see the bottle in the dark, but after the first sip, I can tell it's good stuff. Chablis, maybe. Andy probably doesn't want to say anything about it: the days of bringing round bottles of wine and cooing over the label and the contents are behind us. I'd have drunk my own paint thinner if Andy had poured it.

He sits next to me and touches my elbow. 'How are you doing?'

I turn away and look out at the garden. A strip of moonlight slants across it, a blue so alien it shouldn't exist.

He coughs and takes a sip of wine. 'Have you heard about Jack?'

'The police arrested him this morning. He said he'd been climbing in the Lake District. He's still saying that Ollie took Evie. I don't know any more than that,' I say.

Andy has been speaking quietly, but now he lowers his voice even further. 'He called me. You know, his one phone call? He wanted Gill to represent him. They can keep him for thirty-six hours without charging him.'

'Do you think he had anything to do with it?' I can't stop the tremor in my voice.

Andy shakes his head. 'He sounded terrified. He was crying. Swore blind he didn't know what had happened. That he'd never hurt Evie. Says he's loved her since she was little. He genuinely didn't seem to have a clue — he didn't listen to the news or read a paper or even see another person apart from his mate over the last two days. And because he was travelling in the early hours of the morning, he didn't stop at any services. That's what he said, anyway. For what it's worth, I believe him. Fucking irresponsible to drive all night and then plan to teach a class of thirty seven-year-olds.'

My heart is pounding. 'But if he's telling the truth, then who has Evie? I have to speak to him.'

'Gill's not taking the case, by the way.'

I nod. 'Tell her thanks.'

'Don't be daft. Course she wouldn't have represented him. I thought you should know. Can I do anything to help? Anything. Just name it.'

He sounds desperate. I shake my head. He slides off his stool and hugs me. I can feel his tears, wet against my hair.

'Is everything okay with Ollie?'

I shake my head.

'I saw the paper this morning   '

'It's not true,' I say. 'Ollie lied to the police about where he was. At first. But he'd never hurt Evie.'

''Course he wouldn't. You're both under a lot of stress. Do you and Ben want to sleep at ours?'

'Thanks. We'll be all right.'

'I'll call you in the morning,' he says and grips my hand tightly.

I sit in the dark and drink wine and feel lonelier than I've ever felt. Losing Evie is like cutting out my vital organs, my heart, my soul. At some point, I crawl upstairs and into bed, without undressing.

Ollie rolls towards me.

'Did you have sex with him?' he asks.

I close my eyes and grind my teeth and try not to scream. Someone has taken our daughter and that's what he's lying here thinking about. Worse, not *someone* – Jack is still saying that Ollie took her. I swallow down bile.

'No.'

'Did you want to?'

'Yes!' The word explodes out of me. 'But I decided not to. I chose you. I chose our family.'

He reaches out for me then and, even though I've still got my top on, I feel as if a fleet of spiders are creeping beneath the surface of my skin. I slide onto my side, away from him.

# TUESDAY: FOUR DAYS AFTER

When I wake up, my body feels like lead, my mouth thick and gritty. My head aches when I move. It could be the wine or it could be the start of the migraine I thought I'd avoided on Saturday. Ollie isn't in bed and when I look in Ben's room, neither is he. The duvet has been pulled back and there's an indentation on the mattress in the shape of his body, as if he'd been snatched as he slept. My heart constricts.

I run down the stairs and Bella leaps up at me, thinking I'm playing. Ben is in his high chair.

'Mummy!' he shouts and waves a breadstick at me.

Ollie is cooking. There's the smell of freshly brewed coffee. He's squeezed oranges and defrosted blueberries. They've exploded in an unctuous purple goo in the bowl.

'I'm making pancakes,' he says. 'We need to eat, keep our strength up.'

I'm about to protest, to say that the last thing I feel like doing is eating, but then my stomach rumbles. I've eaten almost nothing since Friday. I sit at the table next to Ben, and Ollie sets maple syrup and a plate in front of me. I eat pancake after pancake, hot and sweet, crispy on the outside. It reminds me of our Sunday mornings before we had children. Ollie would always cook pancakes – in exactly the same way – even though I'd tease him and demand thick, soft, Scotch pancakes for a change. Or maybe a croissant. We'd read the papers; sometimes we'd go back to bed afterwards, or we'd meet up with friends and have a pub lunch or visit an art gallery. Those leisurely Sundays, of chilled beer, rosé in the park, lattes and carrot cake in a cafe, newsprint on our fingers, seem as if they happened to another woman, a different couple.

When I finally stop eating, Ollie sits down to have his pancakes. It's only then that I realize Ben is still in his high chair. This is not like him – normally he hates being strapped in for a millisecond longer than necessary. I lift him out and he sits quietly on my knee. I hug him tightly and, while I'm enjoying cuddling him, a small part of me wishes he was tearing round the living room shouting his head off. We should go back to see Dr Kapur, I think, kissing the crown of Ben's head.

'They've given me compassionate leave. I'm not going in.'

He piles blueberries on his plate. He always used to insist on crème fraiche, but we haven't as much as a yogurt in the fridge. Ben's eaten nothing but Weetabix and cheese sandwiches for the last couple of days.

'I've made a start on these,' Ollie tells me, gesturing to the haphazard pile of cards that have accumulated over the past two days.

The thought of looking through people's platitudes, condolences via Hallmark, makes me feel sick. I push them away. Used envelopes in muted shades of pink slide to the floor.

'I want to talk to Jack,' I say. 'They wouldn't let me yesterday but maybe they will today.'

Ollie stops, his fork midway to his mouth.

'I'll come with you.'

'Someone needs to look after Ben.'

Ollie has only eaten one mouthful. He stretches out his hand towards me. 'I'm sorry,' he says. 'I haven't been here for you and Ben. And Evie.'

I take his hand out of force of habit. His skin feels lizard-like against my palm.

'Let's talk about it later.'

'I mean it, Zoe. I can see I pushed you away.'

I don't respond. I don't have any spare space in my mind or my heart to deal with Ollie. I don't know how I feel about him any more, but I do know that now isn't the time to make any decisions. And I'm trying not to say something I'll regret later.

He says, 'Why the hell is Jack still saying I took Evie?'

'I don't know. I'll find out. If they won't let me speak to him, I can talk to Collier again.'

I have a shower as hot as I can bear and dress in clean clothes. There are still a couple of paparazzi camped on our street but no one approaches me. I think Collier has slapped some kind of injunction or restraining order on them. I can imagine him growling at them. I'd be intimidated if he wasn't on our side.

'Zoe. Glad you came. I was just about to send Ruby to pick you up. How's the lad?' he says, when I get to the police station. 'Ruby says you think Haris poisoned him, and that's how he ended up in ICU.'

'He did poison him! Did she tell you about the spindle tree in his garden?'

I have to believe it was Haris. Because to go along with what Jack says happened is unthinkable. Collier gestures to a chair. Clegg sits next to me, stretching out his long legs. We're in the same room I've sat in to speak to the two detectives every time we've come here: it's small with linoleum tiles and bars against the window. The walls are painted a horrid creamy-yellow, the paint thick and clotted. We're sitting in the police version of comfy chairs around a coffee table, as if to emphasize that this is a more informal meeting.

'It's not enough, Zoe. It's not proof. Your little boy could have found those berries almost anywhere in Ilkley and eaten them. Those trees grow all over the place.'

Collier pulls over another chair and Clegg shifts his feet awkwardly, shuffling them under the table.

'I wanted to tell you in person. I'm afraid Haris is going to be released later today, Zoe.'

'You don't believe me.'

'We have no evidence. We've nothing to tie him to your daughter. The DNA results came back this morning. He's not related to Evie. He's not her father.'

'What?'

'I can't hold him any longer. And we've had to scale down the alert on the ports and airports.'

Collier gives me a look from beneath his eyebrows. The hairs are wiry and unkempt. I imagine there's no Mrs Collier to help him keep them under control. Clegg looks away. He's not yet hardened to other people's pain.

'But –'

I can't take it in. Evie has the same colouring as Haris; the same green-brown eyes, dark hair, olive skin – Collier said so himself – the same artistic temperament.

'Could the lab have made a mistake? They do, don't they? They get things wrong. DNA can be contaminated.'

I was sure he was her father. Even if he's not her father, it doesn't change the fact that he took her. He was obsessed with me. He wished he could destroy me when I didn't want to have an affair with him. He tried to kill Ben. And he's taken Evie as revenge. How can I convince Collier? How can they not see? Surely Ruby has told them what happened between me and Haris? There's no point hiding anything now that Ollie knows the truth.

Ruby comes in with a tray of tea. She hands me a cup made

just the way I like it – weak and milky. I've never drunk this much tea in my life.

'I'm sorry, Zoe,' she says. 'I told DCI Collier what you told me about Haris and your relationship. But he's right. We have no proof. We can't find any evidence that Evie was ever with him, or even met him. We have to move on.'

'We still have Mr Mitchell in custody,' says Clegg.

'Haven't you found out any more?'

'The friend he was with vouches for him – once he got to the Lakes. We're trying to track down any other climbers who might have spotted him. He can't prove he left when he said he did, and that he didn't take Evie with him. Although Forensics haven't found any evidence she was in his car or his tent,' says Collier.

'Can I speak to him?'

'I'm afraid not. But I do have something else I wanted to talk to you about.'

My chest tightens. What is Collier going to tell me? That he thinks Jack Mitchell really did take Evie? That his climbing story was a cover for whatever he did with my child? Or that Jack handed Evie to my husband before he left? Collier gives me a manila folder.

'Take a look at these.'

I open the folder slowly. I'm not sure what to expect. Something terrible. There might be blood. I don't want to see whatever is inside. The last time Collier showed me photos, it was a mugshot of Haris; it was how I discovered he'd done seven years in Leeds Prison. I try to swallow but saliva sticks in my throat.

The first photograph is of Evie. It's black and white. She's smiling. She's wearing leggings and a vest. She has her back to the camera and is holding something – a blanket or a shawl. The edges of the fabric are slightly blurred as if she's going to throw it. She's looking over her shoulder and laughing. In the second one, she's wearing a tutu and a vest; her legs are bare. She's fallen backwards, as if into an explosion of tulle. Her eyes are closed and she's giggling. You can see the long, lean length of her thighs; the edge of her knickers. In the third photo she's wearing pants and a vest and nothing else. She's stretched out on the sofa. She's smiling.

There is one more photo. I pick it up slowly. My hands are shaking as I turn it over. In this one, she's serious. She's looking at herself in the mirror. She's adjusting her tiara; in the other hand she's holding a wand. There's a lost innocence about her and a certain weariness; she looks like a child beauty queen. She's wearing strappy sandals and a shiny dress. It's the *Frozen* outfit, the one she wore to Ben's party, the one I found a fragment of on the moor; the one I didn't buy her. In the mirror is the reflection of the man taking the photo. His face is partly obscured by the camera. It's a good one – a Nikon SLR – same as mine. The flash has gone off, so his features are blurred behind a star of light. It's given the dress sharp edges and shrunk Evie's pupils to pin-pricks as if she's been drugged. But I can still tell who it is. Jack Mitchell.

'We searched his house,' says Clegg. 'There's lots of photos like this – children half undressed, putting on costumes. Your head teacher has gone through them with us. They're all kids Mitchell babysat for or childminded after school.'

'There's nothing indecent, as such,' says Ruby. 'Nothing else that would incriminate him on his computer. Only these photos.'

Collier takes the folder from me.

'I need to speak to him.'

'I'm sorry. I can't let you do that,' Collier says again.

I'm shaken by Collier's revelations and I don't notice her. She's so close to me, she's able to reach out and touch me. When she puts her hand on my arm, I start. I'm aware of the smell of lilies before

I realize who it is.

'Zoe, is there any news?'

It's Hannah. I've walked out of the police station in such a daze I almost careered right into her. I wasn't aware of the time – it must be the children's break. It was only last Thursday that I did the school run and already I've lost track of the things that used to bookmark my days.

I shake my head and wonder whether to tell her what the police said about Jack. I don't know what I think about it myself yet. I don't trust my own instincts any more.

Hannah is so pale she looks ill – maybe she's coming down with a bug. Looking after Evie's class on her own must be exhausting. What can she be thinking about Jack? She glances away from me and winds her scarf more tightly round her neck and hooks it over her head. It's cold and she must have forgotten her hat.

'They've released Haris, haven't they?'

I nod.

'I wasn't sure whether to tell you this, but—'

'What? What is it?'

She looks back at me and the winter light catches her pale green eyes. She grips my arm again. 'It's something that Evie said before... before... You know I said I was trained in play therapy? I gave her some dolls—'

'But I didn't ask you to do any play therapy with her.'

She bows her head and lets go of my arm. 'Yes, but I didn't steer her into a role-playing session, honestly. I just gave her the dolls. I asked her to tell me a story about them.' She bites her lip.

'What did she say?' There's a heaviness in my chest. It hurts to breathe.

'She said they were a family – a mummy, a daddy and a little girl called Evelyn.'

'No baby brother called Benedict?'

'No.'

'And what happened in Evie's story?'

'I don't know whether to say anything now. I shouldn't have started telling you...'

'Just say it. Please.' I want to shake her, to make her tell me, although inside I'm cringing.

'She said that the mummy and the daddy took their daughter up onto the moor. They had a picnic. They'd brought all of her favourite food – cheese sandwiches on white bread with the crusts cut off and strawberry-pink cupcakes – and when the little girl had finished eating, she looked around for her mummy and the daddy. But they'd gone. They'd left Evelyn on the moor by herself.'

It's as if Hannah has punched me in the stomach. I take a ragged gulp of air.

Hannah says, 'I'm so sorry, Zoe, I know it sounds hurtful, but I think she was trying to work out some abandonment issues. You know, because of the adoption.'

'Why are you telling me this now?'

I want to say that it's none of her business: Evie knows we love her and we would never leave her. Or is she implying that Ollie and I abandoned her on the moor? 'In Real Life,' as Evie would say.

Hannah looks as if she's about to start crying. 'I wondered...' She looks away and her scarf slips from her head; her blonde hair gleams like gold. I think of Rapunzel and all the other doomed princesses that Evie is obsessed with. 'They've stopped the search across the moor, haven't they? I thought – perhaps Evie has run away? All her stories are about the moor. She could be there. You should tell the police to keep looking!' She grips the sleeve of my coat. 'We can't give up.'

I pull away from her. How dare she imply that Evie has run away from *me*?

'I will never give up,' I say, and walk swiftly away from her, back up the hill, my throat constricting tighter and tighter.

Should I ask the police to resume their search of the moor? Could Evie have simply run off? No, she's got our child all wrong; Evie writes stories about the moor but she wouldn't hide there. I try not to think of that other, fictional little girl, eating cupcakes and then turning round to see she is entirely on her own in the middle of the moor, with only the rowan trees and the stonechats for company. A fictional child, maybe, but one created out of my daughter's imagination.

Ollie is cleaning the house when I return. There's a ferocious intensity to the way he's wiping down and buffing the stainless steel. Ben has a cloth too and is copying him.

'He's got pictures,' I say. 'Photos of Evie.'

Saying the words out loud makes me feel leaden.

Ollie is very still.

'What kind of photos?'

Ben takes the opportunity to run over to his father and plant a dribbly kiss on his cheek. Ollie sits on the floor and pulls him onto his lap.

'Black and white. Artistic looking.' I swallow uncomfortably. My breathing has grown laboured and shallow. 'Wearing that *Frozen* dress. And one of her in her vest and knickers.'

Ollie pushes Ben off and rushes outside. I watch him through the French windows, raging, kicking the chestnut tree, howling and sobbing. Ben starts crying too. I pick him up and cuddle him. We should do something with him. Make buns. Get paints out. Roll Play-Doh. He's used to being at nursery in the mornings, with lots of other children and organized activities. I wait until Ollie has calmed down and then I go outside and we stand together in the cold, wet garden, holding each other and Ben until our son toddles off and starts chucking sand about and gets some in his eye.

Later that afternoon, Ruby calls. I pray it's good news.

'Yes?'

'Zoe, I'm ringing about Jack Mitchell.' She pauses. When I don't say anything – I can't, I'm holding my breath – she says, 'He's been released. There isn't anything to charge him with. No concrete evidence. Just those photos. They look bad but they're not pornographic. And there's nothing else on his computer that's incriminating.'

I let the phone drop to my side. Evie has been gone for four days and we're no closer to finding her. I stand and look out of the sitting-room window, across the valley. It's dark already, with a chink of light over the hill. The blades of a line of wind turbines catch the last remnant of the setting sun.

Ruby's voice is muffled: 'Zoe? Zoe?'

Jack Mitchell. The last person to have seen my daughter. Now that he's been released, suspicion is going to fall back on my husband. I disconnect the call.

I've always wanted to do well with my art, but I've never been much of a planner. I didn't plan my career, or map out my life. I wanted to paint and I wanted Ollie and I wanted to have children. Ollie is the one who plans, who wants things to be orderly, who likes to take charge and be in control. Ollie chose our house and organized the interior design. I was just thankful I had somewhere beautiful to live and, if I'm honest, I always felt a little guilty at having so much when me and mum had so little. Somehow I've ended up in the latte-drinking classes.

But what's happened to Evie, to us, has taken away the small amount of order, the semblance of control I did have over my life. I feel lost, adrift, with nothing to cling on to. I'm literally helpless. How can I find my child? What can I do to save her? The police had two suspects and now they have none. They're bound to be suspicious of my husband again. And Ollie, who was once my anchor, is no longer a stabilizing force in my life. I need him to be. I need him to be there for us. I need my marriage to work. And all I have is hope – that we will find her, that Evie's still alive, that we will be a family again.

'I'm going to Jack's,' I tell Ollie. 'He's been released.'

'I'm coming with you,' he says.

'No, I can't take —'

'We'll bring Ben.'

He's grimly determined and there's no point arguing with him.

We drive to Mornington Road. It's just two streets over from the house Mum lived in before she died: a row of identical narrow, red-brick houses. There are no front gardens, the doors open straight onto the pavement; most evenings, there'd be kids playing out, kicking balls up and down, cycling trikes along the road. Skipping. Who skips these days? Now it's dark and cold and the streets are choked with cars. There's no one around. Our breath freezes in a cloud around our faces when we step out of the car. I pull my coat more tightly around myself and dig my hands deep into my pockets. Our footsteps echo hollowly as we walk in silence down the street.

When Jack comes to the door, he looks terrible. His skin is grey and waxy. Two nights without sleep, one of them in a cell, is the least of what's happened to him.

His bottom jaw goes slack when he sees me and then he stutters, 'Zoe. Ollie.' He looks as if he's about to cry. 'I'm sorry.'

'Where is she?' Ollie shouts.

'I don't know. I don't know.' His voice goes high-pitched at the end and cracks. He looks up and down the street and then shuffles backwards. 'Will you come in? Please. Just for a moment.'

Jack has knocked through the wall between the sitting room and the kitchen and it's one open space, with a modern-looking breakfast bar at the far end. It's all painted white – even the wooden floorboards are white. I stop. I've been here many times before but I've never given it a thought. I'm looking at it with different eyes now. I put Ben down and he runs over to a white Ikea set of shelves with fuchsia and lime-coloured canvas drawers full of toys and children's books.

There's a chest at one end, almost dominating the room. On the wall opposite are three framed black and white photographs of children. They're close-ups of their faces. The kids are smiling, eyes wide and bright, tiny teeth breaking through their gums, their smooth skin glowing. I wonder if he has hung the other pictures. If I walked round his house, would I find a framed photograph of my daughter in a state of undress?

He sees me looking at them and shifts uneasily.

'Can I get you a drink? A cup of tea?'

'Sit down, Jack,' I say, and he does.

Even the sofas are white but they have bright green and pink throws over them. There are some fake flowers in a plastic vase on the mantelpiece but nothing else, no clutter. I can see why children love being here: there's space to run around, but it's small enough to feel cosy; there are no dark corners, nothing they might break, and the focus is on chairs to jump on and toys to play with. Ben tips up one of the boxes full of toys and laughs with delight at the clatter they make as they fall across the whitewashed wooden floor.

Jack clasps his hands in his lap and stares from me to Ollie. He looks as if he's going to be sick. He's a small, slight man. I never knew he was into rock climbing, but if it really was what he was doing in the Lake District, it's the perfect sport for someone as light and sinewy as he is. When I thought of him as a child-man, almost in a state of arrested development, I meant it mentally – that he preferred the company of children – but now I see I must have been thinking of it as a physical trait too. Jack has curly hair and large brown eyes. His features are elfin-like, his skin smooth, with stubble poking through in a sporadic pattern as if he hasn't sufficient testosterone to generate proper facial hair. I know from the head teacher that he's in his early to mid-thirties, but he looks younger. Then again, you couldn't put an age to his face or frame; he looks timeless, or out of time, like Peter Pan. Or Dorian Gray.

'I promise you,' he says, 'I've never hurt Evie. I'm so fond of her. And those photographs – I guess the police showed them to you – there was nothing indecent about them. None of her naked. She was playing. She loved dressing up. I'm not a paedophile. They were all taken with her permission. I deleted any she didn't like.'

A shudder runs through me. 'A seven-year-old can't give you her permission. You should have asked me. You should have spoken to me about them.'

'You're right. I should have. You can have all of them. The prints and the digital copy. I'll delete everything from my computer.'

I think about how long Jack has been looking after Evie. Since she was two. How many photographs are we talking about? Five years of a little girl's life.

'I swear I didn't touch her. Not like that.'

I try and look at Jack as if I've never seen him before. It's horrific to imagine that the person you trusted with your child, the man who is your daughter's teacher, could have abused her – but surely I would have noticed? Wouldn't there have been a difference in how she acted? She wouldn't have been so excited about going to

Jack's if she'd been frightened of him. And then I remember the day I found the card from her father. She hadn't wanted to go to Jack's then. I'd ignored her.

'What happened?' Ollie asks. 'The night she went missing. You said I picked her up.'

He shakes his head. 'I said her *dad* picked her up.' He's wringing his hands now. 'I'm going to lose my job, aren't I?'

Ollie explodes, half rising from his seat. 'Do you think I care about your fucking job? Just tell me where our daughter is!'

Ben jumps, frightened by the shouting.

'I don't know. I promise I don't know.' Jack pauses. 'I was in a hurry – I was going climbing in the Lake District with my friend. I didn't want to get there too late. I didn't know the way and I didn't want to put my tent up in the dark. I can't believe it now. I thought that was important at the time. I wish I could go back to Friday—'

'For fuck's sake, Jack. Who took Evie?' Ollie yells.

'I don't know! I thought it was you, but... We were the last people in the building. Everyone else had gone home. The receptionist had given me the keys to lock up. We went into another classroom so we had a view from the front of the school, out onto the road so we could see as soon as you or Zoe arrived. I was sitting at one of the computers, looking up climbing routes, and trying to get hold of my friend to tell him I was going to be late but I couldn't get through. Evie was standing at the window, watching for you. She shouted, "My daddy's here!" I saw a car pulling up. Evie was so excited. I thought she must have been really worried about Ben and being left at school like that. She started jumping up and down and she ran over to the door. And then I got through to Stefan, my climbing buddy. I thought I wouldn't get another chance to speak to him – I'd been trying for so long – so I took it. I took the call and I waved goodbye to Evie. That was the last time I saw her.'

'So you didn't check? You stayed inside, on the phone, and waved her off?'

'I thought… you know… we were expecting a car to pull up. She said it was her dad. I trusted her.'

'You trusted her? She's fucking seven. You should have checked.'

'I know. I would give anything—'

'I want to get this straight,' I interrupt. 'She said her daddy had come to pick her up and that's what you told the police – knowing they would assume Ollie took her. But, really, you let her go to a parked car outside the school on her own, without looking to see who was in that car?'

'Yes.' It's a whisper. 'I thought, if I told the truth I'd lose my job. But then the police found those pictures – I'm going to be fired anyway. Evie *said* it was her daddy. Why would she say that if it wasn't Ollie waiting outside for her? Even if she was mistaken, wouldn't she have come back inside when she realized it wasn't him? When I went to lock up, the car had gone. And so had she.'

'Did you even see the car?'

I can barely hear him when he replies. 'No.'

'But I told you—'

And then I realize that I hadn't. I never told Jack that Evie had been contacted by her biological father. I never showed him the card or explained about the presents from her 'real' father. Jack's act of negligence is my fault.

'And the pictures?' asks Ollie. His voice is thick with loathing.

Jack glances at the chest. 'It's full of costumes. I was trying to express the joy of that experience, you know, when a child transforms from being themselves into whatever they're imagining in their magical world.'

'You c—'

I put my hand on Ollie's arm to restrain him.

'The costume,' I say urgently, 'the *Frozen* dress. We think she was wearing it when, when—' I can't finish the sentence.

'I loaned it to her,' he whispers. 'She loved it so much, I said she could borrow it.'

I squeeze my eyes shut. I can imagine him giving Evie the dress to stave off one of her monumental tantrums. And Jack wouldn't have told me because he didn't think like that, he never thought of things from a parent's perspective, only the child's.

And, if I'm being brutally honest, I don't believe he was deliberately taking indecent pictures, they're too artistic; he's managed to capture that magical moment when a child's mind spins into a make-believe world. But actually, what Jack did is steal something – a child's innocence – whilst creating something darker that will resonate with the adults looking at these photos: themes of sexuality and death, the leitmotifs that run through fairy tales, the stories that we tell ourselves about our children.

Jack starts to cry. 'I'm sorry. I can't forgive myself.'

Ollie is getting to his feet and I think he's going to punch Jack, but instead he scoops Ben up then bangs the front door open and strides out, cursing under his breath. I glance back at Jack. He's curled up in a ball on the sofa, hugging himself like a child.

Ollie drives like a maniac down the narrow streets, a dark mass of fury.

'Stop!' I say. I want him to slow down before he kills us. 'We need milk.'

The shops are all shut and the centre is practically deserted. Ollie pulls up at the bottom of Cowpasture Road, round the corner from the newsagent's opposite the school, where I bought Ben's sandwich the other day. I leave the two of them in the car. A couple of the lights aren't working so parts of the store are in semi-darkness, whilst the rest is incandescent beneath the strip lighting. I hesitate in front of the rack of tired-looking vegetables, cloudy grapes and puckered oranges. We need to do a proper shop so I only buy the things we have to have for breakfast, but I also stick in a cheap bottle of wine, the price tag in neon-pink.

Jack's picture is on the front page of several newspapers. 'Did the teacher do it?' screams one headline. The *Guardian* has gone for a different tactic: there's a map of Ilkley showing the line of the river in relation to Evie's school. 'In the case of missing school girl, Evie Morley, an inside source claims the River Wharf will not be dredged because the police have insufficient funds.' I'm never going to buy another paper in my life. They're all so full of shit.

The woman who serves me is Bengali. She has a headscarf pulled so tightly round her face it cuts into the flesh of her cheeks. Her nail varnish is chipped and dark red and she has the faded remnants of henna on her hands. She doesn't look at me or speak as she rings through my shopping and places my purchases in a blue plastic bag so thin I know it'll break. I think about my mum; how she would talk to everyone she met. It used to embarrass me as a child; by the time she'd bought her groceries she'd know if the cashier was married or divorced and how many children she had. Now I try to copy her. It's only polite. But today I don't have an ounce of energy to engage in small talk. I don't even thank the woman as I take my change. I stop momentarily at the door, thinking of what Jack has told us. I take a breath – and then I realize where I am.

I turn back to the woman. She's talking in a low voice to someone behind her. 'Excuse me,' I say as I return to the counter. The other person steps into the shadows and disappears into another room. 'I was wondering – my daughter is missing. She was taken from the school on Friday. I thought – you're so close, I mean, you're practically opposite – you might have CCTV footage? There could be something on it, anything that would help identify the man who took my daughter.'

She's looking at me now, her eyes dark and inscrutable. She glances down at the pile of local newspapers on the counter, as if my story is still on the front page.

'I'm sorry,' she says, 'the police came and they asked us that question already.'

How stupid of me. Collier told us they were checking all the CCTV footage; of course his team wouldn't have overlooked such an obvious location. 'So they didn't find anything?'

She shakes her head, not left to right as I would, but a kind of wobbling figure of eight.

'Okay.'

'I'm sorry,' she says again. 'I hope they find your little girl. When you see her, give her this.'

She snatches up a Chupa Chups lolly from a stand in front of her and holds it out to me. It's the kind of sweet Evie loves and only ever gets in party bags because I refuse to buy them for her. I take it from the woman and, for a moment, I'm frozen to the spot, clutching it to my chest.

The cold bites into my face and seers my throat as I leave the shop and turn the corner into the wind. I put the lolly in my pocket and wipe tears from my cheeks.

A voice calls, 'Wait!'

A young girl is running towards me. I don't know who she is and I look around, thinking she must mean someone else. She stops near me, breathing heavily. She's dressed in black. She's not wearing a coat and she wraps her arms around her chest.

'I'm sorry about my mum,' she says. 'She was embarrassed.'

'That's okay. I understand,' I say, realizing she must have come from the newsagent's.

The girl shakes her head, as if I haven't got it. 'The CCTV is broken. It doesn't ever record anything. The police told her off about it when they came round. She didn't want to tell you.'

'Oh,' I say. The disappointment is crushing. I'd thought I could get Collier to take another look at the footage, now that I know a man who was not my husband did pick our daughter up, right outside the school gates. I've got to call him. I get out my phone.

'It's Anita,' says the girl.

I look at her in confusion and then I remember, she served me last time I went into the newsagent's. It comes back to me now — her severe fringe, the acne, her self-consciousness. In the orange light from the street lamp, her skin looks worse, shadows and scars from her spots spread across her jaw and cheeks. She's shivering.

'Thanks for telling me. You should go back, you're cold.'

She glances behind her as if her mother might be coming to fetch her. 'You don't remember me, do you?' She's sullen. I'm about to contradict her when she says, 'You came into my school one day and gave a talk. About your art? You showed us some of your paintings?' Her voice rises at the end of her sentences.

'Yes, I remember.' I spoke to the sixth-formers at Ilkley Grammar earlier in the year. I don't recall this girl though — but then, why would I? There were over three hundred students listening to me. I'd been petrified with nerves, angry with Jenny for arranging it, and telling me it would only be a handful who were studying for Art A level. I hadn't expected it to be the whole sodding lot of them.

'You inspired me,' she says shyly.

Christ, I think, is that what this is about? She's found out my daughter has been missing for four days — and she wants to speak to me about a career in art?

'I started taking photos after that.'

I shift impatiently. My hands are frozen. I should have worn a scarf or brought a hat with me. I need to get back to Ben and Ollie.

The girl is shaking. She looks behind her again and licks her dry lips. 'I was taking pictures the day your daughter went missing,' she says.

'What? What did you see?'

She shakes her head. 'Nothing, I didn't see anything. But you asked for the CCTV footage and we haven't got it. I just thought – I was taking photos outside on the street, in that little park, near the school. I don't know. It might be nothing.'

'What might be nothing? If you saw something...'

'I didn't. But *you* might see something – it's probably not helpful at all...' She thrusts an object at me. I hold out my hand. It's a memory stick. As soon as I take it from her, she turns and runs back down the road. The street lamps give her twin shadows, splaying out either side of her, and then she turns the corner and disappears.

I run back to the car so quickly, I'm out of breath. 'We need to tell Collier. He doesn't know Jack lied,' I say.

Ollie says nothing, driving faster and faster. I shut my eyes and clench my hands in my lap.

I let Ollie put Ben to bed. I hope it'll help him calm down. I get out my laptop.

'Look,' I say, when he comes back downstairs, grey with exhaustion. 'A girl – Anita – one of the sixth-formers at Ilkley Grammar gave it to me when I went into the newsagent's. It's all the photos she took around the school the day Evie went missing.' They start downloading onto my laptop. There are hundreds. She hasn't edited or deleted any of them. 'It might be nothing.' I echo her words. I can't get our hopes up.

Ollie looks over my shoulder. I click on the Information button.

'I can narrow it down to the ones taken around the time Jack said Evie was picked up.'

I make a folder and drag the pictures taken from 4 to 6 p.m. on Friday into it – just in case there might be something in an earlier photo. There are sixty-three. Ollie pulls up a chair and sits down next to me at the dining-room table. We go through them one by one and then we run them again as a slide show. I'm not sure what we're looking for. I get distracted by the actual photos themselves. The girl has no talent. They're snaps, almost random, but taken with a semi-decent camera. I can't see the point of them. They're not framed properly; I don't know what the subject is supposed to be. You could vaguely say they're street scenes, but since it's Ilkley, they're not particularly gritty or urban. There are bare branches and benches, flower beds and litter; people crossing the road, double-yellow lines; a woman on a mobility scooter. If I were being kind, they remind me of the video of a plastic bag dancing in the breeze that kid in *American Beauty* filmed. I don't feel kind. I put my head in my hands. They're worthless. I'd tried not to hope there was something in them, but I couldn't help myself.

'There!' says Ollie, and jabs the space bar.

The picture shows the railings in front of the school. There's a car bumper in the bottom right corner of the picture. It's slightly blurred as if it's in motion. The photo was taken at four minutes past five. He moves on to the next picture. This one is a close-up of railings and shadows. A cliché. The car isn't there. I swear. Ollie, more patient and methodical than me, selects the following photo. It's similar to the first but the framing is different, it's not so tightly focused, and the car's in it again. It's five minutes past five. The car is still blurred. You can't see what model it is or the driver.

'Can you do anything with it?' asks Ollie. 'I don't know how these things work.'

I import the picture into Photoshop. I enlarge the part with the car and lighten it. I sharpen it, then save a copy. I take the new copy and sharpen it further. I add some contrast and boost the highlights.

'Look, you can see the numbers on the reg now,' says Ollie.

I sharpen and add more contrast until we can make a stab at what they are.

Ollie writes down two different versions of what the registration could be and snatches up his mobile.

'Are you calling Collier?'

'I will. But I'm going to ring Gill first.'

'Why?' I ask. We haven't spoken to Gill since I went to see her on Sunday afternoon. 'She hates us for not sticking up for Andy.'

'She'll get over it when she calms down. She knows the score.' He starts dialling her number. 'Gill's bound to have some contacts that could help us – or access to DVLA software herself. I'm sick of the police not telling us anything. Can you see who the driver is?'

I shake my head. All the sharpening and boosting of the contrast has been good for the hard-edged numerals but it doesn't work for the driver. What was a blur is now an abstract pattern of light and dark, not even recognizable as a human face. I revert to the original photo and make a new copy. This time I work on the section of the car where the driver is. This is much finer work and it's frustrating, because whatever I do doesn't seem to help make him identifiable. After Ollie speaks to Gill he hangs up and comes over. I've enlarged the picture so much, it's become abstract. I turn it black and white. Are those eyes or is it a shadow? There are reflections on the car windscreen and the more I work on giving clarity to the man's feature's, the clearer the reflection becomes – which obscures him even further. I sigh. Ollie steps back.

'Zoom back out.'

I do. I reframe the picture so what we can see of the car fills the entire screen of my laptop. I lean back in my chair as Ollie grasps my shoulders and bends forwards.

'Oh my God,' he says.

I swallow and my heart clenches so hard it's painful. We don't have proof that this is the car our daughter was in. All we can say for sure is that this photo was taken around the time that Jack says Evie left him to run to a car, which pulled up in front of the school gates. Now that the photo is a better size, it's clearer, less abstract. Sometimes you have such a fixed idea in your mind of what you're looking for that you can't see the real thing – even when it's right in front of you.

But I can see it now.

'A woman,' says Ollie.

The figure in the car is dressed in dark flowing clothes that shroud her body. She has a scarf bound tightly around her head and across her face. A niqat. Only her eyes are visible.

'Evie's mother,' I say.

We sit in stunned silence.

'But why would Evie go to a woman?' Ollie says. 'The cards were from a man – they were all signed "Daddy".'

'He could be in the car. Whatever the signal was that was mentioned in the last card, Evie must have recognized it. We can't see the passenger side. Her father could even be in the back seat. It would make sense for him to sit with her, if he wanted to reassure her.' Or drug her, I think, but I don't say it out loud. 'And it makes sense that she – or they – are Muslim. The prayer book,' I remind him.

All this time I'd been imagining Evie's mother as a white junkie prostitute from Leeds. But she could be anyone. A respectable young Muslim woman from Bradford, for instance. I think of Yasira. Haris's sister.

'We need to tell Collier. They haven't been searching for a woman. Or a couple,' I say.

Ollie's mobile rings.

'Thanks. I appreciate it,' he says. 'Yes. Yes. Okay. Got it. Gill,' he tells me. 'She says that one of the registration numbers is valid. The other doesn't exist. The car belongs to a man living in Ilkley.'

The impact of what my husband's just said is overwhelming. That car is registered to someone living here, in this town. Is it a wild goose chase or could Evie really be here, in Ilkley? A darker thought intrudes before I can stop myself. *If she's still alive.*

'What did Collier say?'

'He didn't answer. I left him a message.'

'Let me see.'

Ollie holds out the scrap of newspaper. The address is Panorama Drive. My stomach falls away, as if I'm in a lift dropping ten floors at once. It's the other end of Ilkley from where we live; the road that runs parallel to the moor and ends by Heber's Ghyll and the reservoir. The car is registered to Mr G. Hardgrave. It doesn't seem to stack up. Hardgrave is a proper, old-fashioned Yorkshire name; very few ethnic minorities live in Ilkley, and Panorama Drive is one of the most exclusive parts of the town. You'd have to have bought a house years ago, or be extremely wealthy to live there. What are the chances that a young Muslim woman owns a house on the edge of the moor? But maybe she lives with or is married to a G. Hardgrave who could be Evie's father? I keep thinking of her as young, but I have no idea. It's impossible to tell thanks to the graininess of the photo and her niqat.

'I know where this is. I'm going now,' I say.

Ollie shakes his head.

'I won't leave it until the morning. Not when Evie could be there!'

'I don't want to wait either – but shouldn't we hang on until Collier checks it out?'

'I'm going,' I say, shrugging on my coat and putting my phone in my pocket.

'I'll go,' Ollie says. 'It could be dangerous, you have no idea —'

'I don't care,' I say. 'I have to know. I have to be there if she is, if she is—' I can't finish the rest of my sentence. 'Besides, it's late.' It's almost midnight. 'If a strange man turned up on the doorstep at this time of night, they might not open the door. But a woman on her own – I've got to go!'

'Take Bella with you.'

If this weren't so serious, I'd laugh. The idea of Bella protecting me is ridiculous. But it'll help keep me calm to have her in with me. I call her and she comes trotting over.

'Ring me as soon as—'

'I will.'

I unlock the car and Bella jumps into the passenger seat as if she knows I won't protest. It's not as cold as it has been; the air smells moist, of decaying leaves. There's a silver-gold smudge where the half-moon is obscured behind a dense bank of cloud. My hands are cold, but damp with sweat. I'm tamping down my hope, but it's surging through me, threatening to explode. What if Evie is there? A sparse couple of miles away from me. I don't want to think about what state she'll be in. If they really are her mother and father... Even if they've looked after her well physically, she'll still be missing us, wondering why we abandoned her. Will she ever forgive us? Something like this could scar a child for life, couldn't it? I don't want to think about what might have been done to her. If it's a man and a woman posing as her parents...

I don't drive into town; I keep to the top road, skirting the edge of the moor. I can't see it but I know it's a dark, brooding mass is behind the tarn, the trees, houses, a hotel. At the end of Crossbeck

Road, we rumble over the cattle grid and turn onto Wells Road, and now there is nothing between us and the moor.

A small light, somewhere in the centre of the heath, flickers and wavers: Haris's house. The stand of pines that shield him from the town are blowing in the wind and obscuring, then revealing, the light. I wonder what he's thinking. He must have been released this afternoon, no longer held on a charge of child abduction. He'll have spent the time pacing his croft, reclaiming it for himself, like a predator in his lair. He'll have strode up the path to his studio. Run his hands along the smoothest shafts of metal, an old plough share, the teeth from a digger, spinning orbs from bike cogs – and then he'll have ripped down all the photos he took of me and burnt them. He'll have rued the day he first laid eyes on me – the obsession that led to him being cast as a kidnapper or worse.

I don't know how I feel about Haris now. I believed that he was Evie's real father. When he couldn't recreate his original family – his blood-daughter and me, the wife of his prison dreams – I was convinced he'd poisoned Ben and taken Evie to destroy me. But now? I know Collier doesn't believe that Ben was deliberately poisoned, but it seems too convenient – that Evie was taken just at the moment when Ollie and I could not be with her. But maybe Collier is right and that is far-fetched – after all, if I'd managed to get hold of Andy or one of my mum friends, Evie would have been safe. None of them would have allowed her to walk to a parked car without checking who was in it. And there's no need to invoke a poisoner – as Collier pointed out, spindle trees grow all over Ilkley. Ben could have grabbed at one on the way to school without me noticing.

I can't think about any of this though, because I'm on Panorama Drive, and I'm almost with my daughter! I feel as if Evie is calling me. She's just metres away now. I imagine I can smell her, that particular odour of little girl, like suncream and mushrooms. As I'm driving – too quickly – I can almost see an image of myself running supernaturally fast up the hill, my arms outstretched, calling, 'Evie, my love, Evie!' I imagine myself holding her tightly, feeling her ribs, the sparrow-flutter of her heart.

'Mum, your heart is the same size as your fist,' she told me once in delight, and we both made our hands into fists and held them against our chests and bumped them together: hands as hearts.

The road is narrow and dark and tree-lined. On one side is the wood I walked through with Haris. The Tarmac is slick with a mulch of dead leaves. I force myself to slow down. The houses here, as I remember from my walks across the moor to the Swastika Stone, are large, set back from the road, with huge gardens front and back, surrounded by high fences, above which you can make out the tops of trampolines and stately shrubs. There is one like a sixteenth-century manor house, with mullioned windows, another that's modern: a glass wall and two verandas face towards the moor.

I glance down at the piece of paper in my hand. The address is number one, Panorama Drive. I've passed eight and six; the numbers are growing smaller as I go further. It must be the last house on the street. I've never been this far – I suppose I was always so desperate to get off the road, I'd have slipped down that public footpath between two old stone walls to get to the moor, or gone the other way – woven through the wood to return to town.

I park just before I reach the house and call Bella to come with me. This house is different from the others. It's square and solid, with a short stone wall in front of it; it's so close to the road, it has barely any front garden, but behind it; is a large expanse of lawn. It's made of millstone grit, like ours, but it looks austere. The door is set in the middle, a window either side. It's three stories high, with two attic windows that have their own little roofs. They might have been the servants' quarters in former times. Could Evie be here?

There's a single shrub in one corner, near the gate. There are no lights on and it's hard to see as the nearest street lamp is some distance away. The road ends abruptly just past this house, in a steep, grassy wall. The reservoir must be on the other side. It's not a place I'd want to bring up a child, I can't help thinking – the moor out the back, a wood in front, a sheer-sided reservoir to the left, all at the end of a lethally steep and narrow street without a pavement. It's exposed – the wind hits me as I step away from the car, whistling straight off the heath.

The flagstones leading to the front door are slimy with algae and, in my haste, I nearly slip and fall. I ring the doorbell and hear it clang and echo. I wonder if Evie can hear it too. Is she sleeping? I look up at the windows, but they're shrouded by curtains and there's no movement of the fabric. I ring again and again, and when still no one comes to the door, I bang on it with my fists. What if they've left already? Put Evie in the car and taken her somewhere? I try the door but it's locked. I keep knocking until I feel the skin on my knuckles split. I'm about to go round the back, when a light blazes above my head and the door opens. My heart misses a beat.

An elderly man is standing in front of me. He's wearing paisley pyjamas and a burgundy dressing gown and slippers. His white hair is ruffled and his pink scalp shines through.

'What on earth do you want? Making all this racket.'

'I'm looking for Mr G. Hardgrave.'

'This is he. What do you want at this time of night?' His voice is loud, as if he's slightly deaf or was a headmaster before he retired.

I pause. I'm not sure what to say now. This isn't what I expected – although he does look like a typical resident of Panorama Drive.

'My daughter has gone missing —'

'I'm sorry to hear that. But I haven't seen any unattended children. Goodnight.'

Mr Hardgrave starts to shut the door.

'Wait! You might have seen it on the news. She went missing on Friday. After school.'

'I don't watch the news any more,' he booms. 'Certainly not the local news. I'm sorry about your daughter but I fail to see why you're bothering people at night.'

I'm so desperate, I step forward, ready to push my way into the house. 'Do you own a car with the registration—' I unfold the piece of newspaper Ollie has written the number on.

He cups his hand behind one ear. 'You'll have to speak up. This blasted hearing aid is on the blink.'

I read out the number as clearly and loudly as I can without shouting at him.

'Yes. It's parked in the garage round the side. What has that got to do with your daughter?'

'She may have been picked up from school by someone driving that car. A Muslim woman. There might have been a man in it too.'

'Utter rubbish. That is my car. My wife and I drive it. You can clearly see I'm not Muslim and my wife certainly isn't either. I'm not in the habit of lending my car out, before you ask. Now goodnight.' He slams the door shut.

I stand for a minute in the garden and I want to weep. I was convinced that Evie was here, in this house. Did we get it wrong? It was so hard to see what the letters and numbers were. Maybe our best guess was not the real registration number of the car in Anita's photo. I walk to the end of the road; my feet sink into the mossy turf round the edge of the reservoir. I climb to the top of the slope and look down. Its black surface is scarred with ripples from the wind. It's impossible to tell how deep it is. I stand and stare at the moor. The wind keens and the clouds scud across the sky, shades of shale and slate. There are no stars. I stand there and I cry as if I will never stop.

———

The lights are out in our house when I return, but, as I let myself in, I feel Bella shiver against my leg and thump her tail. Ollie is sitting on the sofa in the dark. He gets up and hugs me tightly. I'm surprised by the fierceness of his embrace. I let myself lean against him, take comfort in the familiar contours of his chest. He kisses me on the top of my head.

'I was worried about you.'

I'm grateful for this moment of care when he wants to know about Evie above all else – and why she's not with me.

'I called Collier straight after you'd gone. He said the car belongs to an elderly Caucasian couple who've lived at that address for thirty-odd years. He's going to send someone over to interview them in the morning, but it looks as if we got the number wrong. I emailed him the photos. They might have some software that could decrypt it.'

I nod. I feel utterly defeated: emptied, hollowed out. Ollie takes my hand and we walk upstairs together. As we go, I see a photo next to my laptop on the dining-room table. It looks as if it's an abstract work of art, slices of dark and a band of light; a fragmented pattern. And then I realize – Ollie's printed Anita's picture. It's the reflection on the car window and, beneath it, a woman's face: the woman who might have taken our daughter.

We go into the bedroom and climb, exhausted and spent, into bed. Ollie rolls onto his side so he's facing me.

'Do you remember when we first brought Evie home?' he says. 'She was so tiny. Her whole fist was the size of my thumbnail. And her eyes were enormous, as if they were too big for her face.'

'Yes,' I whisper. 'Such a strange colour. The green was starting to show through the blue already so they looked kind of cloudy.'

He reaches for my hand and laces his fingers between mine.

'She was só still. Do you remember how worried we were? She never cried and she hardly moved. Just lay there and stared and stared.'

'Yes.'

It's like a story he's telling me. Like the 'Story of You' that I tell Evie – only this is the parents' version.

'We were shattered. We'd been in the hospital with her constantly, watching her in that little Perspex cube. What was it called – an incubator – like she was a creature from Outer Space, growing in a laboratory—'

'Or a princess in a glass box—'

'—when really she was a drug addict. She must have been so tired from fighting the addiction – her poor little system – and when we took her home, she was so fragile and so silent! And then, do you remember the day your mum came round? We were both worried, all we'd been doing was frowning at Evie, and your mum just held her and smiled and smiled at her—'

'And she smiled back.'

'It was the most amazing smile I've ever seen. All gums and huge eyes – and she was happy!'

'So happy! As if she'd suddenly realized that she was okay. It was going to be okay.'

We lie, our legs and arms intertwined, holding each other tightly.

'It's going to be okay,' whispers Ollie into my hair.

# WEDNESDAY: FIVE DAYS AFTER

In the early hours of the morning, I wake. I lie rigid with tension. Ollie's arm and part of his leg are still draped over me and I feel as if I'm being crushed. I manoeuvre his arm from my chest and he grunts in his sleep and rolls over. What if the woman was working *with* Haris? He poisoned Ben to get us out of the way and then he left for Leeds – to set up his so-solid alibi. Meanwhile, she took Evie and is waiting for him – perhaps she thought they'd be together on Monday but the police delayed their rendezvous. But now – now that he's been released... I won't be able to sleep with this turning over in my mind.

I get up and shower and dress. Collier is not going to re-arrest Haris simply because I've had an idea at 4 a.m., or search his house again the day after he's let him walk out of Ilkley police station a free man. He'll need something to convince him. If I knew who this woman was, or what the connection is between her and Haris... I decide to ask Jack and go to the school and see if anyone knows who she is. If someone has been stalking Evie, then one of the teachers might have noticed her before – or maybe it's a coincidence and she's a friend or relative of one of the parents and not involved in our daughter's disappearance at all.

It's too early to call anyone. I make coffee. I scrub Ben's high chair. Ollie fed him last night and it's still smeared with fromage frais and sticky with orange juice. The area around the table looks like a small bomb in a cereal factory has detonated. Ollie only polished the kitchen cupboards. I end up cleaning the entire room. When I open the fridge, it's almost empty. There's the milk, yogurt and juice I bought yesterday; margarine, the rind from some parmesan, a wizened chilli, and half a can of baked beans. I could go to Tesco – it'll be open in ten minutes when nothing else in town will be – and get back in time to give Ben his breakfast before I call in on Jack and go to the school. Leaving at this time means I won't bump into anyone I know. And I can't sit here doing nothing.

Tesco at the best of times is soulless – but it's so much worse at six in the morning. It's not as empty as I thought it would be. Who the fuck shops at 6 a.m.? The fluorescent lights flicker. The shelf upon shelf of coloured cans make my eyes go funny. Everything is hard and shiny and there's so much fucking choice. Why do I have to choose from thirty kinds of granola? Do I want Country Crunch or Rude Health? Raisins and almonds or tropical? Goji berries and chia seeds or Strawberry Surprise? I'll just buy the Tesco range – that'll be easiest. No, wait, there's Tesco Finest*, Tesco Everyday Value and Tesco Free From. What can be so damn fine about granola? You eat it every day and what could it be free from? It hasn't got anything unhealthy in it! What could one possibly take out? Actually, we don't need any fucking granola. We can eat Weetabix. I drop a box into my trolley.

I start to feel waves of panic wash over me: I have no idea what we do need. I don't give a shit about what we eat. I don't even want to eat. I don't know where anything is. I can't make sense of the chaos in my head – it's as if a fog has descended and I'm incapable of joining up the dots – that if we need Weetabix, we'll need milk. Then there's lunch to think of and tea and after that more lunch and tea and snacks – food for Ben; food for Ollie. An endless circus of meals. I grip the handle of the trolley and try to focus. I wish I wasn't here. Shopping for me and Ollie and Ben. Not Evie. If Evie were with me, what would she choose? My mind goes blank. Beyond fish fingers I can't think of anything. She's been gone for four days and five nights. I panic, thinking I can no longer remember what she likes to eat. And then I do. Evie's favourite meal is garlic bread, the tear-and-share kind that Tesco's does in a tray; pizza, peas and sweetcorn, ketchup, followed by vanilla ice cream with strawberry sauce that you have to squirt from a plastic bottle and it always emits that farting sound, which makes her squeal with laughter, blow raspberries and pour even more syrup over her dessert. Topped with marshmallows – if I'm ever soft enough to buy them for her.

I'm starting to breathe faster and faster. If Evie were here with me now, I'd buy her marshmallows. I would drown her in marshmallows. I'd let her eat them for breakfast, lunch and dinner. I miss her so much. I'm starting to wonder whether there's any point in anything any more. Why would I want to be in a world without my child? I'm leaning my forehead on the sharp bit of the trolley, the bit where you're meant to hang your handbag, if you'd remembered to bring it. Tears and snot are dripping off my chin. I can see my scruffy Converse sticking out of my baggy jeans and I notice I'm wearing odd socks. One is stripy and the other has polka dots. I'm not even sure they're both mine. It's exactly the kind of thing that would have made Evie laugh – and that makes me cry even more because I just used the past tense. About my daughter.

Someone taps me on the shoulder. From my position leaning over the trolley handle, I can see this person's shoes. They're the comfy kind you get from specialist shops; flesh bulges between the gaps in the straps. The jeans she's wearing are too pale and wide and short; there's a gap where her ankle bone should be, her calves are encased in skin-coloured tights. I stand up. She's square and wearing a maroon fleece with a zip at the front; her face is doughy.

'I saw you on the news,' she says. 'Your little girl is missing, isn't she?'

I pull a damp tissue out of my pocket and wipe my face.

'Yeah.' She looks around the supermarket, as if checking for an audience. 'I knew it was you. I said to myself, that's the woman off the TV whose daughter was taken. You haven't found her yet, have you, dear?'

I shake my head. 'Not yet.'

'They said they're still looking. Seven, isn't she? Pretty little thing. Doesn't look like you.' I grit my teeth. 'Well, I just wanted to say, we're all praying for you. We're praying you find your little girl.'

'Thank you,' I say, gripping the trolley, ready to push it away from her as fast as I can.

'I read that book, the Madeleine McCann one? Most sex offenders dispose of the kid less than a couple of miles away from the site of the abduction. They haven't found her body, have they? So either he's hidden it well, or there's still hope.'

I lose it. In the middle of Tesco.

'Evie is not dead! My daughter is not fucking dead!' I scream at her.

Her eyes widen and her mouth puckers. She's affronted at my outburst. I manage to control myself enough not to yell obscenities at her.

When I get home, Ollie takes my one paltry shopping bag from me and unpacks it. He places the items on the table: a box of Weetabix and a bottle of vodka. He doesn't say a word.

'I can't find Hannah,' I tell Audrey, the school secretary. 'I've just checked her classroom and it's still locked, and she hasn't replied to my texts. I thought she'd be here by now.'

Audrey had buzzed me in earlier, even though I don't have a child with me. Tragedy can do that to people: make them react in strange ways around you. Now she looks harried and I wonder if it's me. That is the other thing I've noticed: no one knows what to say, and, rather than say the wrong thing, they say nothing and look away.

'She's not here. She called in sick,' Audrey says. 'I'm trying to find a supply teacher.'

For once, her fraught expression has nothing to do with me.

'Oh, I hope she gets better soon. You haven't seen this woman, have you?' I show her the photograph Ollie printed out last night.

She shakes her head. 'I don't recognize her but it's hard to tell. Is it…?' She doesn't know how to phrase it.

'It could be nothing. She was in a car that pulled up outside the school on Friday night.'

Audrey nods and gives me a look full of sympathy. 'I'm sorry I can't be more helpful.'

'Well, perhaps you could be. Can you give me Hannah's address? There's a chance she might know who it is – the woman could be a friend of one of the parents. She might have seen something.'

Audrey shakes her head. 'You know I can't, Zoe.' She looks as if she might cry at being put on the spot like this. She glances up and down the corridor, but no other parents have arrived yet. 'You could ask someone who knows her well, though. Have you heard, Jack's been released?'

She gives me a wobbly smile. She's not sure I'll want to speak to Jack. I nod and thank her.

'I'm going to go round and see him too,' I say.

When I'm in the car, I dial his number.

He clears his throat before answering. 'Zoe. Is there any news?' His voice is hoarse, as if he hasn't spoken since we talked. He sounds both fearful and hopeful.

'No, but I have a photo of a woman who pulled up outside the school, around the time you said Evie left you.'

'Want me to take a look? See if I recognize her?'

He's so eager to help. No matter what he does, though, he's never going to forgive himself. And I'm not sure I ever will.

'Yes. I want to show it to Hannah, too, but she's off sick. Can you —'

'I'll text you her address.'

'Thank you. I'll be with you soon.'

I wonder where Hannah lives. The cheaper houses are the old mill workers' terraces, where Jack lives and my mum used to – but I doubt Hannah could afford one on a teaching assistant's salary. She probably lives in a shared house, or lodges in one of the larger properties in Ilkley. I imagine her in one of the grand houses by the River Wharfe, in someone's garret, overlooking the park and the tennis club. But then, there's no reason she'd actually live here, is there? She could be in any of the surrounding small towns – Guisley, Menston, Otley, Burley – where I grew up.

I check my watch. Ruby has arranged for us to do another statement to the press at two this afternoon. I'll need to be back in time to wash and change into clean clothes, maybe even put matching socks on – and we have to drop Ben at Andy's and then write and rehearse our statement with Ruby. I should probably go straight to Jack's now – if there's time I can see Hannah – otherwise I'll have to wait until after the press release.

I turn the key in the ignition and my phone rings. I think it's going to be Jack but it's Ruby.

'Zoe? I'm outside your house. Where are you? Ollie said you'd gone out but he didn't know where.'

'Can I give you a call back?'

'Listen, Zoe, it's really important you stay at home. We need to know where you are at all times. Also, I've got the name of a therapist we use. A grief counsellor. We've found him really helpful in situations like these. Can you come back? We could —'

I can't breathe. Grief is not generic, I am not a case history, I want to scream at her.

'I don't need a fucking grief counsellor,' I say. 'Evie is not dead.'

I hang up and check my text messages. There're two from Ollie wanting to know where I am, and a missed call from home. The third one is from Jack – it's Hannah's address. At first, I'm confused. I think Ollie must have sent it too. I double-check. No, it's definitely from Jack and he's put 'Hannah's address' at the start of the text in a teacher-like way. My heart lurches. I wind through the back streets onto Wells Road. In spite of the mild night, it's growing colder by the minute. The damp Tarmac is developing a glassy sheen, where few people have driven, and the dew is turning to ice. The wind has picked up. A flock of gulls is scattered over the moor. A few dank leaves cling to the bare branches above my car; eddies of them swirl across the windscreen. I ease into first gear and inch up the steep road. There's no way I can go to see Jack first now that I know where Hannah lives.

I pull up outside one Panorama Drive. There are frost flowers blooming in the corners of the windows and the grass in the front lawn is sharp-edged with ice. Could Hannah White be the Hardgraves' lodger? Ollie and I might have got the car registration wrong but it does seem like an odd coincidence. I'll call Collier as soon as I've spoken to them to see if they've found the real registration number. Either way, coincidence or not, I have a feeling Mr Hardgrave will not be pleased to see me again.

I ring the bell. This time I hear light, quick footsteps across the wooden floor in the hall and the door opens. An elderly woman stands in front of me. Even though it's early and she must be retired, she's dressed with precision – in a tweed skirt, a pale, shiny blouse and a baby-pink cardigan. She has a silk printed scarf knotted around her throat, pearl earrings, and her hair is set in that strange, helmet-like way that some older women favour.

'Can I help you?' she asks.

She has an aristocratic accent – there's no trace of Yorkshire in it.

'I don't suppose you have a lodger, do you?'

'What a strange question. No, we do not.' She starts to shut the door, frowning with displeasure.

'Wait!' I put my hand out to stop her. 'I'm looking for Hannah White. Her colleague told me she lived here.'

She stops and looks me up and down. 'Who might you be?'

'I'm Zoe Morley. Hannah teaches my daughter —'

'Oh.' Her face changes. 'Yes. I saw you in the paper. Your little girl has gone missing.'

'Yes.'

'And you were round here last night, asking my husband something about our car.'

'Is Hannah here? It's really important that I speak to her. This is the address Jack Mitchell gave me but I don't know if it's a mistake and maybe he's missed a number out and she's at another house on Panorama Drive. Do you know where she lives?'

'Have you tried the school? You said she taught your daughter.'

I wince at the way she's used the past tense to describe Evie. I try to keep my voice even.

'Yes. They said she's off sick today.'

'They shouldn't have given you her address.'

'They didn't. Jack gave it to me. He knows it's crucial I speak to her. Hannah might be able to help us.'

I'm growing increasingly desperate. She seems to know who Hannah is, so why is she being cagey with me?

Mrs Hardgrave glances behind her and half closes the door.

'Hannah is our daughter. She was living with us. We've got a self-contained flat so she's been able to come and go as she pleases.

It's in the attic. She wanted more independence though. She moved out recently.'

I hadn't realized that Hannah is married. It seems odd that Mrs Hardgrave didn't say 'Hannah and her husband.' She seems too young to be divorced. I guess she kept her husband's name. I try to concentrate.

'Can you please give me Hannah's new address? It's really important.'

'If she's ill, I'm not sure you should be disturbing her, but—' she holds up one hand, the knuckles crooked, the veins raised, 'I can see you want to speak to her. If you wait one moment, I'll come with you. I'd like to see if she needs anything. Do you mind dropping me back here afterwards?'

I shake my head. I'd say anything at this point. Mrs Hardgrave disappears inside and shuts the door behind her. I blow on my hands and stamp my feet. I look up at the house, at the peaked attic windows. Now I'm here in daylight, I can see a wrought-iron staircase that spirals from the top floor, round the back of the house. Hannah must have had a fantastic view of the moor from there. I wonder what would have made her give up a rent-free flat in such a stunning location when she would only have had minimal interaction with her parents.

I wonder if this is going to lead anywhere or not. The woman in the car might not be connected to Evie at all. Even if she is, how likely is it that Hannah would recognize her? If the woman in the niqat knows Haris, I doubt Hannah would be any help since she's doesn't know Haris – she said she'd never heard of him when I told her whose preview I was going to when she babysat for us. But then there's the car registration. Could Hannah have lent her parents' car to a friend?

Mrs Hardgrave returns, wearing a matching tweed jacket and carrying a casserole dish.

'If she's not well, she's probably not looking after herself properly,' she says, giving me a tight smile.

On the way to the car, I fight the urge to take Mrs Hardgrave's elbow since the pavement is so icy – she doesn't look as if she'd welcome my assistance. Once she's fastened her seat belt and tucked a tea towel round the dish, which she rests on her lap, she says, 'Do you know Valley Drive?'

'Yes.'

'Well, head there and then I'll direct you.'

'I appreciate this,' I say.

I look back at the house one last time. I half expect Mr Hardgrave to be staring furiously out of the window at me. And that's when I see it. The single shrub in the front garden, the one I'd seen the outline of last night. It's a spindle tree. I grip the steering wheel and remember Collier's words: it's a poisonous plant that grows in practically every garden in Ilkley. Mrs Hardgrave doesn't speak as we drive through town. I wonder if she hasn't commiserated with me because, like everyone else, she can't think of what to say.

We turn into Valley Drive.

'I didn't know Hannah was married.'

'I beg your pardon?' she says. Her voice is brittle.

'White. She's Hannah White.'

'Oh. I see. She changed her name after she left home. She didn't much care for Hardgrave.' Her tone is dry and final. She angles her body away from me and stares out of the window. 'Slow down. It's left after the Wool Secretariat.'

We pass a huge, glass-fronted building. Directly over the entrance is a massive sculpture in bronze turned green-gold with age. It's of curly-horned sheep; the largest ram faces outwards, two stories high. The metal mural runs round the sides too, telling the story of wool, depicting the textile trade in a Soviet Socialist Realism style. The Wool Secretariat is what my mother called this building too,

I think, even though it's now owned by some chemical company. I turn left as instructed and left again. Weirdly, the street we are now in is Rombald's View. The flats here are built of pale orange brick, with bars masquerading as verandas in front of the windows. There are no gardens, only a hedge and parking spaces. Over this soulless block looms the Secretariat, panel after panel of glass. It feels creepy, as if we are being spied on. Although I can't see a single office worker, I can make out acres of strip lighting.

'Park here,' says Mrs Hardgrave, pointing. She hands me the casserole for a moment while she clicks open the gold clasp of her clutch and takes out a set of keys. 'Hannah may be in bed,' she says.

If she's trying to make me feel guilty, it doesn't work. I don't care how ill Hannah is – and she can't possibly be too sick to take thirty seconds to look at a photo and answer my questions. I know she'll want to help. She loves Evie.

Mrs Hardgrave rings the bell but when no one answers the intercom, she lets us in. The stairs are covered in that hard-wearing brown carpet you find in municipal buildings. I hate the austere, modernism of the place, the miserliness of the size of the windows, the cookie-cutter layout of the building. I'm aware that I'm focusing on these trivial details to block out thoughts of Evie and to tamp down my hope that Hannah will know who this woman is. Or come up with reasons why the car was registered to the Hardgraves at Hannah's old address… and who was in it.

On the top floor, Mrs Hardgrave stops outside the door to Hannah's flat and knocks crisply. When there's no reply, she unlocks it.

'She must be very ill,' she says. 'Wait here.'

The door opens straight into a sitting room. I step inside and close it behind me.

My phone rings in my pocket. Ollie. Another missed call from Ruby. I turn it to silent. There's a small kitchen and a bathroom leading directly out of the living room. Mrs Hardgrave puts the casserole on the counter and walks to the far end, disappearing into what I'm guessing must be Hannah's bedroom. I set the black and white photo of the woman in the niqat on a coffee table and look around. The floor is covered with fake wood. Apart from the table, there's a small TV and a brown sofa and armchair, an uplighter lamp in the corner and an Ikea bookcase with a lamp on it and a few books. There are net curtains hanging in front of the window, which looks out onto the street. To say it's spartan, would be an understatement. There's virtually nothing here that would give any indication of Hannah's personality. It looks like a show home. The only thing missing is a vase of fake flowers.

Mrs Hardgrave is frowning. She pulls the net curtain aside and looks out. 'Her car's not here. She must have popped out to the shops.' Her shoes make virtually no sound as she goes back into the kitchen and puts the casserole in the fridge. 'We might as well wait. I doubt she'll be long. Shall I make us a cup of tea?'

'I'm going to call her,' I say, taking out my phone. I can't stay here.

'She's probably buying herself some Lemsip and paracetamol, poor darling. Leave it a few minutes, I'm sure she'll be back soon. There's no point ringing her if she's driving.'

I pivot on my heel. The only splashes of colour are the framed photographs on the white walls. I walk over to one. It's a majestic-looking snow-capped mountain; the sky behind is a brilliant blue. It's not a snap – it's beautifully framed, floating on white board and with a white-waxed wooden frame. The artist has signed it. I look at the next one. It's also impossibly exotic-looking. It's of apricots drying in the sun. My heart starts to beat in my chest; it's so loud I feel as if Mrs Hardgrave will be able to hear it. The one on the opposite wall is of a string of chillies, ruby-red, beginning to shrivel in the sun. They're identical to the pictures Haris has in his house. They're framed the same way, too, and signed by the artist. I remember thinking I'd never seen a name like it before; what was she called? It's definitely the same person: Hajar Abyadh. They're all pictures of the Hunza Valley in Pakistan, similar to the photographs Haris bought to flesh out the lie that he'd spent the last seven years in Shangri-La.

There's one more photo I haven't looked at. It's on the wall by Hannah's bedroom door. I walk over to it. The sky is the same shade of cerulean-blue; there are orange flowers in the foreground. It's the same photo as the last card Evie received, telling her to wait for the signal. I'm breathing hard now, as if I've been sprinting. This must be the connection. Haris knows Hajar Abyadh. Hajar Abyadh is the Muslim woman in our photograph. And Hannah must know her too. She may have lied to me about not knowing Haris. Did she introduce him to Hajar? Whatever the truth is, Haris and Hajar have taken my child and Hannah must know how to contact Hajar. But why use the Hardgraves' car?

I ring Hannah, but there's still no answer. I hear Mrs Hardgrave come out of the kitchen. She's standing, a cup of tea in each hand, looking down at the photograph. Carefully she sets the cups down.

'Your tea,' she says. She stops when she sees the photograph I'm looking at.

'Do you know where Hannah is?'

'No, of course not. She's probably in that pharmacy on Valley Drive. I understand you're agitated, but I don't believe she'll be long. It's not like Hannah to take time off work. Do you take sugar?'

'No, it's not, is it?' I say, because I suddenly have a stream of images of Hannah at the start of the school year: of her with a red nose, tissue in hand, her voice nasal; bent over double, coughing; pale and husky-voiced, sucking throat lozenges. There are so many bugs that you catch from children, particularly if you haven't been a teacher for long, and Hannah struggled through all of them and came to work.

'Why don't you tell me what this is about?' Mrs Hardgrave gestures to the photo and stands still, her feet in her orthotic shoes tight together, her gold-ringed hands clasped in front of her.

I have a cold, sick feeling in the pit of my stomach. There's something I'm not getting. There's something I'm missing. This place gives me the creeps. It's so unlike where I imagined Hannah would live...

I wheel round and bang open the bathroom door. It's empty. It's small, with only a shower and a toilet. I catch sight of a chrome wire basket; not the kind of bin you'd normally find in a single woman's apartment, where she'd want to hide the detritus of her life from view: all those cotton buds and make-up wipes and sanitary pads... There's something in the bin. I lift it out. It's an empty box of dark brown hair dye. I drop it immediately. I run into Hannah's room. She's not here. Of course she's not here. I'm starting to feel really frightened. Because I know who Hannah really is and where she might be now.

'What on earth are you doing?' Mrs Hardgrave is behind me.

The window is open a fraction and the net curtains are billowing; an icy breeze funnels through the gap so the room smells of frost; there's not a trace of Hannah, of her beautiful lily perfume. The bed is made, the bedspread neatly folded, lilac cushions scattered across it. It's not like the bed of someone who is ill and has crawled out to the nearest Boots for ibuprofen. There's a wardrobe and a chest of drawers and two side tables with a lamp on either side. Above the chest is another photograph of a mountain range in Pakistan. I throw open the wardrobe door. There's a shalwar kameez hanging up, slightly wrinkled as if it has been recently worn, the scarf puddled on the bottom of the wardrobe. I swing round and start yanking open all the drawers. In one of the side tables, in the drawer that normally holds a Gideon Bible in a hotel, there's a book. It's not the Bible. I take it out and turn it over in my hands. I'm trembling.

'I'm going to have to ask you to leave,' says Mrs Hardgrave.

I hold it up so she can see it. It's a red prayer book, the same as Evie's. It's not hers, though: there's no inscription inside.

Mrs Hardgrave's face seems to cave in upon itself. She pauses for what feels like a long time and then she says, 'In Pakistan they call her Hajar Abyadh. It was the name they chose when she converted to Islam. Abyadh means "white" and Hajar is "stone". She had to be like a stone – hard and strong – to defeat her drug addiction.' She's pale and shrinks into herself.

'Did you know?'

'No, I did not,' she says, attempting to muster some spirit, but she can't meet my eye. She pulls her baby-pink cardigan tightly around herself.

'Where is she?'

'What you don't seem to understand is that I lost my daughter when she was eighteen and became a drug addict. She left home. Moved in with some degenerates in a squat in Leeds... I didn't hear from her for two years. Two years! Your daughter has been missing for five days!'

I want to shake her. The need to find Evie, to find Hannah, is overwhelming.

'Hannah only contacted us when she was twenty to tell us that she was pregnant,' continues Mrs Hardgrave.

She's gazing out of the window at the Wool Secretariat. She misses my murderous look.

'She was still on drugs. I advised her to give the baby up for adoption and, at first, she was happy to go along with that. She could barely care for herself, let alone a child, and she was so young. But when her daughter was born, she fell in love with her. She called her Mary.' She frowns and the lines around her lips deepen, her face sags. 'She changed her mind about the adoption at the last minute, but I wouldn't let her. She's never forgiven me.' She looks at me then, her pale grey eyes full of loathing. 'After you took her daughter, I suggested she change her name, make a fresh start. That's when she became Hannah White. We've become accustomed to it now. It's been seven years. She lived with us for a short time but it was extremely difficult. She was still on drugs, stealing from us, selling our possessions to fund her habit. She hated me and Geoffrey – well, the two of them have never seen eye to eye. She read somewhere about this Shangri-La, this community in Pakistan, where everyone is healthy and lives until they're at least a hundred. They only eat organic food. The water is pure – straight from the heart of the glacier. The Hunza Valley. Of course, when she got there, she saw it wasn't like that at all. They were like any developing country – in need of better education, health care and more to eat. But those people cured her, you know.'

She picks up her cup of tea and takes a sip. I want to knock it out of her hands.

'My husband and I didn't see Hannah again until she turned up on our doorstep two years ago, saying she'd trained as a teacher. We were delighted, of course. She'd been drug-free for years. She'd taken her A levels, done a PGCE. It was a new beginning. We offered her the flat in our house, rent-free. We thanked God for returning our daughter to us. I didn't realize she was a Muslim.' She holds up one thin, lined hand. 'But I'm not surprised she converted to Islam. That community helped her when no one else could or would. I don't agree with it – we brought her up as strictly C of E – but she always was rebellious. She refused to go to church from the age of thirteen. My husband still doesn't know. He'd have disowned her. I told her to keep it a secret. A few weeks ago, she said she couldn't hide her true self any more. I begged her not to tell anyone, particularly not Geoffrey. We had a huge row and she moved out. That's the last time I saw her.'

'I don't believe you,' I say. 'How does she know Haris? Why does he have the same photographs in his house?'

'They're stunning pictures, aren't they? I'm afraid I don't know anyone called Haris. Hannah was trying to raise money to support herself while she was applying to work as a teaching assistant at Evie's school. She took her photographs along to a Ms Jennifer Lockwood who owns the gallery in Ilkley. Ms Lockwood said she wouldn't represent her – but she bought a full set of her pictures. Maybe she sold them to the gentleman you mentioned.'

I see it now – the landscapes of the Hunza Valley that would make Haris's lie look compelling and safeguard Jenny's reputation.

'But how did she find *us*? How did she find Evie?'

Mrs Hardgrave looks ashamed for a moment, but then she rallies. 'You and I had an appointment,' she says. 'It was shortly after Evie was born.'

I remember now. We'd wanted to learn something – anything – about Evie's family, so that we would have a story to tell her about where she'd come from. The social worker had set up a meeting with Evie's grandmother.

'But you never showed up!'

'I discovered that Hannah hadn't told the truth about where she was from on the forms. She'd said she grew up near Bolton in Lancashire. The social workers thought that was far enough away from Ilkley, where you were from originally, for the adoption to go ahead. I didn't want them to know she'd lied. I thought I might accidentally give her away. In any case, I couldn't bear to meet you. I didn't want any kind of emotional tie or connection to you. But you're wrong. I did go to the meeting. I saw you through the half-open door. I stayed for a couple of minutes and listened. When Hannah was at her lowest, her most despairing, I told her what I'd seen.'

'What did you tell her?' I whisper.

'I described you. I'd overheard that you were an artist. I recognized your accent. It wasn't hard for a clever girl like Hannah to find out who you were.'

'My God! She engineered the entire thing!' I scream into Mrs Hardgrave's face, unable to contain myself for a second longer. 'She sent Evie presents and cards from "her daddy" so everyone would think Evie's father took her.'

'You can't blame her for wanting to give her only child a present!' says Mrs Hardgrave.

She's animated and, for a moment, I see what she'd have been like as a younger woman, how she must have looked when her cheeks were firm and unlined and there were no shadows beneath those large, grey eyes; I see her daughter in her features.

'She manipulated us all! She poisoned our son, Ben! She needed a diversion so she could take Evie – she used the berries from the spindle tree in your garden.'

'You have no proof of that! Hannah loves children.'

I can see it now. Haris had nothing to do it with it; the fact he'd been stalking me was a helpful coincidence for Hannah. He created a diversion. But didn't she use that time well! Looking after Ben for us, so she'd know exactly what stage the investigation had reached – and getting close to us so no one would suspect her. And once Haris was released, she knew it was time to leave with Evie. She could be fleeing the country right now.

'And you helped her,' I say, as I push past her.

Where are you going?' The surety in her voice has gone.

'I'm going to find her.'

'Let me come with you,' she says.

'No.'

I open the front door and I'm about to run down the stairs, when she hobbles towards me. 'Please. I want to help you find her.'

'Then tell me where she is,' I say.

She hesitates for a moment. 'The airport. She's taking Evie to Pakistan.'

And even though this is what I suspected, I'm frozen with fear. If Hannah takes Evie with her, we may never find her again.

'It looks like a wonderful place: the Hunza Valley.' She sounds wistful, as if, in spite of her tweed skirt and sensible shoes, she wished she too could have trekked through a glacial valley and eaten apricots picked fresh from the tree.

'Not for my daughter! You have to tell me when she's leaving.'

Mrs Hardgrave glances at her watch. It's on a thin gold chain and the face is minute. She peers at the hands and I want to slap her.

'It depends which flight she managed to book. The next one's in forty minutes.'

I race out of the flat. She's slower than me. She clutches the bannister rail to help her down the stairs.

'Please,' she calls again. 'Wait for me. I can help.'

I ring Ollie and explain as fast as I can what's happened, then tell him to ring Collier. I'm still speaking when Mrs Hardgrave eases herself into the front seat of the car. 'Bring Ben. Don't let him out of your sight. I'll see you there.'

Mrs Hardgrave glances at me. Her face is pale and a layer of powder cakes her skin.

The one advantage of Hannah's flat is that it's close to the A65. It's mid-morning and the traffic is light. I can get to the airport in twenty minutes if I put my foot down. It's twenty minutes more time than I've got. I feel sick with fear that I'll be too late. The roads are icy – they haven't been gritted yet – but I have to hope that enough traffic has passed to keep us from skidding. Mrs Hardgrave's knuckles are white. I press the accelerator to the floor as the car struggles up the steep climb below Otley Chevin. I glance up at the lowering grey sky, heavy with the threat of snow. Above us great grey granite rocks are lined up on the skyline; so similar to the Cow and Calf, these massive outcrops look as though they too might tumble down this treacherously steep hill and smash us to smithereens.

'Hannah kept Evie in your flat, while she waited for the right time to take her out of the country,' I say.

'Why would she do that when she had a place of her own?' Mrs Hardgrave says.

'Because it diverted suspicion away from her. She couldn't take a child to her flat – it's overlooked by all those other apartments and by the Wool Secretariat. And the neighbours living below her would have heard Evie during the day. But it was a fantastic alibi – coming and going from her new place without a child. And she could easily hide Evie in your house.'

'She was not in our house!'

'With the moor behind you, the reservoir next to you, a wood in front – no one would have noticed Hannah taking Evie there, or heard any noise during the day when she was at work or at our house. She borrowed your car to pick Evie up from school. As you said, she could come and go as she pleased. And how else to explain the scrap of fabric on the moor? Jack lent Evie a *Frozen* costume, and Hannah must have taken it to make her feel at home. Evie escaped, wearing her princess outfit. But Hannah found her and brought her back. She never meant Evie to stay in your flat on the edge of the moor for so long – she thought she'd be flying to Pakistan at the weekend. But Evie was there for four whole days. Your husband wouldn't have heard her, particularly not if his hearing aid wasn't working properly. Or if you broke it. But there's nothing wrong with *your* hearing. Once you realized that Evie was there, you helped Hannah. You covered for her. You thought you could win your daughter back.'

Mrs Hardgrave twists the gold crucifix on the chain round her neck. We pull up at the traffic lights at the top and I drum my fingers impatiently on the steering wheel. I hope to God that Collier and Clegg, with their flashing blue light, reach the airport before I do.

'May I see a picture of her? Of Evie?' she asks.

'There's one in my purse,' I say through gritted teeth.

It can hardly matter now. It might even do some good – win Mrs Hardgrave over so that she helps us find Hannah in time.

My handbag is in the footwell; she opens it and looks inside without touching anything, then delicately takes the photo out of my purse. She holds it with both hands and strokes the picture with her thumbs. The gesture reminds me of when Evie went on a school trip to Hesketh Farm Park. She'd come home, brimming with excitement, and described how you have to hold a baby chick, cupping it in the palms of your hands, leaving your thumbs free to caress its feathers.

'She's beautiful,' Mrs Hardgrave says. She continues to hold the photograph and wipes away a tear with her handkerchief.

We're here. I screech to a halt outside the entrance. I abandon the car and Hannah's mother and run inside. How can I find Evie? I can't get through Security. I scan the departures board of Leeds Bradford Airport but there are no direct flights to Pakistan. Hannah would have to get a connecting flight but I don't know where to. If you were going to the Hunza Valley, which airport is nearest? I have no idea. Would Mrs Hardgrave have told me if I'd asked her? The only place I've ever heard of in Pakistan is Karachi. My only hope is that they haven't left yet.

Once Haris was released without charge and the alert on the airports scaled down, Hannah would only have had a small window of time to book tickets, so she might not have been able to fly yet. Even so, no one has been looking for a *woman* travelling with a small girl. I run over to the nearest security guard.

'I think my daughter is being smuggled out of the country. I need you to check the records, see who is booked in to fly or if anyone has already flown to Pakistan. A woman with a small girl, about seven years old.'

'We don't fly to Pakistan,' he says.

'I can see that! But you must have a list of connecting flights.'

'Which airport?'

He's young, with a broad, Bradford accent. His name tag reads 'Jareed Akbhar'.

'I've no fucking idea, Mr Akbhar! You might have heard about her on the news. Evie Morley. She's been missing since Friday. I believe she's been or is about to be smuggled out of the country. I need you to start looking for all the connecting flights to *any* city in Pakistan.'

Jareed, who is tall, with a buzz cut and close-cropped facial hair, bends slightly towards me. 'Ma'am... checking all the women with small children who have flown or are about to fly to any airport in Pakistan on any connecting flight—'

'Peshwar or Islamabad,' says a voice behind me. 'They're the nearest international airports to the Hunza Valley. Start there.'

I swing round. It's Clegg. Collier is a few paces away, lumbering towards us, a man whose girth doesn't make running easy. He's on his mobile. Clegg jerks his thumb at him.

'He's on the phone to the airport police. Won't be long. And Ruby is on her way.'

I hear someone calling my name. It's Ollie, carrying Ben, running towards us. When he reaches us, he leans over to kiss me and Ben stretches out his arms.

'I came as soon as I could.'

I cuddle Ben and inhale the scent of his soft hair. He smells of Johnson's baby lotion and Cheesy Puffs. Over his blond curls, I see Hannah's mother, standing a few feet away, holding her clutch like a shield.

'Come with me,' says Jareed.

He takes us through to the control room and sits down at a vacant terminal. He starts typing and scrolling through screens. He speaks to another security official, who joins him. Collier comes over.

'They're going through CCTV,' he tells me.

The wait is interminable. Ben wriggles and arches his back. When I can no longer hold him I pass him to Ollie.

'Two flights left this morning,' Jareed says. 'There's one more, connecting from Manchester. Boarding in five. There's no one called Evie Morley on the plane and she wasn't on the previous flights.'

He looks up at me and then at Clegg.

Collier says, 'Search for a woman travelling with a child aged seven or eight – but no other companion.'

'That will take time, sir,' he says.

'We haven't got time!' I shout. 'The plane's boarding in five minutes!'

Jareed shrugs off his jacket. He has sweat patches under the arms.

'Put a hold on the flight,' says Collier.

Jareed glances at an officer who'd been listening on the other side of the room. 'Bit above my pay grade.'

His superior holds his hand out to Collier. 'Dave Ludlow. We need sufficient grounds. Is she a terrorist?'

'How about child abduction?' It's Ruby. She's out of breath; her dark curly hair is sticking out in all directions.

Ludlow picks up the phone and dials through to the gate.

I'm looking at the CCTV footage, not the one Clegg and a security guard are going through, but the live feed from the airport.

Jareed asks me quietly, 'I don't suppose you've got any idea what name the woman who's abducted your daughter is using? Any ideas at all?'

'Try Hajar Abyadh.'

'Can you spell it?' He starts checking the flight details. 'Nothing under that name for the flights that left yesterday.'

My eyes flick from screen to screen. There are so many people. It's hard to focus. Please let Evie be here, please let me spot her.

'No one called Hajar Abyadh is on today's flight either.'

I look down at him. I was so sure that was the name she'd use. 'What about Hannah White?' says Ollie. 'Try that.'

I shake my head. 'It's not Hannah, she won't be using Hannah. Can you show me the gate for Manchester?' I ask Ludlow.

He points to screen seven. 'It's that one, love.'

It's a small room, with four rows of seats. It's packed. People are queuing down the middle, ready to board. I can't see all the passengers who are standing and waiting, so I scan everyone in the seats. My heart is thudding, the beat pulses in my teeth. What if I miss her? What if I can't see her and she gets on that plane? We might lose our daughter for ever. I'm looking for a woman in a hijab with a child; a woman with long brown hair like my daughter's, and a child, my child, who I know so well. I know every inch of her body: the dimple in her right cheek, the freckles in the shape of a flower on her forearm, her bony collar bone, her elfin face, her wide-set eyes. There are so many women wearing shalwar kameez, draped in scarves, carrying or ushering children. I can't see her. I can't see Evie.

I look round the office we're in. Ben is crawling under the tables; the room is packed – there's Collier, Clegg, a couple of other officers, and several security guards – all focused on the screens in front of them. The police alert with Evie's photo is posted on the wall. Mrs Hardgrave is standing in the corner, the light from the CCTV screens flickering over her face, glinting on the gold cross round her neck.

'You said you wanted to help.'

'I do. It's why I'm here.' Her tone is clear and crisp but it doesn't hide the tremor in her voice.

'I don't mean help Hannah, Mrs Hardgrave, I mean help Evie. You need to tell us Hannah's name.' Mrs Hardgrave is silent. 'You said she changed her name but you weren't talking about her Arabic name. What was her real name?'

She hesitates fractionally. 'Jane Hardgrave.'

'Jane Hardgrave. Travelling with a child,' I say to Jareed.

And at that moment I see her. Even though she's swathed in fabric, her petite frame shrouded in a voluminous shalwar kameez that hides her curves, and she has a scarf tightly wrapped round her face, I recognize her. The long straight hair showing underneath, which she dyed brown last night, those pale green eyes, the small straight nose, her soft, plump cheeks; for one moment she seems to be looking right at the camera. And my heart starts to break because I see then, for the first time, how like Evie she is... there is no question about it, Evie looks like her mother. Her real mother. Hannah drapes the scarf over her face and disappears into the throng, dragging a small girl behind her.

'Evie!' I shout.

'Jane Hardgrave,' Jareed says, reading from the screen, 'travelling to Peshwar with her seven-year-old daughter, Mary Hardgrave.'

Collier is bellowing but Ludlow is already on the intercom, and while we all watch the screen, two of the check-in staff peel away from the desk and walk down the room towards Hannah White, née Jane Hardgrave.

Collier, Clegg and Ludlow run to the gate. Ruby commands an electric car and demands Jareed drive it. Ollie, Ben, Ruby, Mrs Hardgrave and I climb aboard. Ben is entranced by the flashing lights and the siren, and stands on Ollie's lap to try to touch them, screaming with delight. Ollie, clutching him to his chest with one hand, reaches over to hold mine with the other. His face is wet with tears.

'I can't believe it. I can't believe we're going to see her in a minute—'

I grip his hand tightly. 'It's like she's been missing forever.'

I can almost sense the imprint of her body, how she'll feel when I hug her. I can't believe that Mrs Hardgrave is with us too.

She's sitting directly behind me. I want to slap her; I even start tensing my fist, but Ben plants a spitty kiss on my cheek. I lift him onto my lap.

'I really thought she'd have flown under her Arabic name, Hajar Abyadh,' says Ruby, frowning, 'especially as she's dressed as a Muslim.' Mrs Hardgrave looks at her as if she's an imbecile. Ruby's eyes widen. 'Of course! It's difficult and expensive to get a fake passport and she had a copy of Evie's birth certificate, so she used her original passport and got Evie one in the name she gave her when she was born.'

Jareed takes a shortcut closed to the public. We barrel through a door and back out into the main body of the airport. We're surrounded by people. The noise is overwhelming. Jareed puts the siren back on and tourists, wheeling vast suitcases and hauling bags with travel pillows bursting out of them, move slowly and with bad grace, out of our way. We must be so close to the gate, I want to leap out of the car and sprint towards my daughter. I know I can't – we've been given strict instructions to stay put until we get to the departure lounge, since we haven't cleared Security.

'She must have been planning it for years,' says Ollie. 'Tracking Evie down, getting a job at the same school as her, befriending our daughter so she would trust her—' He chokes on his words and can't continue.

I take the prayer book out of my handbag and slap it into Mrs Hardgrave's lap.

'Your daughter might need this where she's going.'

She flinches but says nothing.

We're at the end of the departure lounge and the gate is in front of us. The place is so crowded, the car is moving slowly. I leap out and start running towards the entrance. Two airport officials step forward but Ruby is behind me. She flashes her badge at them and they back away and I'm inside.

'Evie!' shouts Ollie. He's behind me, holding Ben.

She's there, sitting on the seats at the side with a female police officer. She's wearing a beige shalwar kameez with a dark brown chiffon scarf, edged in gold embroidery, draped around her face and neck. She doesn't turn towards us and I falter for a moment, and then I'm next to her, crushing her against me and whispering, 'Evie, Evie, my love,' over and over again. She's unresponsive and when I look at her properly, she stares up at me, wide-eyed; her pupils are pinpricks and her irises are glassy. Hannah would have had to give her sedatives over the past few days to keep her quiet and to get her on to the plane.

'Evie!' Ben screams. He wriggles out of Ollie's grip and comes toddling over, his arms outstretched. 'Evie!'

He hurls himself at her, his arms wrap tightly around her stomach. She looks down and gives a goofy smile of recognition. When she tries to touch him, her hands are floppy, as if she has no control over them. Then she holds out her arms to me and starts to cry.

'Mummy,' she says. 'My mummy.'

They drag me away from you. I hold on to you for as long as I can, but they prise my fingers from your arms, from your clothes. I'm screaming. I can't breathe. The pain is so intense. It takes two of them to hold me. A large man comes over, his face is red, his eyes are grey. He's accompanied by a younger police officer, tall and thin with ginger hair. I try to look past them, to you, but they bar the way.

The older man clips handcuffs on me. He says, 'I'm arresting you, Hannah White, née Jane Hardgrave, for attempted child abduction. You have the right to remain silent when questioned. Anything you say or do may be used against you in a court of law—' And when he's finished reading me my rights, he leans forward and whispers, 'The sentence is seven years. We'll be pushing for the maximum penalty.'

I start to cry. How much have I gone through to get here, to this moment? Leaving my parents and my home town, everyone and everything I knew, giving up my identity, travelling to the other side of the world to a country that was alien to me. Under that harsh sun my pale skin burnt; my hands, unused to manual labour, blistered. As the drugs left my system, I had hallucinations, convulsions; I thought I was going to die. But what kept me going was the image I had of you: my baby girl. My daughter. One day old. Stolen from me.

I swore that I would get you back. Whatever it took. However many years. And I did it. I defeated the drugs. I became a valuable member of the community in the Hunza Valley. I converted to Islam. I made a pilgrimage to Mecca. I prayed to Allah for my little girl to return to me. I struggled through university. I searched for you.

After I'd graduated I came home to see my parents for the first time in five years. My mother broke down and apologized for helping to take you away from me. She told me she'd seen the woman who adopted you, and that she was a blonde artist from West Yorkshire.

'She had the same horrid accent as those children you used to play with at school,' she told me.

When I did some research, I found Zoe Butterworth, and then I knew Allah was on my side, because she had moved back to Ilkley with her two children and her husband. I was trying to find out her address when I saw you playing in a park by the river; I've told you this bit already, haven't I? How the shock of recognition was so strong, I thought my heart would stop. How I knew who you were immediately. My flesh and blood. My daughter.

I tried and tried to get a job at your school. I waited an entire year for a vacancy. I spoke to the head repeatedly. In the end, I buried my pride and told my father, your granddad. He talked to the school's board of governors, and in September I started work as a teaching assistant in your class.

Even then, when I was so close to you, I had to be careful. I couldn't show you any favouritism. I couldn't sit you on my lap and sing to you. I couldn't buy you a birthday present. I had to wait and watch and plan and pray. I researched poisons. It had to be something that couldn't be linked back to me and was commonplace in our part of Yorkshire. It was your granddad who gave me the idea: I watched him pruning the stupid shrub in our front garden and when he saw me, he used it as an excuse to give me a lecture on the spindle tree. He has a PhD in chemical engineering. Talking at me is his way of trying to be fatherly. He must have thought it had worked for once. I baked the berries from our tree into biscuits. It wasn't that I wanted Ben to die; it was just that I didn't care if he lived. Please remember that he is nothing to you. He is not your brother.

I pretended to be your father. I sent you cards and gifts from your 'daddy' so that no one would suspect. No one would be searching for a young woman with pale green eyes and blonde hair. It worked even better than I had hoped: that stupid bitch, your fake mother, had an affair with a man who was perfect as a suspect. I knew then that it was another sign that Allah was on our side. And you accepted my explanation: that I would be your mother and father. I would be your all, your everything.

My plan succeeded. I've had four days of bliss and one night of hell, when you were lost on the moor. But even then, I found you. I know you better than anyone else. Better than you even know yourself. We were reunited. My daughter. The love of my life.

'Let me speak to her!' I say to the officer. 'Please! One last time. Let me say goodbye.'

He shakes his head and signals to the men holding me. They drag me away. I look back over my shoulder, hoping for one final glimpse of you. Your head is bowed, your hands clasped together on your lap. You're dopey with drugs. I had planned to stop giving them to you once we reached Pakistan and we were safe. But even so, even though you're sedated, I want you to acknowledge me.

'Mary!' I shout. 'Mary, my darling!'

This is what hurts the most: you do not cry. You do not call 'Mummy'. You do not even turn your head in my direction.

# FIVE MONTHS LATER

# MARCH

When we walk in, the place seems more spacious than usual. My pictures are large against the white walls. Jenny has spotlit them perfectly, offsetting their austerity with garlands of fairy lights over archways and around the central desk. There are flowers everywhere, tall vases in the corners, packed with velvet-green moss and vibrant pink peonies, their blowsy flowers in full bloom. The preview for my exhibition is going to be tonight. This afternoon, though, is all about Evie.

'Sweetheart, these are my paintings,' I say, leading her in.

We're going to have a quick look round and then go for ice cream. I hope it'll feel like a special, grown-up treat to her. She holds my hand tightly and doesn't say anything. I wanted to bring her this evening but Ollie refused. He said we shouldn't disrupt her routine. Ollie isn't coming either. He didn't want to leave the children with a babysitter. I understand – of course I understand – it's only five months since Evie was abducted. I can't bear the idea of leaving her and Ben with anyone. But I did want them with me. And I wanted Ollie to come.

Evie and I walk around together, stopping in front of the pictures. There are a couple of men still working, hanging the paintings, and a caterer, setting out wine glasses and jugs for water. Evie doesn't let go of my hand. She is silent.

'What do you think of this one?' I say, with forced jollity.

The paintings don't even look like mine: there's something distancing about seeing them in a gallery. But it's not just that — it's the tones I've used, the darkness, the depth of despair. It's as if someone else painted them. This one is called: *I wish I were a girl again, half savage and hardy.*

'Good,' says Evie, with a little shrug.

I remember when we found Evie again; hugging and hugging her as if I would never let her go, lifting her up and clutching her floppy, drug-limp body to me, feeling her raspy breath against my neck. And over her shoulder, I saw Mrs Hardgrave standing watching us, clasping her clutch squarely in front of her with both hands. She hadn't demanded Jareed drive after the airport police when they led Hannah away. She'd remained where she was, a few metres from our little family, her eyes fixed on Evie. Of course, I thought, it was always about Evie. The granddaughter she'd lost. The little girl she'd have done anything for — even concealing her hiding place, lying to the police, to me, tinkering with her husband's hearing aid. Would she have flown to Pakistan, too, telling Geoffrey she was off to 'see the sights, one last time'? I squeeze my eyes shut for a moment and snap them open. I try to focus on being here, now, with my daughter.

'So when you're a grown up, you can be a sculptor and have your work in galleries like this one.'

My voice is high and bright.

Evie doesn't reply. Ollie is right — she needs routine, stability, love. She's lost both her teachers. She found her real mother and then her mother abandoned her for the second time. She thought she'd discovered her real father, but he was a lie. It's easier to say what Evie won't do now, rather than what she will do.

She won't sleep without a light on.
She won't go on the moor.

She won't go anywhere unless it's been planned and we've told
    her about it several times.
She never plays with dressing-up clothes.
She can't stand the sight of anything to do with the *Frozen* movie.
She no longer plays with other children at school.
She won't speak to adults apart from me and Ollie.
I can't stop her from biting her nails until her fingers bleed.
She won't leave my side when we go out.
She won't hug or kiss us; when she thinks I'm not watching, she
    pinches Ben or pulls his hair.
She won't talk about what happened.

The child therapist we spoke to said not to push her. Occasionally
Evie will ask questions. She was with Hannah/Jane for five days but
much of that time she was on her own, because Hannah was with us,
or at school, or driving to and from her empty apartment by the Wool
Secretariat. The police let us see Hannah's flat. Every time I think of
Evie locked in that tiny, cold attic on the edge of the moor I want to
bite my own fingers until they bleed. Hannah, herself, hasn't spoken
since her arrest. The trial is next month. I'm not sure I'm strong
enough to go. Ollie will be there. He's withdrawn his application for
partner of the firm and he's already booked time off work.

'I want to see that bitch sentenced,' he'd said with uncharacteristic
venom.

If it's a really bad day, I think about Evie on the moor, alone,
in the dark, wearing only a thin, blue, princess dress. The police
estimate that she was outside by herself at night for about five
hours until Hannah found her.

These are the things Evie has said:

Where is Pakistan?
Why does Miss White want us to live there?

Would you have visited me?
Why did Miss White say you were my fake mummy?
Is Miss White really my mummy?
When I grow up will I call Miss White Mummy?

It's not much in five months. The list of what I think Evie really wants to ask but can't, and may never be able to is even shorter:

Why didn't you find me?
Why did you leave me there?

So I can understand it: she clings to me and at the same time she acts as if she hates me. But understanding my daughter's behaviour on a rational level doesn't make it any easier.

'Just give her time,' Ollie said, when I cried to him about it. He sounded impatient, no longer the gentle, reassuring man he used to be.

I need to give him time too. He hasn't forgiven me. Sometimes I catch him looking at me and his expression is unfathomable, as if he doesn't know who I am, as if I'm not the same woman he fell in love with fifteen years ago, as if I've betrayed his trust. Which, of course, I have.

Jenny comes over, her crimson-soled heels ringing out.

'Darling, let's have a quick word before this evening,' she says.

I extricate my hand from Evie's.

'I'll just be a minute, love,' I say. 'Why don't you look around by yourself? You're safe here.' I give what I hope is a comforting smile.

Evie looks at the door, locked behind us, the solid presence of the men working. Jenny and I pass the hidden entrance at the back of the gallery and I feel a blush creep up my cheeks and neck as I remember stealing through the kitchenette and kissing Haris behind the car park. Once we reach her desk, Jenny runs through the names of the guests: these are the people I need to concentrate on speaking to: members of the press, dealers, buyers.

She clutches my elbow mid-sentence and says, 'I didn't invite Haris, by the way. You do know I don't represent him any more?'

'Dropping him was the least you could do,' I say.

She hesitates for a fraction of a second and then continues. That's as much responsibility as she's going to take for her part in derailing my life.

'Don't worry about remembering everyone's names, I'll bring them to you. Now, anything else I can say to potential buyers? Have you started work on a new series?'

I shake my head and she looks disappointed. I haven't been able to paint much. I'm okay with that, really. I need to focus on Ben and Evie right now.

I've stopped walking across Rombald's Moor. Although I worry I might bump into Haris, that's not the main reason. I spend a lot of time following the path alongside the River Wharfe, past the tennis club and the golf course. Bella chases the ducks and I'm looking forward to the summer and dense verges of cow parsley and Himalayan balsam. It feels safer.

I've started going further afield too; sometimes taking Ollie and the children with me at the weekends. We mostly go to Bolton Abbey and amble through Strid Wood, admiring the churning gush of the river as it pounds over the rocks; the swirling pancakes of foam above Guinness-brown pools. On those occasions we act like a normal family of four. We squelch through the mud and then go to the cafe for hot chocolates. We are an averagely good-looking, middle-class couple with a beautiful girl and a gorgeous boy and a lovely liver and white springer spaniel. No one watching us would see past our Boden Breton tops and our Joules wellies and guess that both our children are damaged in some small but significant way.

'I've done one picture,' I say. 'It's not finished. I'm not sure—'

Jenny holds out her hand for my phone. I swipe through the photos until I find it. It's a departure for me. It's full of motion – of the river, the dappled light, the wind in the trees – and it's also filled with colour: purples and pinks, magenta and lime, lemon-yellow and cobalt. She inhales and turns to me, her red lipsticked-smile wide.

'This is wonderful. You need to do more like this. We could have another exhibition next year.'

I shake my head. 'I'll let you know. I can't really...' I trail off.

She's about to say something but she thinks better of it.

I look around for my daughter and feel what has become a familiar ball of panic burning in my chest. I need to be constantly aware of where she is every second. That exit out the back – there could be a car waiting! I'm breathing faster and faster as I scan the room.

'Where's Evie?' I say sharply.

Jenny looks at me in surprise and then her features soften. In the time we've been talking, Evie could be halfway to Leeds Bradford Airport! She wouldn't go anywhere on her own. Someone would have had to take her, force her... I march through the gallery, towards the second large room. I can't see her here either. I swing round and head towards the smaller section off the central gallery and halt at the entrance.

She's here. She's concentrating so hard, she hasn't seen me. She's built a sculpture right in the centre, using the materials she has to hand: wine glasses. She's laid them out in a grid and stacked others, three, four, five high. It's not a pyramid – it's far too random and precarious. She's got her tongue stuck in the corner of one cheek, as she carefully pours red wine from a bottle into the glasses. She must have found an open bottle. There's water in some of the other glasses already. I bite my lip to stop myself from calling her name and making her jump. I try to relax my shoulders. I admire the strange beauty of her creation: the way the fairy lights strung from the entrance sparkle from the rims; how the spotlights pick out the tonal dimension of the burgundy Merlot and the clear water, the fluidity of her sculpture, spreading wave-like across the gallery floor. And I admire my daughter: her long dark hair, her wide-set green eyes, her caramel-coloured skin. She is perfect.

'It won't be long until she has an exhibition of her own,' murmurs Jenny, peering over my shoulder.

Thank God she isn't angry.

Evie looks up and her face changes from intense concentration, as she's jarred out of her semi-trance state, to surprise, guilt and then defiance. She stands up. I know instinctively what she's going to do. I can see it playing like a movie in slow motion: her face will twist and she'll aim a kick at her sculpture; the glasses will tumble and some will shatter, red wine will splash the white walls and arc across my paintings. I close my eyes for a second and swallow.

'It's time to go for ice cream,' I say softly.

Evie hesitates, almost swaying, as if she's unbalanced, as if she's undecided what she's going to do, as if she no longer knows what she feels. And then she walks over to me, holding out her hand for mine.

# ACKNOWLEDGEMENTS

My thanks go to Sarah Hilary, who brainstormed the original idea for *The Stolen Child* with me. Maddie West, my first editor at Corvus, read the synopsis and gave me excellent feedback. At every stage in the writing process, I've been helped and encouraged by my agent, Robert Dinsdale, of A.M.Heath. Sharon Lewis read part of an early draft and made insightful comments. My fellow writers, Claire Snook and Emma Barton-Smith, helped enormously, offering apposite suggestions, pointing out flaws with both precision and kindness, as well as cheering me along. Paul Whitehouse, Susie Painter, Sabina Bowler-Reed and David Cohen all helped with the technical aspects of the novel, from police procedure to poisoning to adoption. Artist, Elaine Jones, patiently answered my many questions about her work and how to juggle a career in the arts with bringing up small children.

*The Stolen Child* has been guided to publication by my wonderful, kind and clever editor, Louise Cullen, who also makes a lovely lunch date! Nicky Lovick has corrected my dodgy grammar with humour and aplomb. A huge thank you to the sales team behind Atlantic Books, and the marketing and publicity department, masterminded by Alison Davies.

At every step of the way, my husband, Jaimie, has been supportive and encouraging, whilst my daughter, Jasmine, has kept me endlessly entertained, reminding me what it's all about. Thankfully, she's slightly too young yet to be comprehend the emotional resonance within the poem that inspired this book: for, my darling, the world's more full of weeping than you can understand.